MW01136460

Playing School

by
Dean Caputa

A teacher's account of daily classroom
struggles in our inner city public schools

authorHOUSE®

AuthorHouse™
1663 Liberty Drive, Suite 200
Bloomington, IN 47403
www.authorhouse.com
Phone: 1-800-839-8640

First published by AuthorHouse 6/9/2008

ISBN: 978-1-4343-6652-8 (sc)

Printed in the United States of America
Bloomington, Indiana

This book is printed on acid-free paper.

Dedication

This book is dedicated to all public school teachers, particularly those in the inner city, who toil each day in anonymity in their attempts to educate children in a morally challenged society.

I also wish to thank the journalism department at the University of Arkansas at Little Rock for opening my eyes to the world. I offer a special thanks to UALR history professor, Dr. Harold T. Smith, for encouraging students to consider the teaching profession. I want to salute my former teachers, Ms. Cady, Ms. Stewart, Ms. Polk, and Mr. Bennett at Baton Rouge's Riveroaks Elementary School for introducing me to my love of research and writing.

Finally, I would like to thank my wife, Liz, for having to live with my cantankerous behavior while writing and editing this book over the course of five summers.

"Our youth now love luxury. They have bad manners, contempt for authority; they show disrespect for their elders, and love chatter in places of exercise…They contradict their parents, chatter before company, gobble up their food, and tyrannize their teachers."

-Socrates, Fifth Century B.C.

Preface

This book idea came to me one crisp, fall day in October 1995. I was working as a part-time sportswriter for a college sports magazine while teaching social studies full-time as a teacher. I had just completed daily interviews with coaches on the football practice field where Louisiana State University was wrapping up preparations for an opponent. It was then I got word from a member of LSU's Sports Information Department that my editor wanted me to visit the Pete Maravich Assembly Center to cover basketball practice, only days into their pre-season.

As I made my way across an empty parking lot toward the PMAC, I noticed a young lady working in a cramped parking booth outside. Her blonde head was buried in a book, apparently studying, as a new Lexus pulled up and honked its horn to gain her attention. The young lady looked up, pushed a button, and the red and white-striped mechanical arm lifted allowing the driver to enter.

As I walked closer to the young lady, I recognized her as one of my former students from Baton Rouge Magnet High School. She was studying. The driver of the car I recognized as a forward on the school basketball team and one of the most highly recruited players in the nation. It occurred to me, obviously more as a teacher than a sportswriter, that there was something very wrong with this scene.

The young lady (we'll call her Amanda) graduated from an institution, which at the time, had ranked as the fourth-best high school in the state. Students who did not earn and keep a 2.5 GPA at BRMHS were asked to return to mainstream public high schools. Consequently, competition among students was keen. The extremely diverse student population did not find Ebonics, slang words, trousers falling off their backsides, or failure in the classroom as an option in a life that could offer them much by simply graduating. It was not unusual for representatives from Virginia, Harvard, Yale, Duke, Vanderbilt, Tulane, Texas A&M, Miami, Notre Dame, UCLA, and a host of other outstanding colleges and universities to recruit graduates on a daily basis. Gaining admission to an in-state public university for many of the students I taught was not a first choice. They were that good.

Amanda was middle class and not qualified to earn a scholarship to the out-of-state school she wished to attend. Not unhappily, Amanda decided to attend LSU. At that time, there were no state-funded college scholarships, or TOPS (Tuition Opportunity Program for Students). To make financial ends meet, she worked as a parking booth operator for minimum wage. She studied to kill the boredom of her thankless job and to guarantee continued academic success.

The basketball player, on the other hand, was not academically gifted, hardly excelling at a Baton Rouge public high school, except as a player packing his school's gym with record crowds and college coaches drooling over his athletic prowess. His grades were just average and he had to take the ACT more than once to qualify academically. Most sports media members and close observers to the recruiting fiasco surrounding this talented player knew he would struggle to stay academically eligible.

Nevertheless, college coaches phoned and sent their letters of interest to this player by the bushel. He could have gone to college anywhere he chose. He could have literally gotten out a map of the continental U.S. and tacked it on a wall, thrown a dart at the map, and gone to college in the city closest to wherever the point of that dart hit. Pick a state. Select a conference. Name a school. He could have attended any of them with a simple phone call to a head basketball coach. He eventually selected LSU.

Amanda? No one knew her name. She was just one of a lengthy list of nameless students attending college to prepare for a future in the workplace. She eventually graduated LSU and worked hard each day without so much as a pat on the back. She did not get a scholarship offer and no one gave her a new Lexus to drive to her classes each day. She read the textbooks, wrote the term papers, studied the endless pages of notes given by demanding professors, and never missed classes. She was the epitome of what a college student should be.

Watching Amanda work in the small glass enclosure, I realized there was something very wrong with our educational system and its distribution of awards. On that October day, watching Amanda push a button earning minimum wage to stay in college so a spoiled brat of a basketball player with slight academic talent could park his undeserved Lexus nearest an entrance to the gym was too much. Amanda deserved to be at LSU and was financially fighting to stay there. The basketball star had an array of choices available to him. It made no sense. I would eventually learn, through much experience as a teacher, that one enemy in education is those who purport to direct the system and feed it.

It reminded me of an incident I experienced in December 1978 as a member of LSU's marching band. The band stood patiently under the goal post in the end zone of the Liberty Bowl in Memphis, Tennessee, preparing for a pre-game march while watching the football team conduct drills in preparation for their opponent, the University of Missouri. I watched my classmate and good friend, catching balls tossed from the quarterback. He was so athletically gifted. I admired him. But we both got into some academic trouble weeks before and I wanted to know about his final grade.

After class one day our professor informed us in a callous tone we both needed to make an 'A' on the final exam to pass the class. We had both failed the midterm exam and she urged us to study. An immature student, I decided to study for the first time. I asked my football friend if he wanted to study with me, but he shocked me by declining the invitation. I thought that strange since failing the test might affect his football eligibility. However, I had my own problems and I was going to solve them. I went home and studied very hard for three straight days. I committed myself to studying hours with note cards. I read the ten chapters I should have read during the entire fall semester at least twice. I was committed to passing even if it was with a dishonorable grade of 'C'. I wanted to stay in the marching band and that meant being a successful student.

When the final exam was administered, I was so prepared I cramped my hand writing the answers down so fast. As I got up from my desk to turn in my five-page exam, I walked by my football friend. The look on his face was one of frustration as he challenged himself to games of tic-tac-toe. There were blanks where the essays were to be written. I knew then he would not pass the class.

When report cards came out two weeks later, I got a 96 percent on the speech exam earning me a 'C' in the class. Now as I stood with my saxophone in the midday sun of a chilly stadium I had to ask my friend about his grade. I fought my way through three lines of band members and yelled out to him as he caught passes, "What did you get in speech class?"

As if I didn't know. He heard me and ran toward me in uniform to shake my hand before replying, "Man, I passed with a 'B'!"

He smiled proudly before returning to pre-game practice. I stood there stunned. Not only was it mathematically impossible to earn a 'B' in the class, I knew for a fact this football player turned in an empty paper full of X's and O's from a game of tic-tac-toe! How could it be? Simple. The system was corrupt. I began accruing evidence of that as a college freshman. Amanda was learning it, too, only in a different way.

As an inner city public school teacher today, I can sadly inform the reader that ineffective state administrative leadership and student apathy are the main enemy to public education. As an educator with fourteen years of experience teaching nine subjects in five different high schools in two parishes (counties), I have witnessed more than I care to remember. It is little wonder we have a very serious "brain drain" in Louisiana. Many of the state's problems, I believe, begin and end at home and in our classrooms. It's easy to blame the teachers and school administrations. That's the popular thing to do.

The problems with our educational system, however, are far deeper than one might imagine. Our problems are as much political as cultural and reflective of the dizzying times in which we live. We teachers, particularly the public school species, are legislated by the unknowing, hired by those with unearned arrogance to do the impossible for the ungrateful, while being chastised for the failures of parents who blindly believe in the innocence of their spoiled children leaving them to be reared by perverse television and Internet programming designed to blunt the imagination of a bankrupt society, drunk on materialism and immediate self-gratification.

More often than not, our state educational leadership lack practical teaching experience. Often, their comments and policies consistently undermine teachers and destroy their morale.

I read in a July 25, 2004, Baton Rouge *Sunday Advocate* edition about the impending exodus of East Baton Rouge Parish School Superintendent Clayton Wilcox to Florida. One paragraph in the article aggravated me. Wilcox said, "…the embrace of technology has been slow…just one in four teachers use technology everyday in their classrooms, (Wilcox) estimates."

Estimates? The sentence alluded to the notion that all teachers *had* technology in the classroom, but *chose* not to use it. I thought about my own classroom use of technology while reading that ridiculous blanket statement. The fact of the matter was I did not have a computer in my classroom during my first eleven years of teaching. When I got one, it was due to a grant written by my wife who got them donated.

Computers? They are an overrated expense.

One of my dear friends is a professor at Southeastern Louisiana University. He agrees with my opinions of computers in classrooms and directs his frustration at those believing technology will save education with a sign posted on his office door. It reads: *"Technology in the classroom makes bad teachers look good."*

It's true. I was in a high school library one afternoon in late May 2004, when I overheard a student teacher, who was working on her degree in education, bragging about the new PowerPoint presentation she made to a history class concerning the Vietnam conflict. When I quizzed her about her knowledge of the content being taught, she knew only slightly more than the students. She didn't know the capital of South Vietnam, didn't know the difference between the Viet Cong and the North Vietnamese Army, knew almost nothing of saturation bombing, Vietnamization, Americanization, the Ho Chi Minh Trail, or when the U.S. fled the country. But she could push those buttons on the PowerPoint presentation. Is this effective teaching? Technology disguised her ignorance.

I am afraid colleges are teaching prospective educators more about useless theory and how to integrate the Internet into the classroom as an entertainment tool more than challenging their subject knowledge. Too many graduates don't know enough to *teach* a class without the use of technology. Show me a teacher who knows their facts, can quote famous and infamous individuals, can recite interesting stories not found in textbooks, can recall formulas by memory, and can point to a location on a map within seconds, and I'll show you a teacher who can send your kids to Ivy League schools. I believe the best teaching involves using only a piece of chalk and an overhead projector. My students, past and present, are expert at taking notes and asking questions, just like I know they will in college or trade school.

I understand the need for the use of the Internet and other forms of technology in the classroom. I am not a classroom Neanderthal. After all, this book was written on a computer. However, technology should be the cheese on the education pizza, and not the entire pie. Technology should be part of the educational process. Instead, we see more school systems emphasizing computer usage over taking notes and analytical thought. One would also be amazed at how many high school students cannot use the index of a textbook, a table of contents, or type a cohesive sentence. But they can use a computer "mouse" and download highly objectionable material with ease. I find that frightening.

As a 1970s high school student, I remember an invention that was supposed to revolutionize education. Its presence in the classroom was going to endear students to education, and provide a visual aid, as well as entertain. As a resource tool, it was said to be most invaluable. That invention was a VCR. My generation of test scores did not rise. The fanatical overuse by teachers eventually passed. After graduation, we entered college armed with what we remembered reading and researching in books (remember books?), and what we wrote and edited in class.

I am reminded of what I read in Morris Berman's book, *The Twilight of American Culture*, about the decline of American society. In it, he related a story about a college professor at a Midwestern university who was shocked at how many college students had never read a novel.

Berman wrote, "...how long before he has a student who asks him, 'what's a novel?'"

I'll trump that by asking, how long before we have students asking, "What's a book?"

Unfortunately, the Internet and other forms of technology are the latest passing fancy for the experts to hang their proverbial hats on. If you don't believe me, check inner city public school test scores. Those marks consistently fluctuate, regardless of parish, students, or socio-economic backgrounds. Is technology important? Absolutely. Should a teacher's classroom worth be based on how much technology is used and how many computers are present on a given campus? No way. Believe it or not, there are teachers like myself who don't lean on technology. I read a great deal about what I teach and I have a degree in what I teach. It's simple—I don't hide behind technology. I know my subject areas well. There should be something said for old-fashioned reading and teaching. This style, which is now being discouraged by the "experts," can work again if we exercise some common sense.

I don't want to abuse education's misguided love of technology. Let's share the guilt.

In March 2004, some members of the Louisiana Board of Elementary and Secondary Education (BESE) wanted to offer provisional high school diplomas to students who completed their high school courses, but could not pass the Graduate Exit Examination (GEE), which is the state mandated test of basic skills required for graduation. A Louisiana legislator sponsored the bill during the 2004 session based on the idea that some students worked very hard to graduate high school and attended classes every day performing at peak efficiency, but just could not pass GEE. Therefore, it was reasoned, a provisional diploma—not to be confused with the graduating variety—would make them feel better about themselves as they entered the working world. Hence, a provisional diploma would insure their self-esteem and slow dropout rates.

As a teacher I was shocked at the reasoning. Were they assuming students needed some type of false social reinforcement? Did those individuals rise to their position with a provisional diploma? I think not. Trust me as an educator, many inner city students will choose the path of least resistance. Their goal, sadly, would be the provisional diploma.

This BESE member assumed students attended class regularly and just could not pass GEE. Check the attendance rates of those failing any test. The majority of failing students miss far too many days of school.

BESE may have meant well, but could have inadvertently weakened a teacher's authority while regulating them to highly paid baby sitters. BESE and that legislator's voice, thankfully, were silenced with a veto. Ideas such as these come from our legislature. They make many of the rules in education. BESE members behave like academic monarchs. Their crowns are hardly respected by most inner city public school teachers.

I strongly believe the worse thing we educators can do in society is to socially promote high school students in a highly competitive, increasingly multilingual world sharply creased with technology. When my students get angry at me for pushing them too hard in class, I unsympathetically remind them that I don't care one bit what they think of me at age sixteen. I do, however, care a great deal what they think of me when they reach age twenty-five, are married—possibly with children—and have rent to pay. Being denied a job and the ability to support a family because one is not skilled is harsher than my words could ever be. In Louisiana, many in our population are unskilled, poorly educated and it is costing the state business and respect.

BESE member Leslie Jacobs of New Orleans knows this and works tirelessly to improve education in Louisiana. Appointed by former Governor Mike Foster's administration to serve the BESE, she is outspoken on educational issues, often critical of teachers, and has been labeled an "expert" on education. Expert? Would it surprise one to know Jacobs has never taught a grade school class? A former member of the Orleans Parish School Board, she has never reported to the same school and taught them for 180 school calendar days, been cursed by a fifteen-year-old student, been assaulted while breaking up a fight, been ridiculed by a parent because she had the nerve to question a student's commitment in the classroom, never fundraised or washed uniforms at 10 p.m. on a school night for a sport she coached, or graded hundreds of papers per week from students who simply did not care about the value of an education.

I don't know much about medicine and have never administered a drug to anyone, but I guess if the current Louisiana governor wishes, I could gather some of my teaching contemporaries and we could interpret endless pages of data and make "expert" recommendations to the state Department of Health and Hospitals.

My point is clear. I don't want to be led into battle by a commander who has never seen a shot fired in anger. I don't want to work on a construction job for a foreman who has never perspired over the wooden handle of a shovel. I don't want to be coached by one who has never played the game. Teachers do not want to be led or criticized by those who have never performed their job. Is that too much to ask?

Then there are the parents—if you want to call what many of them insinuate as parenting. When educators set up a parent-teacher conference concerning a child's grades or behavior, one might be shocked when they fail to show up. If parents do show up, some literally weep, professing to teachers, "I just can't control her! I don't know what to do!" If the parent cannot control the child, what are teachers expected to do? Teachers can't hire the tutors, take away car privileges, or set and enforce curfews.

Once I met with a mother of one of my failing students. Exasperated, she asked my advice on how to discipline her fifteen-year-old son. The husband had abandoned the family and she voted me her proxy husband. I asked if her son had a computer or a car. She explained he did not have a car, but he did have a new computer and he loved to play video games. I told her to confiscate the video games and make him use the computer for school projects only and under her strict guidance until his grades improved. Her response? "Oh, I'd hate to do that to him," she said meekly as she dried her tears. "He loves to play on that computer so much. I think that would be a bit cruel." Weak.

Attempt to phone a parent only to be stunned at how many numbers have been disconnected. If a teacher does happen to reach a parent by phone, would it surprise one that it's the teacher sometimes on trial by the parent for "failing to understand my child like I do! I know my child! He would not do that! You cannot continue to tell me that and expect me to believe it!" Increasingly, teachers are often sorry they bothered to phone parents in the first place. Needless to say, the child in question rarely improves.

I think students simply need to go home and study the work their teachers tirelessly present to them each day. Their parents need to get more involved in their lives. They are increasingly in short supply.

An example of the stupidity reminds me of nine families in Orleans Parish (New Orleans) in March 2000, claiming the state standardized test, LEAP, is racist because an inordinate number of minority students fail the test each year. At the time, a student only needed to score "approaching basic," on the exam to pass to through the eighth grade and are given many chances to take it. If students fail standardized testing, it's because it's designed to protect them from ignorance and social promotion. The test is about mastering basic skills, not building a race car fueled by green vegetables and water. But the Orleans Parish parents, calling themselves "Parents Against Testing Before Teaching," predictably filed a lawsuit claiming students failing LEAP suffered "…undue stress, embarrassment, humiliation, social isolation, and educational deprivation"—words obviously written by an attorney. One should have heard the parents speak on the issue. Their vocabularies made sixth-graders sound like Washington D.C., lobbyists.

Nearly 38,000 students statewide failed LEAP in 2000, representing one in every three who took it. Despite what many claim as racist, it is proof that the test needed to be given. The students in need of help were identified. However, some believed a lawsuit would better serve their needs rather than helping their children to read better and calculate equations. During summer 2007, the NAACP picketed the state capitol in Baton Rouge demanding an end to standardized testing because too many students were failing. What was the message to students? Why not help tutor them during summer instead of leading a protest?

There is little explanation concerning poor statewide test scores. Disconnected, spoiled students, poverty, the state's populist mentality, and parental apathy are an attempt at an explanation.

The news media, however, are no friend to teachers either. Talk radio hosts often influence the public into believing the pubic school system should be run like a business.

I remember one caller's tantrum, "If I'd a run my business like them-there teachers run their classrooms I'd be broke. Make 'em accountable!"

Teachers cannot be expected to run their classrooms like a business if they are not allowed to operate like a business. Let teachers pick their students like a business hires and fires its employees. Let teachers pick their start times and implement their own brand of strict discipline and watch them succeed. No, they are handed a roll book on the first day of school to teach students with no fear of authority, little respect for education, and many caring nothing for their future. Teachers are expected to reach them and educate them. There are success stories, for sure, but it's becoming increasingly difficult to produce in inner city schools.

East Baton Rouge Parish's newest superintendent, Charlotte Placide, remarked to one local news magazine in June 2005, "When we change the culture…then we will have a successful community."

She's right, but how do we change Louisiana's culture? It won't be easy if it can be done at all. The state is stereotyped nationwide for a reason. Louisiana has made itself comfortable at the bottom of many of the nation's lists for decades. When we change the state's culture we can eradicate litter, our over-dependence on oil revenue and gambling, lower our insurance rates, decrease our reliance on our charity hospital system, decrease crime and our out-migration, and get the grass cut and the trees pruned along our interstate highways more often. Educators are entrusted to help move the school system in that positive direction, but changing the culture begs for more allies not always present in our living rooms.

I would pay money to videotape a state education "expert" teaching in inner-city public schools today, and I don't mean as a guest speaker or as a substitute for two days. I mean reporting each day without fail to the same class for about one month. No support from a qualified teacher would be allowed and no police officer for protection. Just issue them a grade book, a subject manual, a box of chalk, and thirty-two students who are not enrolled in honors classes and let the magic of teaching begin. They would be shocked at what students would say to them, what they know, what they don't know, and what they think is important. They would learn high school students look up to and know more about rap artists than they do political leaders. They can't locate or spell "Massachusetts" on a map and too many think the nation's capitol is in Washington state. The numbers of parents who do not care to support them socially or academically would further shock them. I think they would learn quickly there is no teaching fad of the day, formula, theory, or data to help teachers save students not wanting to be saved.

When I taught at BRMHS, I helped send Baton Rouge's best students to college. Was I that good of a teacher? Today I teach in the inner city where I hope the kids don't mind coming to school with some regularity and at least pass most of their classes. Am I that bad of a teacher? The answer to both questions is a resounding, "No." My success and failures often boil down to a personal commitment and a commitment by the people in whom I am entrusted to teach. I am committed. The majority of my students are not.

On a positive note, however, our state legislature has made great strides in promoting education. They have given students an opportunity to earn college scholarships, if only after achieving modest academic success. They have given birth to a thriving community college system. They have given teachers pay increases and instituted a standard of reform many other states have attempted to emulate.

TOPS requirements, however, could be raised in a state that annually faces budget shortfalls. When I suggested to two legislators in 2003 that raising TOPS requirements would save the state money by allowing only the state's best to attend college, they agreed, but admitted to being politically paralyzed to make that come to fruition.

I related a story to those legislators about the abuse of TOPS bonus money students could earn with high grade point averages. I know of two young female students earning TOPS bonus checks of between $700 to $900. The money was not used to purchase necessities for college. Instead, the money was used to get breast implants, courtesy of the state of Louisiana. Who is in charge?

Despite some obvious improvements in secondary education, Louisiana still carries terrible burdens it may not unload in our lifetime. Nationwide, the story is almost as dismal. A quick look at some statistics, and our present culture, is shown below.

*According to a "Kid's Count, 2006" survey, Louisiana listed 28 percent of its children living in poverty and 13 percent living in "extreme poverty" or income below 50 percent of the poverty level.

*In 2005, "Kid's Count" listed 20 percent of Louisiana's citizens between ages eighteen and twenty-four as "disconnected," meaning they are not attending school, are not working full-time or part-time, and with no degree beyond high school.

*"Kid's Count, 2005" also lists Louisiana as having 42 percent of its children living in families where "no parent has full-time, year-round employment." The study also cited 19 percent of Louisiana families where the head of the household is a high school dropout.

*According to a recent study by the non-partisan group, "Public Agenda," 34 percent of American middle school and high school teachers have considered quitting because of the lack of student discipline on campus. Many teachers interviewed called their job "crowd control"— not education. Fifty-two percent of teachers said there's an armed police officer on their campus.

*"Public Agenda" also revealed the majority of American parents see society as "an inhospitable climate for raising children" because of the declining morals. Parents in the study said they worry more about protecting their children from negative social influences than they do paying their monthly bills.

*According to the National Center for Educational Statistics, almost 1.1 million students were home-schooled during the 2003-04 school year, reflecting a 29 percent increase since 1999. Thirty-one percent of parents home-schooling their children said they did so because of the environment of regular public schools.

Over the decades, these statistics seem not to change much. We should be outraged with the numbers, but few public school parents show interest in helping. Parents will stand in line for football tickets but do not attend school functions like Parent-Teacher Night, a band concert, or a school play. True, some parents do care, but there are not enough of them—not nearly. Ask an inner city public school teacher for verification. One may not like what one hears.

Another report for "Public Agenda" entitled, *"A Sense of Calling: Who Teaches and Why,"* reflected the thoughts of teachers with less than five years' experience. Not only did the report accurately suggest teachers did not choose their career because it was a last resort, they taught because they loved it. All teachers have heard the horrible definition of what some want to believe they are, *"Those who can, do. Those who can't, teach."* What Public Agenda President Deborah Wadsworth wrote about the 1997 survey was simple and accurate. I also consider it invaluable advice in Louisiana, a state struggling to remove the scrapes and blisters from being near the bottom of the nation's academic statistics for too long. Consider Wadsworth's discovery of teachers:

"The strength and vibrancy of their morale and motivation are striking. It seems almost criminal to ignore what they have to offer by turning a deaf ear to what they have to say."

I think teachers would love to be asked, just once, what they think of the policies and procedures the "experts" advocate. Teachers are the real experts. They don't get to choose whom they teach. They don't select the conditions. They accept them and do the best they can. They don't select their leadership, and are granted little, if any, parental support. Oftentimes, they don't even have enough desks and textbooks, especially in the early part of the school year. They purchase many items out of their paychecks because they understand education is expensive.

This book was written for them. It's a collection of stories the legislators do not want to hear, BESE members cannot locate in their data, the public may not want to believe, and the media either does not know about or finds too controversial to report.

I am the only teacher crazy or stupid enough (pick your choice of word here) to write about my experiences in a fictional way. The events related in this work are based on fact. The stories are upsetting, funny, shocking, sad, disgusting, uplifting, immoral, and corrupt.

This book was not written to save the educational world. I'm not that arrogant. Many will belittle me in my effort to reveal the real problems in our inner city high school classrooms and the daily grind of teachers. It will prove easier to discredit me than to admit these problems are real. Some will praise the effort as admirable. Either way, I'm satisfied it will be read. It's the truth.

Whether one likes reading the truth or not, I know three things concerning education:

1. There are too many powerful individuals afraid to relinquish their power, even at the expense of the young student masses.
2. Those *not* in education have a radically different notion of what they *think* goes on in a teacher's world rather than what really does.
3. Just as importantly, there is no magic to save the school system. Only old-fashioned common sense can prevail,

but the culture of the new millennium is kryptonite to civility.

It's important to note—do not be angry with the author for writing these stories. I am only the reporter and witness to the events. If you must be angry, be angry about the fact teachers must deal, on a daily basis, with what you are about to read. Be frustrated with me, not at me.

In any event, we teachers will keep trying anyway—with or without the respect we deserve. It's what we do.

Dean Caputa
August 2007

"Knowledge in the form of an informational commodity indispensable to productive power is already, and will continue to be, a major—perhaps the major—stake in the worldwide competition for power."

—Jean Francois Lyotard, "The Post-Modern Condition"

August—"Can You Be Bought?"

It was only 6:50 a.m. when thirty-year-old Tory Leblanc drove into the parking lot of East Side High School. The temperature was already eighty-three degrees and climbing with 90 percent humidity. The heat was already becoming intolerable on a sunny day with no clouds on the horizon. As far as Tory was concerned, August 11 was just too soon to welcome students back to school. The heat was proof of that. There was a time when school began with the first college football weekend. In Baton Rouge, that would not occur for at least another three weeks.

Tory wondered whatever happened to the month of August on the education calendar as she pulled her car into the teacher's parking lot. When she was a student in the late 1980s, the school year did not begin until at least mid-August. There were literally two weeks or more that teachers and students could count as vacation during the year's hottest month. With the advent of pay increases to teachers, the school system and the state erased August. Slowly, but surely, the school calendar had been rolled back. Teachers always joked among themselves they were not given raises at all. They believed they were simply given more pay for more work.

As Tory exited her red SUV, she grabbed her leather satchel and a plastic bag full of lunch items. As she locked her vehicle door, she glanced over her shoulder at the mighty roar moving into place in the empty parking lot. Like tanks moving into battle position, one, two, five, eight, eleven, seventeen yellow buses full of students pulled into the parking lot in a long line and stopped at the curb one at a time. The

1

students aboard were already proving to be a noisy bunch. They were not allowed off the buses until 6:50 a.m. when most of the faculty would be at school to take duty positions.

Tory could smell the overwhelming fumes from the buses as they shut off their engines and waited for the morning bell that would release drivers to run additional routes. It was a nauseating odor. She held her breath as she cut between two buses and stepped up to the sidewalk that made a path toward the school office. The heavy morning dew lay still on the dark green grass sparkling in the sun that continued to rise higher in the light blue sky. The student parking lot behind her was filling up quickly. Some of the cars could be heard for long distances as the oppressive bass from radios blared obnoxious rap music. The decibels thudded against the sidewalk and taunted Tory's every step.

Like all public school teachers, Tory had ten weeks off during summer and already missed it. She could not afford to go on vacation, did not own a pool, and did not entertain out-of-town company. There was nothing particularly interesting about the summer she missed. What she missed was the freedom those ten weeks allowed. Tory could simply walk the mall and window shop, sit in a dark movie theatre alone in the cool air-conditioning and watch a movie on a hot day, jog around the beautiful homes nestled around University Lakes or spend all day at the health club. Or, she could simply stay up late at night and read a book or watch an old movie with no interest in the time. It was not exactly exciting living, but the beauty in summer was that most everyone else was working. For Tory, Sunday, Monday and Friday were all the same during the long, dull days of summer. It felt like she was cheating life when her summer paychecks were deposited in her bank account twice per month. The summer months were as much a vacation as it was a mentality. That was over now. The school year, with all its promise and frustration lay straight ahead.

Tory walked into the office and checked her teacher mailbox. In the middle of the wooden maze was an eight-inch square with "Leblanc" typed underneath. It was full with memos on what to do on this first day of school. There were updated student rolls and an additional room key. There was paperwork to fill out concerning students with learning disabilities. There was a textbook list to fill out. The library wanted teacher lists of those wanting overhead projectors. There was paperwork to fill out concerning any lab fees extended to students. Lesson plans for the first three weeks of school had to be turned in by day's end. There was a small sheet to fill out identifying any fundraisers and field trips considered. There were duty lists to adhere to, new dress codes to follow, and student handbooks to pass out and have students sign. There were e-mails to read and return, much to sign, get signed, passed out, collect, advise, initial, count, file, fill out, approve, teach, number, monitor, assist, alphabetize, and turn in. It was mind-boggling.

Tory was also East Side High School girl's assistant basketball coach. As a coach she had even more lists to attend to about the sport she coached and the one she would be "volunteered" to help with when her basketball schedule was complete, such as collecting admission or working concession stands for other sports.

As assistant coach, she assisted with uniforms to order, fees to collect, game schedules to make out or update, district meetings to attend to, insurance cards and medical paperwork to pass out and collect. Drug cards, emergency cards, parental consent forms, and transportation forms had to be signed and dated and turned in to the state high school athletic association on deadlines.

Tory stuffed all that paperwork into her satchel and greeted some of the new teacher arrivals making their way into the office. She then walked out of the glass door when the morning bell rang granting the 500 students crammed on the buses, about 50 percent of the school's population, permission to disembark. Tory picked up her pace trying to beat the mass of teenagers rushing toward the Commons area. As students took the three steps needed to exit the buses, the cursing began. Duty teachers and administrators greeted students with reminders to tuck in shirts and remove scarves and hats from heads. Boys were reminded to pull up trousers literally falling off their backsides in the perverse gangster style in which it was intended. It was a terse reminder to Tory of the economic class of students in which she was entrusted each day and the enormous task ahead of her.

Within minutes, Tory entered the paneled walls of the teacher's lounge as the portable air-conditioner hummed. She placed her food in one of the three refrigerators provided while inhaling the brew of fresh coffee as some teachers gathered around for their morning fix of mock adrenaline. Tory resisted the temptation to drink it. She was already feeling anxious and did not need its hot content filling her veins.

She hastily headed into the building dubbed, "McCall Hall" in memory of the school's first principal, some four decades before. She entered the hallway and was greeted by an outdated bulletin board exclaiming to all, "Have a nice summer!" with two well-drawn palm trees sitting on the edge of a sandy white beach. Tory wondered which beach the kids had on their mind when they stapled up the project in May, but she wished she were there wherever it was. The fact was the school year had begun and morale was already low among many teachers.

For the second consecutive year, the teachers in East Baton Rouge Parish public schools did not receive a pay increase. The state Board of Elementary and Secondary Education and its overly complicated formula, the so-called Minimum Foundation Plan, for extending pay increases to teachers did find money to dole out to many in most of the state's sixty-plus public school systems. Ironically, teachers in the parishes who were already among the highest paid got even more money. All Tory and her contemporaries saw during summer months was a letter reminding teachers their medical benefits would increase, their class sizes would rise from an average of twenty-seven students per class to thirty-two, and a reminder of the immense pressure from the state to increase East Side High School's test scores or the faculty would face some form of career discipline. In addition, Tory agreed to take on an additional prep due to summer teacher layoffs as the school system failed, for the fifth consecutive year to balance its budget. As usual, the school system balanced the budget on the backs of teachers in the form of increased workloads for the same pay. Like a corporate soldier trapped in a cubicle, teachers were asked to do more for the same money.

Tory found her room by remote control. She was in her sixth year of teaching at East Side High School, all of which had been in Room 134. She turned on the lights with one hand while placing her keys in her satchel with the other. She looked out the window at a view of four trees that had grown a bit taller over the summer. Those four broad leaf maple trees would be her view and year-long companion providing daydream material on those weary days to come. Tory would watch the leaves of those trees go from dark green to yellow to litter at its trunk.

The branches would then stand naked in a frozen chill. She would watch them bud again and then open into leaves the size of small dinner plates before another school year would conclude.

Her classroom was as ancient as some of the history she taught. Only four of the eight windows could be opened—the others were broken and in need of repair since she took possession of the class. The shades covering them were in tatters. The twenty-eight-year-old light fixtures seemed to eat bulbs much more quickly than they should—one fixture blinking off and on at will for no reason. The room was in need of paint, and the doorknob was often difficult to negotiate with a key on most days. With the advent of computers came the need for more electrical outlets. The school system met that need, but the metallic tubing holding the wires were exposed and quite an eyesore. There were cracks in some of the walls, proof the foundation was faltering. The wall clock was permanently set to 3:10.

While unpacking, Tory glanced at her watch and realized that in two minutes another bell would ring and students would move into the building to begin their first day. She was nervous, excited, scared, hopeful, and alert.

Tory then heard a knock on the frame of her door as she pulled items from her satchel and placed them on her small wooden desk stained with graffiti. Standing under the doorframe was Margaret Sexton, a thirty-one-year-old science teacher from across the hall who reintroduced herself after the lengthy summer.

"Hello, remember me?" called Margaret, now in her seventh year at East Side High School. "How are you?"

Margaret and Tory had a great deal in common. Both had taught about the same length of time, had begun teaching at East Side High School at nearly the same time, and were newlyweds. They were both tall brunettes and extraordinarily cute. The boys had their eyes on them at all times. Margaret and Tory hung out together when time allowed, but that was rare. Funny thing about the pair though, as much as they liked each other they never spent time together away from school. Their relationship was purely professional, but they got along famously. Naturally, their August introduction resembled a family meeting at Christmas in an airport terminal after a lengthy absence.

The two hugged and held each other and laughed. Tory needed the interaction. She was on edge, and just for a minute before the students flooded her room, Margaret made her relax a bit. The two made small talk as only women do. They talked about the health of their marriages, where they did not go on vacation, and how quickly the summer sped by them. They said the same thing teachers all over the nation say on the first day of school.

"The summer went by so quickly!" Margaret said as if it were newsworthy.

"I know!" replied Tory. "I can only hope the school year goes by just as quickly."

The two then laughed at their own attempt at teacher hallway humor before pledging to meet in the teacher's lounge for lunch to catch up.

"Hey, hey!" came a voice from across the hallway. "What's all this noise I'm hearing at seven o'clock in the morning?"

The booming voice came from Randy Berlin, the assistant football coach and freshmen English teacher. He was a burly man in his early fifties, but did not look the part. He had all of his hair, a bit of a belly, stood about six feet and had arms as hard as hammers. He also had a knack for telling stale jokes that were better suited for students of 1970s vintage. He was "old school" to be sure—meaning, he was a bit out of touch with the realities of the modern student and the social baggage they now carried. But he was a competent teacher, a master organizer, and his students were scared of him. Again, Coach Berlin was in the midst of making a corny joke. The gesture, however, was well intended to welcome Tory and Margaret back to school.

"I thought students understood that they were to wait outside until the bell rang," Coach Berlin said as he pointed at the women and then the double doors leading outside.

Of course, everyone made their obligatory laugh as the bell interrupted them. All at once, the tone of all three teachers changed. It was time to get serious.

"Okay, let's get to work!" Coach Berlin said excitedly to no one and everyone.

Through the double doors on both ends of the hallway, students and their loud chatter entered. Tory always likened the second before the morning bell rang as a disturbed ant pile. If one took a stick and placed it inside the large mound of ants there is initially no movement. But within seconds, ants erupt from all locations and move in many different directions. Students did the same as they made their hallway entry look more like an attempt on their part to take over the school rather than a move toward their first-hour classes.

"There's ugly, old Coach Berlin!" one male student said to another hoping he could be heard as the coach stood in the doorway under his nameplate.

Coach Berlin knew the boys and knew they were picking on him, but he decided to have some fun with them as well.

"Come here, you two!" he said motioning them to move toward him.

"He said it!" the taller kid said pointing to the other.

"No way, dog, I didn't say shi…uh, nothin'," with his eyes as wide as saucers.

Coach Berlin walked up to the taller student sticking his index finger in the boy's hulking chest asking, "How old are you, son?"

"I'm sixteen," he said, not understanding where this attempt at a reprimand was going.

"Well, it took me fifty-three years to get this ugly!" Coach Berlin said. "It took you only sixteen!"

Four or five students walking by laughed heartily overhearing Coach Berlin's joke at the expense of the two being questioned.

Coach Berlin even laughed at his joke as the two boys walked away nodding their heads and vowing with a smile, "Okay, Coach, we'll get you. We won't forget! Sho' won't!"

Coach Berlin waved them away. It was harmless fun, but a reminder to students that teachers were not a bunch of bookworms hanging out at the library on Friday night. They, too, had a sense of humor and were quick-witted. Some teachers, especially the male coaches, had an intimidating presence and proved to be more than equal to the task of defending themselves from practical jokes.

As the number of students and the noise they delivered increased in the hallway, Tory, Margaret, and Coach Berlin watched them file by. Which students moving toward them would be theirs to teach? They knew the reputation of some of them and hoped they did not enter their room. To their dismay some of them did. How they dressed and how they entered the classroom would be some of the early signs to note when assessing the personality of classes. And make no mistake, classes developed personalities.

First-hour classes were usually the best behaved and with the most absences. Dozens of students routinely found themselves late and entered class after the tardy bell rang. Some were late because a bus may have developed mechanical trouble or got stuck in rush hour traffic. Mostly, student tardiness was due to simply not being able to get out of bed on time. Disruptions, along with morning announcements, were often at a peak. For the most part, however, first-hour classes were still sleepy despite the noise made when entering the building. There was something about settling in a desk at 7:05 a.m. that broke a student's early morning morale. They were listless and appeared fatigued. Because of that fact, behavior was rarely a problem in the early morning hours. Overall grades, however, usually proved to be the lowest because attention spans were at their worst.

Second, third, and fourth hours were often the best classes of the day. Students were beginning to wake up. Disturbances were fewer after 11 a.m. as late check-ins slowed. Teachers were also more awake, too, and everyone appeared more in the flow of things. At this time of day—lunch and the break—their stomachs began to rumble. Quite simply, there had not been enough of school by lunchtime to bore students accustomed to a litany of ten-second sound bites commonly found on bad television.

After lunch, fifth and sixth-hour students took on another character. Most of the older students—the seniors—had left for the day having satisfied their minimum daily requirements to graduate. What was left of the student population was sixteen-year-olds and younger. They were louder, more aggressive and immature, and more prone to fighting. With a belly full of food they had been reenergized. By noon, some students were no longer in the mood to be at school. To entertain themselves they often looked outside of accepted behavior.

By seventh-hour, most students could prove to be out of control. They could smell the end of the school day. As they watched their wristwatches and its second-hand tick closer to their 2:30 p.m. release, they became increasingly inattentive, even if there was a test the following day. Their attitude reflected a lazy man's creed of, "Don't do today what you can put off until tomorrow."

Which classes would reveal their character on this first day? Tory wondered as her class began to fill with students.

One by one they filed by Tory as she stood in the doorway greeting them with, "Good morning."

Some returned the greeting. Most did not. The usages of manners among young people were often not taught in the home and its lack of use at school was proof.

Finally, the tardy bell rang as the few students scrambling in the hallway suddenly dashed to the open doorways before they could be counted as tardy. Some students were lost as they glanced at their schedules and slowly walked by looking up at the room numbers posted above doors.

"Good morning, students, and welcome back!" the principal said in greeting the 1,110 enrolled via the intercom. "Please stand for the Pledge of Allegiance followed by a moment of silence."

The students slowly rose from their desks. The looks on their faces showing interest in pledging allegiance to their country was severely lacking.

"I pledge allegiance, to the flag, of the United States of America…"

Tory noticed two boys in the back of the room who remained seated with their heads down on their desks. She left her position in the doorway under the American flag and walked toward them. She did not like being interrupted during morning reflection.

"…And to the republic for which it stands…"

Tory leaned over and whispered in the ear of junior Jeff Palmer to stand out of respect for the nation. Jeff wore dreadlocks and had red eyes in his sockets. He had holes in both of his ears where earrings normally were attached when school was out. He raised his head and wiped the sleep from his eyes as he slowly rose. He did not like being disturbed, but he had been out partying the night before until nearly 1 a.m. He was hardly ready for a first day of school. When standing, Jeff stretched rather than participate in the Pledge of Allegiance with the other students.

Tory then took a few steps toward the windows and tapped sophomore Matthew Kent on the shoulder—a student with tattoos running down both of his skinny arms. He did not budge. He was playing dead.

"…Indivisible with liberty and justice for all."

Matthew still had not budged at Tory's request.

"Son, please stand for the pledge," Tory said softly in his ear as she tried to shake him again.

"Students, please remain standing for a moment of silence," the principal asked.

"The pledge is over, lady!" Matthew said in an ugly tone as he quickly rose in a sitting position.

"Well, then stand for the morning prayer, please," Tory asked too nicely.

Tory knew this kid could be trouble and did not want the first minutes of first-hour on the first day to be negative. She would speak to him in private later in the hour.

Matthew began to stand as the prayer ended at the principal's request to, "Please be seated." Everyone did sit on command and Matthew smiled at Tory. It was round one between them in the battle of wills and he thought himself the victor.

"You see, you make me git up fo' nothin'!" he said to Tory in a half-sleep. "Why you be getting' stupid on me?"

Tory ignored the remark, turned around and walked to her desk to be seated as she listened to the principal welcome the students back to school and reminded them of some simple rules teachers would soon be asked to explain in detail. When he was through with announcements, Tory found herself in front of thirty-five students for the first time in ten weeks. They were sitting in every desk available and at a large rectangular table with six orange plastic chairs situated around it. She wondered where she would put any additional students if the guidance office enrolled any late arrivals. There almost assuredly would be late arrivals in the weeks to come.

The state and the school system advertise the average class size to be about twenty-four students. Most teachers knew that figure to be a bad sell to a gullible news media and parents. Tory's average class size over the last three years averaged thirty-one pupils. Most teachers in the five major disciplines of mathematics, social studies, English, science, and foreign language experienced the same numbers. There were never enough desks to accommodate all the students.

Tory slowly rose from her desk as all students, except Matthew, stared at her. She was on trial with the students and she knew it. They were looking for her weaknesses. They watched her intently wanting to see if she was going to be one to push around or one in which they would have to stay on guard. Tory, like most teachers with any experience, knew the first few days—indeed—the first few minutes, were critical to gaining or losing respect. In a perfect world, students obeyed their teacher's wishes because they were the older authority figure. Those days were long gone in inner city public schools.

On the other hand, if a teacher proved too tough the students would rebel, either internally or externally. Being a public school teacher required being more than a teacher. Many times they would be required to play the part of police officer, counselor, mother, father, coach, mentor, drug enforcement agent, psychologist, fundraiser, sociologist, and parole officer. No one said it was an easy job. That multi-tasking of the profession made teaching as attractive to some as it was, sometimes, painfully frustrating to others.

"Class, welcome back from the dog days of summer," Tory said. "I'm going to be your geography teacher this year. My name is Tory Leblanc and this is my sixth-year of teaching at East Side High School. We won't waste any time because there isn't much of it."

Tory then put her hand on the white board where she had written notes for the class to follow along as she spoke. First on the list was "attendance" followed by "testing." It was time to explain her classroom culture.

"Class, attendance is getting to be a huge problem at every school in the parish," Tory explained. "Students think coming to school is an option. It is not. It is required, but I know some of you will miss as many as ten to twenty days this semester alone. If you miss eleven days unexcused this semester, regardless of your grade, you will fail. That is not my rule. That is the school's rule. If you don't think it's fair, take it up with the principal. And let me add, even if you miss, say, fourteen days and get six excused, that means you really only are unexcused for eight. You might think you're in the clear, but even if you are excused you will have missed too much school to expect a good grade. How can you miss that many days, excused or unexcused, and expect to pass? It won't be easy, let me tell you. It is important that you be here. It should be the most important thing in your young life."

Tory registered the look on the faces of her pupils. They sat stone-faced seemingly caring little for the information or the warning from the teacher they would meet with for the next 180 school days.

Tory continued, "Tests. We will go through about half of the chapters in this book," she said holding the navy blue world geography textbook above her head. "Each of you will get one if you want it. All you have to do is say you want one and I'll check you out a book. You may keep it for as long as you wish. If you want to turn it in after one day, one month, or keep it all year, it is up to you. I'll be giving you more than enough notes to pass your tests, but that requires you to be here every day. If you check out this book and lose it, you will be responsible for replacing it at a cost of fifty-five dollars. You will not be extended a report card or allowed to transfer to another school, or even graduate until your debt is settled with the school system. If you die, we will send the bill to the coroner's office."

Some students chuckled at Tory's joke. She took note of those who did as having some form of intelligent life. Most probably did not laugh because they did not know what a coroner was or did.

Tory had heard stories that an increasing number of students checked out textbooks with the intention of selling them to pick up quick cash. It was also not uncommon for a teacher to issue as many as 150 books to students in the early days of a new year only to have about twenty students "lose" textbooks by year's end. The loss of textbooks each year was a huge expense for the school system and the taxpayer. Recovering money from lost textbooks was virtually impossible, although the school made every effort to do so.

Next on the list was "grading" and "supplies."

"If you look at the bulletin board to your right," Tory said as she pointed, "you will see the grading scale. If you fall below 60 percent, you will fail this class. There is also little extra credit given. Some students use it as a crutch to raise their grade point averages with two weeks remaining in a school year. I don't do that. I reward longevity. Do you know what that means?"

No one stirred. Thirty-five students stared at Tory with blank expressions. She had just used two words this morning that most of this class of high school freshmen and sophomores did not know—"coroner" and "longevity." It was a sign of things to come.

"Longevity means I want students to work hard all year long, not just at the last two weeks of school when they realize they might fail," she explained. "Work hard over the entire year, not just before report cards are passed out and you realize you might be in trouble. Let me tell you, guys, I don't respond to tears and sad stories like, 'My momma is going to beat me.' Finally, try to remember I am here to help you. I don't care what TV or the music tells you, teachers are not your enemy and I am not here to babysit. We don't have to be angry at each other and we don't have to distrust each other. That is not what school is about, so don't believe the garbage society is telling you about what school should be so you can entertain yourselves. Fight for your education. Fight to succeed. Ask me questions if you don't understand. That's what I am paid to do. Okay? Education can be fun. If it is not fun, fine, but we don't have to make each other miserable. We both have a job to do. I will do my job. The question is, will you do yours? Only you can answer that."

Matthew raised his hand. Tory did not ask for questions yet. Somehow she knew his raised hand meant trouble.

"Matthew, hold your questions until I'm through," Tory asked. "I might answer it before the end of class."

Matthew ignored the instruction and asked a question, nonetheless.

"Can you be bought?" Matthew asked in his attempt to be the class clown.

"Bought?" Tory asked.

Some students began to snicker.

"Yea, if I don't do good, what does it take to pass this class? 'Cause I can get whatever you need, you know?"

Some students giggled louder. Some did not. They knew Matthew and they knew his comment to be serious. Tory looked at Matthew very hard. Her thick reddish-brown lips were pressed together and her blue eyes were stern. It would be the kind of look an educated or mature individual would register as one of strong disapproval.

Matthew returned her look beaming a smile. He was trying Tory's patience. He wanted to be noticed. He was also serving notice to the rest of the class that he was attempting to wrestle control of first hour. Matthew failed four of seven classes the year before, including a geography class. Over the summer, he did not go to summer school to make it up. He had obviously not grown up either, and his failures obviously meant nothing to him. Tory decided to begin to battle Matthew's attempt at wit. She squared her shoulders and stood facing the class with her back to the board.

"You can play tough guy if you want, young man, but I know that you failed geography last year," Tory said in a tougher tone. "If you don't want to be here, Matthew, then don't come back to school tomorrow. As it stands now you can leave class and report to the office now."

"What I gotta' go to the office for?" Matthew said in disbelief. "I ain't did you nothin', bitch!"

"Uh, now I know you have to go," Tory said as she moved toward the door and opened it for Matthew's exit.

"You don't talk to me like that!" Matthew continued as he pointed at her. "I do as I want in this world!"

"Yea, yea, whatever you want people to think, Matthew," Tory said with the door open and the steel doorknob in her left hand. "Don't forget your book sack. It's doubtful you will return today."

"I ain't got no books!" Matthew yelled to her as he walked by. "You been on my case since I walked in class! I won't forget this! You'll be hearin' from me!"

How could anyone be on Matthew's case after just a few minutes of school's first day? It was his only defense and it was a lame one. What bothered Tory was Matthew's threat. It was too early to know whether he meant it or would follow through on it.

Matthew mumbled his complaints about Tory Leblanc as he walked down the hallway en route to the office. He disturbed other classes as he strolled by. Several teachers halted their opening day instructions and opened their doors to check on the disturbance, including Elizabeth Hilliard, a middle-aged American history teacher.

"What the hell you lookin' at!" Matthew said as he extended his finger at her as she stepped toward him. "Go back in class and do your job!"

"Hey, boy, I know you did not just talk to me like that!" she said, her voice rising in anger. "Come back here and talk to me like a man and not some little punk!"

Elizabeth, a heavy woman with the gift of attitude when prodded, was being disrespected in front of her students on opening day and she did not appreciate it. She was a no nonsense kind of teacher. Most students respected her mostly because they were afraid of her. They were smart to do so. Matthew, however, never stopped moving toward the office.

"You got two problems now, son," Elizabeth warned as Matthew moved away from her at a quick pace. "Whatever you are going to the office for is one problem. And I'm the other."

Matthew now had his back to Elizabeth as he moved toward the hallway door. He no longer listened to her as he began clapping his hands and singing in rhythm to a rap song he undoubtedly heard on the way to school. In effect, he was tuning Elizabeth and civilized society out of his crazy world.

Female teachers could not afford to be disrespected. Once the word got out among the student population they might be a pushover in the classroom their jobs became much more difficult. Male teachers, on the other hand—even bad ones—often got more respect simply because they were men. It was not fair, but more than a handful of female teachers reluctantly admit that it's true.

Elizabeth returned to her class with a scowl on her face. Tory, with her head sticking into the hallway, saw the confrontation between Elizabeth and Matthew, but retreated to her silent class. They were dumbfounded by Matthew's behavior on the first day of school. Tory studied the looks on the faces of her pupils.

"Is he always like that?" Tory asked the class. "Is this normal behavior?"

Their heads nodded 'yes' before a hand went up in the back of the room. Tory pointed at Allison Teague giving her permission to speak.

"You don't have to be worryin' 'bout him too much, Mrs. Leblanc," she said frankly. "He gonna' miss a lot of school."

"You've had him in other classes before?" Tory asked Allison.

"Yea, and he be rude to everyone. That the way it is wit' him."

Tory appreciated the explanation and respect of Allison. This was not the way the first day of school was supposed to be. Tory went on teaching her class for the remaining thirty-five minutes. It was not even 7:30 a.m. and only hour one of day one.

Summer was only hours retired, but Tory missed it already. Her limbs were still tan from spending time at the pool just a few days before and her hair was still a bit bleached from the sun. She was in her classroom now staring at maps, a shelf full of textbooks, and colorful bulletin boards. Lazy summer fun, the pastel bathing suits, and the smell of suntan lotion were now memories from another past summer. Even though somewhere not far away some lucky individuals were still carrying summer's torch, classroom teachers seemed to possess a mentality that once school began all the simple frivolities of summer were deceased. The weather would be changing soon and talk of another football season was once again dominant in the city. Tory finished eating lunch at her desk while the radio played, and she was just beginning to close her sleepy eyes on her first lunch shift on her first day when the bell rang for her fifth-hour class to begin at 11:30 a.m.

She slowly stood from her chair and stretched hoping to reinvigorate a body that had not yet become accustomed to full-time work. Two months of summer vacation is like part-time retirement. With no alarm clock to disengage the summer slumber and used to treating each day as if it were a Saturday, it was a bit difficult to get back into the routine. But Tory knew it was only a matter of time before she would be back in fall semester form.

Students began to enter her class as Tory strolled toward the open door. During this hour she was again to teach freshmen, the most unruly and most immature group a teacher could face in a given day. They entered the classroom smug believing there was something special about them. They were just a year removed from some sort of presumed elite social status at their middle school that granted them unwarranted arrogance. For whatever reason, too many of them carried that over to high school where it was not respected or understood by teachers or the upper classmen in the student body. Nevertheless, it could take teachers days to break them of their childish antics, if it could be done at all.

The students filed in and immediately sat down. Some students dropped their books on a desk and returned to the hallway to be seen by friends and taking the chance of being tardy. Tory redirected them back to class informing them that once they were in class they could not leave it, even if the tardy bell had not rung. When the tardy bell did ring, three girls began to run to the classroom door. While Tory spoke to them about the school rule concerning late class entry, she watched a male student move by them and exit her class and then walk toward the end of the hallway. Tory had two problems to deal with, but had to chase and challenge the male student. Tory chose to speak quickly to the girls before turning her attention to the young man moving away from her at a rapid pace.

"Girls, you are late," Tory warned as she backpeddled from them. "I'm not going to do anything about it today, but beginning tomorrow you will be entered on the roll as being tardy, got it?"

Tory could really do nothing more. It was only the first day of school and she did not know their names to mark them tardy. The girls nodded their heads that they understood Tory's warning, but she knew from their body language they did not really care. Besides, Tory had more pressing matters as she watched the young man move down the hallway.

"Young man, please stop," Tory called out as she closed in on him from behind.

He did not even turn around to dignify her instruction.

"Please wait. I must speak to you. Stop now, please!" her voice began to have a sense of urgency.

The young man finally stopped, rolled his eyes, and turned to look at Tory. The look on his face told her he was not to be denied. He appeared highly frustrated. He was going somewhere and to compromise with him would be a waste of effort. As Tory moved toward him his face registered anger. She was not afraid of him, but had to be careful not knowing anything about him. Tory prodded gently.

"Where are you going, young man?" she asked.

"To the office," he replied coldly.

"But why? We haven't even started class," Tory explained. "I haven't even called roll. I don't even know your name."

"You don't need to know it. It doesn't matter anymore."

With that, he turned away from Tory and began to move toward the building's exit. Tory walked with him as another duty teacher, Brenda, moved toward them.

"Brenda, I have to take this young man to the office," Tory explained to the duty teacher. "Would you watch my class for a second, please?"

Brenda Aguillard taught French and was on duty patrolling the hallway when Tory made the request. With Brenda now watching her class, Tory could take the time to try to get to the bottom of why the young man walked out of her class. The two walked side by side as they moved outside toward the school office into the brutal 102-degree heat.

"I don't understand why you are leaving. Would you at least tell me that?" Tory asked as the two walked briskly.

The two did not make eye contact and Tory began to feel more like a nagging mother than a teacher.

"Look, I just decided to quit school, that's it! Okay?" he said staring straight ahead with determination. "I don't want to be here anymore. I'm going to get a job or somethin', I don't know. I just don't want to go to school anymore. Would you leave my ass alone?"

"You quit school?" Tory replied ignoring the cursing. "How old are you? What do you think you can do to survive without an education?"

"It ain't none of your business. You don't have to worry about learnin' my name and I ain't coming back!"

Tory held open the main office door as the two entered the chilled room as a dozen parents were enrolling their children late. Tory explained the situation to the office personnel as the many parents and students looked on. While Tory spoke, the young man sat down in the only empty chair available awaiting his fate. The parents stared at him quietly as he was temporarily the subject of attention.

As Tory left the office she wondered why a young man at the tender age of fourteen or fifteen years of age would declare he was quitting school. Not that it mattered, but perhaps he was older. Or, maybe he wanted to transfer to another school. Tory could only wonder, but there was nothing she could do. The public school dropout rate in Louisiana was among the highest in the nation, but Tory never had a student quit school on the very first day. She put it out of her mind promising to focus on the students who were in class as she strolled quickly back to her classroom.

The bigger item in Tory's mind centered around the large number of people in the main office waiting to enter the crowded guidance office to enroll their children. Why parents did not enroll their children before school began during the quiet summer months was always a question among school administrators. Tory also knew there would be "new" students enrolled as late as mid-September. Many would not be transfers from other schools; just students that decided to personally extend their summer vacation at the expense of their academic status.

As Tory moved past the guidance office she saw it was crammed with parents and students. The school's administration had so much to do on the first day of school dealing with the students they knew were coming. Having to deal with a walk-up, late-arriving group trying to gain admittance was incredibly taxing on them. In fact, so many students enrolled and transferred to various schools, the parish school system did not officially tabulate the number of students present and submit it to the state until October 1.

The transient behavior of the public school system was very hard on teachers. Tory had already been e-mailed, like the other teachers in the school, a list of nine students to be stricken from the rolls for various reasons, but having made contact with the school to verify such. Tory had already added eight new students since 9 a.m. and the day was still three hours from its conclusion. Now, she had another student quit school before she knew his name for reasons she would never know.

It was not an unusual beginning to the first day of school or the most difficult of her career, but it was an interesting one. It was a day the superintendent was almost sure to explain to the news media this afternoon as one that was quiet, streamlined, and pristine with all teachers exploding with optimism as eager students awaited instruction. Tory could only laugh as she moved back into the hallway to return to her class. What was told to the news media by the school system mouthpieces was in the general area code of the truth, but the phone number was not always accurate.

After the first day of school was completed, Tory overheard four teachers discussing the first expulsions of the year as she walked to the parking lot. It took just one day for East Side High School to expel two male students and suspend two others for lengthy periods. Two were expelled before 7:15 a.m., having arrived at school drunk, one vomiting on the hallway floor outside of his first class, and the other vomiting near the office when he was summoned to appear before the assistant principal. The two suspensions involved boys "skipping" their final class of the day and breaking into the lockers of football players who were working out in the weight room nearby. They stole sneakers, cell phones, and about seventy-five dollars in cash before two team managers caught them when entering the locker room to prepare for after-school football practice. There was one fight involving two males between afternoon classes that took three teachers to break up. Their fate was not yet known. The teachers went into detail about the incidents and greeted the problems with a shrug of their tired shoulders. Tory did not stop to ask questions. Like most experienced inner city teachers, she was numb to such antics and there would certainly be more of the same as the year went on.

"There is an old saying that the course of civilization is a race between catastrophe and education. In a democracy such as ours, we must make sure that education wins the race."

—John F. Kennedy

August—"Soccer should have never been invented"

The students chattered among themselves as they sat in scattered desks waiting for further instructions. The bell had rung to end the day as more athletes walked into the cramped room without windows in the core of the school just after 3 p.m. The open classroom door revealed hallway floors in the process of being mopped by the custodial crew. Trashcans were full and spilling onto the horrible green-stained carpet that was a vestige of a more prosperous 1970s public school system. Seated players reached out for handshakes and "high-fives" from those entering. The noise level in the room began to pick up.

In all there were twenty-one students representing different cultures. The classroom more resembled a meeting of the United Nations than they did the East Side High School boys soccer team. Nine players were Caucasian, three were black, four were Vietnamese, two were Palestinians, two were Hispanic, and one was a foreign exchange student. Only two in the group were freshmen revealing a serious question about the sport's survival at the school.

Last season's captain and most vocal of all players, senior Terrance Wright, asked another player as he noisily entered the room, "What's up, dog?"

It is a common expression of affection used and accepted among the lower socio-economic groups or the middle-class students striving for acceptance. Terrance, along with most on the team, was very middle-class, but had been barbarized nonetheless.

Junior Jesus Estevez, short in stature and darker in complexion, extended his fist as a handshake. The two boys bumped their fists out of respect to each other.

"Just chillin'," Jesus responded as he threw his body in the desk next to Terrance, appearing more tired than a senior citizen.

"I didn't think you were coming back to play," Terrance said. "Word was you were through with this team and were going to stick with 'select' teams only."

"I know, I know, but I didn't want to let the team down," Jesus said in mock exasperation.

"You just did, dumb ass," Terrance said in a joking manner not allowing Jesus to get the best of him. "You showed up."

"Hey, say what you want, but if I don't play you guys don't score, you know?" Jesus shot back with his head slightly cocked.

The comment brought laughter from some players in the room who knew Jesus and Terrance were good friends. Jesus slumped in his desk and laughed at his own joke. Jesus was a clown on a team that was funnier than it was good.

The team was an athletic joke. In seven years of existence the boy's soccer team never had a winning season. They had never even experienced a break-even season. The soccer team not only lost matches, they lost them badly. In fifteen matches last season, they lost thirteen and scored a mere eleven goals, revealing the worst statistic in the eight-team district. Part of their failure was due to a lack of talent. Most of the quality players in their attendance zone enrolled in private schools that routinely beat them. But the most significant problem resided in the school's athletic director, Ray Gatewood, who served double duty as head football coach. Coach Gatewood hated soccer and considered it a threat to the survival of western civilization. Coach Gatewood had made it his personal mission to undermine everything associated with the game. His success with doing so showed a gift with being insensitive and narrow-minded.

"What are we waiting on, man?" Jesus asked Terrance in a slight Honduran accent while staring at an empty doorway. "I've got to be at work in an hour. I can't be waiting around."

Terrance did not answer looking around the room at the three new faces. Two of the players were small, skinny, and still waiting for their pubescent growing spurt to liberate them from their middle-school physique. None of the veteran players spoke to the new guys. Terrance then glanced over at the largest of the three new players wearing the black and white T-shirt of the powerful Spanish football club, Real Madrid.

Without raising his hand to point, Terrance signaled to Jesus with his head to look at him asking, "Who's that guy?"

Jesus spun his body around in his desk to look at the young man, a new face, who was sitting quietly in the back of the crowded room full of noisy chatter. None of the other students spoke to him as the soccer team anxiously waited for the first meeting of the season. The young man's build was muscular, his face was pale and covered with blond hair, and he appeared taller than both of them. Terrance and Jesus turned to face the front of the class before revealing their thoughts.

"Either he's a foreign exchange student or too stupid to know better than to be here," Jesus said, revealing a lack of team pride and a growing impatience with having to wait for the start of the meeting. "We'll find out soon enough."

"Why wait?" Terrance asked as he looked over his shoulder at the new student. "Hey, you! Yea, you."

The young man with gray eyes and short blond hair raised his chin slightly in recognition of Terrance. He was glad to be noticed, a stranger in North America in need of friends.

He paused before asking in perfect English, but in a thick European accent, "Yes, what can I do for you?"

"Where you from, man?" asked Terrance curious about a teenager with such perfect diction.

"Poland. Warsaw. You know where that is?" he answered hoping to deepen the conversation.

Terrance did not know where Poland was. He had never heard of Warsaw. So he inquired to Jesus, whose grade point average was only slightly better than a dead man.

"Do you know where Poland is?" Terrance asked Jesus.

Jesus shook his head indicating he didn't know, and then asked, "I thought he said he was from Warsaw?"

Both lost for words, Terrance did the only thing he knew to do. He asked.

"Where's that?" Terrance asked.

"It's in Eastern Europe," the anxious reply came from the back of the room.

"Are you any good at soccer?"

"I think so."

"What's your name?"

"I am Ivan Stralnovic," he said pronouncing the name "E-von Stral-ni-vich."

Jesus looked at Terrance and laughed sinking his body in his hard-plastic yellow chair.

"Well, he sounds like a soccer player," Jesus said turning his body toward the front of the room. "I wonder if he'll take your position, because he can't have mine."

The lack of response from Terrance or Jesus made Ivan feel unwanted. He did not understand just how insensitive and ignorant too many American teenagers really were. He would have an entire school year to learn that.

Terrance was last season's captain and was likely to be again, during his final season. He felt some responsibility for the team. He was the most vocal player on the soccer team and one of the most popular students in the school. His medium-length brown hair and solid build make him the school heartthrob. He was also the target of football coaches who constantly nagged him to play inside linebacker in their "34" defensive scheme. Each year head Coach Gatewood asked Terrance to go out for his squad of dwindling players and each year Terrance turned him down. Terrance enjoyed turning down the request of the football coaches because he hated Coach Gatewood so much. The soccer players respected and admired Terrance for denying the request of a man they believed to be at the heart of their team's problems. Terrance wanted only once in his four-year high school term to win more matches than Coach Gatewood did football games—a feat not yet accomplished.

Terrance was glad to be a senior because he did not know if soccer would survive at the school, or be allowed to survive. The soccer team at East Side High School was the most mistreated team in the metropolitan area, thanks in large part to the ignorance on display by the school's football coaches and players who strutted the sprawling campus with unparalleled arrogance.

They often verbally abused the soccer players with greetings like, "Here come the fags!" or "Soccer should have never been invented."

The comments were often followed with laughter. Never mind that the first football game recognized as American was played with a soccer ball between Princeton and Rutgers in 1869. It was five years before American football even allowed running with the ball. The first American football games involved significant kicking of a rolling ball. Those affiliated with football at the school did not know that small fact. School coaches heaped their misdirected hatred and jealousy of the world's most popular game on the backs of the easiest target: fourteen- to seventeen-year-old boys having no defense against grown men. What was worse, however, was the coaches were supposed to be entrusted with nurturing open minds. Instead, they were teaching intolerance to gullible football players drunk on gaining their coaches approval ratings—a rating gained by insulting athletes that anywhere else in the world would hail nothing short of celebrity status. Mix the situation with a principal, also an ex-football coach, and the soccer team was at the mercy of those who did not grant it.

Terrance, however, felt he was now physically big enough and mentally tough enough to challenge those ugly remarks. Either that, or he no longer cared what anyone thought having fought and lost too many verbal battles with the gridiron boys.

As an underclassman, however, Terrance was often taunted in the locker room as he dressed for soccer practice each day. He never forgot the nasty comments directed toward him. Nor did he forgive those who aimed them at his once fragile ego.

That did not keep Coach Gatewood from recognizing Terrance as one of three soccer players who could help his team better compete in a six-team football district that fielded three private schools and one suburban school loaded with talent. Coach Gatewood knew his team was having increasing difficulty with that competition with each passing year and resented the addition of soccer to the school's sports menu. He strongly believed his school was better off focusing and competing strongly in a traditional American sport like football rather than scattering its thin manpower pool. Quite simply, soccer was a competition he did not want to contend against. Its popularity threatened to upset the future athletic power structure comprising the good-ole-boy network of which he subscribed.

The chatter in the room began to idle when Coach Gatewood entered the room. He was a tall, young man carrying a five o'clock shadow on a face whose crown was covered with sandy short-cropped hair. Being a physical education coach, his arms were powerful from working out in the weight room each day. He carried a scowl on his face as his chosen characteristic. It was his definition. He exuded intimidation as a social defense against officials, pain-in-the-ass players, overbearing parents, and his fellow coaches. His mood was unpredictable and often monitored by his staff as it was important to know when he was approachable. If Coach Gatewod had worked in the brutal corporate world of scheming, distrustful, competitive professionals, he would have fit in perfectly.

Coach Gatewood did not like the task ahead of him. He had to address the boy's soccer team about completing and submitting eligibility forms in the absence of a soccer coach. As athletic director he was instructed by Principal Berling to perform this duty and he hated doing so. It was Coach Gatewood's intention over the summer months to quietly disband the soccer program after the third head soccer coach quit in as many years. All three coaches voiced their disgust over the lack of support from the school's administration. Coach Gatewood orchestrated the demise of the soccer program by refusing to cooperate with it. He did not allow the team to play home games on the football field thus denying them the right to collect an admission fee and making even a small profit. When the team's parents organized one weekend selling jambalaya outside a large grocery store to raise money for uniforms and to become financially solvent, Coach Gatewood quietly, and legally, confiscated that $2,100 bank account over the summer months. He used the money to upgrade the football practice field, although the soccer players and their parents had yet to learn of his latest transgression against them. In past years, he also charged the soccer team an annual fee of $300 dollars that the team bank account could barely meet to re-sod the football field he did not allow them to use. Ironically, the money was taken from their school account just weeks before the start of spring football practice. It was a power play against the soccer team he could utilize without asking.

In short, Coach Gatewood was a cruel man who had not yet grown up. He foolishly believed the purpose of the school was to field a football team that would impress his coaching peers and perhaps gain the attention of a college coach wanting to add him to their staff. After five years of coaching football, that dream had not materialized for him. He was privately resentful of it. His reputation preceded him and many high school and college coaches found him lacking persona.

As he stood in front of the boy's soccer team, he looked them over for football prospects forfeiting the original purpose of his meeting with them.

He pointed to one player with his powerful right arm before rudely asking, "Why didn't you come out for football this year, son? We're practicing right now. First game is in two weeks."

Obviously startled, the young man was a sophomore standing about five-foot-nine, and weighing 165 pounds. Completely intimidated, the young man did not respond. Instead, he shrugged his shoulders with his eyes wide open. With the exception of Terrance, the players sat up straight in their chairs awaiting Coach Gatewood's next pointed question and hoping it would not be directed at them. But Coach Gatewood spared them, realizing he was not able to sell football to these young men just eight weeks before the start of their season and six weeks into his. Instead, he adjusted his demeanor moving from brusque to simply disapproving.

"All right, listen up," Coach Gatewood told the young players as he shuffled papers never once making eye contact with the team. "I don't want to be here and I don't want to do this. I had hoped we had this problem taken care of over the summer, but I think you've got a coach coming. I don't know when you'll meet him and I don't really care."

That much, the players believed. As he spoke to the team in a rude monotone there was nothing but misplaced intolerance in his voice. He rarely made eye contact with the players and spoke as if he would rather be at home weeding his garden on a hot August afternoon than showing the team any courtesy whatsoever. Quite honestly, Coach Gatewood did not perform all the functions of his job title and got away with it.

With the flick of his wrist, Coach Gatewood then tossed two red manila folders packed with numerous forms on a messy desk to his right. The folders landed flatly, spilling its organized contents.

"There's your forms," he said. "Pass 'em out. Fill 'em out. Your coach will collect them."

He then turned to walk out of the room. He was almost out of the door when he finished his thought process aloud.

"If you'll excuse me, I've got a real sport to coach now."

Coach Gatewood was out of the door and down the hallway by the time any of the soccer players stirred. The young men were in shock at how rude he could be, and how smug he was toward them. He cared little of the opinion of others and proved to be a horrible example to young men about how to lead or behave as a role model. His job title was athletic director, but the last thing he was to many players and coaches at the school was a director of athletics. What he did was direct his ego and his football program, in that order, to the top of the food chain at the school at the expense of other programs. Coach Gatewood had alienated himself from those who could help him. He was the butt of students' jokes. Other teachers snickered at him behind his back as he acted as an athletic Neanderthal. He had the title to negotiate the athletic program for the school's twelve sports in any manner he saw fit without question. He was without character. Coach Gatewood was his own god and he worshipped regularly. He even went as far as to refuse to vote "yes" at the last Louisiana High School Sports Association meeting to allow the increasingly popular sport of bowling to be officially recognized. He told the school bowling coach it was his intention to end the school's participation with the sport.

"I don't want *that* sport in my school," he had told the bowling coach just days prior to the statewide vote, even though eight students made up a school team just one year removed from winning the district's unofficial title; a title eluding the football program over the last six years.

My school. His school. Coach Gatewood thought it was all about him. Coach Gatewood never understood that the purpose of the school was to introduce new ideas to young minds; to expand the immature thinking process of teenagers and to make them comprehend the much larger world around them.

When his players were injured in football games they became ghosts. Coach Gatewood had no more use for them and treated his wounded as if they had let the team down. He refused to speak to them in the

28

hallways and did not inquire to the extent of their pain, both physical and mental. However, he insisted they be at practice or face being removed from the football team. He wanted his players available to be abused at his whim.

He only attended basketball and some baseball games—sports he recognized. Track, softball, wrestling, tennis, golf, cross-country, volleyball, gymnastics, and soccer be damned. He not only did not support the coaches of those respected teams with his mere presence, he did not even speak to them. He slightly acknowledged the school band, but only because they spilled the school's fight song into the autumn air when he took the field for Friday night games. He did not attend any band concerts or offer in any way to help that struggling organization make money to survive in the face of stiff budget cuts that directly affected it. No, he was not decent enough for that. Coach Gatewood saw the band, like the rest of the school, as a small arm that played some vital part in the success of the football program.

Terrance thought he should say something after Coach Gatewood's exit, to explain that his behavior was not something shocking in the least. But he was worried that his ugly attitude toward the soccer team might force some of the younger players to rethink playing for the school. Terrance sat up in his chair and noticed no one moving to leave the room. The other athletes stirred little. It was as if they were waiting and hoping that there was more to being a part of the soccer team than what had been revealed.

The team had not met their coach. They only learned that they had one and had no information as to who that might be. The papers they needed to fill out for eligibility were still scattered on the desk and no one knew how to fill them out or what vital instructions were attached that would help them do so. There was no information on practices, uniforms, fees, jamborees, deadlines—nothing. They felt unwanted. That much was made clear. They were not respected. The new players did not understand why. A few began to mumble as they stood up. Then the silence was broken.

"What an asshole," another said quietly in summing up the meeting, if it could be called that at all.

"Are you gonna' play?" another asked.

"I don't know," was the response.

"I don't need this," said another.

Terrance realized very quickly what Coach Gatewood had done. He had begun to dismantle the soccer team before the first practice began. Terrance was not going to allow that to happen. He stood and moved to the front of the room. He held up his hands, but the words did not come out. For a second, he knew what it was like to be a young teacher. He wanted to gain control of the situation, but was too young and inexperienced to do so. As players began to rise from their seats and move toward the door, Terrance summoned a voice from deep inside. Jesus sat up straight in his chair knowing Terrance was about to put his reputation on the line. He wondered if his friend could pull the motley group together and organize it before the players left the room for a long school year of anonymity.

"Excuse me, guys!" Terrance said with his palms up. "Excuse me."

The players were all standing now and had gathered near the door. They turned for a second to see who was making the effort to hold them together as a team. They listened, hoping he could, although they realized he was a mortal student.

"I've been on this soccer team for three years and we have never had this many players show up for a first meeting," Terrance explained, although he was telling a lie to get their attention.

No one moved. Some even moved toward the center of the room as if they were going to sit down again, but they stopped short of that. Terrance knew he had their attention and did not want to lose it. He was the team's captain and for now, the team's coach and advisor. He was smart enough to know that what he said next would either save the team or lose it. He decided the direct approach was best. Besides, it was the only way he knew to communicate with players slightly younger than he was. Jesus quietly closed the heavy wooden door in an attempt at team privacy and as a show of support to Terrance.

Terrance continued, "I know Coach Gatewood made a lot of you angry. That's what he does. If you quit the soccer team now then he wins. He wants you to quit. He expects you to quit. I don't want you to, okay? We don't want you to."

Terrance then motioned for Jesus to stand next to him as a show of strength.

Terrance went for broke. He decided to say whatever he must to get their names, positions, and classifications for the coach they hoped would arrive tomorrow. He wanted to get all the information he could so as to track down these players in the future if need be. Terrance was not shy by any stretch of the imagination, but it was not in his character to play any other part on the team but captain, a position that held more in title than in substance. For today, Terrance had to be more.

Terrance motioned to Jesus to get a piece of paper from his shredded yellow science notebook. Jesus quickly pulled a piece of lined paper from the spiral notebook and handed it to Terrance, who was growing more nervous by the second. Terrance then held the paper over his head.

"Before you leave, I want you to write your name on here and your phone numbers," Terrance said waving the paper high. "We will get in touch with you. Don't leave without signing this. We will have another meeting, a serious meeting next time, with our new coach. I promise."

Terrance did not know if that was true or not, but he had to say something to lure these players back the next time a meeting was called. He could not have these players believing that every soccer meeting was similar to this one. Terrance wanted to win and to do that he knew the team needed something it had really never had, and that was bodies in uniform.

As the players leaned over the classroom desk, they wrote down their names and phone numbers in messy print as they were asked to do. As each one rose to leave, Terrance thanked them and said something nice, even if he didn't mean it. He did not know many of these players. Most were new, but he wanted to make a mark on them.

"Dominick Vaccarro," Terrance recited as the skinny freshman completed his name in blue ink, "I heard you could play, man."

"I try real hard," Dominick said with a grin.

"Well, we'll need you. I hope you'll stick with it."

"Coach, don't scare me none."

"That's what I want to hear."

Jesus enjoyed the response, too. He extended Dominick a high-five as he left the room.

In all, every player signed up to play soccer. A soccer coach was expected to arrive at some point. Terrance turned what should have been a disastrous meeting into a positive one. What he did not know was the soccer bank account was emptied of funds. That was something the new coach would be forced to reckon with soon. It was something that would raise the anger levels of the veteran players to new heights. There would be no speech to remedy that one.

"He who opens a school door, closes a prison."

—French poet Victor Hugo

September—"She was the victim in a love triangle and lost out"

Tory had spent much of her planning period sitting in the guidance office waiting for a parent to show up for a conference concerning her child. It was not unusual to wait, but the parents of Matthew Kent were ten minutes late and Tory had many things to do, including attending a girls district basketball meeting and grading ninety-four geography tests taken earlier in the day.

Tory sat in the green cushioned aluminum chair listening to a senior argue with one of the guidance counselors about why he should be allowed to drop his calculus class, even though he signed up to take it. This senior did not understand or simply refused to acknowledge he was the one who filled out the schedule card in May of last year. The classes were his to choose. All the guidance officer did was meet the request, but he continued to argue as if he thought he could actually win the verbal altercation. Tory wanted to stand up and slap the increasingly rude young man knowing he probably treated his parents that way at home. He probably did not think a teacher was worth even a modicum of respect.

"Billy, for the last time, it was not I who filled out your schedule card," school counselor, Denise George, explained for the third time. "You filled it out and we are not allowed at this late date to accommodate any changes without the approval of the principal. And he is not going to approve it, I can tell you that now."

"Well, I want to talk to him!" Billy said in a sassy tone. "I don't like this class. The teacher is too hard and you made a mistake putting me in his class! I'm not going back to his class. Suspend me if you want, I don't care, but I'm not going back!"

Denise toyed with the pearl strands around her tanned neck and again tried to sink into Billy's head that he could not get his way. High schools are not in the business of giving students the teacher of their choice or time slot they may like. They simply place the information into a computer and let those results dictate a student's given schedule. Billy's voice began to rise as if he thought the possibility of a temper tantrum might scare the guidance officials into making an exception for him.

"Billy, where are you supposed to be this hour?" Denise asked, as two other counselors slowly made their way out of their office to stand behind her to offer support.

"Don't worry about where I'm supposed to be!" Billy verbally snapped at her. "Worry about my schedule and I'll leave you alone!"

"Well, you can talk to other people like that, but you are not going to get your way with me like that," Denise said in a stern, but professional tone. "You need to leave. Now!"

"You don't know who you are messing with!" Billy said as he spun around and pushed the glass door open so hard he could have smashed the glass when it hit the brick wall behind it. "Mess with me and see what happens!"

What Billy said in leaving could be constituted as a threat and could have far-reaching consequences, but Denise chose to ignore it. The other counselors mentioned how rude Billy was while reiterating to each other the rules that were in place regarding schedule changes.

Meanwhile, Tory continued waiting and glanced at her watch. She was in no mood for this type of disrespect from a parent. She had many things to do and the least a parent could do was be on time for a meeting.

It was bad enough Matthew was rude to her and failing her geography class in a consistent manner. Now, the parents she was slated to meet were displaying the same type of behavior in a different way. They were late for a meeting with Tory and there was no explanation as to why. Tory waited anxiously and reflected on the very young school year.

With five weeks having elapsed from the school year and just one week prior to the first progress reports being delivered to students, Tory was already frustrated. Of her 160 students, over 40 percent were failing. Of the 60 percent who were passing, only seven students had earned an 'A.' Among all students, twenty-three had already missed more than nine days of school and fourteen had already earned time in the discipline center for major infractions against the school rules. Another thirteen students had missed her class having to spend the day in the school's time-out room for a variety of minor offenses. The figures were not unusual, but frustrating and demoralizing to teachers just the same. It was only September.

Tory had already called many parents to inform them of their child's behavioral problems or academic difficulties, but most either could not be reached or there was rarely any improvement after communication was successfully made. Most parents made the obligatory remarks to Tory about that type of behavior or failure not being tolerated. It was just rhetoric to impress Tory, and other teachers, into believing solid parenting was taking place in the home. The fact was parents today appeared incredibly weak in dealing with their offspring, exercising just slightly more control than teachers. At least parents had the right to take away phone privilieges, dating, and car privileges. Teachers could only make phone calls and hope changes would be made. For teachers, "hope" was a lonely and unreliable partner.

Then there were the Matthew Kents of the world who had missed five of seven tests days due to unexcused absences and simply failed the two he did take. He had already been suspended once for fighting in the school gym during physical education over who was going to take the ball inbounds during a basketball game. Matthew had problems. He was rude, ignorant, volatile, unpredictable, loved to play the part of the school bully, cursed aloud, and was rumored to be involved with the drug culture. His choice of friends was horrendous and he verbally abused most teachers, especially females, because he believed he could get away with it. Ironically, it was Matthew's family who phoned Tory and other teachers wanting to meet with them about their child's complex and erratic behavior. Tory was the first teacher on the list, but while Tory kept waiting, her paperwork was backlogging.

Finally out of frustration, Tory slowly rose and told Denise she was leaving.

"If they show up I'll be in my room grading papers," Tory told Denise, who was seated directly in front of her just a few feet away. "I cannot wait any longer."

"I don't blame you," Denise said in agreed frustration. "It's not unusual for parents to do this. They don't even have the courtesy to call and cancel."

"This was a group of parents I really needed to speak with," Tory said in frustration, "because he is a real pain."

Denise nodded her head in agreement.

Tory excused herself and slowly walked back to class thinking the opportunity to help a student was wasted. She really needed help with Matthew, but there would be none forthcoming. On the way to her classroom she saw a football coach holding one kid by the arm as blood dripped from his nose. She heard another student taunting him from about fifty feet behind while another male teacher physically restrained him.

"Yea, mother-fucker, you betta' be gittin' away from me," one student yelled to the other at the top of his lungs. "If'n it wasn't for these damn coaches I'd finish what I started in the locker room! Believe that!"

The bleeding student said nothing as he held many brown paper towels over his nose. The coaches said nothing as they attempted to manhandle the two into some sort of civility as they marched them to the office. Tory never flinched as she watched from afar. It was just another day in the life of an inner city public school teacher. The coach and the teacher tried very hard to restrain the students, while at the same time, they tried to keep from getting blood on their own clothes.

"Yea, bitch, I ain't through with yo' ass!" the more verbal of the two boys continued. "Ain't nobody can save, ya' either!"

As Tory slowly walked to her classroom, she was unaware of the actual time. She was so focused on the amount of time wasted while waiting on a parent who was not coming to meet her for a scheduled meeting, she lost sight of how close she was to teaching her final class of the day. She picked up the pace as she moved in the hallway toward her classroom, now realizing she was not going to be able to grade any papers. Before she could think her next thought, the bell rang for seventh hour, the last class of the day. Tory rubbed her eyes and then pulled her glasses off of her tired face. Students spilled into the hallway around her as they left their sixth-hour classes. They were oblivious to her presence as their conversations were often lewd. There was no way to catch a student in the act of cursing or threatening anyone simply because there were too many students bunched together. As always, not one student would dare tell on another.

"Hey, nigga', go fuck yo' self!" one male student could be heard yelling to another. "I be knowing where you live!"

"I know you ain't talkin' to me, bitch," the reply came from further down the hall followed by mock laughter.

"Why you trying to be white?" another screamed from a distance.

"Whore!" a female voice was heard to say from near Tory's door before a playful scream went out.

Students screamed and laughed over the slamming of lockers and shuffling of feet as they made their way to their final class. Tory wanted to catch those students making those vile remarks, but it was the way some students bonded with each other. As crude as it was to do, some students found it possible to do so.

Tory opened her door as students filed into her class and other classes. Her presence slowed only some of the horrible language. Some students entered Tory's class behind her and sat in their desks. Others dropped their books on their desks and immediately walked out to stand in the hallway to see friends and be seen. It was a move by students that was never understood by teachers. The boys lined up against the hallway wall as if, magically, a party van full of scantily-clad voluptuous girls were going to show up and they were afraid they would miss out. In reality, the girls just walked by the boys hoping they would flirt. When they did, they made every effort to ignore them. It was harmless, high school fun. It was also an easy way to pick up an unnecessary tardy.

When the tardy bell did ring, the hallway was full of dozens of students racing to various doorways hoping to sneak into class unnoticed. The teachers were there to record their gamble in their roll books.

Tory had no tardy students to record this hour, so she simply shut the door and sat down at her desk to call roll for the noisiest class of the day. When she began calling roll, students began to speak among themselves a bit lower, not so much out of respect for their teacher, but out of fear of accidentally being marked absent and having to explain it to the school disciplinarian the following day.

"Abbott," Tory called out.

"Here," came the reply from the back of the room.

"Boudreaux."

"Here."

"Calais."

"Here."

"Dickinson."

"Present."

"Everett."

No reply, but Tory knew he was in class because he had walked right past her while she was on duty in the hallway. She tried again, but did not look up from her roll book so as not to break her rhythm.

"Everett."

No reply.

"Everett."

Tory could see him out of the corner of her eye. This was a silly game she sometimes played with Spencer Everett, another of her troubled youngsters who was failing school academically and socially. Spencer liked to aggravate Tory by not answering the roll when called. It killed time and gained him attention, albeit negative. Tory had warned him about this type of failure to respond before, but naturally, he shrugged it off believing he could do anything he wanted. He had reason to think he could. The system favored irregular behavior. Liberal educators had a label for it and corrupt attorneys always could explain it away in a tired rendition of socio-economic inequality. In fact, Spencer's behavior was just rude in failing to respond to a teacher hired to call roll and perform a job function.

Over the summer months, Spencer had been arrested for breaking and entering a home while the owners were away on vacation. The sad part of it all was Spencer knew the family all too well. He stole jewelry that was never recovered, two television sets that were recovered but damaged, and let the family dog out of the yard in an effort to open the gate and make a fast getaway when discovered by neighbors. Ironically, it was the barking dog that tipped off police. Spencer was hiding inside a covered ski boat three houses down the street. The judge gave Spencer a warning and community service, which he laughed about aloud in class as having never performed. Spencer was trouble and his mother had absolutely no control over him.

Tory was not about to lose this "game" with Spencer, no matter how incredibly childish it was. She was going to call his name until he tired of hearing it, hoping he would respond.

"Everett."

No reply. Tory would repeat his name all hour if she had to. She was not going to allow Spencer to dictate to her when and if he should reply to his name being called when other students had to. Sending him to the office for the offense would result in nothing more than a chat with Spencer about being respectful and it would be wasted paperwork on her part. This was a silly offense not worth sending a student to the office about, but aggravating enough for the teacher demanding respect.

"Everett."

There were some giggles in the class and some exasperation.

"C'mon, man, answer the lady," begged one student to Spencer sitting near Tory's desk.

"Everett."

"Yo," Spencer finally said in a very low tone.

"Everett," Tory continued.

"Yo," Spencer repeated a bit louder.

"Everett."

"What do you want now?" came the reply from Spencer in an arrogant tone.

One student caught on quickly wanting this spar to end.

"She wants you to say "here' and to do it with respect, man," said another student near the door of the smallish classroom.

Tory thought to herself without looking up from her roll book that at least one student understood exactly what the problem was.

"Everett."

"Here!" Everett finally responded in a loud, rude form.

Tory never missed a beat.

"Flanigan."

"Here."

"Lloyd."

"Here."

Tory was back in rhythm and did not surrender her class to Spencer's antics, although it did cost her some self-respect.

As she began to continue with the roll call, the noise in the class began to get a bit louder than usual, even for seventh-hour. One pregnant sixteen-year-old was showing another a final list of names she had selected for her unborn. Most students had their notebooks ready for class as they spoke. However, most of the noise was centered near the long row of windows that looked out into the school's courtyard of trees. The sun was shining directly on the students, further illuminating the argument between two girls. Tory looked up and did not know whether to continue to call roll and hope the argument would fizzle out or move the students immediately.

"Girls!" Tory yelled out. "Shut up now before things get out of hand!"

The girls paid no attention to Tory and she began to sense that the situation was already out of hand.

"Look, bitch, you don't know me to be talkin' to me like dat," one girl said to the other.

"I know's you ain't be talkin' to me like that!" the other replied in defense while moving her head from side to side, "'cause if'n you is I'm gonna kick the hell out of you in front of all yo' friends!"

"Bring it, girl, if you think you be bad enough!" came the reply.

Both Tomeka Evans and Andrea Smith were not academics, but they had never been discipline problems for Tory. She knew they were both from lower socio-economic backgrounds and did not have a lot going for them, but they further enhanced their future defeats by refusing to take school seriously. Both students were failing, but Tomeka—Tory's pet project—still had a chance to pass if she would spend even just a little bit of time studying. Tomeka always promised Tory she would study more, but she never did. Now both girls were threatening each other without any regard whatsoever for the consequences.

Suddenly both girls stood up over their desks situated just a few feet apart. Both had their hands out to their sides almost inviting a punch from the other. Tory began to get a bit frightened. She could smell the recipe that promised to produce one hell of a fight and she did not know if she could physically handle it. Tomeka was seventeen-years-old in the tenth-grade and weighed in at about 220 pounds. Andrea weighed nearly the same and neither was over five-foot-six.

"Girls! Girls! GIRLS!!!" Tory repeated. "That is enough! Please sit down!"

Neither girl looked in Tory's direction. The class was becoming anxious. The tension was building. It resembled a Las Vegas "weigh-in" the eve of a heavyweight boxing match. The girls were still threatening each other and getting louder.

Tory then moved around her desk and moved toward the girls as the other students watched in utter amazement. They knew the history between these two girls. Tory did not. As the teacher, she could not wait another second to respond.

"That's it, Tomeka, get out of here now and go into the hallway!" Tory said as she leaned over at the waist for effect.

"Fuck this!" Tomeka blurted out as she moved toward the door while looking over her shoulder at her adversary. "I ain't goin' to the hallway. I'm going to the mutha' fuckin' office!"

"Now I *have* to take you to the office," Tory replied as Tomeka moved past her. "You just gave me no choice but to do so."

"I don't give a shit!" Tomeka said defiantly as she moved past her teacher, about one-hundred pounds lighter. "Do whatcha' gotta' do!"

Tomeka never took her eyes off her adversary, aware that a cheap punch could land on her at any time.

Tory had never been in such a situation. It was like something out of a bad movie. She readjusted her disposition, took a breath, looked at the class and with as much decorum as possible addressed them.

"Guys, I have to take Tomeka to the office, so please stay in your seats and wait for me to return," Tory said calmly, but in obvious irritation at the way the end of her day had unraveled.

She then turned to Andrea, the other party to this potential fight, and said as she pointed to her, "Young lady, stay here. Do not move from that desk. We'll call you down to the office in a moment and get to the bottom of this."

"Mrs. Leblanc, she called me a..." Andrea explained in an aggravated tone as she rose from her undersized desk.

Tory interrupted, "Andrea, tell Mr. Nutt. I don't want to hear it. Please stay seated."

Andrea then turned to walk out and catch up with a fast-moving Tomeka already moving away from her. Tory ran to catch up. When she did, she stepped in front of Tomeka to stop her advance. Tory believed she had a rapport with Tomeka, although an uneasy one. Tory asked the obvious question.

"Tomeka!" Tory asked as she moved in front of the student's imposing physique. "What was all of that about? You have never behaved that way in my class."

Tomeka, who stood eye to eye with Tory never looked into her face. She simply waved Tory away as she stepped around her before saying, "You don't want to know, Mrs. Leblanc."

The two of them paced quickly down the empty hallway as students occupied classes on either side. Tory could hear other teachers instructing their classes and tried not to interrupt them.

"Tomeka, what is going on for you to behave like that?" Tory begged again attempting to hush her voice.

"Leave me alone!" Tomeka commanded before issuing another threat to Andrea as if she were present to hear it. "I'll kill that ho', bitch! Talking to me like I was some kind of trash! Stupid ho'!"

Tory could not control Tomeka and wondered what she could do to halt the war of words, but Tory now had a larger problem, literally. Tory sensed movement behind her and noticed Andrea had left class without permission and snuck behind the two of them in an obvious attempt to sucker-punch Tomeka as she moved with her teacher. Both Tory and Tomeka turned at the same time.

"Andrea!!!" Tory said in surprise and in a voice desperate for an authoritarian tone. "I told you to stay in class!"

Andrea ignored Tory and directed her attention to Tomeka who was sizzling with the kind of rage only a street girl like these two could understand.

"I told you, bitch, I was going to get you and I am going to settle this right now!" Andrea warned as her eyes bulged from a face that meant what it said.

"Fuck you, bitch! I don't scare that easy, especially..." Tomeka started to say, but never got to finish.

Andrea then lunged at Tomeka throwing punches as fast as she could. Tory was in the middle and completely caught off guard. She was determined to stay between the two girls and keep them apart, but with nearly 450 pounds of female attitude scuffling around her, Tory was outgunned and she knew it. As she struggled to keep the girls apart, she continued to ask them to cease fighting.

"Stop it! Stop it now!" Tory demanded in as serious of a voice as she could muster while trying to avoid being hit.

Punches landed from all sides, but they all hit the thirty-year-old teacher, not one landing on its intended target. Tory was hit in the head, neck, breast, and shoulder. She was hit eight times and the punches were beginning to take their toll. Tory kept her head down to avoid being hit while she pleaded for the two girls to stop. It was a useless tactic.

Tomeka began to punch back at Andrea landing several punches at the air to either side of her head and at Tory, who continued to get pummeled. Out of nowhere, English teacher Allen Kirby appeared and grabbed Andrea from behind. Andrea was caught off guard and began to buck at the waist as Allen held her around the chest in a bear hug.

"Leave me alone, motha' fucka'!" Andrea demanded as Allen held her tightly.

Allen never said a word and never lost physical control of Andrea.

Tomeka had calmed a bit when she saw many teachers arriving on the scene to help Tory. Regardless, Tory grabbed Tomeka by the arm to usher her out of the hallway, never losing her grip, but losing her breath. All along the hallway other teachers and students popped their heads out to witness the altercation, but Andrea continued to fight like a scorned woman.

"Let me go! I want to kick her ass!" Andrea screamed at everyone and no one.

Tory finally got Tomeka to the double doors leading outside as Daryl Nutt, the school disciplinarian, approached them with his walkie-talkie in hand.

"You got it under control?" Daryl asked a panting Tory.

"Yea, now I do, but for a while there I was in trouble," Tory said with her right hand still gripping Tomeka's left arm.

"Take her in my office and have her wait for me," Daryl instructed as he waved them by.

As Daryl moved toward McCall Hall, he could see in the distance Allen holding Andrea around the waist as she was still cursing and out of control, but now getting assistance from another male teacher.

"Mutha' fucka', I said to let me go or I'll kick your ass, too," she threatened to Allen, who had a reputation for being in total control of his students.

Two other male teachers stood by in case control of Andrea was lost. The fight was over. All that remained was calming Andrea and learning the history that set it off.

Tory had left Tomeka in the office and had to walk back to her class past the two men now holding Andrea. Tory never made eye contact as Andrea continued to scream and threaten all involved. She hoped for a better end to a tumultuous day that produced verbal sparring with several students for nothing more than the fact that they thought they could get away with it. She lost most of her planning period and a chance to grade her test papers waiting for parents to show up who never did and did not have the courtesy to cancel the appointment. She broke up a terrible fight between two girls who absolutely lost their minds. She had a headache from the punches she had taken to the head and still had a meeting to attend and forty minutes remaining in seventh-hour to teach. She was not in a good mood, but Tory did it anyway because that's what she was paid to do.

As she entered her room, Tory saw everyone in their desks. No one stirred. The class was quiet. Even Everett Spencer kept his mouth shut. Tory then sat down at her desk as if nothing ever happened and finished the roll call. What happened, however, would be the talk of the school for the next twenty-four hours. It was a good story. High school gossip was better than Oprah Winfrey, except the kids witnessing a given action could directly relate.

An exhausted Tory entered her class, sat down at her desk and continued to call roll as if nothing had happened.

"Landry."

"Here."

"Melancon."

"Here."

"Milton."

"Here."

Tory taught geography. Although the students were actually well-behaved for a change, it was doubtful they learned anything. Several had been writing notes while Tory was away dealing with the fight. One student was drawing pictures at his desk. Two girls in the back of the room had been trading notes back and forth believing Tory did not see them as she returned to teaching. She did, but was too tired to stop it after a day like this one. Three students slept at their desks. In thirty minutes, a textbook chapter was completed. A test was announced two days in advance. A review would take place tomorrow, she told the class before the bell rang. Most students seemed completely disconnected from her words and efforts to educate them. They said nothing. They packed away their notebooks, pens, and conversations, and turned openly to sex, jobs, drugs, fighting, dating, cruel jokes and idle threats toward each other.

Following the afternoon announcements the final bell rang. Classes were dismissed for the day. The hallways once again filled with noise, slamming lockers, running feet, and vulgarity that could not be traced. The students filed by Tory as they did five times per day. None told her goodbye, thanks, or go to hell. Teachers, to many students, were just furniture. It hurt to be thought so little of, but that was the sad fact of the new millennium at East Side High School.

When the class emptied, Tory packed up her books and stuffed them into her satchel. She sighed and moved to turn out the lights. She then straightened her desks into the neat rows she liked. She turned off the air-conditioning and stood alone in the quiet darkness. She wondered how many more years of apathy and reckless behavior among students she could possibly take.

She threw her heavy satchel over her shoulder and opened her door. As she put the key in the lock, she saw Daryl Nutt, the assistant principal, moving toward her. Maybe he had an explanation as why the fight broke out. Sure enough, Daryl called out Tory's name as she removed her silver-colored key from the door.

"Tough day, wasn't it, Tory?" Daryl asked as he moved toward her.

It was the obvious observation, but Tory did not challenge the remark.

"I've had better," Tory said as she fumbled with her keys.

She then pulled her long auburn hair from her eyes and looked at Daryl. It was time to ask.

"Daryl, what was all that about between Andrea and Tomeka?" Tory asked.

A smirk creased Daryl's face. He tilted his head and tried to keep from laughing. He then looked down as if he was embarrassed.

"You mean you don't know?" Daryl asked, never looking up.

"No, I don't," Tory said in a matter-of-fact tone.

Daryl stood up, made eye contact, and folded his arms like he had a good story to tell. He did not disappoint.

"Well, Tory, those two girls were lovers last year," Daryl said to Tory's shock.

Daryl let the shock sink in. He knew he just blew Tory's innocent mind. Tory was not naïve by any stretch of the imagination. The news just stunned her more than Andrea's punch to the back of her head.

"Oh, yea!" Daryl continued, knowing he had Tory's complete attention. "You see, there's a whole gang of lesbians in this school and they love on one another. Tomeka dumped Andrea over the summer when she fell for a girl at some private school. Andrea walked in on them when they were having sex. I heard they fought at some party last weekend and someone called the cops to break it up. Andrea's always threatened to beat up Tomeka's lover, but Tomeka kept seeing the girl. I think the private school girl's name is Nicole. I'm not real sure.

"Anyway, Andrea promised to get even and picked today because it would have been her first anniversary with Tomeka. Andrea told Tomeka she was going to find Nicole alone one day, beat her ass, and then screw, uh, well, have sexual relations with her. Girl-on-girl rape, I guess. Andrea, well, she was the victim in a love triangle and lost out."

Tory stood in silence. She had been teaching long enough to be numb. However, there was always a new story to shake any teacher's confidence in his or her ability to simply maintain control of a class and teach the students inside of those walls each day. Daryl was telling Tory a story that shook her faith in the public school students she was now teaching.

"It's not your fault this happened, Tory," Daryl assured her. "This was going to happen sometime today and time was running out. Andrea was going to get Tomeka today and she couldn't do it after school because she had a bus to catch and she lives on the other side of the city."

Tory stood and said nothing. She was speechless and continued to study Daryl's face in the hope he was telling her a bad tale to make her laugh. Daryl laughed all right, but at Tory's expression of disbelief, not at the story he told because it was fact.

"It's a different day, isn't it?" Daryl said as he chuckled and walked away toward his parking lot duty.

Daryl moved away from her as Tory stood for a second with her keys dangling in one hand. She then slowly walked in the other direction to go to her vehicle and a basketball meeting. She knew kids fought. That's what they sometimes did, but they usually fought over a place in the lunch line. Maybe one kid threatens another over a suspicion of theft. They may become cruel towards each other in a war of words that gets out of hand. But Tory had never heard of a fight between two lesbians caught in a love triangle. It was almost too much to digest, even for a veteran teacher like Tory.

"In this state, there is nothing more important than providing our children with a strong and sure educational foundation. Education is poverty's mortal enemy. It is the number-one ticket out of poverty. Education opens the door to better jobs and is the foundation for successful economic development."

—Louisiana Governor Kathleen Blanco

Late September—A Series of Knots

It was an ordinary day and an ordinary class period as far as Tory Leblanc was concerned. As usual, she taught her third-hour civics class with ferocity. Although primarily a geography teacher, Tory taught one section of the intricacies of American government each day. She enjoyed the break in the monotony of instructing geography four hours daily. A change of pace in one's daily routine, regardless of occupation is always welcome. For Tory, teaching how the local, state, and federal government worked and interacted was a needed respite from the grind of the day.

As Tory moved from white boards posted on both ends of her classroom with marker in hand, she pulled down colored maps, used various overhead projector transparencies to enhance the lesson, and delivered a handout to students all in the hope they would be more engaged. The education experts nationwide all believed students, more now than ever, needed to be entertained while being taught. Teachers could not compete with Internet web sites, Oprah Winfrey, or expletive-filled early afternoon reality shows. Teachers knew that, for sure, but the pressure on educators to produce amusing learning was greater than ever. Even though there was only so much they could do in the form of classroom entertainment, teachers continued to try to rally students to the cause of learning. Learning was work. Being successful is work. And most inner city public school students were allergic to work as much as any success it enhanced.

It did not take long into the hour for Tory to recognize that she was more excited about the lesson than were her lazy students. As she continued to verbalize the definition of how a president could be impeached and what it meant, it was not lost on her that more than one-half of the students no longer were paying attention. Two students were sleeping. She raised her voice and became a bit more animated in her sublime effort to awaken them and gain their eye contact. It was an effort in vain.

"You see, guys and girls, 'impeachment' does not mean throwing a president out of office, even though the word sounds like it does," Tory explained to the class. "Think about the word, 'impeachment.' It sounds like the public is telling the president, 'You're fired!' In fact, the word means 'to accuse' the president of doing something illegal in office.

"It's kind of like sending a student to the office. We're not expelling you. We're telling you that you did something wrong and that the school is aware of your mistake and you had better not do it again. Congress would not tell President Bush, 'Hey, George, you are impeached so get your luggage and leave the White House.' No, Congress would be telling President Bush if he were to be impeached that he has been a bad boy and that the nation is aware of his error. Got it? Is that clear? Do I need to repeat it?"

No response. Some students were writing down her words in the front of the room, especially the same three students consistently excelling in the class. Another two in the rear of the room were exchanging notes. Tory only hoped the notes exchanged were about the day's lesson. The remaining twenty-nine pupils were writing something in their tablets to be sure, but their body language failed to disguise their disinterest in the subject. Many were not making eye contact with their teacher as she spoke. When they wrote in their notebooks they did so in a manner Tory knew was not keeping pace with the lesson. Most likely, many students were writing only some of what was needed to keep from revealing their lazy nature.

Tory did not take their apathy personally. She knew in her years of experience that some students were not at school to learn. Even though it was early in the year, she had already identified which classes and students were the best and which were going to be miserable failures regardless of her methodology. That was just the way it was.

Tory continued to teach, even if it meant teaching only students who seemingly cared.

"Let's talk about former President Bill Clinton," Tory said looking at the class for a spark of any kind. "He was impeached because of his affair with a White House intern, or worker, named Monica Lewinsky. Remember that story?"

Some of the students perked up. They began to laugh and make eye contact with each other.

"We all know what the president and Monica Lewinsky did, so let's not discuss it," Tory instructed the class trying to make a point as some students snickered. "What is important here is…"

"Man, Bill got a blow-job!" roared John Wilson, a troubled student with pale skin highlighting chest and back tattoos of fire crawling up his neck near his ear lobes.

Tory froze while many in the class laughed. She did not appreciate John's attempt at humor, especially from a student not having passed a test the entire year with nine unexcused absences to date. Tired and more than frustrated, Tory ignored the remark knowing that a trip to the office would result in nothing more than a one-day visit to a time-out room. There was no point in sending him out of class given the loss of momentum she was trying build.

"Okay, John, we all know you're here," Tory said sarcastically looking directly into the eyes of the underachieving pupil. "You can stop now. What you're telling us is all reruns."

"I'm just trying to contribute to the class, Mrs. Leblanc," John said with his palms open as if he were surrendering to police, a stance in which he was quite familiar having been arrested twice at age fifteen for assault. Now age seventeen, John had learned next to nothing about social skills and was a danger to himself.

Tory shot back quickly, "John, want to make a contribution? Try contributing to one of the worse grade point averages in the school by passing at least one test this year. Just one. Okay?"

The class groaned their approval of Tory's remark. It was entertainment to many of the students. It reminded them of those common reality shows in which they were so familiar. They enjoyed what they perceived as a verbal competition between an adult and a student. They hoped the spar would continue and interrupt their boredom. They were disappointed. The showdown was short-lived.

Tory thought it strange how just minutes before the class had almost no pulse. They were academically dead. However, just as immature children with no social skills are expected to be, they rose from their slumber to pay homage to the use of a perverted phrase by a punk student toward an aggravated teacher defending her lesson and personal morality.

"Like I said, we all know what Monica and President Clinton did in the White House," Tory continued. "My question to you is, should we have impeached the president for what he did? Remember, he is married, and when questioned about the incident, he lied. Then he backtracked and said he didn't really lie, he just kind of made a regrettable error. What do you think, class? Was he fit to be the leader of the nation, or not?"

Two hands went up immediately and Tory was grateful for the interaction. At last, she thought, the class was responding. Tory pointed her hand at sophomore William Kellog, who placed his hand on a desk full of notes before answering.

"I don't care if he gets what he got or not," William said with conviction. "I mean, as long as he does a good job as president it don't matter to me none what he does in his private life. You know what I'm saying?"

Tory ignored the poor usage of the English language. She noticed many students nodding in agreement followed by several statements of, "For real, man."

"But what does that say about his character?" Tory asked.

"Who cares?" William added. "That don't interest me none at all."

Tory pointed to junior Les Carter, taking civics for the second consecutive year after failing last year due to excessive absences. The previous school year Les missed thirty-four days during the spring semester. It was not a record for missed days in Tory's class, but Les was hardly positioning himself for all-American academic status.

"Hey, yo', if he be messin' around on his wife that be their problem, not mine," Les added looking for support from and pointing at William.

"I agree with him. Just run the country and I ain't caring what he did."

"But I ask again, what does it say about his ability to run the nation?" Tory asked. "Whether you like President Clinton or not, he lied. He lied to us all. What does that say about him?"

Silence. The class did not know how to respond to Tory. So she did what she did best by creating an analogy the class could possibly relate to.

"Look, let me put it this way," Tory said now realizing she had most of their attention for the first time. "Let's say tonight you go home and watch the 6 p.m. news and see me in an orange jumpsuit with 'East Baton Rouge Parish Prison' written on the back. I am handcuffed and being escorted to jail by sheriff deputies to be fingerprinted."

"I'd like to see that, for real," John said with a huge grin.

The class was smiling at whatever example their teacher was pursuing, even though it was completely unrealistic for Tory to be able to do this on a consistent basis.

Tory continued, "The television news reporter at the scene tells you that public school teacher, Tory Leblanc, was arrested on the East Side High School campus with possession of marijuana with intent to distribute. They also report I was released after posting $100,000 bond."

"Hey yo', why you didn't sell me some?" laughed John aloud.

Again, the class laughed and Tory ignored it.

"Now, the next school day I report to school as if nothing happened," Tory explained, "and when you walk in this room tomorrow for civics class I tell you to open your books, be quiet, and get ready for my instructions. What would be your response?"

The class made it quite clear to Tory they would not listen to her as they shuffled their papers and made juvenile comments to that effect.

"I ain't doin' nothin' you say do," said one student.

"Me neither!" another said in mock laughter.

"My mom would not let me come to school if one of my teachers was a drug dealer," another said.

The remarks continued and Tory bathed in them. She smiled because the classroom energy, however brief, was full scale. Tory was now ready to make her final point.

53

"Okay, you would not listen to me, that's clear," Tory said. "What I find so funny is this: if I break a law or I'm accused of breaking a law, you admit you would not have any respect for me at all. And you shouldn't! I did nothing to keep your respect. But, if the president of the United States involves himself in unethical behavior, cheats on his wife, lies to the American public, and then admits he made an error, you are okay with that. Is that what I am hearing?"

The class was getting the point.

"Let me get this straight, you expect a thirty-something-thousand-dollar per year high school teacher to be near perfect or you have no respect for them. None! But if the most powerful man in the world representing the most powerful nation in the world cheats on his wife and lies about it and tries to get away with it, you have no problem with it. Does that about sum it up? You would not want to impeach him?"

Tory was pacing the class and pointing her finger at the class making strict eye contact with them.

"Here's the other problem," Tory reiterated, "if the president lied about his relationship with Monica Lewinsky, is it possible he's lied about things we don't know about? If a man lies to his wife, he will lie to anyone about anything. Would you agree? Do you really want this type of person in leadership? You said it didn't matter what he did in his personal life, but it does matter. Do you see this now? If it matters what I do, don't you think it should matter how the president behaves? You place more pressure on me than you do on the president. And just so you know, I voted for Bill Clinton twice. So don't go home thinking I am trying to change your opinion about the man. I just want you to think about how you would treat me if I were arrested like I explained. You would be very cruel to me! I know you would! As for the president, would you really not be in favor of impeaching him? Think about who you are and how you look at issues. Who are you? What do you stand for? What do you want from your leadership?"

Tory's questions were thought provoking, but felled the class. Perhaps, Tory thought, this form of stimulation was a bit over the intellect of her below-average pupils. Theirs was a generation lost in perverse music, push-button entertainment, and elementary humor unfolding the obvious. Challenging their minds led many students to a quick retreat. They did not want to be academically stimulated. They wanted to be entertained. Tory did, in fact, entertain them on this day, even though it was not her intention when class began. In the end, the kids enjoyed themselves and Tory received feedback from her lesson. It was doubtful many students could comfortably tie the lesson's two laces concerning impeachment and a constituent's obligation to bind a president to morality and ethics. For many of Tory's students, the day's lesson was a series of knots serving only to amuse, and not to unravel.

"Once again, Louisiana has been ranked near the bottom in a national survey of child well-being across the country. The low ranking should be a call to action, but the cause of improving the lives of children in Louisiana cannot simply be an obligation of government. Improvement must come from the involvement of churches, neighborhoods and, most importantly of all, the families where many of these children face tremendous obstacles…it's not a problem easily addressed by government. But it's holding Louisiana down, and it will continue to do so until more of us begin to make better choices."

—Baton Rouge Advocate editorial, July 10, 2006

October—The first day

Brent Masters never gave much thought to being a teacher. He had just graduated college with honors and wanted to enter LSU's business school to work on his MBA, but money was in short supply. Like many before him, getting a job and going to college at night seemed to be the path to take. All through the summer, Brent applied for corporate jobs in three states and four Louisiana parishes, including East Baton Rouge Parish. By late September, it was obvious the job market was proving tougher than he ever envisioned.

Many college students, diploma in hand, attacked the job market with tenacity, only hours after throwing their caps and gowns into the air marking the end of their undergraduate studies. Armed with a bachelor's degree and a tremendous graduation speech from former U.S. President George W. Bush, Brent believed the market would absorb someone with his qualifications and work ethic. He wanted to "Make a difference" and "Dare to dream" and employ all the great quotes delivered by the distinguished faculty and guests that challenged them during graduation exercises.

Four months later the diploma was framed and hanging quietly on the wall with the rest of the pictures. The quotes had been shelved, long stuck to the pages of a scrapbook memorializing graduation day. Brent learned the hard way, unfortunately, that he was one of thousands of resumes sitting in piles in obscure filing cabinets in corporate offices throughout the Deep South. The fact was the bills were piling up and he needed a job—any job.

With encouragement from his mother, a retired public school teacher, and his father, who once taught science and coached high school football, Brent decided to travel a road not part of his overall plan. His mother, with connections to the school system, had learned of a job opening at East Side High School. All Brent needed to do was visit the East Baton Rouge Parish public school office and meet with one of several in charge of human resources. A job teaching Spanish at East Side High School was offered on the spot and Brent accepted without knowing much about the school or its reputation. All Brent knew was that he might be up to the challenge and would now able to pay his bills on time. Who knows, he was told by many in the profession, teaching may have been his dream job without his even knowing it. More than one teacher had fallen into the profession through non-traditional routes.

The teaching of foreign languages, like Spanish, was labeled as a "critical need" statewide. One need not be certified to teach in critical need areas. All one needed was proof of having taken enough college classes to push students enough to challenge them. Brent did not possess one minute's worth of experience. He did not really understand what he was getting into. His mother, however, sold him on the idea of helping students who did not have his affluent upbringing. Brent was a product of the private school system. He was still young and naive enough to believe he could breathe hope into the lives of many kids whose home life and future bordered on hopelessness. Brent, now enrolled in night classes for certification, was to begin work October 1, replacing several substitutes who had been on the job since school opened.

On the morning of his first day, Brent reported to the office promptly at 6:30 a.m., some thirty-five minutes before classes began. He was introduced to the administrative staff and walked to his classroom by Principal Adam Berling, a twenty-four-year veteran of the public school system. As the two walked up the stairs to the second-floor classroom, Brent appeared nervous and Principal Berling was aware of it.

"Nervous or anxious, Brent?" Principal Berling asked Brent as they tackled the staircase one step at a time.

"It shows, huh?" Brent answered while nervously adjusting his silk tie.

"Yes, it does," Principal Berling said never taking his eyes off Brent and using hand gestures to illustrate his point. "Look, keep in mind these kids have not had a Spanish teacher all year. We are in the eighth week of school and they really have not learned a word of Spanish. The students you are teaching are freshmen. About 80 percent of them did not take Spanish in middle school. So, anything you teach them is going to be new to them. So, don't worry. You'll know enough to get by and help them. Trust me."

Brent found it strange that Principal Berling appeared to be selling a job that was no longer on the market. He had accepted the job, but Principal Berling played up the job as if Brent had fallen into a proverbial career goldmine. Closer to the truth, he probably was afraid Brent would quit after the first day.

The school needed a Spanish teacher desperately, especially at this late date. Many of the students were issued passing grades on the first six-week progress report passed out in late September based on mere attendance. There was simply no way to grade the students accurately without a qualified teacher. Brent realized students were going to be far behind where he thought they should be. As they entered the classroom, Brent noticed the disorganization of the bulletin boards and desks. It was a sign of chaos.

"Here are your textbooks," Principal Berling immediately pointed out to Brent as he flipped on the light switch in the back of the room. The books were on a shelf near his worn wooden desk. Brent noted that the green and gold color on the binding was nearly falling apart. How old they must have been, he could not guess. Brent then observed the view outside of his room. Barely overlooking the treetops was the green manicured football field covered with morning dew and bright sunshine. It was a beautiful sight. Inside his room, the sight was not so pristine.

Trashcans had not been emptied. The desks were not in neat rows. Many of the letters haphazardly stapled to the bulletin board were out of date. There was graffiti on the board written by bored students. Some read, "Mr. G. Sux!" or "Kevin and Kaley 4-Ever!" Another simply read, "Fuck you." Simple messages left by simple students unaware of how far they were out of life's mainstream.

Principal Berling erased the board when he noticed Brent reading it. Neither of them acknowledged the juvenile phrases.

"These need to be passed out today, if you don't mind," Principal Berling ordered and suggested at the same time. "The books, I mean. We didn't see the need with all the teachers they've had so far this year. We hope you'll stick around to collect them at the end of the year."

Principal Berling was fishing for a positive response. He did not get one.

"How many teachers have they had so far?" Brent inquired.

"I've lost count," Principal Berling said as he took it upon himself to help Brent place a textbook on each desk. The textbooks they passed out were entitled, "Introduction to Spanish" as the clock pushed to 6:50 a.m., just ten minutes before the bell rang to start the first-hour class.

"That many?" Brandon said as he unpacked his briefcase and laptop computer, a habit picked up in private school that he was never able to beat.

"Well, we get a substitute and keep them for a couple of days and then they are scheduled to be someplace else," Principal Berling said. "Then we get another and another and the kids don't know from one day to the next which teacher they are going to have on any given day until they walk into class."

For a brief moment there was silence. Principal Berling wanted to know Brent's thoughts and he was not divulging any.

"I know what you might be thinking, 'This is a hell of way to run a school.' Right?" Principal Berling asked before answering his own question. "But the state, and this school system in particular, are very short of qualified foreign language teachers. We get what we can get and make the best of it. Our most qualified instructors are teaching the juniors and seniors and readying them for TOPS and college entrance examinations. Many of them are already teaching six classes with no break. We've placed quite a load on them already."

"I thought teachers only taught five classes per day," Brent asked as he feverishly straightened up the disorganized class left from the previous day.

"They usually do," Principal Berling said as he pulled the cord on the window blinds in an effort to get them even and add a semblance of order to a classroom he hoped would now turn the academic corner. "But with the continuing budget cuts, teachers across the parish are either going to have to teach multiple preps or accept an additional class with the understanding they could forfeit their duty in return. It makes for a heavy load and they don't get extra pay for it, sadly. That's the way it is."

Brent quickly looked over his teaching schedule for the second time. It appeared he had only five classes of Introduction to Spanish. He did not have a duty post and did not ask to carry one. Principal Berling read Brent's mind and explained to him why.

"You don't have duty during fall semester because, again, we had too many teachers filling this job," he continued explaining as he tightened the cord on one of many broken window blinds. "I didn't want to overburden them. They had enough to worry about just being here. I don't want to overburden you, either."

Principal Berling clasped his dusty hands together and looked straight at his newest employee.

"Look, just teach to the best of your ability," he said sympathetically. "Bring any of your concerns directly to me, and I'm sure things will work out fine."

With that, Principal Berling shook Brent's hand and offered him, "Thanks for being here. We need you and good luck."

With that he exited the room. Brent was finally alone and began to get even more nervous. The classroom, however, was coming together nicely. The board had been erased and Brent's name had been fixed to it for students to learn. The desks were in four neat rows of seven facing the front. A textbook had been placed on each desk for each student to claim. Brent's desk had been neatly arranged. The room's two bulletin boards had been stripped of cluttered paper. Brent wanted the room spartan proving to students he was organized and ready for his first day. It was an impression he knew was important to make immediately. Brent did not want to appear as another in a long line of substitutes.

Whether he would stick with the profession he did not know. He would simply weigh each day at a time. No matter what, he promised himself he would stick it out at least until the end of the year.

The bell rang to begin classes and Brent looked up at the ceiling as if he were searching for the noise he could not see. Principal Berling quickly returned with another piece of advice. Brent was hoping he would stay until the students were seated, but the old man knew he needed to tackle the first moments on his own. Principal Berling never entered the room. He just stuck his head in as he leaned over at the waist.

"Oh, by the way, Parent-Teacher Night is two weeks from today," Principal Berling said. "Put it on your desk calendar. You'll need to be here on that Monday from 6 to about 8 p.m., okay?"

Brent nodded his head that he understood. Brent would need at least two weeks to learn the students' strengths and weaknesses.

The principal then disappeared in the corridor now filling with early morning rays of sunlight.

Brent could hear the students moving up the staircase. Lockers began to slam. Footsteps grew louder as they grew nearer. Brent's heartbeat began to race. His palms grew slightly sweaty. He wanted to appear cool, but he was a nervous wreck.

Never in Brent's life did he think he would be a teacher. As a student, he never considered what ran through the mind of any of his teachers. Never. Now, he was one and he had to admit he was intimidated by his own insecurities. Would he be able to handle the students? Would the students accept him? Would he be able to handle behavior problems? After all he was just a scant five years older than a high school senior. Could he teach them anything? Would they like him? Did it matter? Was he in over his head? Brent would not be able to answer any of these questions for many weeks.

Brent left his laptop screen open and on. The wallpaper was set to a 1920s autumn morning in New England with a one-room schoolhouse nestled under the orange and red leaves. It was a scene from a simpler time—a time when a teacher's authority actually stood on its own. Authority came with the job title and was respected by all. A sick society, poor parenting, and liberal judges browbeaten by special interest groups had eroded those days.

Brent moved into the hallway to watch the students file by.

As some of his students moved into his room, one female student giggled with her hand over her tiny face before exclaiming, "I wonder how long he'll be here."

To which a male student walking behind her replied, "Who cares?"

Brent said nothing as he watched the students move into his class.

"Are you the new teacher?" asked a teacher from across the hallway.

With that statement two teachers then walked toward Brent to introduce themselves. Handshakes were extended and small talk lent levity to a strange situation in Brent's short work life. They assured Brent he could do the job despite knowing nothing about him. It was a nice gesture on their part, but it was going to take more than kind words to give Brent the confidence he needed.

When the tardy bell rang, Brent entered his room and the students were seated as the announcements began. Brent sat at his desk as students spoke aloud. Most were not listening to the announcements Principal Berling was making—comments regarding changes in football and marching band practice times, Beta Club meetings, today's lunch menu, and a plea to do a better job regarding the wearing of the school uniform. The final announcement was the one that made some students comment aloud.

"...students interested in applying for an academic scholarship offered by the organization 'Black Opportunity' need to see a guidance counselor by the end of the week to fill out a questionnaire. The college scholarship is for African-American students only. Have a good day, students. That is all."

A loud click on the intercom indicated the announcements were over. Brent was now on stage. He was alone. It was his turn. His teaching career officially began.

Near the window, a white male who looked like an unmade bed with his uncombed long, brown hair, could not pass up the opportunity to aggravate the black students.

"Hey, yo', why y'all get scholarships because of your skin color and we don't?" he asked begging for a response that would result in an argument.

"'Cause we special, that's why, fool!" said a black male sitting in front of him never bothering to turn around.

"What'd ya'll do to get scholarship chances?" the white student asked again. "All ya'll done is to be born black. That ain't nothin' ya'll went out and did. You were just born that way and they give ya'll money for it. Now, that ain't right!"

"Shut up, trailer trash!" said a black female laughing from across the room.

"That's discrimination, that's all it is and it's legal to do that against white people, even trailer trash like me, huh, girlfriend?" he said smiling and directing the comment at the female labeling him trailer trash. "Maybe I want to go to Harvard or something. Maybe I want to go to, uh, uh, a community college or something."

Some students chuckled at the verbal jabs they were tossing at each other. Brent doubted the white student could spell "Harvard." The comments were made with no malice, as far as Brent could see. Everyone sat listless as they directed their remarks like darts thrown at a board pinned to the wall. They were obviously comfortable with each other, maybe too comfortable, but Brent had to stop the mindless chatter before the students wrestled control of his class.

It was time for Brent to play teacher. It was his moment. Brent looked at the students and decided to say nothing until roll was called, which he did without incident to the twenty-eight students present out of thirty-two in his roll book. It was a good thing for the absences, too, because there were not enough desks to accommodate them all.

Brent posted the four names absent on a piece of paper and pinned it to the heavy wooden door for office workers to collect. He then turned to observe the students looking for a way to get his attention so he would speak to them.

The students appeared in clusters. About six students had their heads on their desks and were sleeping. Others were talking quietly having moved their desks disrupting the neat rows to facilitate socializing. Brent took a deep breath, clapped his hands together like a coach, and announced, "Class, straighten up your desks, face the front, and listen up, please."

The students appeared startled at first. Brent sounded like the authoritarian figure they had yet to meet in their Spanish class. Brent waited for them to settle. He shook the body of one young female who did not pick her head up off the desk.

He pressed on the shoulder of her red sweater a little harder until she reared her head and exclaimed in an aggravated tone, "I'm up! Leave me alone, man!"

That got the attention of the rest of those sleeping and socializing who proceeded to move their desks into their proper position.

Brent took a deep breath and tried to remember he was a college graduate. He was an honor student and was once a hell of a high school fullback. He was in his 20s and was no longer a kid, despite a baby face that betrayed him. He was dressed in tan-colored khakis, a traditional white button-down collared shirt with a blue and green tie. He looked the part of the 1980s preppie when conservatism and Ronald Reagan were all the rage. He also looked like a yuppie professional who would be more comfortable in an entry-level position in a Poydras Street tower overlooking the Mississippi River near New Orlean's French Quarter rather than in an East Baton Rouge Parish public school. But here he was standing alone staring at twenty-eight underachieving students. They had very little in the way of discipline and had learned less than nothing to date, despite their grades. He began to feel as if the perspiration was going to blast out of his heating forehead. Brent was afraid his apprehension was going to show and the students would pick up on that fear and exploit it. He took a breath.

"Guys, I'm Brent Masters and I'm going to be your Spanish teacher for the rest of the year," he said. "I am not a substitute. You will see me here tomorrow and the next day and next week."

No one budged. There was silence, even if it were only apathy. He continued.

"I understand you have had quite a few teachers and have not learned very much so far," he said. "Is that right?"

"Yea, man, and we like it that way," said a white male with a shaved head sitting near the door. "Don't wanna do nothin'."

The voice from that immature statement came from freshman James Tanner, who appeared scruffy with his shirttail hanging out in the back of his tan uniform pants. He was not wearing a belt, a school requirement. The shoestrings on his filthy black and purple Nike sneakers were not tied. In fact, the tongue of the shoes was open revealing one gray sock and one white one. He had his left hand on the steel doorknob as if he were ready to escape class rather than study within it. James was slumped low into his desk with his head resting against the back while his feet stuck out far in front of him. He was a mess of a person.

Brent could not allow James to challenge him so early in the year or so early in his career. He had hoped not to be challenged like this, but it was inevitable. Brent was on trial and resented being so from a jury of snotty teenagers with a penchant for arrogance and ignorance.

"Your name?" Brent asked looking directly at the rude voice interrupting him.

"James," came the reply.

"Well, James…"

"Bond. James Bond," interrupted James, now eliciting some nervous laughter from the room.

But Brent was clever, too. If James wanted to match wits with him it was a battle he was going to lose. Brent's ex-fraternity brothers were more clever and quick-witted than most of the civilized world. James did not have a chance and was too stupid to know it.

"Well, Mr. Bond, you may be 007, but I'm 008," Brent said to James in the most sarcastic tone he could muster. "That means, in case you are brain dead, and that's my guess, that I've replaced you because, just like 007, your jokes are dead, and so is your run of this classroom, got it?"

The class busted out in laughter in respect for Brent's quick comeback.

"Ohhhh, mannnn!" they exclaimed almost rattling the windows.

"James, you don't run this show," Brent continued with steely eyes that hit James like daggers. "You may have poo-pooed all over your substitutes, but I'm not them and I will not hesitate to toss you out."

With a smile from ear to ear, James said in a slow, lazy tone that was the trademark of his entire character, "You can't lay a hand on me."

"I don't want to touch you, James," Brent said. "I don't have enough disinfectant."

More students in the classroom reacted to the shock humor. One male student looked at James and said as he shook his hand at the floor, "Ohhhh, for real, this dude don't be playin', man! He ain't playin.'"

"Sho' don't!" said another student a lot less impressed with the incident.

However, the class continued to howl in laughter. Students slapped their desks and slumped over at the waist covering their faces with their palms as if to suggest they really did not want to laugh, but had to. They thought Brent was going to be a hoot. Brent did not back down from James and sent a message to the rest of the students he was not employed as their play toy.

"Can we move on now, guys?" Brent asked the class politely. "I'm bored now and I'd like to get some work done."

Brent spent the remaining time explaining the outline he had written on the white board in red and black highlight markers. He explained his attendance policy as well as that of the school's. He identified the grading scale and had the students fill out forms indicating they had received textbooks. By the time the class ended, they had read the first section of Chapter One and were orally tested on its six pages. Brent assigned homework and even gave the class the last five minutes of the hour to begin working on it if they chose to. Things were going well when the bell rang to dismiss class. Brent had initiated more learning in one class than the students had seen all year. Whether they learned or not, Brent felt good that an effort had been made.

As students filed out of separate doors, Brent heard his name mentioned by the students. Some of the comments utilized his name in vain.

"His name isn't Brent Masters, it's Brent masturbate!" howled one student after he was safely out of sight in the crowded hallway.

That did not upset Brent. It couldn't. It was a tired joke he had heard most of his young life. He knew some students were resentful of teachers trying to do their jobs. That was a fact. He knew enough about teaching to know that. Brent had served notice to those students that changes were going to be made in Spanish class. He was the boss, despite his inexperience. He was going to teach the way he was taught and there was very little in the way of clowning when he had attended high school.

Three female students then approached Brent's desk in appreciation of his efforts to teach a class that had been gaining ground in the wrong direction. Brent would show his appreciation.

"Mr. Masters?" came a voice from behind him as he watched the students depart for second-hour class.

Brent turned and saw a girl behind him. She had straight hair and wore enough makeup to make her look more like a woman than a fifteen-year-old high school student. Brent was struck by her looks and then her manners.

"Thanks for trying," she said in a sincere voice. "I mean it. Some of us want to learn and haven't learned anything since the first day of school. We did more today than we have all year. Some of us do want to make something of ourselves."

Brent looked at the other two girls to measure their opinions. They both shook their heads in agreement.

"Don't worry about James," she continued. "He's like that in all of his classes."

Brent was grateful for their efforts to make him feel welcome. He had reached some of the students and they were smart enough to know it. What's more, Brent knew they viewed the morning as a turning point in their learning process. Brent was validated. He felt better. Instantly, he was confident of his efforts.

"Thank you, girls. I will try to keep it that way," Brent offered. "So, what are your names?"

"I'm Michelle," the girl said before motioning to the others. "This is Wendy and this is Octavia."

They both responded uncomfortably, "Hi," and then stared at the floor.

"Well, we've got to get to class before we're late," Michelle said with an awkward wave. "See ya' tomorrow. Bye."

The other girls were in tow behind Michelle. Brent guessed they were all close friends and were excited for the change. Brent was that change. He began to think that maybe he could reach some of these kids. He chuckled as he straightened several of the desks that had been pushed around by the students' exit. He then walked to his desk where his laptop sat open for the last hour. Brent did not have a second-period class. Like many teachers he was going to use his planning period to review his notes. He viewed his laptop thinking about how he would handle his third-period class before being stunned at what he saw.

There on his screen sat a typed message that shook him to the core of his being. It read:

"Would you make me your sex slave tonight? I'll meet you anywhere."

Brent sat for a moment. He read the message over and over. He wanted to wake from the shock. Who would do this? Why would someone do this? Did a student really want him to perform the act? Were they waiting for a response? Was it a sick joke designed to upset him? When did they write it? How did they write it when he was so near them from the moment they entered the room? It mattered little because he had no idea who wrote it. He could not begin to even guess because he did not know the names or tendencies of his first and only class ever taught.

What's worse was even if Brent found out the name of the student who typed this horrible message to him and turned that person into the office for discipline, he or she could easily claim Brent typed the message. After all, it was Brent's laptop computer. It could be easily explained away as a young male teacher trying to coax or blackmail innocent high school females into lewd acts. If the media learned of the situation, Brent could find himself cast as an alleged pervert soliciting sex from a student. To do nothing might encourage more sexual harassment from the student. And it was, sexual harassment, but few might believe him. He had only been on the job as a teacher one hour of his first day. Did the school's front office know enough about Brent's character to protect him? Would they stand behind him? It would be his word versus that of the high school student in question and Brent knew he might lose. Brent did not want to be in that situation.

He leaned back in his chair and stared at the message. He was angry. He stared out the window into the morning sunlight as it began to beam through the windows and bathe the floor of his second-floor class. He sat alone as he heard the second-hour tardy bell ring and the voices of teachers rising over the sounds of books slamming on desks as instruction began. Part of him wanted to walk down the stairway, get into his car, and never return. It would be easy to do. He could simply disappear as quickly as he had arrived. His emotions were as volatile as the New York Stock Exchange. From the moment he stepped onto the campus just ninety minutes prior he had experienced fear, doubt, a bit of anger, frustration, a determination to succeed, vindication and welcome from three students, and now vulnerability. Some student revealed his weakness. Brent felt as helpless as the message was intended.

Brent could not go to Principal Berling with this problem after one hour on the job. Brent knew he must ignore the incident and *hope* it would not happen again. He felt defenseless. He also learned that he could not turn his back on his students for a second, even when he was on hallway duty for a few minutes between classes, which is likely the time the pornographic invitation was typed on his laptop.

However, there was a bigger question to ask himself now. Was this the job for him? Did he really want to teach the rest of his life? A few minutes earlier, Brent felt like a champion against ignorance. He did not want to judge the entire teaching profession and any career in it he aspired based on an incident that may never happen again—but it did happen. Perhaps, Brent thought, this was the nature of the job in all its glory. Maybe this is the type situation teachers complain about constantly to those who choose to ask them of their problems and actually listen to them.

At the moment he felt beaten by a silly high school student playing treacherous games that could cripple his young career and his stalwart reputation. It was only 8:10 a.m. of his first day. Already Brent realized the idea of a career in teaching was most improbable. He knew that after just one day.

> "A society that hopes to remain both ignorant and free, in a state of civilization, expects what never has been, and what never will be."
> —Thomas Jefferson

October—"There is a God and I'm not Him"

It was late in the school year for a parent-teacher night, but the third Monday of October was the time to invite concerned parents to meet the faculty and administration of East Side High School. It was a moment for parents to meet with the principal and teachers personally, pick up class syllabi and a school dress code manual, listen to each of their children's seven teachers present instructional strategy, learn of student expectations, review the textbook, ask any questions, and offer any advice. Students were told not to attend school with their parents. Teachers were told not to discuss grades with parents because it consumed too much time. It was a night specifically designated for adults to become acquainted with the culture of the school and for those interested in improving the grades and performance of their children and aiding the teacher in maintaining classroom order.

At 6:15 p.m. sharp, parents filed into the school's auditorium and listened to Principal Adam Berling and the school's two assistant principals give speeches about the mission of the school. Parents were assured their children were receiving an excellent education, if they wanted one. Parents were also assured their children were being taught by a certified, highly qualified faculty. The speeches sounded corny, perhaps, but they were necessary. Parents needed to hear from school officials that they were in charge of the school, not the students. They wanted to hear that discipline was meted out fairly and in a consistent manner. Parents wanted to hear it. School officials needed to say it. It was safer for both parties that way.

A bell schedule was followed whereby parents had five minutes to reach their children's seven classes and ten minutes to meet with each teacher. It was a night filled with lost parents rushing through hallways looking for classroom numbers posted above doorways. Teachers and administrative staff helped them find their way through the maze of corridors so they would not arrive tardy and waste precious, and limited "class" time.

East Side High School had a student body population of 1,146 as of October 1. Spanish teacher Brent Masters, now only in his second week on the faculty, leaned against his doorway hoping to meet as many parents as he could. He wanted to address discipline issues and get suggestions from parents as to how they wanted to handle certain issues. He wanted to speak with parents about how far behind his classes were. He wanted to assure parents that he would work constantly to ensure their children would catch up as soon as reasonably possible. He also wanted to make certain no one knew or even mentioned the invitation to a sexual encounter left on his laptop computer his first day at work.

Brent had a checklist of things he wanted to say on a white-lined note card. His oral delivery to parents would take about five minutes leaving another five minutes for questions. He also had a list of names of parents he needed to speak with—parents representing students in desperate need of help. Brent *wanted* to speak with them. He *needed* to speak with them. It was the only way his job was going to be more productive. It was the only solution to the poor behavior that regularly fed the hunger of student indifference—an appetite knowing no limit. Brent wanted his class on a proverbial diet.

Other teachers chatted in the hallways awaiting parents as they moved slowly along corridors brightly lit against black windows reflecting the early darkness approaching daylight savings time. Brent was tired. He had been at school since 6:20 a.m., had taught five classes and had one hour of duty. His twenty-five-minute lunch period offered little in the way of rest. Like the other teachers, he was not getting paid for an extra two hours at school, but it was one of many things expected of teachers for no additional money. Most teachers knew if they could improve a student's grades, behavior, or both, this unpaid after-school effort would be worth it.

Brent hummed the "Monday Night Football" theme song, an autumn must-see ritual in his home that he was missing, as he thought about what he was going to say to the parents of Jeff Weber, a socially defensive creature who believed the world was out to get him. Jeff was rude all the time for no apparent reason. It was his chosen personality. A student could simply ask Jeff for the time of day and he would snap back at them, "Get your own freakin' watch, dude!" Brent pleaded with Jeff to understand that life was much easier to live and friends were easier to make by simply glancing at one's watch and delivering the time politely. Jeff actually argued with Brent over the issue many times. But then, the two argued about everything. There was no real dialogue—just one personality playing offense and the other playing defense in a game often in wasted overtime.

"If I don't want to give someone the time, I don't have to!" Jeff would bark sarcastically at Brent when corrected in private. "No one can make me! It's a free country, you know? Yes, I think I read that somewhere!"

To which Brent would reply, "Yes, it's a free country. People are free to label you an idiot. Girls are free to ignore you and not date you. Guys are free to beat the hell out of your snotty little attitude if they choose. Employers are free to hire someone other than you. You are also free to be popular and courteous. Which would you rather be? It's a simple choice to me, Jeff."

"Look, I don't want to be in some stupid picture in the school yearbook labeled "Most Friendly" or "Most Likely to Succeed" or some of that other stupid crap!" he would tell Brent while looking at his teacher's shirt and tie. "And I don't want to wear *Leave it to Beaver* silk ties like you do everyday. So get off me, Ward Cleaver!"

It was a mindless conversation filled with emptiness for Brent. All he wanted to do was make Jeff agree that he needed to change his behavior. Brent knew the first step to improving anything was to admit one had a problem. Jeff would not take that first step. When questioned, Jeff would become more coarse and abrupt. It was the signal of a bigger problem. Brent needed to find out from Jeff's parents if they had the same problem with him. If so, how did they handle it? If they did not know, then they needed to know. In any event, Jeff had made two 'F's' on his chapter tests and two 'F's' on quizzes. Brent needed to alert his parents to their son's obvious problems and now.

There was Erik Dobbs, the only sophomore in a class full of freshmen, and the only student to make a 'D' on his last six-week progress report. With only substitute teachers in place before Brent took the job, students were given grades based on attendance only. Everyone in the class got at least the inflated grade of 'A' or 'B.' But in the first six-week period totaling thirty days, Erik had missed ten days of school, unexcused. If he missed another two days unexcused he would fail all classes for the fall semester as early as mid-October. Since Brent had become the Spanish teacher, Erik had not missed a day of school, but he slept in class frequently. Brent could not seem to keep him awake. Brent needed to make this information known to Erik's parents, and perhaps set up a conference with the school's guidance counselor.

The most-weird student in Brent's class, and maybe the entire school, was George Malovich, who cut his hair in a Mohawk-style in the past week, which is against school rules. Forced to comply with school dress codes and change his chosen hairstyle, George then shaved his head. He wore clothes that were three sizes too big for him and a denim jacket that exclaimed to the world, "Bite me!" until it was confiscated by school officials. Three days later he then wore another denim jacket so filthy no one wanted to rub against him in the hallway. This jacket lamented the phrase, "Fat, Ignorant, and Proud!" silk-screened on the back. This time school officials confiscated George's jacket and sent him to the discipline center for three days of reflection, which he did not attend.

Brent could not figure out what made George's mind work, except the drugs students constantly insinuated he was taking. When Brent questioned George, he would often place a dumb look on his flabby round pale face and stare into "nowhere-land."

Students would giggle at his strange behavior and remark, "Too much drugs last night, George?"

Through the laughter, another student would respond for George in a mock sluggish manner that only drug inducement could guarantee.

"Yea, dude, I'm such a good customer they gave me a 'buy one, get one free deal.'"

There was more hilarity at George's expense, although he did not seem to mind. The class always laughed at their own judgment of George who was pronounced guilty without saying a word in his own defense. Brent thought George liked the attention regardless of whether he was involved in illegal substances or not. Some students reveled in attention, even the negative kind for which they may or may not be accountable. George was failing Spanish and Brent was desperate to speak with his parents.

Pamela Fernandez was another below-average student, but she possessed unpredictable behavior. Two weeks prior, on a field trip to the downtown museum with an art class of twenty-six, students viewed a five-foot tall replica of Michelangelo's nude statue "David" that was making its tour of the nation. Pamela listened to the museum curator explain the Italian Renaissance work in detail as the student-crowd gathered around the icon. No student laughed. It was art, some of the finest in the history of the world. The class also knew in advance they would view the naked work and had signed permission forms from parents to be in the museum and learn about a world much different from their own. However, when the class viewed the next exhibit in the museum, Pamela stayed behind to admire "David." When she noticed most were no longer looking, except a few boys who were as sick as she would prove to be, she leaned into the statue, wrapped her tongue around David's "penis" and feigned oral sex. She would not have gotten caught except the boys daring her laughed so hard they drew the attention of the museum's security officer who caught Pamela in the "act." She was turned over to the school's assistant principal who sent her to the discipline center for five days. Worse yet, she gave the school a terrible reputation. During those five days of suspension, Pamela refused to do the Spanish homework assigned in the discipline center and received five 'F's.'

Brent had other parents to speak with, although none of them possessed the problems of Jeff, Erik, George, or Pam. Nineteen others had grades of 'F' and another six had already missed anywhere from eight to ten days of school, unexcused. Brent had to tell the parents of these students about their children's problems whether they wanted to hear them or not. The truth was that some parents really didn't know about any difficulties facing their offspring. Whether those parents were disconnected from their children's lives or had been deceived, Brent could not wait to meet them. It was time to set the record straight.

As he looked around, Brent could see many parents moving toward him slowly. Then a bell rang which signaled the official beginning of the reason for their being there. An announcement from Principal Berling was made alerting teachers that his meeting with parents was complete.

"Teachers, the administrative meeting in the auditorium is completed. Parents should be moving in your direction. Assist them in their quest to find classrooms. Thank you."

Head baseball coach, Randy Phelps, sensed Brent's nervousness and broke the monotony. From across the hallway he took the short walk over to Brent and offered him a final piece of advice before the parental politicking began.

"Remember, some of these parents are going to ask about grades, so tell them you don't even have the roll book with you," Coach Phelps said. "They have to make an appointment to discuss that. Otherwise, they will keep you all night. Got it?"

"I got it, Coach," Brent said with confidence. "I just want to meet all these parents. I have to tell some of them…"

Coach Phelps smiled at Brent's naiveté. He knew his advice to Brent sounded more like seventh-inning instructions to his team than two adults in conversation. His tanned and lined face then broke out in a broad grin and interrupted Brent.

"Whoa, what a minute, hotshot," he said with the palm of one hand extended toward Brent like a traffic cop. "I hate to tell you this, but most of these parents are not going to be here."

"But it's parent-teacher night."

"I don't care if it's, 'Let's Eat All the Steaks We Can for Free Night.' Most of these parents will not be here."

Coach Phelps hated to tell Brent that, but it was the truth. He was in his twelfth-year at East Side High School and had never seen it any differently. Parental attendance was getting worse every year. He looked at Brent and it appeared his remark somewhat deflated the idealistic first-year instructor. Coach Phelps was going to say something to soften the obvious blow to the younger teacher.

Coach Phelps had seen it all in his twenty-two years of teaching English and eighteen years of coaching. He was a four-time district coach of the year, his winning percentage was over .600, he read nearly ten novels per year by authors like Alexander Solzhenitsyn, Victor Hugo, Winston Churchill, Fyodor Dostoyevsky, and Ernest Hemmingway. He could quote Emerson, Pushkin, and Dumas. He knew as much about literature as he did a squeeze play and a sacrifice fly. He was no dumb jock coach and he loved his job, but not much excited him or deflated him any longer. Nothing shocked him when it came to student or parental behavior in today's public school system. He had broken up his share of fights, been cursed by too many parents much too involved in the baseball life of their children rather than any academic aspirations. His car had been vandalized four times in his career by students who did not like him for either not starting them on his teams or by students angry over his stringent classroom discipline. On three occasions, parents physically intimidated him after close baseball game losses. Last year he awakened one morning in late May at the end of the lengthy baseball season to two dozen eggs splattered over his house and truck. Paint damage to the three-year-old truck was in excess of $3,500. In short, he was a seasoned teaching veteran who learned not to expect much, to walk away from potential trouble, and to see it coming—more often than not—before it ever erupted into an uncomfortable situation. Like good, experienced people in any business, passing along advice to those less so, was a rite of passage that could save those who heeded it much pain in their careers. However, he realized his last comment to Brent was too harsh, but no less true. He had to be more positive even though it was going to prove fiction in the matter of an hour.

"Some of them will be here, Brent," Coach Phelps added in assurance.

Coach Phelps' follow-up remark did not help Brent's sudden mood change.

"How many do you think will come?" Brent asked sincerely while the first group of parents passed them by.

"I have five classes with 152 students total," Coach Phelps said. "I look for about fifteen parents to show up. That's about how many attend this thing every year."

Brent's expression changed to one of near horror. He looked at Coach Phelps and repeated, "Fifteen? That's it?"

Coach Phelps nodded in agreement not wanting to be right, but knowing he would be.

World history teacher, Gloria Hampton, began to laugh from across the hall, but not in a way that was cruel towards Brent's obvious lack of experience. Aside from her name, Brent knew little of her in the eleven days he had been employed at the school. Gloria was in her late fifties with thirty-three years' experience and could retire at any moment. Brent knew she knew what she was talking about and it frightened and disappointed him. With her many jeweled fingers folded over her pressed white blouse and red scarf draped neatly around her neck, Gloria took a few steps toward the two men without crowding them. She was as direct as Coach Phelps and had to be because time was short.

"Brent, do me a favor and walk toward the door at the end of the hall and take a look at the parking lot," she instructed as she pointed in that direction. "Tell me what you see."

Brent paused for a second and then moved toward the double doors just a few steps to his right. Coach Phelps and Gloria said nothing as the heels to his black, tasseled, dress shoes knocked in rhythm against the hard tile floor. He stopped, peeked out of the glass door overlooking the staircase and small parking lot and noticed it was just under halfway full of vehicles. There were still many parking spots left empty and there was no sign of traffic filing onto the campus. The streets lining the campus were growing dark and quiet. A lone, young female jogger with her collie dog on a leash ran down the middle of the blacktop street in bright orange sneakers. That scene said it all. Brent became more disheartened. He turned back toward Coach Phelps and Gloria and did not say a word. Neither did Coach Phelps or Gloria. Brent had gotten the point and there was no need for anyone to say anything further.

Some parents began to enter the rooms of the trio, including Brent's, but the flood of parents Brent thought would eventually fill the hallway never occurred. Brent stuck his head into his own room and saw just five adults. There were three males and two females. The clusters in which they chose to sit in the small desks appeared to represent just three of his thirty-two first-hour students. He then moved across the hallway and glanced into Evelyn's room and counted six clusters of parents representing the same number of students. Before Brent could peek into Coach Phelps' room, the coach held up one finger at Brent.

"I've got one parent," he said before smirking quietly and repeating it for effect. "I've got one parent."

"Take a breath," Gloria said to Brent as the three disappeared into their rooms to address the parents who chose to attend. "You'll be fine."

Then the "tardy" bell rang and another announcement was made.

"Teachers, all parents should be in first-hour classes. Remember, you have ten minutes to introduce yourself and field questions. That is all."

That was Brent's sign to meet with the parents and present his expectations to them. As he entered the room, he heard Coach Phelps and Gloria welcome the parents. They knew he was shocked and now in painful recognition of the fact he was not going to be able to reach students and improve their lives as he had envisioned. Absentee parents were a barrier to student achievement. Even a rookie teacher like Brent knew that.

Brent quickly remembered parent-teacher night when he attended private school. The hallways were packed with parents and there were often not enough desks for them to sit in. Parents lined against the back of the classroom walls. Sheriff's deputies were hired to direct traffic on and off the campus. Parking was a problem. Interest among parents in their children was not.

Over the next ten minutes, Brent did what he was expected to do. He outlined his procedures and expectations and never met the parents he needed to meet with most. Not one of those on his note card had showed up. While he spoke enthusiastically to the few parents in his room, he calmly discarded the index card in recognition of what was and not what he hoped.

During the entire evening he only met the parents of thirteen students. Coach Phelps met with parents representing nineteen students—according to him, the most he had met in years. Gloria met with the parents of twelve students. Numbers like those were reflected around the school regardless of age, race, subject, or student classification. Numbers among honors classes were slightly higher, but nothing to brag about.

It was beginning to settle into young Brent's mind that all the legislation and expert advice from those who ran the state's public school system might be in vain. Teachers were not the primary tools in solving the educational problem. Parents needed to be a willing teacher's apprentice to aid that effort. He realized that in eleven short days of teaching and one parent-teacher night. In two short hours, Brent was now a wiser teacher. What he wanted was to remain idealistic. The teacher he was slowly evolving into was now more realistic.

As the night ended, he began to straighten up his room and reflect. He thought of a script line in the movie, *Rudy,* delivered by a priest who had befriended the main character, Rudy, a physically small student-athlete who wanted to play football for college powerhouse, Notre Dame. Brent felt like Rudy and that priest's council was something he now needed to employ to make sense of it all.

"Have I done everything I possibly can?" Rudy asked the priest in the movie. "Can you help me?"

The priest responded to Rudy, "Son, I've come up with only two hard incontrovertible facts—there is a God and I'm not him."

For Brent, it was not just a movie script. It was wise council.

"From the morning to the evening, careless of the sun or of the rain, the spectators…remained in eager attention; their eyes fixed on horses and charioteers, their minds agitated with hope and fear for the success of the colours which they espoused; and the happiness of Rome appeared to hang on the event of a race."
—Roman historian, Edward Gibbon

Early November—"Your hero is here!"

What remained of the crowd at East Side High School's Hurricane Stadium was ill at ease. Mostly, they were the parents and friends of the players, and some teachers, left to cheer on the team during a game about whose outcome had long been decided.

Some parents, mostly fathers and guardians of the football players, screamed unsolicited advice to coaches standing on the sidelines near enough to hear the criticism—some of it vulgar. Parents, particularly men who had played any sport in their youth, always seemed to think they knew more than the coaches. They believed by yelling advice aloud it would jar whatever common sense they felt a coach was lacking into calling the right play from the right formation with the proper personnel. Although there was no way East Side High School could overcome its 31-7 deficit to Bienville High School late in the fourth quarter, the pent-up anger swelled in the bellies of some parents living their athletic lives through their kids. Many of these parents had never attended a parent-teacher conference or made a phone call to the school regarding the academic progress of their offspring. Communicating with coaches, however, was another matter when the balance of a football game and all its implications lay in rubble as the clock wound down on the final contest in a season gone wrong.

"C'mon, Coach, put in Lester Hayes and give him the damn ball!" one parent yelled with his arms crossed over his ample belly and his legs stretched over empty bleachers that just one hour before was crowded with fans. "He ain't played the whole game! He's your best weapon!"

To which another parent immediately responded, "Throw the ball long, Coach. You got nothin' to lose at this point!"

"Lose! That's all this bunch knows how to do!" another man yelled from the top of the old, worn, aluminum bleachers.

Run the ball. Pass the ball. Put Lester Hayes in the game and let him carry the ball. Throw the ball to Lester. Punt. Go for the first down on fourth down. Quit. Fight. Pass to the left. Run the option right. There was so much advice from well-intentioned parents to tired, overworked, and poorly paid coaches going into the sixteenth hour of their workday. And there were still another two hours before they would make their way home to the scratching a.m. radio sounds of the statewide football scoreboard show and a warm shower.

The coaches said nothing to the unkind remarks hurled at them. They knew their players were watching for their reaction. They knew the players heard the ungrateful fans. To combat the pressure, the coaches made wisecracks at the remarks while the game forwarded to its undeniable conclusion.

"That's why you should get an education, gentlemen, so you don't sound like those people when you are their age," the adult trainer said to everyone and no one while watching the players on the field.

The players giggled and shook their heads at the trainer's remark hoping it was not their parents acting so foolishly.

Wrapped in a dark blue and silver rain jacket to combat temperatures dipping into the upper thirties, assistant head coach, Randy Berlin, adjusted his headset and cap while senior tailback, Myles Dugas, attached his chinstrap to his silver helmet reflecting the bright stadium lights. Myles was an average student who played sparingly throughout his four-year high school career. His claim to fame was he never missed practice and the coaches counted on him to be a team leader despite his lack of statistics proving his mathematical worth to the team. Growing up without a father figure, Myles—like too many kids—was raised by his mother, Glenda Payne, sitting quietly in the stands allowing the verbal bullets targeting the team to fall harmlessly on her soul.

She knew the truth about the team, even if the remaining overzealous parents did not. East Side High School did not have the talent to compete with high schools like suburban Bienville High School. White flight and urban apathy relegated the better student-athletes to various schools throughout the metropolitan area. East Side High School was no longer fulfilling its quota of capable football players, and truth be known, was lucky to have the thirty-two players dressed out to form a squad to compete. Glenda knew nothing about slots and I-formations, but that fact she knew.

Glenda forced a smile with 1:25 remaining in her son's high school gridiron career as the coach issued him instructions he had heard in practice 1,000 times before. This time, of course, Myles would get to run the football against a team dressed in orange jerseys trimmed in green, rather than against his friends in a midweek scrimmage on a dark field sitting adjacent to the on-campus stadium.

"You ready?" assistant coach Randy Berlin asked an overly excited Myles. "Calm down, son. Calm down. Let's go, 'Slot left, I-Shirley, toss-sweep on one.' That's 'Slot-left, I-Shirley, toss-sweep on one.' Okay? Let's go!"

With a slap on the back of his clean helmet, Myles entered the game for the first time since the Hurricane's 18-7 win over St. Andrews Academy in late September. With an overall record of 2-7, and 2-8 just moments away, Coach Berlin began to insert senior athletes who garnered little playing time during the season and younger players needing the experience. The mix was not a good one in which to attempt to rescue humiliation, but Coach Berlin knew it to be the right thing to do. Bienville High School's head coach, a long-time friend of the East Side High School staff, was now playing his second-string understanding the game was technically over. He understood the need to no longer punish the out-manned Hurricane team or his coaching contemporaries.

Myles entered the huddle where his teammates were bent at the waist waiting for the play.

"Coach said, 'Slot left, I-Shirley, toss-sweep on one,'" repeated Myles nearly out of breath from excitement.

"You gotta be freakin' kiddin' me?" asked offensive lineman, Tanner Liwinski, now standing erect while looking at his coach standing on the sideline. His hands were on the hips of his dirty white uniform pants. His look was one of indignation toward a coach he felt whose game plan was doomed from the moment the Star-Spangled Banner was played.

Myles may have been one year older than Tanner, but everyone on the team was scared of the six-foot-two, 267-pound senior, now receiving letters of interest from several Division I-AA in-state universities. In his best interest, Myles simply repeated the play, but was interrupted.

"How the hell are we gonna' score with a shit play like that?" asked junior quarterback Ricardo Holmes.

Ricardo, frustrated, shook his head in disgust and repeated the play and finished the instruction with, "On one, on one. Ready?"

"Break!" the players stated in unison more out of habit than with conviction.

The East Side High School offensive line walked to the line of scrimmage at Bienville High School's twenty-five-yard-line. The Breaker defensive line outweighed the Hurricane offensive line about thirty-five-pounds per man. In teenage years, surrendering thirty-five pounds per man was sometimes impossible to overcome. At the college level, technique could sometimes overcome the difference. At the high school level, that was a nice fact to sell young players not knowing the difference. To make matters worse, the Hurricane coaching staff believed the best way to defeat the Bienville Breakers was to run the football directly at that team's defensive strength. It was a huge assumption. Now that it was understood the strategy failed, the new play called to flood the weak side, "Shirley," with players and try to force Myles around the left end.

As the players got into position, a few fans filtering out of the stadium stopped near the exit gate directly behind the goal post to watch one final play. Perhaps, they thought, East Side High School could score one final touchdown and soften the inevitable defeat and collect their tattered pride.

Ricardo stood behind his center as the north wind blew against his steel faceguard and studied a defense he had yet to unlock. The end zone bleachers were empty and the light bouncing off the smooth aluminum was blinding. He noticed the defense was playing nine players within four yards of the line of scrimmage—not a good sign for an offense wanting to run the football. Ricardo could change the play at the line of scrimmage, but chose not to.

"Red, 58! Red, 58!" barked Holmes to his offense looking both right and left using a dummy audible. "S-eee-ttt! Hut!"

The snap from center hit Ricardo in the palms of his hands. He turned to his right with outstretched hands and handed the ball to Myles now moving to his left. Myles stepped over a defensive lineman who broke through an attempted block, but fell to the ground trying to roll as he reached for the senior tailback with both taped hands. Myles kept moving left looking for a seam to exploit so he could move up field. He could not find one as he continually ran parallel to the line of scrimmage. Nearing his own sideline, he changed hands with the ball now properly tucked under his left arm as coached. Forced to make something happen, Myles lowered his head running into two Breaker linebackers having a field day making tackles against a tired Hurricane offense. Myles was gripped tightly as he stood upright. He spun his body as much as allowed to fall forward for a gain of two yards. The two receivers designated to make blocks on the play failed to do so.

Staying in bounds the clock continued ticking to 1:02.

"Second-down and eight for the "Canes at the Breaker twenty-three-yard line," the field announcer responded to the play via the intercom.

"Good effort, Myles!" yelled the clapping coaches knowing the senior was giving his all against superior competition. "Let's go! Let's get a score!"

"Hold the damn block, receivers!" yelled the offensive coordinator at the top of his lungs. "If you hold that block, Myles turns the corner! C'mon!"

"Let's go, baby!" yelled a group of dirty Hurricane players now out of the game for a variety of injuries and simple fatigue. "Let's get another one! We can do this!"

The play yielded little yardage, but it was positive real estate nonetheless and only two of 139 total yards of total offense earned throughout the night. Myles bounced up from the tackle and ran back to the huddle while Coach Berlin stepped onto the field and instructed Ricardo near the sideline with another play. Ricardo ran to the huddle and entered the circle of ten players awaiting instructions.

"All right, we're goin' 'split, I-Harry, 22-slant on two. On two!" Ricardo instructed. "Buster, don't drop the ball or I'll kick your ass. You feelin' me?"

Tanner, more frustrated than any player in the huddle, again made his feelings known in his usual brusque manner. Looking at Buster sternly through a chewed steel facemask, Tanner issued his warning to the entire team through the wide-eyed receiver.

"Don't...drop...the...ball, got it?" Tanner said to Buster in his dramatics. "Our esteemed coach is finally showing some guts. Don't slow this offense down."

Sophomore receiver Buster Finnerty nodded his head that he understood.

"The rest of you, make your damn blocks! Okay?" ordered Tanner with his finger extended to everyone in the huddle leaning on his every word.

No one said a word. There was no reason to. The instructions from Ricardo and the threat from Tanner were clear.

Ricardo quickly repeated, "On two, on two. Ready?"

The team responded, "Break!"

The Hurricane offense moved toward the line of scrimmage as Buster moved to his position wide at the far sideline. Buster was one of the most athletic players on the team, but was hardly excited about academics. Entering the previous spring with a 1.2 grade point average, Buster failed four of seven final exams and finished the year with a 1.0. The only way to make him eligible for the fall was to enroll him in summer school, conveniently taught by several private and public high school football coaches who had an understanding to "help each other out for the good of the game." In other words, coaches teaching summer classes were to do everything possible to award players of any football-playing school the grades needed to become eligible. Buster was one of the many recipients of such generosity enrolling for fall classes with a 1.9, enough to qualify for participation in the current season.

"Blue-34!" Ricardo called out to his team in his white slightly torn jersey with blue numerals.

It was another dummy audible for the offense to ignore and confuse the defense.

"Blue-34! S-eee-ttt..."

Myles moved slowly in motion to the weak side to make a block once the snap was made on the second 'hut."

"…Hut! Hut!" Ricardo sounded out in rapid cadence.

The sound of pads clashed and the grunts from the pain and the violence of the collision followed. Ricardo moved back with the football in his hand in a five-step drop. Three steps is the usual rule in running a quick slant pass play across the middle of the field, but the Bienville High School defensive lineman were too tall. Hence, the extra two-step drop was insurance the play had a chance to work at all. Bouncing his body and then pushing off his right foot, Ricardo wasted no time rolling to his right two steps and throwing the ball into Buster's gut as he ran low to the ground six yards down field. The ball was bobbled as Buster fell to the ground, but he recaptured it before being hit hard by two Breaker defensive backs, both of whom had verbally committed to play college football out of state. Buster hurt as he rose from the ground with the ball and raced off the field in pain.

The crowd of less than 200 cheering for the Hurricanes yelled their approval while the band played abbreviated stanzas from the school fight song.

"Third-down and two, at the Breaker seventeen-yard-line!" the public address announcer said.

There were no timeouts remaining and the clock was now down to forty-nine seconds and still ticking. The players wanted to throw the ball, even though they knew it was a risk. The last thing they wanted was a play through the middle of the Bienville High School lineman they could not control physically. A running play would also continue moving the clock. But one receiver left the field and was replaced by a tight end now moving toward the huddle with the new play.

"A damn tight end," Ricardo said with sarcasm within earshot of his teammates. "I wonder what we are going to call."

Coach Berlin wanted to score a touchdown on the ground in the manner in which they drew up in film sessions. An ex-offensive lineman, Coach Berlin wanted to shove the ball down the throats of an adversary he knew to be superior. In his opinion, scoring on a pass play may have been the higher percentage play, but was nothing short of cheating in a game demanding maximum physical contact.

Bienville High School's defense knew exactly what to do. They inserted an additional linebacker expecting a plunge through their defense line. The Breakers wanted to end the Hurricane offense threat in the next two plays and break the morale of East Side High School offense. It was cold and getting more so. The fans were now stopped in their tracks as they slowly walked toward exits behind fences ringing the field. There was some drama left in the game and the Hurricane fans wanted to experience it knowing the next football season and all its promise was nine months away.

"Okay, listen up," junior tight end Tyrone Hughes told the Hurricane players as he entered the huddle. "We're going right at them!"

"No, we're not!" Tanner informed the team.

"I'm with Tanner," said senior offense lineman Bert Cassidy. "I ain't goin' out like this. I want to score one more time."

"Can't do it, man," Ricardo told the two burly linemen looking at his newest tight end. "Coach called a play and we gotta' run it."

Ricardo then looked at Tyrone and asked, "What's the play?"

"Basic, Bobby, Power-24," the tight end said. "Myles is running the ball right behind my block."

"That's bullshit, Ricardo," Bert said. "I ain't never going to get this close to an end zone again in my life and want in. That play won't get me there."

Time was running short and Tanner knew it. The head official slowly walked toward the Hurricane huddle. Tanner grew concerned about a delay of game penalty and became nervous as the man in the black and white striped shirt moved slowly toward them as he glanced at his watch.

"Coach will be really mad, man, you know, if we change the play," another player said.

"Screw it!" Tanner insisted. "Huddle up!"

The players drew a tight circle and listened to the only player with the nerve to shake off a play from the bench and do it his way. Tanner wanted to go to college. He had the size and the grades to attend a major Division I-A institution and had yet to receive letters of interest from any. He wanted more from his football life and knew he could not get it in a conservative offense averaging a mere thirteen points per game. He did not think scoring a touchdown this late in the game would get the college coaches knocking on his door, but he wanted a reputation as a leader, albeit a reckless one. That, however, could prove an attractive quality to some college coaches desperate to win to save his job and looking for a nasty offensive lineman with a desire to win at all costs.

Tanner continued, "Basic, power, 38 dive, quarterback option. Tyrone, you need to be open if Ricardo has to unload. Ricardo, run your ass off and dive if you have to. On one, on one. Ready?"

"Break!"

Tanner knew what to do in a situation where all players agreed it was becoming critical in terms of time. The Breaker defense line placed ten players close to the line of scrimmage. Only one defender covered the lone receiver set to the right side.

"Here they come! Here they come!" the Breaker linebackers warned each other believing a play was going to be run through the middle of the line.

The defense then began to taunt the offense with, "Bring it, baby! Come to mama!"

The Breakers knew a burst up the middle would be stopped colder than the north wind now picking up speed. Tanner set up the offense that way to confuse the defense and his own coaching staff believing Myles would fight his way through the tangle of bodies for a first down in the play they called.

"Red-99. Red-99," came the dummy audible. "Set. Hut!"

The ball was snapped, Ricardo turned left and handed Myles nothing but a fake. Myles dove through the line faking his clutching of the football. His body fell to the turf as Breaker tacklers mobbed him before realizing they had been duped. Ricardo had the ball and was rolling right looking for Tyrone running a crossing pattern to the rear of the right side of the end zone. It was not the proper route. Tyrone was waving his hands that he was open, even though he was not. Had Tyrone run the route in the shallow part of the end zone he would have been open. With no other option, Ricardo would have to run for the needed two yards and a first down. His tired body ached as his knees churned toward the green space that seemed to sprout in front of him. His peripheral vision caught two Breaker defenders moving in from his left and on his space quickly. Ricardo angled his run closer to the sideline hoping to extend his run and get out of bounds to stop the clock. Ricardo needed to reach the fifteen-yard-line for a first down. As he crossed the fifteen-yard-line stripe he sensed the impending violence and stretched his frame as he fell hard out of bounds in the cold grass. The grunts of the players went up as the chain crew moved back from the collision. The official immediately stepped on the sideline spot where the play ended. Ricardo bounced up and noticed the official's foot was just inside the fifteen-yard-line awarding the Hurricanes the first down.

"First down Hurricanes inside the fifteen!" the announcer verbalized with more drama.

The small crowd screamed its approval.

Ricardo jumped up and tossed the official the ball as the band played another twelve-bar stanza. Many fans were now hugging the fence to be close to the action.

As Ricardo ran to the huddle, he looked up at the clock that read, thirty-eight seconds. He was met with a play brought in by Buster, who re-entered the game.

Buster leaned over and whispered to Ricardo, "Coach is pissed, Ricardo. You better not shake this play off."

Ricardo screamed in the left ear hole of Buster's helmet, "Ask Coach if he wants us to give the play back."

Buster grinned getting the point and then gave the play to Ricardo who would repeat it to the team who overheard it.

The new play was nothing more than a sandlot call. Four receivers would move into the end zone, or near it, get open, and catch any ball thrown to them. It was that simple.

Ricardo entered the huddle and wasted no time calling the play.

"Double-slot, Ace…" Ricardo said before being interrupted.

"We know, we know," the other players responded.

"Okay, assholes, on one and pay attention!" Ricardo told the team. "Tanner, make damn sure your guys hold their blocks. If they blitz, guys, the ball is going up. I ain't taking no sack. We ain't got no timeouts, okay?"

No one answered him. They knew the situation and they knew Ricardo had to say it to remind those whose stomachs were now being eaten up by nerves.

"Ready?"

"Break!"

The drums from the marching band were beating out a powerful rhythm as the dancers and cheerleaders screamed high-pitched voices into the night. The fans were on their feet, including the Bienville High School parents waiting anxiously for the game to end so they could embrace their sons and begin thinking about next week's playoff game.

Ricardo walked slowly behind his lineman to the scrimmage line. He looked over the defense and noticed his girlfriend, Jessica, standing along the back fence. The drums stopped beating at the director's command. More of the crowd had shifted to the end of the field where the players fought over ground gained and lost.

Ricardo barked out the signals and took the snap from center. As he took his seven-step obligatory drop, he looked around for an open receiver, but had no time to study their routes. He was immediately hit by a Breaker lineman and hobbled toward the turf, but caught his fall with his non-throwing hand. His wrist was now severely sprained and Ricardo could hear himself scream. He pirouetted, kept his balance and rolled to his left near the East Side High School sideline. His coaches were shouting instructions but in his haste he heard only noise, not advice. Ricardo saw Myles running across the middle open. Ricardo instinctively threw the ball to Myles who caught it in full stride at the four-yard-line and hustled out of bounds. The successful play was greeted with unbridled enthusiasm. Fans, players, coaches, the band, and cheerleaders were hoping for a moral touchdown against a playoff-bound team. With just fifteen seconds left, it was setting up as an exciting finish.

As Myles got off the turf, he tossed the ball to the official who marked the play out of bounds with his foot.

He was met by Coach Gatewood who patted him on the backside and yelling, "Atta-boy!"

Myles was then escorted to the sideline as Coach Gatewood gave instructions to senior tailback Lester Hayes, playing his last game and had yet to see any action in the contest.

Ricardo's heart sank as he watched the transaction as the pandemonium continued around him and his team huddled near him. Most of the assistant coaches, honorable men in their own right, walked away from Coach Gatewood upset with the decision, including Coach Berlin. They were head coaches in other sports and would not have agreed to allow Lester to play. But Lester was bringing in the next play, not Myles. Lester was suspended for the last three games of the season for fighting during the lunch shift three weeks prior. He knocked out the front teeth of a much smaller sophomore who he thought broke in the lunch line. It was Lester's third transgression of the semester. He was also failing five of seven classes and had missed nine days of school unexcused. Lester was a mess of a person, but his athletic value was too great, according to the school powers that be, to permanently dismiss him from the team. When the parents of the abused sophomore threatened to sue the school, the best Coach Gatewood, Principal Berling, and Lester could agree on was expulsion from playing games, but still be allowed to practice. It was a strange arrangement, teaching Lester no moral or ethical value. And now, to make matters worse, the best athlete in the school was making an appearance he did not deserve. To the ignorant crowd, applause went up as he stepped onto the field like a gladiator in the ancient Roman arena.

"First and goal for the Hurricanes at the four!" the announcer said to the vocal crowd.

Myles took off his helmet in shock. He did not play much, had strongly contributed to the team's late heroics, and was now watching nothing short of a hallway felon try to score a meaningless touchdown for East Side High School.

When Lester entered the huddle, he was met with silence. There was justice in the huddle, even if the so-called adult coaching the team failed to digest the signal he was sending to his players.

"Your hero is here!" Lester said to the team as he leaned over. "Listen up! Basic, Debbie, I-option left, on one! On one! Ready?"

There were only claps from a few players as they walked to the line of scrimmage. The only one responding to Lester's call for unity was Lester. Hearing his own voice scream "Break" as they broke the huddle never alerted Lester to how much some players resented his presence in the game. It was not Lester's game. It was no longer Lester's team. In the first six games of the season, Lester accounted for 72 percent of the Hurricane offensive production. But Lester was too arrogant for his own good and the college scouts were backing away from the six-foot-one,

210-pound senior runner with a penchant for hurting opposing tacklers. The team needed Lester, but most players thought the cost too high. Everyone hurt for Myles, now visably upset on the sideline, as he had played his last down for the school.

The players lined up with Lester at tailback. The receivers were split to each side. The tight end was set to the left side. Ricardo took the snap, faked the ball to the fullback immediately forced to lay a block at the feet of a rushing Bienville High School lineman. Ricardo ran parallel to the line of scrimmage, was met by a linebacker, stopped and extended a perfect pitch to Lester running three yards behind him. As Ricardo was smashed to the ground, Lester gathered in the ball in full stride and raced toward the corner of the end zone. At the three-yard-line Lester was hit by two Breaker defenders before a third pushed him out of bounds stopping the clock. Lester gained one yard.

"Lester Hayes on the carry. One yard gain," the announcer told the standing crowd.

There were just eight seconds remaining in the game. Perhaps there was time for two pass plays in the end zone. The Hurricane team knew their coach was going to take one final chance trying to push powerful Lester Hayes into the end zone. What's more, Bienville High School knew it, too.

As the East Side High School offense circled for the game's final play, Lester ran from the sideline with the call from the coaches who picked him up off the turf after the last play. Lester was grinning. Not a good sign as far as the players were concerned.

"It's my ball, baby!" Lester said arrogantly. "My final play is going to be a touchdown, bitches."

The huddle was quiet as the drums thudded in the distance and the crowd revved up stadium decibels. Bienville High School's second-team defense, sprinkled with a few starters, wanted to halt East Side High School's final threat. The offense wanted desperately to score. Coach Gatewood wanted smash-mouth football to triumph. Tanner wanted to throw his hands in the air and walk off the field a final time on a positive note. East Side's fans wanted to feed their gridiron warriors something positive during the off-season to promote a better weight room work ethic on those long, hot summer days. The band wanted to play the fight song over and again believing their cadence and harmony promoted exuberance worthy of a late-game rally. Myles stood alone near the end of the team bench with his helmet off as the game clock slowly ticked away his football career. Lester just wanted, again, to be the center of attention and everyone in the huddle knew it. He was not a team player. Now, reluctantly, his team listened to the call for the final play of the final game of the season.

"All right, baby, it's gonna' be, 'Twins, basic, 38-power.' And block hard for Lester so we can get this score," Lester said shaking his cocky head from left to right.

At that moment, Lester was hated by his teammates. Even at his age and playing four years with the team he did not understand one thing football was supposed to teach young men. Words like commitment, loyalty, work, sweat, pain, honor, dignity, humility, and team, Lester believed belonged in a dictionary, not executed in a game he thought to be made for him and players like him. He thought himself superior to young men his age because he could carry a football and dance his way through opposing tacklers better than most. It never occurred to Lester that organized blocking and execution helped make him great. The game and this moment in time, he foolishly believed, were all about him.

The team broke the huddle and lined up. Fists were clenched around dirty fingers and hands. Time moved as if it were in slow motion.

Ricardo looked over the defense trying to make the Breakers believe he could change the play with the slight study of their formation. The strategy did not work. The defense did not move as they placed all eleven of their players very close to the line of scrimmage. The Breakers knew what was coming and now Ricardo knew it, too. It scared him and his eyes were the mirrors the defense read that made them feel good about their chosen tactic.

Ricardo barked out the signal and his center snapped him the ball. Ricardo turned to his left and pivoted on his left foot. He placed the ball into Lester's hands as the cocky senior moved toward the scrimmage line of piled up, dirty bodies defending and attempting to penetrate a regulation four-inch-wide painted white line in the fading November grass. Lester had the ball secure, took four steps to build up the momentum of his powerful body, and slammed into the line. The blocking was perfect as Lester reached the two-yard line untouched.

Sensing strong resistance, Lester then used his graceful athleticism to take one step and leap over the goal line. As he did, he got careless and lost control of the football. Lester leaped forward, but without the ball. As Lester rolled into the end zone ignored, bodies from both sides scrambled for the loose ball. Mostly, it was orange jerseys fighting for control of it. The Hurricane offense either lay in the grass or stood knowing it mattered little who recovered the fumble. Their final chance at one speck of glory was ruined. The horn sounded ending the game as Bienville players rejoiced after one of their own came up with the ball in one hand extended toward the night sky. The Bienville High School bench ran toward their second-team defense and doused them with respect and pats on their tired uniformed bodies.

Lester watched the Breakers celebrate as he sat on the grass alone with his feet extended. No one went to help him up. Team disunity now returned, sideline players walked toward the tunnel underneath the stands and toward their locker room for a speech from their head coach they did not want to hear. The two head coaches met at midfield for a handshake as Tanner, Ricardo, Buster, and the rest of the East Side High School delegation remaining on the field shook hands with a few opposing players. The fans filed out of the stadium quietly. The band tried to pick up spirits with a final rendition of the East Side High School fight song, but no one clapped or cheered. The season was mercifully over.

Within minutes, half of the stadium lights went dark to save electricity and chase any lingering fans home. As the fans left the stadium, discarded paper and beverage cans were more visible.

Sadly for some Hurricane players, the end of the game that signaled the end of their final season would probably be the apex of their lives. One quick burst of an unknown official's whistle on a cold November evening abruptly signaled that end. As players trudged off the field while spectators made their way out of the bleachers to the cadence of distant drummers, some players wrapped their arms around the necks of fellow seniors. It was time for farewells, the slapping of muddy palms wrapped in tape, and a reassurance of friendship only they could understand, but time would never allow enduring.

A few senior athletes, desperate to continue playing the game they loved, walked off the high school field and verbalized their wish to enter college football as nothing more than a walk-on, perhaps earning a letter or two for special teams playing late in their college career. It was a move they would have to orchestrate themselves. Their head coach played no part and took no interest in helping his seniors move to the next level. With their eligibility exhausted, Coach Gatewood did not return phone calls, e-mails, or questionnaires to colleges showing even lukewarm interest in any of his players. It was a huge commentary on his lack of character, and his players understood that fact and learned to expect nothing from him.

A few players also understood all too well they were being used to advance the career cause of their head football coach. They didn't play the game out of respect and devotion to him or the school. They played because they loved the game and knew it was a means to an end—an end they knew with each passing week. They would discard their cleats and prepare for something greater than a tackle behind the line of scrimmage or being successful on punt coverage. These few players would actually attend and graduate college and finish either with an associate's degree or of the bachelor variety. They would never again play football. They were simply grateful for the game as a brief diversion in their lives.

The majority of these East Side High School inner city footballers would live the remainder of their teenage youth aimless, hoping to catch economic lightening in a bottle. Like too many young people they would look for the easy way out and never legitimately find it. Too many of these seniors would leave the locker room for the last time believing not only their football status had ended, but so, too, had their usefulness to the school. At least one player had already made it known he was going to drop out of school within days of the final game. At least three other players would resume their poor attendance practices now that football season was over.

Football and sports in general, for too many players at East Side High School, defined who they were as people. They were too young to understand the game was only part of their high school lives. It was a chance to compete while making long-term friendships developed in the sweat and pain of weight lifting and running with teammates possessing the same zeal. Their spirit was not born of the school. It was born of the streets from which they came. Football and the controlled violence it provided was the definition of who they were. For most inner city players, the idea of school playing a part in their overall development meant little. They did not attend high school to advance their knowledge. They, instead, attended high school to manipulate whatever celebrity a paragraph in the local sports pages could provide them. Now that the game had ended for them, they lost what prestige high school football afforded them. They were now just part of the student body. They were the ones who would return to games in future years hoping to be seen and remembered for that one play or one game that still meant too much in a future life going nowhere.

> "Those whom the gods would destroy they first make angry."
>
> —Greek proverb

November—Rotten Wood Building Rotten Houses

It was not a particularly good day for Coach Joey Martin. It was one of those days proving extremely hectic. The list of items to attend to appeared endless. Every time Coach Martin tackled one problem another cropped up even more determined to undermine his already taxing day.

Coach Martin was a workaholic by nature. Where some worked to live, he lived to work. Or so it seemed. He simply could not keep still and measured his day's success or failure on how much he could accomplish. He loved his job as a geography and American government teacher and assistant soccer coach. There was simply so much to do if one wanted to excel in both. Procrastination was not his way. He believed challenges were to be met and retired immediately. He often succeeded in his strong-willed way until he succumbed to daily exhaustion.

His wife often joked to friends, "Joey possesses only two speeds—full throttle and fast asleep. There is no between."

He was beginning to gray at his temples and his hair was thinning. Coach Martin's day as a lady's man had passed him by. He was not a very large man. Yet, he possessed large arms and a sizable chest from years of working out with weights to overcome his lack of height. Even today, however, no matter how much he proved himself to others, it seemed he never earned the respect as the athlete he was.

The football coaches joked behind Coach Martin's back that he did not possess athletic talent. They didn't even consider him a coach, per say. They based their ignorant assumptions on his five-foot-eight,

160-pound frame. They figured, wrongly, that he became a soccer coach because it was the only sport he could play in his youth. That was far from the truth, of course, but it's what the other coaches, perhaps, wanted to believe. Soccer was not even a fixture in the community when Coach Martin was younger. He grew up like the other coaches, playing the "big three" sports of football, basketball, and baseball. Coach Martin was one hell of a football and basketball player even in his early thirties. He still possessed a good jump shot, was quick as a cat, and could a throw a football well enough to play or coach those respected sports. But he had grown tired of those games. He had played them all of his life, gotten as far as he ever could playing them even in leisure, and needed a new challenge.

At the late age of thirty-five, Coach Martin was open-minded enough to try soccer one boring summer day and fell in love with the sport. This new game had a grip on him he could not explain. Coach Martin loved challenges and soccer certainly delivered it. East Side High School would need his enthusiasm to assist in bringing credibility to a program that was a joke among other metropolitan area soccer programs. Having already lost two previous jobs in suburban parishes because he did not coach, and having only played the game a mere five years, Coach Martin one day found himself assisting a struggling soccer program that Principal Berling despised and athletic director and head football coach, Ray Gatewood, undermined. Despite all, he was determined to help turn the program around. Never wanting to be head coach due to his grueling class load, he had been an assistant three consecutive years under three different coaches. This year was no different as the school hunted within the faculty for a head coach after the last soccer boss left to take a coaching job in a suburban school system. Reluctantly and without an interview or notice from the school adminstration, Coach Martin accepted the job as head soccer coach and that was that.

Even as an assistant, Coach Martin knew Coach Gatewood used him and the soccer team for a punch line. The tension between him and the other coaches, particularly football coaches, was always there for no other reason than the fact Coach Martin fell in line with a game others considered foreign or were simply unfamiliar.

Rarely did Coach Gatewood pass along helpful hints or guidance in any way. Memos and notices from the state's athletic board rarely made it into Coach Martin's office mailbox.

As a teacher, Coach Martin was simply outstanding. No one, even his detractors, could take that from him. He had a way of teaching and entertaining kids, even the ones who were against learning anything. Even when students were facing expulsion and questioned about their grades by office administrators, Coach Martin's class was usually mentioned as one of the few classes they actually liked, even if they were failing.

Coach Martin was new to the coaching world and only in his third year of teaching at East Side High School, his alma mater. The school had changed quite a lot since he was a student some twenty-three years prior. The school was once a revered institution because of its success and excess. In the late 1970s, and as late as the early 1980s, the school had a student body in excess of 1,500 students in grades ten through twelve. The number of academic awards presented to hard-working students was staggering. Parents did not want to spend money to send their offspring to a private school during that time because East Side High School had so much to offer.

Money was not an issue at the school during this period either. Parents were involved in their children's lives, and boosters and businesses willing to advertise and fill the school's financial coffers were plentiful. The facilities were as good as any in the area. Its teams and clubs won more than their share of games and awards. Student participation was overwhelming. The marching band enrolled over 140 members, not counting drummers, cheerleaders, majorettes, the school mascot, or the 200-plus group of 'Canettes that danced and marched with the band at halftime. It took over fifteen loaded buses to get that musical legion and over eighty football players to some home games played at 4,000-seat Veteran's Field in the Midtown section of the city. The school's gridiron popularity nearly rendered the on-campus football stadium too small for even the junior varsity squad's games.

Traffic control entering and leaving an East Side High School varsity football game of twenty years before once required over one dozen hired sheriff's deputies. Tickets to games were sold out in advance. Students went to games. Parents followed their children. Alumni got involved. The local daily newspaper followed school successes as much or more than any of the twenty-five playing football programs in the metropolitan area.

Coach Martin smiled remembering those glory days as he spied senior newcomer Gary Gonzalez nearing his car. He waved Gary down in the cold early November sun in an effort to get him to join the soccer team during midseason. Gary had transferred from a private school and was considered one of the top soccer prospects in the state. Coach Martin had no one as talented as Gary on his roster. Now, there was a transfer who could infuse his team with a sense of purpose and leadership that it did not have with two-thirds of their games left to play in what was rapidly becoming another losing season for the school.

Coach Martin was using his considerable salesman talents to get Gary to accept the challenge to join his team. After the pitch, Gary told Coach Martin he would talk it over with his family and get back with him on his decision. Gary had a college athletic scholarship wrapped up at a small Midwestern university. He did not need to play high school soccer any longer to prove himself to anyone. Coach Martin sensed Gary's attitude and tried not to press the idea of joining his struggling team. He hoped to appeal to Gary's competitive nature and see him on the practice field in the coming days.

As he waved goodbye to Gary in the student parking lot, Coach Martin felt like a prostitute trying to sell a seventeen-year-old kid on the idea of playing a game any athlete twenty years ago would have begged *him* to play. No, it was not the East Side High School of days gone by. The sad truth was it might never be again.

Urban public school students of the new millennium did not feel any obligation whatsoever to play for their school. Public school sports programs in general, like their academics, were no longer attracting the best. Parents did not involve themselves in their kid's lives as they once did. An increasing number of sponsors no longer proved interested in helping public school sports programs. Money was in short supply and so was the love of playing for one's school. Sports facilities were only as good as a coach could construct and improve with paint, hammer, nail, and limited donations. Coach Martin could not understand it. Neither could any public school coach of any sport in any inner city school. To further complicate matters, academic ineligibility of players was a source of constant concern for coaches.

Watching Gary drive away in his worn, red Ford SUV, Coach Martin hurriedly glanced at his watch. It was 9:45 a.m. and he needed to get back to the office for a parent-teacher conference. He had a million things to do on this day and a meeting with a parent was not going to help him get them done. But it was his job, and quite frankly, he respected a parent or guardian who cared enough to schedule a meeting with a teacher. Unfortunately, far too many parents did not care.

Coach Martin quickly paced the lengthy distance to the office through building two while overhearing several teachers instructing their pupils behind closed doors. By the time he got to the end of the hallway, he saw a student peering inside one of the small glass interior door windows and staring into Jack Meir's English class. Even though he was bordering tardy for his parent conference, Coach Martin could not help but stop and question this improper juvenile behavior.

He crept up behind the female student, Bianca Hargrove, and watched her laughing and pointing through the small glass. Bianca, who did not have her blue uniform shirt tucked into her khaki trousers, was snickering to herself and trying to get the attention of her best friend, Camille Jones, another underachiever, who was in the classroom sitting at her desk. Coach Martin was standing quietly behind Bianca with his hands on his hips waiting to be discovered. When Bianca figured out she was being studied, she turned around quickly and acted as if she had done nothing wrong.

"I wasn't doing nothing,'" Bianca said in a tone that told that she was, in fact, up to no good.

"Bianca, I believe you, because if you were doing anything at all you would not be in the hallway kicked out of class for about the 999th time this semester," Coach Martin replied with just a touch of sarcasm.

Bianca's tone changed almost immediately. She became offensive and her voice rose to decibel levels heard along the entire hallway corridor. That's exactly what she hoped to do. Making a scene was a weak attempt on her part at deflecting her poor behavior to another issue. Bianca would base that issue on how the authoritarian figure, in this case the teacher, would react.

"Man, why you be always getting' in my business?!" Bianca asked defensively. "I ain't did you nothin'!"

"Hey, lower your voice," Coach Martin warned in a hushed tone as teachers nearby began to open their doors to what was becoming an unnecessary confrontation.

"It's not about what you did to me or anyone else that gets you in constant trouble. It's what you do to yourself. I don't care what you did to get tossed out here in the hallway. You are not even supposed to be in the hallway. The school rule says that all students must either be in class or in the office. So, why are you even in the hallway?"

Bianca continued in a very aggressive tone, "Mr. Meir made me come out here, and it's not any of yo' business what I be doin' out here!"

Coach Martin always started his interrogation of a student as nice as he could. He hoped to diffuse any potential ugly situation by simply being nice. He studied the police at sporting events and learned no matter how bad juveniles or criminals behaved on the streets or in the bleachers, the police were always nice. Always. It was a policy he adopted and it usually worked, but not always—especially with high school girls who were experts on being little bitches. Some girls felt like they held the upper hand when being disciplined by adult males. Real or imagined, male teachers were the instinctive enemy of most young, aggressive females.

Bianca also had a lengthy track record and had no fear. It was only November and she had been to the public school discipline center three times, once for fighting a boy larger then herself and scratching him up very badly over seating arrangements in the school cafeteria. Bianca perceived fighting as strength. On the mean streets of her north Baton Rouge neighborhood it probably was strength. In the civilized world she would soon be faced with, Coach Martin knew she had almost no future. East Side High School was full of girls like Bianca who believed a good fight, a loud mouth, an over-protective mother, or a good liberal lawyer could get them in or out of anything they so desired.

Coach Martin, however, didn't have time to play investigator any longer. He was late for his parent conference. He found Bianca's display tiring, boring, and a job that belonged to the school disciplinarian. With no hesitation at all, Coach Martin held out his finger in front of

Bianca's face that told her to follow him to the office. She complied, but not without attitude.

"Take me to da' office and see if I give a shit!" she added with spite as she tossed her head from left to right. "I hate this damn school! You be doin' me a favor getting' me the fuck outta' here!"

"Bianca, I can't stop you from cursing, but would you please do it quietly?" Coach Martin asked.

"I ain't gotta' do shit!" was her quick response. "Write me up and see if I care!"

With that, Bianca marched to the office in front of Coach Martin, who was cursed all the way there. She also cursed the school, the trees, the birds flying in them, Jack Meir, and the judge that forced her to either go to school or the state juvenile institution the students nicknamed "Juvy." Bianca also let her feelings be known to anyone who passed on their way to the office. Predictably, the very worst students with the very worst characters always slowed their pace to a crawl when the office was in sight. It was their way of aggravating the teacher one final time. Students knew they could not be touched, pushed, prodded, or verbally abused. Walking slower than a snail's pace, some troubled students thought, was sure to aggravate teachers having much to do and in a hurry to get it done. Bianca played that predictable part.

While her mouth continued to spit venom, she took about a full two minutes to walk twenty paces. Coach Martin pulled out the sports page rolled up in his back pocket he had yet to read and walked parallel with her. He really didn't read a word, but the impression he intended to give to Bianca was he didn't care how slowly she walked. He would busy himself with other things. That usually angered the slow pacers eventually forcing most of them to abandon their childish mental assault. Coach Martin simply walked with his head down flipping through the sports page moving as slowly as she allowed every step of the way. Matters such as these sometimes proved his job was a ridiculous way for an educated adult to make a living.

When Bianca reached the office door, Coach Martin opened it for her like a gentleman. She entered slowly and immediately began to assume control.

"He cursed me on the way down here!" Bianca said near the top of her voice to no one in particular in a crowded office of students and parents busy with other matters. "And he pushed me, too! What ya'll gonna do about that? Huh?"

Coach Martin waited for Bianca to complete her desperate accusation. He then explained the situation to the teacher on duty and went to his meeting five minutes late. Bianca's loud mouth forced the assistant principal in charge of discipline, Daryl Nutt, to admit her into his office for a conference over five waiting students. Daryl knew of Bianca's potential and did not want it spilling over anymore than it already had.

"Bianca. Bianca!" Daryl's voice roared in an effort to get her attention. "Get in my office now! And watch your mouth, please!"

Daryl pointed his hand at the office door wanting Bianca to move toward it immediately.

"I don't wanna' watch my mouth," Bianca said. "I know I'm in trouble and I don't care! You hearin' me?"

Bianca's mouth continued to display her ignorance and poor upbringing. She wanted to be heard. She wanted attention, even the wrong brand.

"Nobody tells me nothin'," she continued in rapid-fire speech. "I don't get told to do nothin'! I hate this place. Mr. Meir, throw me out in the hallway and then dat stupid Coach Martin come 'round tellin' me this and dat. Fuck him! I hate him! I do what I want. No white trash is gonna'…"

Her voice trailed off as her presence disappeared from the main office leaving behind those remaining to only comment that this time, Bianca, had perhaps gone too far.

As Coach Martin watched Bianca walk out of sight, he overhead a student phoning her mother asking for permission to take a two-day suspension rather than spend one day in the time-out room performing punish work for violating a minor school rule.

"They makin' me do all this stuff and write and I don't wanna' do it," the white female student whispered with the black plastic phone to her ear. "I want to get suspended instead and you gotta' tell the school secretary that it's okay."

Coach Martin knew students were now bold enough to simply walk out of the time-out room—a place where students spent a day performing punish work. Suspension was a better alternative to some students due to sheer laziness, and parents in increasing numbers, were granting their children that permission.

Coach Martin eventually made the short trip through two doors and the guidance office. As soon as he entered their cramped quarters he was greeted by Allison Boudreaux, the guidance counselor charged with the academic supervision of tenth-grade students. One look at Allison told Coach Martin the parent-in-waiting was growing tired of waiting. But she smiled at the tired coach anyway.

"Coach Martin, this is Miss Irene Williams, the mother of Plebius Jackson, who is in your fourth-hour geography class," Allison announced with her hand extended as if the two were meeting for a business luncheon rather than discussing the grades of her apathetic child.

"Nice to meet you, Miss Williams," Coach Martin said as he leaned over to greet the seated parent. "I'm sorry I was late, but I had to discipline a child on the way here and it took more time than I wish it had."

"What happened, Coach?" Allison asked.

Coach Martin raised himself, looked right at Allison and said mockingly, "I've got two words that all of us know all too well—Bianca Hargrove."

As if on cue, Allison, the ninth-grade guidance counselor, Terri O'Dowd, and the secretary all moaned in unison. Irene Williams chuckled to herself knowing she had been privy to something most parents never saw, frustrated teachers.

"A bad child, huh?" asked Irene.

"This girl would have to improve a lot just to be awful," Coach Martin responded.

More laughter was heard as Coach Martin and Irene then excused themselves to the back office for a private conversation.

As the two walked toward the back office for the meeting, Coach Martin took the opportunity to ask Allison one quick question about a new student he had been awarded during the morning hours.

"Allison," Coach Martin asked, "Am I going to get grades on this new student, Kristin Dvorak, so I can enter them in my roll book?"

Allison, without a hint of shock in her voice rolled her eyes and smiled at Coach Martin as if she had a great story to tell, but she got to the point.

"Coach, Kristin does not have any grades in three of her subjects," Allison answered.

"Nothing?" replied Coach Martin, stopping to look at Allison as Miss Williams moved toward the door leading to their meeting room.

"Not a thing."

"But it's the middle of the third six-week period. What have they been putting on her progress reports at Southside High? What am I supposed to put on her mid-term report card?"

"Coach, Kristin will not get credit in any class this semester because she's missed too many days of school. You know, we cannot deny her the right to be here."

A sophomore transfer from Southside High School, Kristin Dvorak, decided to enroll at East Side High School in November after suffering through fourteen weeks of science and civics classes without a teacher. Apparently Southside High School began the year short of certified personnel and used substitute teachers, infrequently, to cover classes and teach to the best of their limited abilities until the school system sent them full-time instructors. With no instructor forthcoming and with nothing else to measure student performance, Southside High School used attendance as the only measure of a student's grade. Although Kristin was a below-average student, she cared enough to withdraw from a school that was failing to award her any grades. To further complicate matters, Kristin had already missed fifteen days of school unexcused. Because of her absences, she had already failed every class for the fall semester.

"This is the third student I have enrolled in the last two weeks that is in my class but will not receive credit," Coach Martin said to Allison. "I mean they are just taking up space in my class."

"I don't know what to tell you, Coach," Allison said as she held out her jeweled hands in frustration. "We have to enroll them if they want to be here. That's the law."

As he shook his head in disgust, Coach Martin followed Irene to a very small office in the back of the guidance department where parents and teachers met regularly. Two people, two chairs, and a phone could barely fit into the room. It was so cramped, in fact, the twenty-five-square feet it provided could be thought of as a closet. Truth be known, the small paneled room was a closet ten years earlier. A shortage of space relegated the area to that of a confessional used in a Catholic church.

The two were seated and Coach Martin closed the heavy wooden door with one hand while digging in his bag for his grade book with the other.

"I'm glad you came to see me about your son's grades," Coach Martin said, looking down into his leather bag full of papers and books. "But I must be frank with you. Your son is not trying at all. No one can convince me in any way that he is. This young man just doesn't want to do the work. Period."

"You've got no argument out of me, Coach," Irene said. "That boy don't do nothing when he gets home. Not a thing! All he do is sit his big butt in front the TV after basketball practice and watch those stupid shows where all those people be screamin' and fightin' amongst themselves. I tell him to study, but he just don't do it. He say he too tired."

Coach Martin appreciated her candor. Teachers never know what type of parent they are going up against in these private meetings. Some parents blame everything and everybody for the mistakes but their children. Irene Williams appeared to be a straight shooter, which would allow the very blunt Coach Martin to speak his mind.

Coach Martin flipped his grade book to the green-and-white blocked sheets inside where he earmarked the spot he wished to review. The room practically made the two involuntarily intimate, but he moved his chair even closer to Irene. Coach Martin pointed at the attendance page. Before he spoke, he realized he had better limit his vocabulary. Irene was as nice as she was concerned, but she was barely educated. Coach Martin, like many teachers, realized with the passing years that about one-half of all parents were only slightly better educated than their children. It was a sad fact that explained a great deal about the difficulty of his profession.

"Miss Williams, your boy has missed nine days this semester already and it is not even the end of the fall semester," Coach Martin explained. "If he misses just two more unexcused days between now and Christmas, he will automatically fail the class. He simply needs to come to school. Academically, he failed yesterday's test scoring a 41 percent. We've taken twelve tests so far and he has failed all of them except one."

Coach Martin took out his solar-powered calculator from the bag and did the math. He slid the digital sum total over to Irene for her to see. It made little impression. Sensing, perhaps, she did not understand what it meant, Coach Martin explained.

"Plebius, as of today, has a 32 percent overall," Coach Martin said with emphasis. "That's not just an 'F,' it's a bad 'F.'"

There was a slight pause in the conversation, as Coach Martin wanted the numbers to make an impression on her.

"Plebius is how old, Miss Williams?" asked Coach Martin.

"He's seventeen," she responded with despair.

"He's seventeen years old in a ninth-grade geography class when most his age are finishing up American history and preparing for the ACT and taking junior class pictures. Doesn't that embarrass him?"

"Nothin' does."

"Does it worry you?"

"Yes, but I don't know what to do about it. The boy won't listen to me."

There was an uncomfortable silence. Coach Martin did not doubt for a moment Plebius refused to listen to his mother, the only person dedicated to being responsible and caring about his young life.

"Maybe you could help him," Irene blurted out.

"How?" asked Coach Martin.

"Talk to him. He ain't got no daddy at home to kick his butt and talk that man-talk to him. Maybe he listen to you."

"Ma'am, I have tried to speak with him. Honest! I have had many heart-to-heart talks with Plebius. And he listens. And he says, 'Yes, sir' and 'No, sir' and all the things a young man is supposed to say when being spoken to by an adult. Then he goes off and does exactly what he had been doing since he's been here at East Side. I do have a suggestion, though."

"What is that?"

"It's hard, but it may need to be done to get his attention. Take him off of the basketball team immediately. He does not need to be playing ball when he cannot handle the academic load. I understand Plebius is failing three of seven classes this semester, including mine. Is that right?"

"I don't know. I ain't got his report card yet. Plebius said he would bring it home when he got it."

Coach Martin about fell to the floor in disgust. He knew many students tossed their six-week progress report in the nearest trashcan minutes after they were issued during their first-period classes. By day's end, many report cards could be seen scattered about the campus like litter. They would be left under desks, balled up and thrown on top of the lockers, in the bottom of trashcans, or blowing in the wind across the campus parking lot. The bottom line was students could not be counted on to take them home. It was too expensive for the school system to mail them to parents who did not get home before their children could hide them anyway. Poor Irene Williams. She was waiting on two progress reports already issued. Coach Martin had to break the bad news to Irene.

"Miss Williams, we've already issued fall report cards twice, the last one about four weeks ago," Coach Martin said slowly, knowing he was breaking some painful news to this struggling single mother. "When we get through speaking, I can take you back into the guidance department and get another one copied for you. Seems to me Plebius not only got a poor progress report, but he's been lying to you on top of it all."

Irene sat stunned in her long, bright brown and soft blue dress. She was no idiot. She knew Plebius was on a fast course to hell. She knew the friends he hung around with and had heard about the trouble they had been in over the years with the police. She knew the girls around her boy were flaunting their sexuality and teasing him wearing clothes that covered almost nothing. She also knew most of those same girls were luring those boys to the bedroom in the late afternoon when parents were still working. Despite all, she believed Plebius had nothing to do with all of that. She explained to Coach Martin that she and Plebius had a long talk over the Thanksgiving holiday. Plebius assured his mother that just because his friends were flirting with jail, drugs, and sexuality did not mean he was. Plebius promised her. Now she realized her only son was a con and now a liar, too. This was not the boy she raised. This was not the type of young man she wanted him to be.

She also knew the only reason Plebius went to school was because of his interest in basketball, in which he excelled. He had already played in five games, and although not yet a starter, Plebius was averaging seven points and four rebounds per game playing a reserve role.

Plebius was tall and muscular. One could hammer nails with his arms. He wore his hair in dreadlocks and often sang outrageous rap lyrics in the hallway that were barely audible. He was not a behavior problem in class, but he was not the definition of "student-athlete." He was just an athlete. At his age, he should have been counted among the junior class. Instead, he was sitting in freshman and sophomore classes attempting to pass courses he should have completed two years prior. With the help of summer school, he was eligible to participate in sports by the narrowest of grade point margins.

Irene, barely a high school graduate herself, was working two jobs to raise a boy her husband abandoned when she was eighteen-years-old, and Plebius was just days shy of his first birthday. She took back her maiden name after the father left, but allowed Plebius to keep the name "Jackson" hoping one day the father would be shamed into returning. He never did. Plebius had never seen his father in person. Only in faded photographs did Plebius see a face that slightly resembled his own. Irene toiled long and hard to teach her boy that life did not have to be as miserable for him as it was for her. It was now crystal clear he was *not* getting that message. It hurt her badly to find that out the hard way.

Devastated, Irene then played her last card. It was a desperate move. She was not comfortable attempting it, but Plebius was her only son and she was looking for any advantage she could gain. She needed some luck and appealed to Coach Martin's good nature.

"Plebius needs help, Coach Martin," she said in a soft, pleading tone. "Maybe you could give him what he needs so he can go on in life, you know?"

She paused almost ashamed of herself for asking.

She then continued, "After all, God loves those who help others."

"I know, Miss Williams, but God also helps those who help themselves," Coach Martin said almost uncomfortably without making eye contact with her.

Coach Martin raised himself from the plastic blue chair, extended his hand for a shake, and thanked her for the meeting. Coach Martin promised to phone her in the near future. It was all he could do. He was not God. He was not Plebius' father. This was not one of those silly movies where the teacher rides into the inner city neighborhoods eventually winning the trust of troubled kids half his age. He did not have a magic wand or some potion that could dispel the problems in her life or that of her son. There was no formula, foolishly taught in university education departments to aspiring, but naive, students who thought they could change the direction of the Plebius Jacksons of the world. In short, he felt as helpless as Irene did.

Coach Martin then ushered her to the front office and introduced her to the guidance department secretary who could copy the progress reports Plebius failed to deliver. He wanted to hug Irene and tell her it was all going to work out fine, but he was not comfortable with that gesture and knew his words were not necessarily true. Coach Martin excused himself as he walked out the guidance office door. He could only wonder why more civic organizations did not flex their muscles and get involved in the lives of troubled African-American students. Here, with Irene Williams, they could attempt to make a real difference in the lives of a young black male desperately needing guidance. But where were they? They were as absent in Plebius' life as his father was.

Coach Martin moved quickly toward his room. He had about ten minutes to gulp down the orange juice and sweet roll he bought for breakfast and to read the morning newspaper. He was in a hurry to do it.

When he finally made it to his classroom, he sat down in his uncomfortable wooden chair, quickly opened the plastic package, and began to gulp down the sweet roll. While chewing, he began to open the top on his orange juice, now warm because of the many morning distractions. He glanced down at the newspaper headline and wanted to choke. It read, *"Study: Bad schools attract bad teachers."* Coach Martin was so enraged he almost choked on his breakfast. He hoped teachers across the inner city area would be as angry. One part of the article stated:

"The report helps confirm what educators have long suspected—the state's most troubled schools are often filled with teachers least likely to improve student performance."

There were quotes to support the article from individuals who had probably never taught a class in their lives. If they had ever taught, it was highly unlikely they had taught in today's environment. These people who work for the State Department of Education, called themselves or were labeled "experts." Coach Martin tossed his unfinished sweet roll into the garbage can and straightened himself. He began to think of those who gather information on these articles. Had a reporter ever interviewed a working inner city public school teacher on these problems? If these experts did go into the public schools and visited with the teachers who were on the front line everyday, and this article showed no evidence of it, Coach Martin knew they would get enough quotes to fill a novel. The article's findings were presumptuous.

These experts from the state's highest education board, the Board of Elementary and Secondary Education, BESE, were usually clueless and many teachers believed that to be true. They are so mired in graphs, charts, education fads, and out-of-state "expert" opinions, they forgot that the job of being a good teacher was also measured in people skills and subject knowledge. Unfortunately for working teachers dealing with low pay, poor facilities, and the horrible parents that send their apathetic offspring to school each morning, it's the BESE members being interviewed by the news media on education reform issues. They were the ones whose opinions seemed to count so much. Coach Martin could only wonder why.

Coach Martin, like many teachers, believed BESE members should be made up of individuals who were actually teaching in a public school. Or, if retired, they must have taught in the last five years at a public school. In either case, they should also have attended public school themselves and their children must have been, or were, enrolled in a public school. That alone would give BESE members more experience in dealing with the public school issues. They would then gain instant credibility with public school teachers.

The problem with the state, he believed, was that too many opinions about state education reform lay in the hands of those who attended schools that were not of the inner-city variety; the same folks that would never condescend to enroll their darling children into the very schools they purport to improve. Who are these people? Where do they come from? How and why are they labeled more expert than the teachers who toil each day, in nearly impossible conditions, only to read a headline in the morning paper such as this? It was demoralizing, especially since East Side High School's test scores were slightly below the state average.

Did it ever occur to the news media that maybe the teachers in poorly performing schools dealt with poorly performing, sometimes violent, and often intimidating students who came from dysfunctional families? Families that live on welfare or where the sound of sidewalk gunshots rock their children to sleep. Did the BESE really believe teachers at better-performing schools could do a better job of teaching if they were to swap places with teachers at real inner city schools? How incredibly ignorant that opinion could prove to be over time.

Coach Martin was past angry now. He was, instead, philosophic. He remembered five years before teaching at Capitol City Magnet High School, a dedicated magnet. Students had to earn a 2.5 grade point average to remain. If students fell below the required average, they would be returned to their community-based school. Competition among magnet school students was brutal. Coach Martin vividly remembered those students crying when they scored less than a 'B' on any test. He remembered the shame in the eyes of students at the end of a semester when some were forced to leave the school due to average academic performance. Capitol City Magnet High School was not the usual school. Parents signed up months in advance to place their kids on their rolls. This public school's reputation was known nationwide and Coach Martin helped many students earn scholarships to the very finest universities and colleges in the nation. Coach Martin wondered if he and the staff at Capitol City Magnet High School were really that good? Of course, the answer was no. He was successful there because students cared about their futures and had the support of their parents. Now that Coach Martin was teaching inner-city kids from poor socio-economic backgrounds who cared little for education or about passing any test, was he really that bad of a teacher? Same answer.

Coach Martin laughed when remembering his own words about teaching, "Give me rotten wood and I'll build you a rotten house."

Coach Martin, like many of the so-called bad teachers this silly newspaper article pointed out was asked to build a Beverly Hills mansion with rotten wood. It was impossible to do. Didn't the esteemed BESE members know that? How could they not know that? Were they that political? Were they that out of touch? Maybe, they were all of the above.

As he gripped the newspaper pages with anger, there was a knock on Coach Martin's partially opened door while his face lay buried in newsprint. It was Betty Manning, the civics teacher from across the hallway. Coach Martin had not seen her all day, but the two were good friends and he could get away with a morning greeting only he could summon at just after 10 a.m.

"Betty!" Coach Martin said in an aggravated tone while holding up the paper. "Did you see this newspaper article? Did you see the headline?"

Betty, somewhat stunned by the greeting, knew better than to interrupt Coach Martin when he was fuming. She had not seen the front page this morning or any other. She did her best to ignore a newspaper she did not like. Betty was young, newly married, and a peaceful person by nature. A brunette with pale skin and a soft voice, Betty had no enemies. Her friendship with the fiery Coach Martin seemed somewhat strange to some, but they spoke the same language when it came to school discipline and academics. They just spoke that language with a different accent, so to speak. Without even asking, Betty knew Coach Martin was angry at something concerning education.

"Oh, what did it say?" Betty asked disaffected in her Southern drawl.

"Those clueless BESE clowns came out with a study that reads, look at this, 'Bad schools attract bad teachers,'" Coach Martin continued. "Can you believe the media bought this opinion? Have they ever spoken with you, Betty? No, and they did not interview me or any other teacher in the state, either, but this is the so-called study's conclusion."

Betty laughed at Coach Martin's tenacity and replied, "Coach, don't give yourself a heart attack over their opinions. Those people don't know what's going on in the school systems around the state. We're just numbers to them. Not many teacher really respects them anyway. You know that. Let it go."

Betty then quickly changed the subject. She had news that Coach Martin had yet to discover and she knew it would upset him. Perhaps her timing was bad. Coach Martin was already in a mood, but she knew she had important information to tell him.

"Now, did you watch the ten o'clock news last night?" Betty asked.

"No, I was fast asleep by then," sighed Coach Martin as his frustration level began to drop.

He dropped the newspaper on his desk and leaned back in his chair trying to catch his breath.

"Well, what you need to see is in the paper this morning," she said.

Betty reached behind her back and unraveled the "Cityscape" section of the morning paper. She laid it on Coach Martin's desk, stepped back, and waited for his reaction. When Coach Martin was finished reading the article, he leaned back in his chair and ran his hand through his thinning hair.

"Unbelievable," was all Coach Martin could say.

The small poorly written newspaper headline read, "Teens arrested in drug bust."

Two students Coach Martin and Betty taught back in October were recently arrested for possession of marijuana with intent to distribute. One student, nineteen-year-old Leon Cascio, apparently fatally shot what he called "an intruder" in the chest with a .38 caliber revolver in a dispute over a drug transaction. The other student, seventeen-year-old Summer Larson, was arrested for evading city police, attempting to hide evidence, and resisting arrest.

It was the second arrest this year Coach Martin knew about involving former students. Leon's arrest, however, did not surprise him in the least. Leon was an overweight kid with an unshaven face and shaved head who had been raised in a dysfunctional home. Leon covered his right arm with tattoos to make himself look macho in front of the rough friends he now called his family. But this family was gangsters making their way in life selling narcotics to school-aged kids. Leon was as much pressured by this new "family" as it was necessary to insure his own survival. Quite simply, Leon was on his own now in life and not doing a very good job of it. Nor could he be expected to.

At one point earlier in the school year, a school guidance counselor asked Betty Manning to keep an eye on Leon. Betty was uncomfortable doing so as she was not equipped in any way to help Leon with his difficulties. Betty was also afraid of Leon, who was unpredictable. Rumor was that Leon slept on a cot in the cold, dirty garage of a neighbor's home. The neighbors appeared only willing to go so far to help Leon despite knowing he was socially drowning.

Leon's parents were divorced. His mother was a crack addict living on borrowed time from an inevitable arrest. His father, forever unemployed, was an alcoholic who forced Leon to leave his small one-bedroom apartment weeks before school began. Alone and unwanted, Leon needed money to survive and school just got in the way of that effort. He turned to the gang culture, and with it, selling narcotics. His drug dealing got him a semi-furnished apartment that was warm, safe, and dry. Leon did what he felt he must to survive in a world that showed him early in life how cruel it could be. In the end, the drug culture sold him out. The city police would be Leon's last customer.

Summer actually had parents at home, but they had long since given up on helping their daughter. She often ran away from home when fighting with her parents. Desperate to gain independence, Summer saved some money and drove to Florida to live with her twenty-two-year-old friend, Glen, whom she had met in Baton Rouge the summer before. The two were barely acquaintances, but Summer foolishly believed sex would cure her problems.

After arriving in Pensacola days after school let out, she almost immediately became pregnant by Glen causing her longtime eighteen-year-old Baton Rouge boyfriend to promise to never speak to her again. Glen practically used Summer sexually every night in exchange for food and shelter. Too young and unskilled to get a decent full-time job, she retreated into a world of despair and drug abuse. She even prostituted herself for extra cash to Glen's Pensacola friends when he was away at work. When learning she was pregnant, Summer told Glen, hoping he would act like a man and help her. Instead, Glen's friends informed him of her clandestine sexual escapades. Glen now had an alibi swearing Summer was not carrying his baby. Summer could not argue too much about it because she knew it might be true. Not one of the Florida boys was going to agree to a blood test. To them, Summer was a cheap whore looking for an exit for her considerable problems. She returned to Baton Rouge and successfully lobbied her best friend for the money to get an abortion. Soon after, she met Leon, and the pair, with a great deal of tragedy in common, struck up a friendship that led to their living together. Now, the living arrangement had gone very wrong.

Coach Martin looked up from the newspaper article and scanned his classroom for the desks where Leon and Summer once sat. It seemed like years ago. Neither was a good student. Leon missed twenty-one days of school by October 1. He always came to school exhausted and now it was clear why. Strangely enough, however, Leon passed Coach Martin's geography class with a 'D,' but was doomed to fail the course due to excessive absences. When Leon learned of his academic fate, he simply dropped out of school.

Summer followed Leon by dropping out herself in a perverse show of support, but neither of them really liked school anyway. School was a bad habit both of them could shake off faster than their immoral, but perhaps mandatory, lifestyle of sheer survival. Teachers were used to hearing stories like this one. As sad as it was, veteran teachers no longer cringed when hearing such stories. They were too common. Teachers have become, like the students they teach, desensitized by the criminal activity, parental and academic indifference, and violence. Eventually, teachers almost expect it from certain students, current and former.

The bell rang, interrupting Coach Martin's thoughts.

"I thought you might want to see this," Betty said as the bell rang for the next class. "One of the guidance counselors showed it to me this morning. Not a surprise, huh?"

Betty left the classroom after a quiet, "See ya' later."

Coach Martin never heard Betty leave as she was off to her own class. Coach Martin sat and stared at the back of the room. He was still thinking of Leon and Summer and what would become of them.

Students soon began to file into Coach Martin's class noisily with dress code violations. Some of them entered without any books or pens in with which to write. It was an omen of the pains to come.

Coach Martin was supposed to be on duty in the hallway between classes, but lacked the motivation to get out of his chair. The sounds of organized chaos marked the time between classes. The slamming lockers and the correction by teachers on duty to the various forms of disobedience were mixed with the high-pitched yells of students as they communicated en route to their respected classrooms. Students loitered until the final seconds that counted down to the tardy bell. Good teachers upheld the rule and marked students tardy anyway. Head basketball coach Dale Jarreau routinely locked tardy students in the hallway forcing them to either go to the office for discipline or simply miss classroom instruction. In any event, it was Coach Martin's job to be at his duty post to help enforce school policy, but he was now despondent after Betty Manning had made him aware of this morning's newspaper article.

When the tardy bell rang, Coach Martin removed himself from his chair like a tired old man. He heard students sprinting down the hallway and then the unmistakable tones that premeditated fights. He gingerly walked to the door and peeked out and remembered the mathematics teacher across the hallway had a substitute on this day. The substitute, thirty-three-year-old Mark Fields, was having a terrible time getting the point across to sophomore Peter Anders that he would have to go to the office for being tardy. Peter was having none of it as he argued with a substitute far in over his head.

"Let me in, man," Peter argued. "You can't keep me out of class. It's against the law!"

Peter then tried to barge his way into class past the shoulder of the slightly taller Mark Fields, who blocked his way by simply moving to his left. Peter backed up and surveyed the situation plotting his next move.

"Look, you are just a sub and you can't keep me out of class, I told you," Peter said in an argumentative way as he motioned with his hand. "Get outta' the way! Now!"

Mark Fields was in a bad situation. He did not possess the experience to deal with this type situation. And yet, his self-respect and credibility as a substitute teacher were on the line in front of thirty-two giggling students watching from their desks not far from the scene.

"Calm down and listen," Mark said calmly. "All I know is the school rule says…"

"Let me in class now or I'm gonna' get strong on you, man," Peter said as he swayed from side to side like a mad man, "'cause I'm a gansta' like that!"

Peter's body language suggested he meant to physically harm Mark if he did not get his way. Anyone who knew Peter knew he would do no such thing, but Mark did not know it. Peter's words and actions could constitute a threat. Coach Martin had seen enough. It was time to rescue the substitute and get on with third-hour class.

"Peter?" Coach Martin asked. "Your name is Peter, right?"

"You know my name, man!" Peter said pointing at Mark and speaking with even less respect to Coach Martin. "Tell this fool to let me in class, dog. I ain't messin' 'round, dog."

He stared Coach Martin in the eye as if he intended to make a real scene for the other students to watch. It was time for Peter to make a reputation for himself. What better way to do it than to make two male teachers back down to his ridiculous demands. It mattered little now. Reputations were on the line. Everyone had something to lose. Coach Martin diffused the situation by treating Peter like a commoner.

"Oh, Peter, I…am…so…scared!" Coach Martin said as he separated his words in a calm mocking sort of way.

Coach Martin suddenly stepped back into character.

"Calm down, Peter," he cautioned. "This is not necessary and is not gaining you anything but trouble."

Peter responded in the only way he knew how—like the want-to-be street punk he was.

"You better respect me, man, 'cause I ain't playin!'" Peter said as if he was still being taken seriously.

Peter then moved closer to Coach Martin in a show of force.

"Let's get this straight right now," Coach Martin said to Peter. "You are the student. The young man that owes us respect, if for any other reasons than our ages. We are the men…"

"Oh, you are a man?" Peter said returning Coach Martin's mocking tone. "I didn't notice."

That was enough for Coach Martin as the class exploded in laughter at Peter's total disrespect of two grown men in charge. At that moment, physical education instructor Wayne Craig walked upon the situation. He was on his break and his timing could not have been more perfect or appreciated.

"Wayne, I'm having a bit of trouble with this boy," Coach Martin explained. "Would you mop it up for me and walk him down to the office? I'll fill out the referral on him and send it down in a few minutes."

"No problem," Wayne said without asking any questions.

Wayne then gestured to Peter with his right hand, "Let's go, boy."

"I ain't no boy, dog!" Peter said.

Wayne shot back, "I ain't no dog, boy."

With that, Wayne put his massive arms around Peter letting him know his dramatization of street tough had come to a boring conclusion. The substitute thanked Coach Martin for stepping in to help as both turned into their doorways to begin class. Wayne's one-armed grip on Peter was fierce and he resented it by producing bile.

"Get your hands off me, dog, I'll sue your ass," Peter assured Wayne, who simply ignored him.

Peter was not immune to trouble. Earlier in the school year he threatened to kill a female English teacher for making him perform his assigned class work. The threat netted him a mere three-day suspension. With "punishment" like that in place for reckless students, how could Peter respect the rules? How could a teacher feel safe?

Coach Martin walked the few paces back to class and filled out the paperwork on Peter's behavior on a referral. Had he waited too long to do so, the school disciplinarian would have interrupted his class asking him to comply immediately to facilitate punishment. Coach Martin hated filling out referrals as they took time away from classroom instruction, but it was a necessary evil. When completed, he sent the referral to the office by way of one of the few students he trusted and waited for that person to return so they would not miss any class work. In all, class began fifteen minutes later than usual because of a simple disturbance.

"Okay, let's get started," Coach Martin stated in a tired enthusiasm to a lethargic class.

Students moaned as they opened their multi-colored notebooks and reached for their pens and pencils. Some students borrowed paper and writing utensils from others with no intention of studying the notes they were all required to take. They took the notes because Coach Martin insisted they do so. Actually studying them was another matter.

Coach Martin's methodology for this was quite simple. If a student had to take notes to get the information needed to pass the test, there would be less clowning during instruction. Many times during classes, Coach Martin saw students attempting to pass love notes or photos to others out of their boredom with school, only to watch the recipient of such a note wave it away without even making eye contact. He also wanted students to attend class. To pass his classes, one must attend school. Sure, the information was in the textbook, but not all of it. Too often, the textbook did not highlight the many details that kept some of the better students interested. Coach Martin presented and expanded those details regularly. The book could not offer that while students studied at home, which many did not do.

"I want to pick up on Chapter 19 in the book on 'How a City Works,'" Coach Martin said with authority as he turned his back on the class and began to draw the Baton Rouge metropolitan area on the white board with experienced precision.

Coach Martin used different colored markers and traced the main city with the surrounding suburbs, villages, unincorporated areas, bedroom communities, various school districts, the metro airport, the river port, shopping malls, the universities and downtown areas. In all, the map was a multi-colored collage. When he was finished explaining, he hoped the students would be able to study it from their desks and make constructive comments about their city.

Coach Martin went into painstaking detail about why "white flight" was affecting many cities across the U.S. He spoke of urban blight, gentrification, zoning, and the current urban trends towards reversing suburban sprawl and local plans to halt it. There was discussion on "eminent domain" and the growth of the "Sun Belt" region of the nation.

The kids were interested—most of them anyway. Coach Martin cited local examples as he defined each term. Students asked questions. Notes were taken. Behavior was good. That did not translate, however, into solid test scores. Quite the contrary. All Coach Martin hoped to do each day was keep peace in the classroom and teach those who wanted to learn. If a student chose not to learn, then all Coach Martin asked of that student was to take notes and not disturb the class in any way. Especially since Coach Martin did not allow students to sleep or lay their heads down on the desk at any time during class, even with seconds remaining in class. It was not allowed. If a student put his or her head down on the desk, out of habit, he would calmly walk by them and rap his knuckles against their desk reminding them of his rule on classroom decorum. In extreme cases, he would kick the bottom of their desk with his soccer foot and scare them. That usually did the trick and either startled or embarrassed the violator of policy.

As Coach Martin continued in the depth of his discussion, he noticed Kendra Ross writing feverishly. That would normally not be a problem except that Coach Martin was now asking students to pay close attention to his explanation of eminent domain. As he used his blue marker to describe newly built streets encroaching on existing private property, Kendra was moving her black pen against a yellow sheet of paper she placed strategically inside of the notebook moments ago that was loaded with pink legal-size paper. Coach Martin continued to explain city policy as he slowly made his way toward Kendra's desk. She never saw him coming as he leaned over her like a tree canopy to the giggles of some class members.

"Kendra, you are *not* supposed to be writing letters to others when you are in this class," Coach Martin said in a forceful tone.

This was the second time in a week he had caught Kendra writing letters to friends. He had cautioned her earlier in the week about not paying attention in class and she agreed to improve. But Coach Martin knew she would not. Kendra did what she wanted. Her overall grade was a pathetic 34 percent. She had already failed each of the eleven tests given during fall semester. The highest grade she had made to date was a paltry 44 percent. She had averaged missing two days per week of school and her total absences-to-date were twenty-eight days unexcused. She probably would fail the class due to unexcused absences alone.

"You know, Kendra, if you had an 'A' or a 'B' in this class, I might let you get away with some things because it would be hard to argue with success, but you are failing terribly and do not seem to mind failing, do you?" Coach Martin said with the intention of embarrassing her in front or her peers.

It was a strategy that sometimes worked, but backfired with the type of student looking for an excuse to quit school.

Coach Martin stood over her smallish desk and into the eyes of a street tough girl who had no fear. She sat in her desk with her four-inch long, bright orange fingernails wrapped around the edge of the desk and stared at Coach Martin, a teacher she tried to like, but whose style cramped hers. In short, Kendra was not going to get away with any of the things she got away with at home. She was beginning to hate Coach Martin. He was too strict for her lazy ways.

Even though Coach Martin was attempting to shame her into performing better in class, she decided to turn the entire situation to her favor by shouting her innocence to all who could hear. With no cards left to play in this poker match, Kendra abruptly rose from her chair.

"I ain't doin' this no more!" Kendra yelled.

"That's right, Kendra," Coach Martin said sternly, but calmly as he backed away from her. "This is what you really want, isn't it?"

Kendra was really getting mad now. Her face was turning colors as her eyes shot like daggers at Coach Martin.

"My mother will be down here and you will be sorry, I promise that shit!" was all her limited imagination could spit out.

Kendra then reached under her desk and grabbed her books. Papers went flying everywhere as Coach Martin now stepped further away. He had never been seriously hurt by a student and did not want that lucky streak broken.

"You ain't shit, Coach Martin!" Kendra said as she moved toward the heavy wooden door. "Screw you!"

Coach Martin moved in her direction but did so by hastily moving down another isle of desks. He did not want to cross a direct path of this psychotic student. Coach Martin beat her to the doorknob, opened the door for her, and let her walk into the hallway unimpeded. He did not want to give her the satisfaction of slamming the door.

Kendra continued to verbally explode as she made her way down what was once a quiet hallway. She even stopped to punch a metal locker and put a small dent in it. Oh yes, Kendra was tough. Even crazy. Which made her doubly dangerous because she was unpredictable. Those were, traditionally, the most dangerous students. The females even more so because there was not much a male teacher could do to stop them physically.

Like many male teachers, Coach Martin knew having to fight or break up a fight involving a female student could result in clothes accidentally being removed. The male teacher in question could then be called a pervert and fired. If a teacher took a physical beating, he might still incur the wrath of the school system or a student's lawyer. The students, whose respect he hoped to maintain, could then question a teacher's ability to control his students. If he accidentally hurt a student, he could be sued. Sometimes there was simply no way to win when in direct confrontation with any student. Retreating was often the best policy.

Coach Martin played it perfectly. He questioned Kendra's behavior and gave her a stern second warning. Kendra chose to go ballistic and leave the class in an inappropriate manner. It was her choice. All Coach Martin did was open the door. Now he had to stop his class to fill out another referral. More wasted time. He sat down to do so before noticing there were just ten minutes remaining in his class.

"Okay, guys," Coach Martin said to his restless, but now energized students. "The party is over. I've got another referral to fill out. We'll stop it here for the day."

The class responded happily with cheers and immediately replayed the entire episode with Kendra among themselves. They would tell many students in other classes about the incident the remainder of the day.

Coach Martin heard one student laugh as he said to another, "Man, Kendra is fuckin' crazy, you know what I mean?"

"No shit, dude," the other student responded. "I would not talk to Coach Martin like that. Maybe I would to Miss Wickersham, but not Coach Martin. He be tryin' hard to make this class fun. Man, Kendra be crazy!"

Coach Martin filled out the referral. As he wrote, he appreciated the comments, even the crude ones, of students who did not know he could hear them. It was true, though. Coach Martin tried hard to make the class interesting. Most of the time he succeeded, but there was always a group of students in each class who did not appreciate him or the opportunity to get an education.

On the other hand, Coach Martin sincerely hoped Kendra would not return to school. She was disruptive in most classes and was failing them all, even physical education. She did not want to be at school. Period. Coach Martin's geography class on a sunny, cold mid-November day was the moment she picked to make her exit.

The last time Kendra excercised her crude manners on another teacher she was suspended for nine days and sent to the parish discipline center, where she did not report. History was likely to repeat itself. There was nothing more a teacher could do.

Kendra was sixteen-years-old. Her future was uncertain and her demeanor uncivilized. Too many students ended up that way, Coach Martin thought as the bell rang ending class and students shuffled their way out while he continued filling out the referral. He taught a total of thirty minutes during this particular class and spent twenty-five minutes on discipline. In his opinion, today's class was a wasted one.

Coach Martin's next geography class was the most rambunctious of the entire day. Every teacher had a class like the one Coach Martin was to inherit in just a matter of moments. Of the thirty-two students in the class, fifteen were failing. Of the seventeen passing his class, thirteen had only a grade of 'D.' Only four students, all female, actually were passing the class with a 'C' or better.

Of the thirty-two students, four males were arrested the previous summer for leaving a party and breaking into a private Christian school. Once inside, along with seven other East Side High School students, they destroyed computers, trophy cases, televisions, VCR's, overhead projectors, water fountains, bathroom receptacles, glass doors, and hallway cameras with crowbars and baseball bats. With the swing of an instrument of force they entertained themselves watching glass, plastic, and wood splinter in various directions. In all, ten were juveniles attending East Side High School. The other involved in this embarrassing incident was a former student. The sheriff's office estimated damage exceeding $500,000. Most in the group pleaded guilty and were sentenced to weekend probation. That is, the judge deemed the ten juveniles too dangerous and immature to be out on weekends unless they were working. Not one student followed the judge's orders. Their parents did absolutely nothing to enforce the court's order. No money was paid to the Christian school for damages. Not one parent offered to pay that school's insurance deductable. When it was all said and done, those student-criminals suffered little. They were not even embarrassed over the incident. In fact, it heightened their reputation in the student hierarchy.

Three other students entering Coach Martin's next class had parole officers for various offenses such as car-jacking and armed robbery. One troubled student was Ambris Washington, a sixteen-year-old whose academic reputation was almost as bad as his criminal one. Ambris put a .44 revolver to the head of a thirty-four-year-old father of two on Jefferson Street one late evening last June and threatened to blow his brains out unless he relinquished control of his Nissan sports car. Ambris left the middle-aged man shaken and in the middle of the street, as he watched his new car moving away from him with a sixteen-year-old at the wheel. Ambris was placed on probation by the judge with the understanding he would keep a detector strapped to his ankle at all times and a promise to stay in school.

The other felon was Quinn Nguyen, a seventeen-year-old Vietnamese kid whose left arm was covered in tattoos scribbled in his native language. Included was the drawing, predictably, of a large fire-breathing dragon. He liked to brag about his late night exploits, but few believed that the five-foot-four, 126-pound Quinn actually did the things he said he did. One night he backed up his image by walking into a twenty-four-hour convenience store, spraying the security camera with tar, and pointing an assault rifle at the sixty-three-year-old clerk so terrified she begged for her life. Quinn must have liked her horrified response to his display of false bravado. He fired one shot into the wall behind the clerk and knocked over a barrel of iced beer and soda as he demanded money. Quinn, knowing he would be arrested, envisioned his name and face on the 10 p.m. news manacled and escorted in an orange jump suit to a waiting police patrol car. The old saying, "Be careful what you wish for because it may come true" applied to Quinn one hot summer night last July. He pleaded no contest, spent one month in juvenile detention and promised to go to school and stay out of trouble. His robbery attempt netted a mere twenty-three dollars and a tough-guy reputation that he relished.

Last, but not least, was Dedra Brown, a fifteen-year-old with short blonde hair. She stood a towering five-foot-eleven, but her figure had yet to catch up with her height. Suffice to stay, she was quite slim but was one of those types who wanted very much to be older than her years. As soon as the school day ended, she immediately entered the bathroom and changed into clothes any hard working prostitute would be proud of. She thought she had the attention of the boys by showing as much bare skin as possible. What they did notice was her lack of figure as much as they did her rock bottom prices on cigarettes and marijuana.

It was known by most students she sold illegal substances on campus, including prescription medication she used to combat depression. But no one could catch her in the act of possession. Dedra was clever and a ring of individuals "had her back," as the students liked to say in describing their protection of each other. Her former school, West Park High School, recommended Dedra for expulsion when she was caught possessing an eight-inch knife, but the principal was too busy with urgent discipline matters to attend the expulsion hearing. Instead, Dedra's lawyer and a school system employee ridiculously hailing as a "disciplinarian" took the principal's place. In the end, Dedra was allowed to return to school based upon what the school system described, "a parent and student's commitment to improve."

West Park High School's many faculty members were livid with the public school system's brand of discipline and the joke of a policy, "Zero Tolerance." Dedra and her parole officer believed she needed a fresh start and transferred her to East Side High School, which could not deny the transfer. In effect, East Side High School inherited West Park High School's problem. That's the way the system sometimes worked—or failed to work.

As the hallway slowly began to empty and the bell was within seconds of signaling the beginning of class, Trey Pablo and Mark Beckham walked side by side, and slowly shuffled up to Coach Martin. Trey extended Coach Martin his hand without saying a word and offered him a note. Coach Martin took the note from his hand, unfolded the torn piece of white notebook paper. It read:

Coach Martin, Please excuse Trey and Mark to go to the gym so they can help prepare for this afternoon's game. Thanks, Coach D. Jarreau

What could Coach Martin do but cooperate? All coaches helped each other as much as reasonably possible. The problem was Trey had already failed geography once. Last year Trey earned a measly 45 percent in the subject. He refused to take summer classes so he could, instead, play on a summer league basketball team with his parent's blessing. Trey was at East Side High School to play basketball and nothing else.

His interest in school went no further than what the hoop's schedule offered.

Last year Trey failed four of seven classes and only became eligible to play baseball during spring, his second sport, because he made three D's, three C's, and a B in fall classes allowing him the needed 1.7 grade point average necessary to be eligible.

Coach Martin looked at Trey and Coach Jarreau's request with a measure of mixed anger and frustration.

"Trey, basketball again?" Coach Martin asked in animated form. "It is not a game. It's a scrimmage. It is *after* school, not *during* geography class. Not to mention that even when you are here in class you struggle terribly. Don't sell me on the idea you will make it up because all it's going to do to you is put you further behind than you already are."

Coach Martin was not going to press Trey much on this matter. He was going to allow Trey to help the coaches prepare for the basketball scrimmage. He knew it mattered little as to whether Trey sat in class or toiled on the basketball court in preparation for a game that was his sole reason for being listed in a high school roll book. Trey's very existence was based on running down the shiny hardwood following an outlet pass. In Trey's twisted world, life was as ridiculous as the T-shirt he liked to wear that read, *"Basketball is Life. The Rest is Details!"* The slogan was cute and Coach Martin was certain it sold well, but it was another in a long list of nonsense fed to students who made manufacturers richer while undermining the kids who bought them, regardless of the sport advertised.

The sadder part still was Trey's parents attended each basketball game religiously. Each time Jim and Elaine Pablo ran into one of Trey's teachers, including Coach Martin who attended most varsity basketball games, they asked about their son's grades. They seemed sincere about their son's struggles in the classroom. Lately, Coach Martin tried to avoid them. During early November, Coach Martin caught Trey cheating on a test and phoned Elaine Pablo at work to inform her of her son's deviant behavior. Her response to her child being caught cheating on a major test? Elaine laughed before exclaiming, "Well, that proves to me he really wants to play AAU basketball this summer! Coach, I used to do the same thing in high school!"

Coach Martin did not find the incident funny. He was burning with anger at wasting the time to phone her while she made jokes. Teachers and education are not jokes. What teachers attempt to do in the classroom is not a joke. Their exams, designed to test proficiency, were not jokes. The fact was that Elaine's attitude towards the incident underlined how little teaching was taking place at home. It reminded him of what former East Side High School football coach Edward Simoneaux once told him during halftime of a championship football game in the Louisiana Superdome two years before. Coach Simoneaux, who taught and coached for thirty-five years in the public school system told Coach Martin, "I've been around kids for five decades and I can tell you one irrefutable truth—kids have not changed. Parenting has!"

Coach Martin believed that opinion to be gospel.

Coach Martin reluctantly signed the paper, returned it to Trey, and allowed both players to miss his class for the second time this semester to prepare for a basketball scrimmage. He was sure it would not be the last time. There was a twenty-seven-game schedule to play out stretching from late November to mid-February. Coach Martin was also certain Trey would fail many tests scheduled along the way. He wondered if Trey's parents would find it funny if he failed a geography class a second time. Would they even care as long as Trey's scoring average was in double digits?

Coach Martin knew one other undeniable fact in his ten years as a teacher: He could not save the souls of kids who did not want saving. He could not help aid parents in efforts to keep their offspring on the path to academic success so long as cleats and sleek athletic uniforms proved more important than notebooks, literature, mathematical formulas, maps, and intelligent classroom dialogue.

Coach Martin sighed, closed the door to his room, and sat behind his desk to call roll for the new hour.

He opened his roll book and without looking up told the class, "Open up your notebooks and let's gets started. I've had enough interruptions today."

At that very moment, there was a knock at his door. Coach Martin was about to lose his temper. He was hired to teach and that seemed to be something he was not going to be able to do on this day. Frustrated, he got up and opened the door to the smirks of the students who knew him well enough to know he was about to lose his cool.

Coach Martin opened the door. An office worker extended a clipboard to him with a familiar sheet of paper attached to it. The format of the paper was familiar with all teachers. It was a "Drop-Add" sheet sent from the guidance office. No new student stood by the office worker so Coach Martin knew a student had dropped out of school. The only question remained was, who dropped out?

Coach Martin took the clipboard from the hand of the young lady and asked, "Who is it this time?"

But the name was clearly written at the top of the page:

"Nancy Hoard. Reason for drop: Transfer to Christ the King Academy."

Coach Martin could only hope Nancy, a petite girl with long, dark hair, and big blue eyes, would stay. She represented the type of student the school no longer possessed. Even the school system admitted publicly on many occasions the need to attract more like her. Translation—the system needed white students to reinvest in public education.

Nancy transferred to East Side High School just four weeks after being asked to leave Metropolitan Prep for reasons described by the office and Nancy as, "Failing to follow school policy." No one at East Side High School really knew what that meant, but rumor was Nancy exchanged words with a teacher at Metropolitan Prep resulting in the need for her mother to meet with school officials, who refused to do so at the time requested. The mother went to school anyway hoping to inquire as to why her sixteen-year-old daughter would incur the wrath of a teacher she never had trouble with before. The teacher then verbally abused the mother, who then complained to the Metropolitan Prep administration who refused her an audience. This mother was paying the sum of $440 per month to send her child to this Christian school hoping to be more involved in her child's education and well-being. It was evident to her at that time she was not getting her money's worth. She simply wanted some answers that were not forthcoming. When it was over, the mother was escorted off the school campus like a criminal. Nancy, humiliated, decided to leave Metropolitan Prep after learning she was going to be suspended nine days and never allowed to tell her side of the story to a callous administration. Neither Nancy nor her mother could live with that type of high school office injustice. Living in East Side High School's district, Nancy decided to enroll in public school the next day.

Nancy surprisingly liked her new school and told Coach Martin just last week that, "East Side's education is a lot better than I thought it would be."

Nancy expected the school to be one where no teaching took place, where a gangland rough and tumble reputation was sadly championed.

Coach Martin once asked Nancy point blank in front of his entire third-hour civics class, "Do you feel like you are getting a good education here at East Side?"

Nancy replied that she thought the teachers were better than those at Metropolitan Prep. That answer did not surprise Coach Martin and kind of shocked his class who, like many others in the community, naturally believed private school academics would be better than that of a public school.

After class, however, Nancy confided in Coach Martin that it was embarrassing to tell her well-to-do friends she was attending a public school, especially East Side High School. Apparently her month at the school only bought her mother some time to locate and enroll her in a school where the family's standing in the white-bread community in which they lived would not be tarnished. Nancy did not even tell Coach Martin goodbye. With the stroke of a pen, Nancy simply dropped from East Side High School and vanished.

Coach Martin opened his roll book and wondered why business such as this could not wait until the end of a day. It was another interruption for a student who no longer even attended the school. But Coach Martin added up her points earned and divided it by the total number of points possible and printed her grade of "76 percent, C" on the line provided and signed his name. Funny, Coach Martin thought, as intelligent as she was, Miss Private School Nancy only earned the average grade of "C." The truth was, often there was really little difference in high school-aged kids, regardless of uniform. He rose from his desk and walked to the door with the clipboard extended to the office worker waiting in the hallway.

"I guess $440 per month doesn't buy such a great education after all," Coach Martin said to a bewildered office worker as he handed her the clipboard.

"What?" asked the teenaged office worker with a confused look.

"It's a private matter, no pun intended," Coach Martin said smiling and waving his hand toward her to let her know he was playing.

Coach Martin knew students like Nancy were the kind who could make a difference at East Side High School. She was clean-cut, upper middle-class, and intelligent, even if she was an underachiever. She was genuinely interested in attending college and had the undying support of her college-educated parents. Compared to what he was teaching now, Nancy suggested a throwback to the golden days of the school. And now she was gone. She used East Side High School to buy time, but was too ashamed to admit she might like to stay. Coach Martin was somehow hurt by that. Was the reputation at East Side High School that bad? Were Nancy's feelings and that of her friends toward the school the identical impression of other white parents who lived nearby but chose not to send their kids to East Side High School? Coach Martin could not fight the world, but it did make him think about how others saw the school in which he toiled each day.

Coach Martin barely got the door closed to begin his last class of the day when sixteen-year-old Ginny Ward, a physically developed junior, grabbed him by the arm and pulled him toward her only to suddenly let go. Ginny had been crying. Coach Martin could see the tear stains on her white shirt mixed with makeup that had fallen on her collar. Ginny got permission from Coach Ed Stallworth to go to the restroom, but instead, she had gone to Coach Martin's class and was lucky enough to catch him in the hallway.

"Coach, I need to talk to you now!" Ginny was nearly begging as her posture slumped forward.

"Ginny, can it wait until after school?" Coach Martin asked.

"No, I've got to get on the bus as soon as school lets out and there's no way I can talk to anyone," she pleaded. "Please!"

Coach Martin, like many teachers worth their stripes, was not going to walk away from any student with that type of overture. Ginny was

134

hurting badly and needed to talk to someone. The way she went about it was a bit underhanded, but teenagers can be expert at being crafty when need be. She knew she could hide behind a written excuse from Coach Martin that Coach Stallworth would have to accept. She was gambling on getting that note.

Coach Martin walked into the hallway and glanced at his watch. It was already 1:50 p.m. There was only thirty-five minutes of class remaining and Ginny was going to eat up even more of his time.

"Coach, I've got a problem at home," Ginny started. "Like, my dad is being such an asshole. Like, I don't know what to do."

Her abrupt introduction to her problem was good news to Coach Martin because he knew she would get to the point.

"Why don't you talk with your mom about your problem?" Coach Martin suggested, knowing that was usually the best place for a teacher to propose a student start with a nagging issue.

"She's my stepmother and she does not like me," Ginny said as a matter of fact.

Coach Martin knew that nearly 50 percent of his students were being reared by someone other than their biological parents. It was a sad fact. A morally corrupt or immature mommy and daddy have sex while excusing any consequences, make a baby, and then abandon the child to the care of grandparents, aunts, or stepparents. For good reasons or bad, it was too easy for many biological parents to forego raising their own children. Many of these proxy parents, unfortunately, see the children they agreed to raise as more than they could handle—especially the grandparents who were more than out of touch and running short on energy in their so-called "Golden Years." The children who should be grateful owed almost no allegiance and offered little respect to those who kept them off the streets and out of judicial control.

Coach Martin hated conversations like the one he was having with Ginny. There was so little he could do. Advice, even if it were good, was cheap. Guidance officers best handled any practical suggestions that could be offered to Ginny. However, Ginny sought Coach Martin out. Many students run to teachers they respect for guidance. They often do not like to admit it, but too often the only time some students are extended a kind word is from a teacher who is not aware of such an impact on a student's life. Coach Martin's words were Ginny's shelter from the street storm.

Ginny continued, "Coach, I told you earlier in the year I wanted to be a veterinarian, remember?" she asked hoping he would nod in agreement and proved she was worth listening to.

Coach Martin remembered. Ginny was a decent student in one of his morning classes. She always seemed to know the answers and engaged in class conversation with frequency. She made B's on tests when she could have made A's. When there was an extra credit assignment to turn in, however, she would forget to do it. Turning in homework assignments was done without consistency. Ginny appeared self-destructive. She was one of the best students Coach Martin had, but she always underachieved, even after finishing the last six-week term with a strong B. After class one day late last month, she told Coach Martin she wanted to care for animals. Coach Martin, an animal lover himself, reinforced that dream, but with the caution that her grades needed to be better than what she was making at that time to enter any competitive veterinarian school. She agreed and hoped to volunteer to work with a nearby veterinarian during the coming summer.

"Ginny, did you ever go to work for that veterinarian near your house?" Coach Martin asked, already knowing the answer.

"No!" Ginny said with anger in her voice. "My stupid dad wouldn't let me!"

"What do you mean he would not let you?" Coach Martin asked curiously.

"He said I couldn't work and I don't have a car to get to work if I could," Ginny said with rapid fire. "That's kind of what I wanted to talk to you about. Over the weekend I went to the university bookstore to look at books on animal care, biology, and stuff like that. They were so expensive and I didn't have enough money to buy them. So, I went home to get more money so I could go back and buy the books I needed. I wanted to read the books and learn as much as I could on my own. When my dad found out I wanted to buy college books about become a veterinarian, he started cussing me out. Like, I left the house crying. Every day since then, when he comes home from work, you know, he calls me names. He calls me 'college bitch' and tells me, 'the only thing good about an animal is that you get to kill one every now and then and eat it.' He laughed when he said it and he knew it hurt me to hear him say that! But he won't stop it!"

Coach Martin was angry just hearing this story. Listening to Ginny, Coach Martin figured the only reason her father did not want her to have books for advanced study on a subject not even offered in high school was due to nothing but ignorance and jealousy. Coach Martin did not have to ask if her father was an educated man, but he did ask, just to justify his intuition.

"Ginny, how far did your father get in school?" Coach Martin asked.

"He only got out of high school, Coach." she said. "Why?"

"Sounds like your father is jealous. He doesn't want you to succeed. He doesn't want you to go further in life than he did. I cannot believe that a parent would not want more for their child, but I've known it to happen to other students."

"I hate him! He's a drunk!"

Ginny then reached into her loose-fitting uniform khaki trousers and pulled out a wad of dollar bills. She sorted them through her small fist and attempted to organize them in some fashion.

When she counted out a sum of forty-three dollars, she handed the bills to Coach Martin and said, "This is for you."

Coach Martin collected the money, gazing at it as if he had never seen cash before.

He asked Ginny, "What do you want me to do with this?"

"Please, go and buy me that book," Ginny begged. "I'll do anything. I'll give you gas money to go and buy it. I'll pay for you to park close to the bookstore. I want to read that book. Like, it's full of things I want to read about and my parents won't take me to get it."

Coach Martin nodded to her that he would cooperate. He scribbled the title of the textbook that Ginny wanted on a rumpled piece of yellow, lined paper. Ginny smiled and that seemed to end her problem for the moment. Coach Martin wanted to ask what would happen to the book if her father found out about it, but he didn't want to tax her emotions more than they already were.

If caught with the book, would Ginny tell her father that a teacher had purchased it for her? Would he get into trouble for overstepping his bounds as a teacher? After all, her father said he did not want her to have it. Who was he to overrule the father of the house?

Somehow this situation was different. Coach Martin was not buying Ginny alcohol, drugs, birth control pills, or some form of immoral materialism. No, he thought, he was helping a teenager hopelessly belittled by an insensitive, and ignorant parent. Too often teachers could not get students to read anything, much less something of substance, and Ginny wanted to read a college freshman-level textbook on animal science. What could be wrong with that? That initiative should be encouraged and Ginny was willing to pay for it from money she had earned. Why would a parent be so ridiculous? It made no sense to Coach Martin.

Ginny thanked Coach Martin and made her way back to Coach Stallworth's room, never having gone to the bathroom.

Coach Martin stuffed the money in his front pocket, walked into his class from the quiet hallway, and asked aloud, "Is everyone here? I don't have time to call roll. There's been too much time wasted already."

"Micah's not here," said one voice in the back of the room.

"Neither is Bart and Cindy," said another.

Coach Martin looked up and asked, "Where is Anisha? Anyone seen her today?"

"She was here first-hour, but I haven't seen her since," answered a student from the back.

"What about her partner in crime, Joshua?" Coach Martin inquired.

"Negative," was the military response from the class's only ROTC student.

Coach Martin hurriedly wrote down the absentees and pinned them to his door as he was required to do at the end of each day. Six absences total coupled with the one the school identified as absent this morning. Not a bad absentee total for a day. On most days, Coach Martin could expect anywhere between five and twenty students absent total in a day. The record for absences in one class hour was held by first-hour totaling thirteen in one day just last week. School attendance had become a major issue in the new millennium. Students, more and more, were seeing their attendance in school as something of an option and parents seemed paralyzed to halt it.

"Let's go, guys," Coach Martin said while clapping his hands together as if he were coaching one of his soccer matches. "Since we don't have too much time to play with today, let's say we quickly discuss what is going on in Iraq. Anyone keeping up with what is going on?"

There was the obligatory silence from the class. Many wanted to say something about the war, but did not want to say anything to expose their ignorance. Coach Martin prodded.

"Come on, guys!" Coach Martin chided. "There are war protests all over the nation right now and some of them are getting heated. There are those who favor the war believing Iraqi dictator Saddam Hussein does, in fact, possess weapons of mass destruction that could very much harm the United States and her friends, or allies as they are called. That could mean nuclear weapons that could be launched and destroy civilization in a matter of minutes. It could mean biological weapons that could unleash deadly epidemics that could spread around the nation in days. It could mean simply providing cash to terrorists who have said publicly they wish to do anything they can to kill Americans and destroy our property or interests anywhere in the world. Terrorists brought down the World Trade Center in New York City. They destroyed large segments of the Pentagon in Washington D.C. You have all seen the pictures and remember that incident, don't you?"

Coach Martin still had the September 11, 2001, front page of the local newspaper with the twin towers of the World Trade Center burning with the unusually large headline screaming, "Terror!" Some students turned their heads toward that image as they listened to Coach Martin deliver his daily lectures that were more like church sermons. He had the students' attention and they loved to hear him speak. To these teenagers, he was simply captivating.

"Movie stars and musicians that you know all too well are coming out against the war," he continued. "However, many politicians in Congress believe the United States has the right to stop Saddam before he attempts another move to control the Middle East. Who remembers what the Middle East has so much of that the U.S. and her allies need to function?"

About half of the class responded in unison, "Oil!"

Coach Martin was pleased. They remembered last week's lecture on international economics. It was a subject the class thought they would not like, but ended up not only listening to but also understanding. Coach Martin was usually thorough in discussing world issues. He did not teach "down" to them. His notes and lectures were detailed enough to use in a junior college classroom. He always believed the reason some kids did not like school was because it was too vague concerning issues of interest to them. The textbooks were sometimes elementary in nature and Coach Martin did not choose to use them often.

"Do these movie stars have the right to protest a war being fought by Americans ready to risk their lives to win on our behalf?" Coach Martin asked. "Do they really understand the issues? Or, are they using their popularity to deliver their point of view to the people, assuming the people respect them enough? How about our leaders? Are they promoting the war so they can justify going into the region and destroying the Iraqi Army again, so the United States can set up the government it wants in an effort to gain access to cheaper oil? How about world opinion? The Russian, French, and German leaders are telling their people and the world that the United States and our president, George Bush, is hell-bent on war. They believe the world should give Iraq more time to prove they are not a threat to the world or the United States. President George Bush said yesterday that the United States has given Saddam Hussein three weeks already to follow a list of demands. Saddam said he would not follow any demands. I ask you, who is right in this issue? Who is wrong? What do you think? There's no right or wrong here so don't be afraid to give your point of view."

Brad Griffin, a smallish student in the rear of the room, raised his hand. Brad, who rarely said a word during Coach Martin's class discussions, apparently found the threat of war interesting to him. Coach Martin had indirectly invited another student into his educational realm. However, he did not want to make an issue of Brad's first time involvement in class topics. The trick here was to treat Brad's inquiry or comment as an ordinary event, and maybe he would feel more comfortable contributing another time in the near future.

"Yes, Brad, what do you think?" Coach Martin asked.

"I think we should go to war and take over Iraq," Brad stated confidently. "Just take it over, take the oil, and then we don't have to worry about the price or availability of oil, terrorism or Saddam anymore. Why didn't we do that a long time ago?"

"Yea, really, dude!" Austin Bennett agreed, sitting directly in front of a standing Coach Martin. "Dude, we could taken over Iraq in about two days, man, and like, make it the fifty-first state!"

The class broke up in laughter. Some students openly agreed with Austin's statement. Coach Martin looked at them with his hands spaced in front of his chest and waved them in order to get the class's attention. They did not notice. The class was too busy laughing. Coach Martin remembered how easily amused they really were. When the laughter died down, he continued.

"Guys, just because you can beat someone up does not give you the right to do so," Coach Martin explained. "I mean, I can beat up most of the people in this room. Well, almost everyone."

Coach Martin pointed at junior Alex Carthon, the six-foot, 230-pound defensive lineman for the football team. The class laughed again, but not with so much enthusiasm. They respected Coach Martin for recognizing his own physical weaknesses. He did not play the part of the almighty teacher. He gave students credit where credit was due. Alex was a huge physical specimen who could destroy any normal man without much effort at all. Alex loved Coach Martin's comment and smiled at the class. To him, it was his only validation as a human being and a young man.

"Just because I can beat up the girls in this room does not give me the right to do it," Coach Martin explained. "Many of the guys in this room can beat up their mothers and sisters, but should you? Might does not make right."

Coach Martin was poised to make his point.

"I want you to think of a bully that you are afraid of," he told the class. "Don't mention any names. Just think of that person and picture them in your head."

Coach Martin paused while the students were thinking.

"Do you have that person in sight?" he asked. "Now, how many of you would love to get even with that person for the things they have done to you?"

Every hand in the classroom went up. Every student in the room could visualize a bully or gangster who had pushed them around at some point in their grade school lives.

"Did you like being pushed around by that person?" Coach Martin asked. "Did that person have the right to hurt you or embarrass you? Of course not! Why did they do it? Because they knew they could get away with it. Did you respect what they did to you, or maybe to a friend? Absolutely not! So I ask again, should the United States be a bully like that? Just because we can push out the government of Afghanistan or invade and conquer Iraq, do we have the right to do it? And here is something else you need to consider and we spoke about this before. Does the United States have many enemies in the world?"

The class agreed that the nation did. They had discussed North Korea, China, Cuba, Sudan, Iran, and other nations openly hostile. Or, not on friendly terms with the U.S. Thankfully, the students remembered those discussions, too.

Coach Martin continued, "If the United States acts as a world bully, invades nations, and takes what it wants because it wants it, or invents a reason to take military action—rightfully or wrongly—even our very best friends will turn against us. That is a problem this nation does not need when going to war. The United States must be very careful that it has most of the world's opinion behind their choice to go to war."

Students were listening. They were giving Coach Martin their complete attention. Every eye in the room was focused on his blue-gray eyes, and hanging on his every word. It never occurred to some of them that, perhaps, the strongest thing a powerful nation could do is to do nothing. Or, gather as much information about a situation before acting. Coach Martin was actually delivering two punches at once. The other point, about dealing with difficult people in everyday life, was crystal clear to some students.

"Think about it," Coach Martin continued. "Let's take Lisa Bordelon here."

Coach Martin pointed to the frail, blonde, sitting in the very front of the class with braces on her teeth. Lisa had no business in a regular class as this one. She transferred in from a private school. East Side High School rarely accommodated transfers into honor's level classes. Coach Martin, as most of Lisa's teachers knew, very much belonged in them. Lisa, on the other hand, wanted to go back to her private, Christian school, but her father had recently lost his job and public school became her only option. She wanted as little attention placed on her as possible, but Coach Martin wanted her involved in class discussions in some form.

"Let's say Lisa called me a bad word in class because I told her to stop chewing gum in class," Coach Martin said. "Now, everyone knows I could take out Lisa with one punch. It would not even be hard to do."

Coach Martin raised his hand over Lisa, she covered her head as if he might actually hit her, and he unleashed a shadow punch with his right fist just inches above her head. His punch was swift as he laid into the palm of his left hand.

"Bam!" Coach Martin acted out in animated form. "One punch across the mouth. I hit her and laid her out cold. Was Lisa wrong to break the rules? Yes she was! Was she wrong to curse me in class? Yep! But instead of sending her to the office, I took it upon myself to administer my own justice. I hit her! My question to you is, am I wrong to do so? Forget that she is a female. Was I wrong?"

The class agreed that he was by nodding their heads. No one mentioned that it was wrong to do so because Lisa, the victim in this pretend scenario, was female. They all knew that if a teacher ever hit a student, or even threatened to do so, it could result in their arrest and firing. That part of the legal process students knew all too clearly.

"What would be the problem for me now?" Coach Martin asked the class.

"Man, you would be in some serious trouble for hitting a student!" Alex said as he punched the air as a show of victory for the student in this classroom trial.

"I'd tell my dad, for sure," Lisa said plainly and calmly with a mock smile.

"We'd be getting a new teacher in this class!" Brad stated correctly.

"That's right!" Coach Martin said. "Even though I was right to be angry at her for the way she acted in my class. The way I handled it was wrong. Even my friends would be angry with me. Not one teacher in this school would stand by me in a situation like this one. It would matter very little to the principal, the school board, an attorney representing Lisa, or a judge that I was cursed and she broke school rules. She may have been wrong, but I was more wrong. And my friends, maybe even my wife, would not stand by me in a show of support.

"The United States may not like the way Iraq is conducting its business in the world. Saddam Hussein may pose a threat to the United States, but we must handle it in a manner that our friends agree with. We must continue to have the respect of the world when we act.

"To answer your question, Brad and Austin, just because we can take over Iraq is not good enough. Do you understand that now? And here's another point to consider; Iraq has friends, too. They may not want to get involved in a war between the United States and Iraq. But what if we do what Brad and Austin say we should do? What happens now?"

"We gotta' fight the other nations, too," said Arthur Jackson, a skinny kid sitting near the window. He had not involved himself in a class discussion in weeks, but he got the right answer on this day. Coach Martin took a deep breath and sighed.

"Thank you, Arthur," Coach Martin said, pointing at Arthur. "You understand. You get it. Good for you."

Arthur smiled in a mocking sort of way at the other students in the class as if he were special.

Coach Martin let that sink in. He had made his point. He hoped that his lecture on current events would make them think about the consequences of using only violence as a way to gain a satisfactory conclusion in a very dangerous world.

"Any questions?" Coach Martin asked. "No? Take a look at the board and you will see the address of a Louisiana soldier fighting in Iraq. If you wish to send him letters, please copy the address, and give it to me for checking. We are not sending poor grammaticism overseas. You will receive some extra credit, not to mention you could make one American soldier happy with a letter."

The address read, "Lance Corporal Joshua Fugler" with the complex military address written next to the name.

Thomas Saddler, another of the class clowns who sometimes made the class difficult to teach, then raised his hand. He had a question and it was not to be interpreted as cute. Thomas really did not know the answer to his question while some students copied the address before time ran out on the class.

"Coach, why does that guy have two first names?" Thomas inquired.

"What do you mean two first names?" Coach Martin asked.

"Well, he's got Lance and Joshua listed as a name. Which one is it?"

The sad part of the question was, not only did he not know, not one classmate laughed. Sometimes the laughter signals to the teacher that at least *some* of the students recognize a situation not meant to be funny. Laughter in this situation would have told Coach Martin that some of the students understood "Lance Corporal" was a military rank and not his first name. The eerie quiet meant that the entire class did not know and was waiting to have the question answered.

"Thomas, 'Lance Corporal' is the rank," Coach Martin explained without a hint of shock in his voice. "His first name is Joshua. Got it?"

"I ain't never heard that before," Thomas said.

"I guessed that much," Coach Martin responded.

Thomas nodded his head that he did understand and Coach Martin tried not to laugh. True, it was a good question, but a sixteen-year-old student should recognize a military rank in print. At least, Coach Martin thought so.

Students knew the names of the various drugs on the street. They knew the characters in many of the absurd thirty-minute, fly-by-night sitcoms they spent too much time watching on television. They could recite the words to every filthy rap song sold on CD, but "Lance Corporal" was just too much for them.

Coach Martin glanced at his watch. It was 2:20 p.m. The final bell would ring in ten minutes. He was just about to stop class early when Brad raised his hand. Coach Martin hoped it was a question about the lecture and not one of Brad's attempts at gaining attention to himself. He was not in the mood. It had already been a long, forgettable day.

"Yes, Brad, what do you have?" Coach Martin asked while the class was still silent.

"Coach, I wanted to thank you, man," Brad said as if he were serious.

"For what?" Coach Martin asked.

"Well, I never thought I would ever use some of the stuff I learned in this class, but I did, and it got me out of trouble," Brad said with pride. "I just wanted to thank you."

There was no way Coach Martin was going to let the story end there. The class attention was now focused on Brad. Coach Martin and everyone in class were dying to know why Brad, a chronic underachiever taking American government for the second time, would thank a teacher he did not like. It was not like Brad, one who was far too busy trying to act cool at the expense of education and others.

"All right, Brad," said Coach Martin. "You've got my attention. What's the story?"

Brad broke out a huge grin exposing gold-capped teeth.

"Well, over the weekend I got into some trouble with the 'po-po', you see," Brad explained in street jargon and muddled English. "You see, me and some buddies of mine was drivin' 'round the city Friday night and the 'po-po' hassled us. They took us down to the jail for possession."

"Possession of what?" Coach Martin asked, not sure he really wanted to know the answer. "Guns? Drugs? Alcohol?"

"Yea," Brad said.

The class busted out laughing. Some students began to hold the sides of their stomachs they were laughing so hard. They knew Brad was no damn good, but to hear him admit it in such a vulnerable way was amusing.

"Yea?" Coach Martin asked. "Yea, what? Was it drugs? Alcohol? Or, was it a gun?"

"All three!" Brad said trying to hide his face, but smiling nonetheless.

The roar of the class grew louder.

Brad was usually very proud of his juvenile antics. For some strange reason he did not relish the attention this time. He genuinely wished to thank Coach Martin for something he learned last week and he could not speak a word without making the class laugh. His face began to get flushed. Coach Martin, arms folded and leaning against his desk, did not know how to respond.

"Look, Coach," Brad said as he sat up straight in his green plastic chair. "Yo, one of my boys got arrested for not telling the 'po-po' about the pistol. Another dude got sent down for underage drinking. And, yo, I got arrested for possession of marijuana."

"With intent to distribute?" asked one student.

"Oh, no. Hell no!" Brad said as he shook his head from side to side. "I ain't never done that before."

"Done what? Possessed marijuana or got caught with it?"

Silence took over for just a second. Brad did not want to answer the question and the class broke up into more laughter. Through the noise, Brad continued.

"Anyway, when the police booked us downtown, they let me make my phone call and I called my parole officer. He hooked me up the next day with my lawyer. When the lawyer got to askin' me questions about the incident I told him, yo, the cops forgot to read me my rights. You know, that 'Miranda' stuff you was talking about?"

"Yes, Brad, I remember," Coach Martin said. "As I recall, you failed that chapter test."

"Yea, you know, Coach, I fail a lot of your tests, but I do listen," Brad said tugging on the ear that would soon bear a gold-studded earring before he got out of the door on his way to the parking lot. "When I told my lawyer that the cops didn't read my rights he checked it out and found out I was tellin' the truth. The officer admitted he had forgotten to read me my rights in all the excitement. Within an hour, yo, I was on my way home, man! I didn't even have to go to court."

Brad smiled and extended high-fives to the guys around him as they laughed in hysterics. Lisa slumped over in her desk embarrassed to be in the same class with those she considered nothing more than mere thugs. The bell rang and students exited the room repeating Brad's tale. They could not wait to tell their friends. Brad's story would be told one hundred times to legions of students.

As students slowly filed out of the room, junior Mike Wilchamp, spoke out of turn yelling at Brad, "Man, I hate wearin' a tie."

Coach Martin looked at Mike with his book sack slung over his shoulder as he pierced his left ear with a diamond stud.

"You don't like wearing a coat and tie?" Coach Martin asked him from across the room.

"I ain't said nothin' about wearin' no coat," Mike said with both hands attending to his ears. "And the only time I wear a tie is when I have to go to court."

"Do you own that many ties?"

"No, I just borrow them from other dudes who went to court before me. We share the same ties. There's only about three of them."

"There's only three ties or three young men sharing them?"

"There's about ten guys that use three ties, but we lost one when Gray Soileau, you know him? He tried to choke a dude with it at a party after he got back from a court date. They got in a fight over a girl they was both bangin'. The tie got all dirty and stuff so we got another one."

"So, who buys the ties when you guys have to attend so many court dates?"

"We steal them from Wal-Mart, Target, Dollar General, whatever. See ya', Coach. Gotta' catcha ride. Later!"

Mike exited in a full stride. Coach Martin stood frozen. He never moved from being propped up against his desk in a standing position. His hands were still fixed across his chest. His facial expression was statuesque. Many things raced through his mind. The idea of stealing a tie to make a good impression in court over an earlier transgression, presumably a felony, was appalling to Coach Martin. Did these students not understand how foolish and dangerous they were living? He knew, sooner or later, Brad and Mike were going to get caught and sent to prison. Coach Martin knew, in the end, all Brad did was buy himself additional time that would soon run out on him and force him behind bars for many future birthdays. The police failed to get another drug dealer off the street. Coach Martin didn't know whether to be upset with Brad or to be proud of him.

With the day now over and the students gone, Coach Martin collected his things and made a hasty exit from his classroom. He began to think about Brad, his parole officer, and the trouble he got into over the last weekend. He wondered how long it would take to see him on the 6 p.m. news handcuffed and wearing an orange prison jumpsuit. Brad, Coach Martin thought, would be lucky to live to see his twenty-fifth birthday.

As he walked through the double doors leading outside, he heard senior Tamara Robertson yell across the parking lot to the captain of the track team, Milton LaBerg.

"Hey, Milty!" Tamara yelled loud enough for all could hear. "Give me a ride home? Please? I don't wanna' ride no bus home today!"

Milton responded jokingly with his back to the girls as he hastily headed to his car, "Not unless you give me some grass, gas, or ass!"

Milton then burst out laughing at his own joke.

"Never mind!" Tamara said laughing before turning to her two friends. "I ain't giving him shit! He's gonna' have to *earn* bed time with me, for real."

The yellow school buses formed a long line in the school parking lot. There were sixteen in all that were to drop students to the many points along their distant routes. Some of these buses would pick up students and take them just a few blocks to Jefferson Park where they would wait as long as thirty minutes for a transfer bus, disembark, and then take a forty-five-minute ride to their homes. In all, some of these students could spend as much as two hours riding and waiting on buses during the course of any given day. But the school system insisted there was no busing going on in the public schools. There's no busing when the parties in the desegregation lawsuit manipulate lines on a map of the city. Many of the students riding buses to East Side High School pass within close proximity of at least two other high schools before arriving at school in the morning. Many students awaken as early as 5 a.m. to catch a 5:30 a.m. bus to school. It's little wonder they make it to school at all.

As he walked quietly to the main office to check his mailbox for messages, Coach Martin watched the buses loading mostly black students. This transportation stupidity was part of a plan agreed upon by the school board in their continued effort to appease the NAACP, one of the plaintiffs in a tired, nearly five-decade-old desegregation case. It was a point of legal and academic peace that not one teacher, parent, or administrator thought could ever be settled in their lifetime. However, it was settled eventually and the damage because of it was incalculable for the entire metro area.

It consistently appeared to public school employees the East Baton Rouge Parish school board was chasing a rainbow in its effort to achieve unitary status for the public school system. The school system kept its aim attempting to hit the target of a legal settlement, but the NAACP daily moved that bulls-eye. In the meantime, attorneys on both sides of the school desegregation case were getting rich. The NAACP was fooling their constituents into believing they had the best interests of the students at heart. And it was the students who paid that legal sum in tiring bus rides in a system dying a slow political cancer. Those bus rides to school in the early morning and home in the early evening exposed them to severe climate changes, uncertainty in the morning darkness during daylight savings time, snarled traffic, boredom, and worst yet, fluctuating attendance practices.

Within five minutes of the bell ringing, those buses carrying roughly 500 students rumbled out of the parking lot. Almost like magic the school attracted a calm about it. The only students left on campus were the usual twenty or so waiting on a ride to claim them and athletes in the back of the school preparing for practice.

As Coach Martin entered the office there was a line of eight students waiting to use the telephone to contact friends or family for rides. It was the only time of day a student could legally use a telephone without permission from the principal.

Coach Martin eased his way around the crowd in the office, angling his book bag in a way as not to hit anyone with its weight of books and papers. He sighed as he entered the next room and looked into the square, wooden slot marked "Martin." Sure enough, there was a note scribbled on pink-lined legal paper that read:

"Coach, I cannot pick my son up from practice today because I am late shopping. Please do it for me. Thanks. Maureen Anzalone."

Coach Martin walked out of the office and thought aloud, "Maureen Anzalone?" He had never met or spoken with her, but she decided for a very tired Coach Martin he was responsible for taking her son home because she was too busy shopping. This irresponsible parental behavior was becoming too common and further taxed his day.

Coach Martin turned the corner of Building 3 and now had his team in sight as they kicked balls around and stretched. He took a few very deep breaths, slowed his walking pace, and disgustedly remembered he was one of the poorest paid public school educators in the nation who some people in the state thought was overpaid and ineffective.

After ninety-minutes of soccer practice ended without incident, Coach Martin informed the team of the uniform situation. Ordered two months before and now two weeks late, the uniforms—really T-shirts with numbers due to a budget that mysteriously disappeared over summer—proved faulty. There was the embarrassing possibility his team may be forced to play their first game, in just one week, in used baseball jerseys the coach of that team agreed to loan to the soccer program.

After dismissing the team, balls were picked up, placed in bags, and taken to the locker room. Corner flags were removed and stored. Benches were returned to the physical education area for use during first-hour class the following day. Portable goals were chained to the fence. Practice jerseys were folded and stored. One at a time young players borrowed Coach Martin's cell phone to call late-arriving parents as dark began to fall. It was all in a day's work.

The time was now nearing 5:15 p.m. Coach Martin still had sixty-seven papers to grade and a coach to call about rescheduling a game. He was tired. This day was not typical, nor unusual. He was hungry. He needed to attend to some bank business in the next hour before closing at 6 p.m. Rush hour traffic was in full spirit and his feet hurt.

Coach Martin chained and locked the gate to the soccer practice field. He was the last to leave practice. He lazily marched to his car and looked up at the orange and yellow sky. The northwest wind began to pick up steam and the blowing wind had a cold tinge to it as it massaged his cheeks. A cold front was expected to blow through bringing rain and plummeting temperatures tomorrow threatening to halt soccer practice.

"Oh, well," Coach Martin said in a voice of surrender only he could hear. "Maybe it *will* rain tomorrow."

After nineteen consecutive practices covering a span of four weeks and a season opener nearing, he wasn't sure if the comment was one of wishful thinking or fatigue.

Two days later on a cold Saturday morning, Coach Martin drove to the university bookstore and bought Ginny the book on animal science she so coveted. He wrapped the book in a white bag labeled, "Gap" so as to not arouse any suspicion from her parents or nosey observers. On the following Monday morning, Ginny almost cried at receiving a book she bought. Even though she paid for it, she treated the package like a late Christmas gift from Coach Martin. Ginny could not speak she was so happy. Now all she had to do was read it at her leisure. She also had to hope wherever she chose to hide it would not be discovered.

"Please exercise some common sense..."

The thirty-year-old intercom crackled throughout the school on a chilly Monday before Principal Berling began to speak. It was nearly the end of third-hour, just before 10 a.m. and he wanted to address the students, notably the senior class, before the bell rang and the majority of them left campus for the day.

"Teachers. Students. May I have your attention, please? Please stop what you are doing and listen to what I have to say because I only want to make this announcement once.

"We are having a problem with students leaving school after their classes are completed, and I'm talking about the seniors who leave early everyday. But it also pertains to others if they fall into the category of parents.

"Students, please do not bring your children to school after you leave school. We have a number of students, current and alums, bringing their children to visit with teachers during school hours. Students, this is a place of learning. It is not the mall where you might run into a friend and show off your children. Do not bring your children to school in strollers or knock on your teacher's doors during school hours to show off your children. Teachers do not have time for that and school is not the place for it.

"Teachers, if a student or former student is seen on campus with children, please send them to the office or send someone to get me so we can escort them off campus. Students, we are not going to discipline you if you are caught on campus with a child, whether it is yours or not. But please exercise some common sense and take care of your family visiting at another time and location. Please don't force us in the office to make this a tougher, and more strict policy. Thank you."

"What education professors told us was that when teachers have problems with order and discipline, it's because they haven't made the instruction sufficiently engaging...They tend to be as idealistic as the teachers they prepare, but they seem to assume a sort of glorified environment in which every youngster comes to school... eager and all a teacher has to do is to nurture their natural curiosity. (Professors) seem content to spin out their lovely theories and leave (new teachers) untested by real world experience."

—Columnist William Raspberry of the Washington Post Writer's Group

December—"These students scare me"

The numbers did not lie. They did not even begin to tell the story of the ineptitude and poor discipline of the lazy students Brent Masters taught Spanish to each day. But the numbers were the only barometer he had that reflected their efforts or lack thereof. Just once it would have been a nice change if those numbers told of a positive learning environment which Brent strived each day to provide. Just once in a great while Brent wanted to teach and have students' test scores reflect his determined efforts. It was not to be. More than once his students failed him, the teacher. Like most inner city public school teachers, he was exasperated by it all.

Numbers were powerful. Numbers explained class sizes, salary schedules, grade point averages, dropout rates, attendance practices, and placed schools in categories that determined and explained their status in comparison to other schools. Brent knew the state school systems manipulated numbers, inadvertently, but often used as the so-called proof by the experts to explain the efforts of schools and teachers. Numbers made teachers look better than they were or worthless in the eyes of an ungrateful public. Some even believed the numbers proved teachers were not doing their jobs well enough to provide an education for the poor, helpless children of the state's public school system. Slowly, Brent was learning about the numbers that many either did not know about or chose to ignore.

As Brent moved his black ink pen over his open roll book full of names organized into hourly classes, he thought about the theories he had learned in college. In college, it was not so much learning as it was indoctrination by professors that could not begin to understand what Brent had already learned in just a short time at East Side High School. Brent wanted his professors to be correct in that there was a solution to the multitude of problems teachers and other workers faced each day. Brent wanted desperately to believe that because his students were not learning that it wasn't due to his inexperience. Brent wanted to identify a problem, expedite a procedure to remedy it, and improve any student's academic problems. He had tried everything. Nothing worked and it began his descent into the cynicism that plagued so many experienced teachers.

Brent was now learning how the entire system worked. It seemed everyone in the school system was accountable and responsible for the improvement of test scores *except* the students. Principals were at the top of the food chain. They could be fired if schools did not maintain discipline, handle and solve financial matters, or meet certain state-mandated academic criteria in a specific time frame. Assistant principals were expected to be on the cutting edge of instruction while implementing discipline and providing a safe learning environment for all. Guidance counselors had to be in touch, both on a personal level and in terms of an avalanche of paperwork, identifying the problems of each student; real or imagined. Teachers were expected to teach multiple subjects in small rooms full of lackadaisical children motivated by nothing except the final bell to end the school day. On the other hand, students were always defined by the media and education officials as "struggling" in a "broken educational system" mired in "mediocrity" and political red tape; a school system refusing to reinvent itself in the face of a changing world that demanded students be better educated to compete in America's complex work force. Brent now knew that image to be a lie. He believed that blame heaped on teachers was misplaced. Students were the problem, although he knew it to be a waste of time and energy to explain it to those blaming him and his peers for the continued plummeting test scores. The media labeled some institutions as "failing schools." What Brent had learned was that schools were not failing students; students were failing in the schools, despite the focus of teachers.

Brent tapped on his solar calculator tabulating the averages of his students, who had just noisily exited the school for the Christmas holidays. Grades were due by day's end and Brent wanted to meet that deadline.

When he completed his feverish efforts, the numbers depressed him as did the stories explaining them. As he examined the figures, he never felt more inadequate. Despite what others wanted to believe about the sad academic plight of students, Brent knew teachers were helpless in changing that. Student culture in most inner city public schools was bankrupt. Parents were often absent in properly directing the lives of their children. Academic failure was simply acceptable in too many homes. There was nothing a teacher could do to reach students who did not wish to be reached. This academic tragedy was no movie with a ridiculous feel-good ending. It was real and it was as sad as it was revealing.

Of the 123 students Brent taught during fall semester, twenty-four failed the course and would have to repeat it. Of the ninety-nine students passing, thirty-one did so with a grade of 'D,' which Brent saw as nothing more than glorified failure. Only three students earned A's.

Of the fifty-five students making grades of 'D' or 'F,' thirteen had missed more than twenty days of school since it began in early August. Another sixteen students had missed at least ten days of school *unexcused,* just one absence short of qualifying them for automatic failure per school policy, regardless of letter grade earned.

Forty-five students failed the 200-point midterm exam, which made up 20 percent of their semester grade. Brent thought those results were next to impossible since he passed out study guides one week in advance of the exam to all students and spent four class days going over it in detail. Brent even allowed students two additional "free days" to study and ask questions in an effort to prepare for exam week. Worse yet, eight students didn't even bother to show up and take their midterm exams. Phone calls to the parents of those eight students produced not one callback, even though the students in question still could have made up the exam before the semester broke for Christmas with a proper excuse.

Brent counted fourteen students who spent at least two days in the discipline center for school-related transgressions. Although those students were allowed to make up their missed work, almost all of them failed in that effort because they simply were not in class to learn it properly.

Six students were dropped from Brent's roll early in the semester—never showing up to school at all. Another seven dropped out of school, one of which was arrested by the city police and booked for a felony charge of attempted murder.

Two others, both age fourteen, ended up pregnant and decided to leave mainstream school, and opted to earn their Graduate Equivalency Diplomas (GED).

Three of Brent's students were expelled for serious offenses. One male student hit a middle-aged science teacher in the nose during lunch shift because he was asked to tuck in his school uniform shirt. The teacher's nose was broken and he was advised not to file a lawsuit because the school system's investigation would be too lengthy and might not support his effort to punish the student-criminal. Another male was quietly arrested on campus for possession of marijuana with intent to distribute. A female student had piled up nine minor offenses in the first twelve weeks of school, compelling the assistant principal of discipline no other choice but to permanently remove her. All three students were only fifteen-years-old.

Overall, during the fall semester the school had placed 278 students in the time out room for 740 various minor offenses, 460 of which were repeat offenders. Thirty-seven of Brent's students spent at least one day in the time out room, twenty-three of those students were repeat offenders causing them to miss additional class time that retarded their ability to compete for better grades.

The worst statistic of all was the failure of students to simply show up at school and take weekly scheduled tests. Brent's classroom rule was like that of most teachers—any student missing a test had seventy-two hours to produce an excuse to retake the more difficult makeup test. Any student failing to follow that procedure was given a grade of *zero*.

It was a method used to force students to take the test on the day set by the instructor rather than allow students to manipulate the system by buying themselves additional time to study. Brent learned there was no quicker way to depopulate a classroom than to schedule a test; it was as if a plague had hit the school on test day. It was not unusual for as many as fifteen to twenty students to miss school on any test day.

Brent made a special mark in his roll book explaining when a student did not test according to procedure and did not produce an excuse to make it up. Brent counted thirty-seven grades in his roll book recorded as zero because nineteen different students just did not like to test at scheduled times. Or, they were not prepared to take the tests and tried to buy themselves extra time by attempting to negotiate with Brent telling him, "I'm not ready to take the test so I'll take it tomorrow." Brent insisted they test immediately or take the zero. Despite the choice, it was a significant reason why so many pupils failed his class.

Another twelve students simply refused to take at least one test during the semester because they simply did not want to. They placed their names on their papers, refused to perform the work, took their grade of zero, and laid their heads on their desks to sleep as others tested around them.

In addition, there was another problem that could be seen only in the daily newspaper's section called, "Police Beat." During the fall semester alone, six of the school's students or former students were either arrested or killed. Their stories generated common talk among numb teachers at lunch keeping track of which students were married before reaching age eighteen, which ones became pregnant or ran away from home, who was jailed, or who was killed. It was the reality of the job and that information kept teachers abreast of who was dangerous and what one could expect. It was a network of information proving most invaluable in the classroom when teachers were on their own with these unpredictable students.

Brent knew only one of the dead, eighteen-year-old sophomore Eugene Wallace. Eugene was far too old to be in Brent's class. He should have already graduated from high school, but he continued to fail classes and repeated grades. It was not unusual for the public schools to find themselves tormented with students too old to be in the grade in which they were listed. Brent taught four students over the age of seventeen who had yet to enter their junior year of high school. Brent's biggest burden of the senior citizen group was trying to teach Eugene, or better, to tolerate Eugene who refused to turn in any work assigned and missed too many days of school to any longer matter. When Eugene did attend school, he was a terrible nuisance, often earning suspension and unmoved by the attempt at discipline. Predictably, Eugene was dropped from the roll and the school due to missing too many days of school. Eugene was still a problem to himself and the world around him. Brent heard the story of Eugene's death from students the day after he was murdered in late November. They knew the details before the newspaper had printed the story and they shared the news with Brent like they were discussing the controversial outcome of a football game. Eugene was selling drugs. Walking home late one night with a wad of cash and pockets full of illegal pills, he was mugged and robbed of his cash and drug stash on the street by another dealer he knew. Eugene was not armed at the time of the holdup, but went home and loaded a glock-pistol he kept under his mattress and went looking for revenge. He never found it. Before Eugene could turn the corner of his block to seek out the thief and retrieve his stolen goods, two young men in a stolen car gunned him down in the street in what police termed a "drive-by" shooting. Eugene fell into a trap in that the murderers knew what Eugene would do and how he would react once robbed.

Eugene left behind a working mother who could no longer control him and a younger sister academically excelling in middle school. Although Eugene had no father figure to maintain a strong presence in the home, the bottom line in Brent's mind was that Eugene knew right from wrong and always seemed to choose the wrong side. There was no suspension for Eugene's lifestyle this time. He was simply dead and that thought ran through Brent's mind as he stared at Eugene's scratched-out name in his roll book.

Just days before, three East Side High School students walked into a suburban convenience store and robbed the clerk of thirty-five dollars before shooting him three times in the chest. The clerk survived and the three juveniles were apprehended and jailed. The shooter was a fifteen-year-old female.

One former student ran up her mother's credit cards while she was away serving in the Louisiana National Guard only to return home to enormous debt. The mother was livid with the newly accrued debt and a war of words evolved into threats. Fearing her mother who was now off active duty, the twenty-year-old former East Side High School graduate waited for her mother to sleep and then tried to kill her with a butcher knife.

Another student, an eighteen-year-old dropout from the previous school year, was found slumped over the steering wheel of his car with a bullet in his head from a drug deal that went awry. Once a stellar athlete for the school, his bloody body was found the following morning with a loaded pistol that had not been fired. The drugs he was selling were stolen by a person or persons unknown.

Brent wondered what he could have done as an educator to rectify these problems. More to the point, he wondered what others expected him to do in rectifying the problems. The problems in the school system were not always about curriculum or theory. These problems were the symptoms of a sick society. Certified instructors or not, master teachers or not, national certification and No Child Left Behind be-damned, Brent knew he could not wake the students each morning and make certain they caught the bus and arrived to school on time. Brent could not make them arrive prepared on test day. He could not make them study. He could not make them bring the necessary materials to class. He could not make them care. Brent did his job and did it well, but the numbers made him look as if he only showed up each day to collect a paycheck. Brent was not short on desire. He was motivated. He was qualified. He wanted to make a positive impression on students and help them develop as individuals. Now, as he leaned back in his aged wooden chair of 1960s vintage, he dropped his pen on the open roll book and sighed. He stared at the five messy rows of classroom desks where students sat just hours before. Brent was too early into his career to burn out. He was too late into his career to believe it would get any better.

While Brent was lost in his thoughts of early retirement there was a knock on the steel frame door to his classroom. He looked up from his desk and was surprised to see his lone foreign exchange student, Rifel, a native of Israel's West Bank. Understanding history, Brent knew to call his home *Palestine* so as to not upset Rifel and respect his culture.

Rifel, like many Arab students his age, looked a bit older than his years. He was only sixteen-years-old and his young face already carried a five o'clock shadow. His eyes were as dark as his medium length curly hair. His physique was average, but he was tall and shy; two traits that appealed to the young girls of all races. Even better, Rifel was extremely intelligent often making grades at or near the top of his classes. He took school very seriously, reflecting the nature of academics in his native East Jerusalem, a hotbed of anti-Semitic and anti-American activity.

While many American kids grew up playing video war games or with makeshift plastic weapons as they ran around their neighbor's homes yelling, "You're dead!" Rifel lived it. He was no stranger to terrorism, poverty, and suicide bombers. He had seen cars lit in flames as he walked home from school as men in scarves ran through the streets carrying AK-47 assault rifles warning onlookers not to cooperate with police or face consequences. Rifel came to the comfort and security of the United States to educate his mind as much as to escape the violence of his war-torn native land, if only for a year. He was one of those students who spoke little, but when he did, everyone listened. Brent knew that to see Rifel standing in his doorway long after the other students had vacated the campus was a sign of trouble. The look on Rifel's face proved Brent was right.

"Hey, Mr. Masters, how are you?" Rifel asked in broken English while trying to be polite and unassuming.

"Rifel!" Brent exclaimed in a pleasant manner as he turned to face his top Spanish student.

Brent rose from his chair and the two shook hands as adults, not in the soul shake reflecting a ghetto manner. Brent loved teaching Rifel because he was a serious student speaking three languages. He represented one of the three 'A' students Brent taught. Rifel was one of the few bright spots in Brent's day. Brent smiled at Rifel anticipating good news.

"Hey, you can't call me Mr. Masters anymore," Brent exclaimed with a smile. "I'm the new assistant soccer coach now. So, it's Coach Masters, and I know you are going to play for us, right?"

Rifel changed his demeanor. He wanted to be happy at his unexpected news, but could not out of respect for his teacher. What he had to tell Brent was going to hurt him and he respected his instructor too much to have to say it. Rifel summoned up his courage and spoke.

"I just came by to tell you to have a happy holiday," Rifel said before changing facial expressions, "and to tell you goodbye."

Brent froze, hoping what he was thinking was not true.

Rifel continued speaking slowly not completely comfortable with his English.

"I recently got permission from a host family in Charlotte, North Carolina, to move there and continue my American education," Rifel said. "I am leaving Baton Rouge and wanted to tell you goodbye. You are a great teacher! I learned a lot from you and I respected you because you understand my people's history and are open-minded. Not many Americans are, you know."

Brent was hurt. He was losing one of his few serious students and a potential soccer player. What Brent wanted to lose was one of the many idiots he taught each morning who believed sagging pants were cute, horrible diction was a ticket to easy success as a rap star, and a misdemeanor or a felony record was something to be proud of on a resume.

Brent was somewhat stunned, but not unappreciative of the situation. He sat back down in his chair and asked Rifel, "When are you leaving?"

"After the holidays," came Rifel's reply.

"But why are you leaving?"

"I just don't like it here. I am very surprised at the school. Well, I should say the students surprise me a great deal."

"What surprises you about them?"

Rifel looked at Brent feeling as if he were on a job interview and did not like the questions posed by the boss. He did not wish to answer them believing the response would anger his favorite teacher. Brent prodded further and did his best to make Rifel comfortable.

"C'mon, Rifel, you're leaving and I'm not going to be mad at you," Brent said. "I just want to know why my favorite student is leaving."

Rifel paused before smiling and then explained carefully.

"These students scare me," Rifel said before making another short pause to register the look on Brent's face. "I came to America to be challenged. Instead, I sit next to students who cheat and steal. They make fun of their instructors who are trying to help them. They are lazy. It makes me sad for America because this is not what I expected from such a great nation. Many people have told me this is not what the country is really like, but it's all that I see. I want to go to a place in

America where students are more like me. I hear Charlotte, in North Carolina, has a good school system—better than here. I wish to go there and further study so I can perhaps earn a scholarship to university."

Rifel then pointed at the empty desks in the classroom and continued, "These students are dangerous. They are not concerned with their futures."

Brent wanted Rifel to respond and got more than he bargained for. He had opened up more than he ever had before. Maybe it was because he had nothing left to fear, and if anyone knew real fear, it was Rifel. He was leaving Baton Rouge and it mattered little to Rifel what anyone thought of him at this point, except for Brent. Brent wanted the truth in all its glory. Rifel delivered.

"I understand, Rifel," Brent said in a reassuring tone. "I can't argue with you even a little bit. You are right on every count. I wish you the best and I will miss you."

"I feel like I am letting you down," Rifel said as he reached out to shake Brent's hand a last time. "I think you are a great deal like one of my teachers in Jerusalem. That is good. He is a great man, and a wise man. I guess I did not expect that from an American instructor."

Brent could not say anything further without being emotional. He did not see Rifel as a Palestinian, an Arab, or a potential terrorist working for organizations like Hamas or Hezbollah. Like Brent, Rifel, too, was open-minded enough to see Americans as people, and not an arrogant superpower intimidating the world into complying with a political doctrine or an image of what the world should be. He was just a tired, scared kid a long way from home wanting to avoid a life on the mean streets of the West Bank. He did not want to grow up throwing rocks at Jewish settlers or burning effigies of the United States president. He wanted to educate his mind through travel and study. What bothered Rifel so much was the stunning discovery that American students he met at East Side High School did not. They were both ignorant and arrogant of all things important, including the struggle surrounding the survival of his culture. Rifel knew there was another side to America. There was an America unlike the thugs at East Side High School. Secretly, Rifel wanted to attend college in the United States, although he had no idea how he was going to go about doing so. What he did know was his dream to continue his study abroad required he be challenged by students with the same dream. He did not see enough of those examples in his current situation, so he changed it.

"You will be missed," were the only words Brent could manage to summon as Rifel waved with the parting words, "Thank you."

"Take care, Rifel."

With that, the two forever parted. Brent stayed seated in his chair. He now had loneliness to keep him company with the despair he had before Rifel visited. Brent did not want to work anymore. He just wanted to go home. It was after 2 p.m. and many teachers had already left early for the long Christmas break.

Explaining to those in other professions how close teachers can sometimes get to their students is difficult to explain. The bond is not physical. It is mental and sometimes emotional. Sometimes the student does not even know the teacher feels that way toward them. Teachers need to be needed. When a student is mature enough to accept the responsibility of being a serious student and allows a teacher into their world long enough to share knowledge, while inspiring them, is special. Watching students grow, learn, and ask deeper questions about a subject they previously knew little or nothing about could invigorate a teacher more than a pay raise. Rifel was one of those students. He was now gone for good.

The multitude of Brent's troubled, underachieving students remained for him to revisit in spring. Brent did not want to think about that at the moment. It was a time to play Christmas songs on the radio, throw a log on the fire to ward off a night chill, watch college football bowl games, visit with family, and to reflect on another frustrating semester with no promise of change in the new year.

"The obscure we see eventually, the completely apparent takes longer."

—Edward R. Murrow
1940s American radio news correspondent

January—Dribbling through a Technological World

It was a bitterly cold Friday afternoon—the kind of biting cold one could expect in the Deep South. The humidity was moderate and the temperature was dropping. January in Baton Rouge can be more frigid than others around the nation could imagine. The map shows the state on the Gulf Coast. Common thinking suggests that because there is rarely snow it could not possibly be uncomfortable in the Sun Belt during winter. Locals, however, know if one were to calculate the humidity, wind chill factors could plummet into the upper twenties. Even transient northerners would reluctantly agree Baton Rouge had freezing days that rivaled midwestern cities, even if the number on the temperature gauge was not as competitive.

The grass was brown. The trees were stripped bare, standing like imperfect black and dark gray creatures against a light gray sky. The silver clouds moved quickly across the atmosphere as another front prepared to enter the area and guarantee to chill the population on this night. Extensive rain had beaten the grassy human paths that crossed the campus into muddy trails.

The holiday season was gone. Even though it was just two weeks removed from Christmas carols and multi-colored lights that livened up the dreadful winter landscape, it seemed a forgotten period now that January had arrived. Teachers were settling into a routine that would not be upset until the two days off for Mardi Gras, seven weeks away, and spring break some fifteen weeks away. This was the monotonous home stretch and the toughest teaching period of the year.

Brent Masters walked the long distance toward the football field that also served the soccer team while wrapping his green, heavily insulted parka around him with his black gloves. His cheeks were frozen as the late evening sky began to slightly dim. In the distance he could see the boy's head soccer coach, Joey Martin, slowly walking behind the striping machine laying bright orange lines on dormant brown grass. It was almost 4:30 p.m. and he had promised to help Coach Martin paint the field for the weekend match. Time was running short as darkness promised an early arrival. Brent had soccer assistant coaching responsibilities in his new job and he was late to help the boss.

Brent walked past the eight-foot high rusty chain link fences that lined the so-called sports complex of the school. They ran long distances around the edge of the football field, the gym, baseball field, practice field, and the track looking more like prison barriers to keep students in. The fence was hardly aesthetically pleasing to the eye.

As he passed the baseball team's practice field, he saw a water hole that drowned a home plate he knew was there, but could not see. The unpainted wooden benches built by coaches years before had been knocked over by either the heavy cold wind or the many unwanted after-hour visitors to the school. There were holes in the black webbing making up the batting cage sitting along the first-base side. A huge pile of mud represented what would be the pitching mound when spring thaw emerged.

The grass was flattened, not so much by cold of winter, but by the treads of the lawn mower operators that continually cut grass through the winter months. Brent wondered how much the school system or the school was paying for that unnecessary service at this time of year. Whatever the cost, Brent thought it a waste of money.

As he made his way down the fence line closer to the football field, he could see and hear a work-out taking place on the outdoor basketball court. Brent thought it far too cold to dribble against the pavement in this weather. The bouncing ball must have felt like a rock rather than thirteen pounds of inflated rubber. He looked at the rim in which the two men were shooting and noticed it was rusting against a worn and torn white net that needed replacing. It seemed to matter little to the participants lightly dressed from working up a sweat.

One of the men looked up and noticed Brent. Wearing a purple sweatshirt and shorts with white knee-high socks, the smaller of the pair waved Brent toward the half court they were playing on.

"Hey, Coach Masters!" he screamed over a baseball cap shifted backward on a close-cropped haircut. "C'mon over!"

Brent immediately shifted directions with his hands now in his pockets. He had to get out to the field to help Coach Martin, but he had been identified by a friendly voice and Brent had to pay his respects. As Brent moved closer, he noticed the player handling the ball was freshman Leonard Dawson, who was in his third-hour Spanish class. Leonard went into the air with the ball in his right hand and the larger man batted it down to the concrete pavement.

"Get that junk outta' here, boy!" the defender said, slightly out of breath. "Now I'm going to show you how to make a play. I'm even going to tell you that I'm going to move on your left side and make the basket anyway. Watch!"

"Give it your best shot, dad!" Leonard said with his hands near his knees and his body bent at the waist just like they do in the overly televised NBA.

"Watch this!" Leonard's father said, as he did exactly what he said he would. He moved to Leonard's left, stopped on a dime, pulled up and leaped high into the frigid air and let the ball go with a flick of his wrist. Brent had played a lot of basketball in his life and knew this man was gifted. The ball arched high and just over the hands of Leonard, who was pushing six feet tall at age fifteen. The ball went through the rim not touching the torn net as it then bounced hard on the poorly striped concrete court.

"One day you'll be able to stop my junk," the father told his athletically inferior son. "Someday you'll be able to 'ball up' like your old man."

Leonard issued a bounce pass to his father in what was obviously a "make-it, take-it" game. Brent stopped on the edge of the court as the wind whipped against his still body. It was getting slightly darker and Brent stood frozen wondering how these two could play in this weather.

"What's going on, Coach Masters?" Leonard asked, staring straight ahead while guarding his father, who stuck his buttocks into his son's face and slowly backed him under the goal.

"Looks like you've got your hands full," Brent observed.

"Want to play me?" asked Leonard.

"Are you kidding?" Brent said. "Too cold."

"Naw, you're too scared, that's what you are," Leonard laughed as his father hit a turn-around jump shot from deep inside the lane.

As the ball fell through the rim, it began to bounce away to the court adjacent to the one they were playing on.

"Who that is?" the father asked in imperfect English to his son as he retrieved the ball.

"That's my Spanish teacher," Leonard replied, pointing at Brent, who waved at the father.

"Hi," Brent said.

The father never acknowledging Brent as he dribbled back to mid-court to take the ball in. Leonard was too immature to properly introduce them. Brent was feeling like it might be up to him to do the honors. Brent felt awkward about doing it, but he was an adult and a teacher. He would try and press the introduction.

"I teach Leonard third-hour," Brent said to the father as he dribbled against his son in another effort to score another basket.

Brent was again ignored.

"Can you stop me? Don't think you can! Can you stop me?" the father asked moving from his right to his left. He used head fakes and stutter steps, but Leonard did not go for them having seen the moves many times.

"Bring it, old dude!" Leonard taunted.

"Keep me in front of you!" the father instructed. "Don't let me get around you!"

"Yea, I wish Leonard was as good a student as he was a basketball player," Brent said hoping to arouse some interest in the father. "Hey, Leonard, do you ever practice Spanish by any chance?"

Nothing. Neither of the two responded to Brent's obvious attempt to garner interest in Leonard's underachieving academic status. Brent began to feel very uncomfortable. He had requested two parent-teacher conferences with this very parent on both the second six-week progress report and mid-term report cards and that request was disregarded. There appeared to be nothing more Brent could do to get the parent's attention. He had seen all he needed to and all he cared to.

"See ya', Leonard," Brent said as he turned away from the action.

"Ya' sure you don't wanna' piece of me?" Leonard asked Brent again as he set up to guard his father.

"No, thanks. See you in class on Monday."

"Later!" Leonard said as his lighter frame tried to stop his dad from moving into position to make another short jump shot.

As Brent walked away it was obvious the father did not seem concerned with Leonard's grades or meeting one of his teachers. Either he did not care about his son's grades, or he did not know about them. When a teacher makes a comment aloud to a parent about comparing a family's commitment to basketball over that of their child's elected subjects, they should take the hint and the opportunity to inquire. Leonard's father did not.

What Brent did know was when he was in high school he would have avoided his teacher like a plague, especially when with his parents. It would not have mattered to Lloyd and JoAnn Masters one bit if they were shopping at the mall, attending a football game, or at a restaurant. They would have gone out of their way to introduce themselves to his teacher. They would have *wanted* to know if Brent was working up to his potential.

As far as Brent was concerned, it was further proof of what he was once told by a long-time teacher just weeks after the incident involving his laptop computer. The teacher told Brent it was not the kids who had changed over the years. It was the parenting. Brent agreed with that synopsis. Only three months into his teaching career, he also strongly believed no amount of legislation, at any level of government, could save a generation orchestrating their lives around the need for immediate self-gratification.

As Brent moved further away from the pickup basketball game, he could hear over his shoulder the father challenging his son.

"What you've got to do is square your shoulders as you approach the shot!" the father instructed without patience. "Place your left foot toward the goal and your right will follow. Keep your balance. Make sure you go straight up with both hands on the ball. Stay balanced!

Don't lean into your shot! Now, go straight up and flick your wrist like this. Then…"

The decibels of the instruction became too difficult to hear and Brent did not care to listen any longer. He was disgusted. Leonard had failed Spanish at the mid-term. Now just a week into the spring semester, Leonard's habits had changed little. He scored a 66 percent on his test Thursday. That was enough to earn a 'D' on Brent's ten-point grading scale. If Brent preferred to use the East Baton Rouge Parish grading scale, Leonard would have earned his fourth consecutive 'F,' since a score of 69 percent and below mandated it.

Brent, now somewhat demoralized, stepped onto the soggy turf of the field now making a squishing sound beneath his feet as he walked. He approached Coach Martin with a handshake until he saw orange paint splattered on his gloves. The two laughed.

"It's not just cold. It's messy out here, too," Coach Martin laughed.

Coach Martin turned and began to walk slowly behind the striping machine along the sidelines with Brent in tow. Brent noticed that much had been done. It appeared his boss did not need much more help. Brent realized he was very tardy and felt bad about it. After all, he was expected to help and it was rude not to be on time.

"What can I do to help out, Coach?" Brent asked.

"You can start shaking up these paint cans as we walk," Coach Martin instructed. "They are almost frozen and the paint is not coming out cleanly."

Brent picked up two aluminum cans. He began to shake them vigorously. The cans were cold and hurt his hands as he gripped them tightly. They felt more like tubular ice cubes. Brent's limbs ached as he shook them and slowly walked behind Coach Martin. The orange paint flowed out evenly from the striping machine's spigot fixed just six inches over the turf. It released a beautiful line—the regulation four inches in width. It took incredible patience for Coach Martin to keep the line straight while walking along the saturated field. This dirty task was one of many that fans, players, parents, and those at the school board never see coaches perform, but expected.

"You do a good job at this," Brent observed attempting to break the silence as the wind howled from the north.

"I'm learning," Coach Martin said.

Brent changed the subject to kill time and tried to forget that he was freezing.

"So how did you get stuck with this job?" Brent asked. "Let's face it, I mean, no one wanted to be soccer coach."

"I know, especially under the conditions," Coach Martin said.

"You are referring to..."

"I am referring to the fact that Terrance Wright practically begged me on the first week of school to coach the team. I don't know a damn thing about soccer, Brent, but I knew if I didn't do it, Coach Gatewood was more than ready to sack the program. I don't know what I am doing, really. I'm just trying to help out, but I am paying a price for it."

"So, why are you doing it?"

"When Terrance, you know him?"

Brent nodded his head that he did as Coach Martin continued his work and a slow walking pace.

"When he told me how many kids had signed up to play, I couldn't walk away," Coach Martin answered while looking straight ahead. "Besides, there's a stipend. It's not much, but it's something. Of course, out here freezing my ass off painting a field in this wet muck is making me rethink whether I made the right decision."

Brent chuckled at the remark. He knew there was a stipend for coaches, but soccer head bosses earned only three percent of their gross pay. For Coach Martin, his stipend was $1,100 per year before taxes. The money was dispersed in his bi-monthly checks and came out to an additional forty dollars per month over a ten-month pay period. Divided by the number of hours he would have to work to field a competitive team—which included washing uniforms, field preparation, team scheduling, student-athlete paperwork, four after-school practices per week from mid-October through early February, game day preparations, paying officials, organizing bus travel when it was necessitated, fund-raising, ordering team supplies, and transportation of players when parents refused to involve themselves in their children's lives—it came to less than two dollars per hour. That sum was significantly less than the minimum wage. Worse yet, Coach Martin could expect only scorn from the school's athletic director who was paid to direct athletics, thus the title. The energy tax on his personal life was also proving enormous and affecting his overall daily classroom performance. The school system did not compensate some coaches well for their enormous efforts. Coach Martin was already learning that hard fact and had already decided he would not coach the soccer team the following year.

"Did the administration ask you to coach?" Brent asked.

"You're kidding, right?" Coach Martin answered as he stopped for a short break to warm his hands by rubbing them together rapidly. "Look, you know how I found out I was coaching?"

Coach Martin did not wait for an answer. He continued as Brent looked on.

"They, I don't know who, stuffed my mailbox with dozens of eligibility forms needing to be filled out by the kids," Coach Martin remembered. "I went to my mailbox one morning and there was all this stuff. I didn't know what it was, when it was due, or what to do. No one bothered to call me into the office and officially tell me anything. I had to figure it out all by myself. Real professional, huh?"

Coach Martin was getting colder as he registered Brent's face for a show of support before he continued.

"Stupid me, I thought Coach Gatewood might actually call me into his office and tell me a few things. You know, about what to expect. Not a chance. It didn't take me long to go from being a regular teacher who blended in around here to a man who was the target of jokes from those not approving of soccer. And there's a lot of 'em. Hey, Brent, I'm no big soccer fan. I know nothing about the game, but I am a fan of kids. I do still foolishly believe in exposing kids to as many clubs, sports, and subjects as we can before they graduate. How else are they going to learn about the world?"

Coach Martin then began walking the paint machine down the field to continue field preparation as darkness fell.

"Coach Gatewood?" Coach Martin asked. "He thinks the school exists for the football program and sees me now as some sort of threat. I've lost a lot of respect for him, but, hey, one and a half billion Chinese don't give a damn."

Brent took it all in. He understood so much in retrospect. Brent realized what Coach Gatewood was trying to do. The head soccer-coaching carousel kept players discouraged, but Coach Gatewood hoped in addition, to compound that by destroying the players' will to play. By not communicating with Coach Martin early in the year, as to whether he would be accepted as head soccer coach, time would make it more difficult to organize the sport before their first practice in late October. However, Coach Martin and Brent Masters recovered and communicated in time to get players to fill out ten forms each as required and turned in the paperwork in time for their first match. The way the entire matter was orchestrated by the school athletic director was childish, but that was the nature of a head football coach who was arrogant enough to believe he would be canonized for sainthood based on his won-loss record. Hurting the school's soccer team exercised his power and sent a message to other coaches of that power. It was an unnecessary show of force that hurt kids. Coach Gatewood was not an athletic director and head football coach as much as he was a pseudo emperor of a once-proud public school football empire that had crumbled into mediocrity.

Coach Martin then changed the subject before placing another can of paint into position to continue his task.

"Hey, I saw you talking to Leonard over there," Coach Martin said.

Brent thought he was about to be chastised for being late by Coach Martin, who had a reputation for being dry-witted to the point of cruel.

"Sorry about that, I..." Brent started to say.

"Don't apologize. I just wanted to know if you taught that kid?" Coach Martin asked Brent.

"Yes, and I tried to talk to the father who practically ignored me. Hell, he *did* ignore me. You know, Coach, it amazes me how a kid can justify spending hours and hours practicing sports or hanging out with friends doing nothing, but can't find the time to study for a class he is struggling to survive in. I've coded Leonard's progress report twice trying to get a conference set up and..."

"Me, too, but you've probably figured out like I have that you are wasting your time with that parent."

"I don't even know his name. He never even looked at me while I chatted with his son."

"You don't know who he is?"

"No. Should I?"

"Not unless you're a fan of litigation."

Brent shrugged his shoulders as Coach Martin stopped to reload the striping machine with another can of paint. He tossed the used can to the ground and looked at Brent for an answer.

Brent repeated with effect in animated form, "I don't know who he is."

"His name is Ed Dawson. Attorney Ed Dawson," Coach Martin said twice for effect. "He's one of the top divorce lawyers in the city and he's very wealthy. His shoes probably cost more than we make in a month's salary. He's a great divorce attorney, but he's twice divorced. Funny, huh?"

"No, 'ironic' would be a better word," Brent chided.

Coach Martin paused before adding, "Seems like he should be doing something else than playing basketball in this weather, eh?"

"Oh, I don't know, just because he's an attorney doesn't mean he's not going to spend a little quality time with his son," Brent said watching the two play basketball in the distance. "Every dad should do more of that. But, funny, his language was that of an uneducated man."

"What do you mean?"

"When he spoke to his son he sounded common. He spoke street slang. I would expect more from an attorney. You would hope an educated man would have manners and a vocabulary to display to his son as the correct way of doing things. He only looked at me once. He asked Leonard, 'Who that is?' when he looked at me."

"'Who that is?'" Coach Martin asked with a laugh. "You would expect more from a parent, too!"

"Yes, especially an attorney," Brent said still shaking two cans in less than enthusiastic fashion. "You think he speaks to the judge that way?"

Brent was having fun now and could not resist making fun of a parent who refused him the courtesy of an audience. Worse, it showed Leonard how little his parent and the public thought of teachers. To an immature mind like Leonard, it could validate the cruelty exercised by students toward their teachers.

"Hey, yo', judge, you the dog if ya' just lay down a lot of dead presidents on my client, yo'," Brent said while laughing at his own joke.

Coach Martin snickered and returned to striping the field. He never looked up from his work, but began to laugh harder. He continued to talk about Leonard as if he knew a secret Brent did not. He did have some information and it was sad insight as to why Leonard struggled in school.

"Brent, I spoke to Leonard just before Christmas..." Coach Martin began to explain.

"You mean winter break, right?" Brent interupted with sarcasm while trying to make a point about his displeasure with the school system's political correctness. "That's what the school system calls it now."

"Like I said, I spoke with Leonard's father before Christmas break and he told me his father woke him up every morning at 4:30 on school days to practice basketball. Can you believe that?" Coach Martin asked. "Haven't you noticed how tired Leonard is in the morning?"

Brent shook his head no. He did not teach Leonard until 11 a.m.

"This kid is failing my class, your Spanish class, and some other classes I can't recall," Coach Martin said. "All his dad wants to do is get him up in the early morning to practice hoops. The kid is not even good enough to play on the school's junior varsity. Even if he was good enough, he's not academically eligible. Ed's dream is for Leonard to play big-time basketball, whether that's college or the NBA, I don't know."

Coach Martin stepped out of character for a second to vocally emulate Leonard's high-pitch, "My dad told me if I didn't make the basketball team next year he was going to kill me!"

Coach Martin paused in his speech as he continued working.

"It's not the first time they've been out here, you know?" Coach Martin continued. "They come out here three times per week. I even once saw Ed put the car lights on so they could finish playing a game of one-on-one."

That bit of information explained a great deal and explained nothing. Brent now understood why Leonard did not understand. Brent still could not figure why an educated man would not take great pains to teach his failing son the value of an education rather than how to make the perfect jump shot. Why didn't this parent call the teachers when requested to do so? Why is the parent spending time teaching his son the rudiments of a game, in freezing temperatures no less? He's not eligible or good enough to play at the high school level. It all made no sense to Brent.

Coach Martin stopped to admire his work and ran his hands together. More paint had gathered around his hands as far up as his wrist. His unprotected hands were chapped, cold, and cramped from pushing the striping machine in precision fashion. He looked at Brent, who was admiring the field. Although the grass had no color, the fluorescent-orange was highly visible under a sky that had faded to near black under the fast fading sunlight. Coach Martin's work was factory perfect. The lines were straight, and the arches and circles were from out of a geometry book.

Coach Martin admired his work and then looked at Brent, not knowing whether the first-year teacher was bored with the conversation or upset with what he thought to be a total lack of parenting. He needed to tell Brent what he knew about Leonard, but didn't want to be the one who forced him to reconsider the teaching profession or to label Leonard as hopeless. He also knew what he would say next would anger Brent. He took one of the paint cans from Brent and began to shake it as he spoke.

"Attorney Ed Dawson also paid an ex-high school assistant basketball coach twenty-five dollars per hour to coach his son two days per week after school and on weekends," Coach Martin added breaking the silence. "The kid doesn't have a language tutor, but he's got his own private basketball coach. Can you believe that? Leonard probably can't say, '*Si, Senor*,' but he's learning the science of shooting free throws."

"Yea, and he knows the language of Ebonics, too," Brent said. "His father is reinforcing that. How can a parent justify that type of behavior? How can…"

"Hey, Brent, I'm on your side, okay?" Coach Martin laughed in an uncomfortable manner and not understanding how Brent got the job as a teacher. "I know this is new to you. I know they didn't teach you this in the College of Education. I know they filled your mind full of useless educational theory and poisoned classroom philosophy that had an answer to every problem you'll face as an educator. But this is how it is. This is not what they teach you in college. This is how it is, and it's not going to change—not in our lifetime, anyway."

Coach Martin then quickly translated his candor to a very negative tone adding, "Not unless we start using common sense in education.

I don't foresee that anytime soon. Besides, I don't think Leonard is going to be here next semester. His dad wants to move him to a Class-C school, you know, where they have only 300 or so students in grades K-12.

"So, not only will Leonard make the basketball team there, he will have a great chance of starting. That's what I heard anyway."

Brent stared at the wiser, older coach. Brent felt like an open book Coach Martin had read many times. His eyes pierced him. He stood shivering as the cold wind picked up velocity. Brent wanted to tell Coach Martin in this moment of trading truths what transpired on his first day in the classroom regarding his laptop, but the "old timer" already knew. There are few secrets in high school hallways.

Coach Martin began to laugh out loud as he turned to move the striping machine in position to paint the eighteen yard "penalty box."

"I heard what happened to you on your first day here with that tramp writing you that nasty note," Coach Martin said. "I think it shocked you. To those of us who heard about it, we didn't even blink."

"No one was supposed to know about that," Brent said, somewhat miffed.

"You can't keep secrets in high schools," Coach Martin said. "The students aren't the only ones who gossip. Either the students will tell the teachers, we'll overhear their naughty conversations, or we'll hear about it another way. Nothing shocks teachers, and the students are not ashamed of telling us. In time, nothing will shock you, either. You'll be completely desensitized. That is, if you stick around long enough."

Brent did not want to admit that he was almost there. He had heard horrible conversations in class just minutes before the bell would ring to dismiss them. Sixteen-year-old pregnant girls talked aloud among themselves about what they were going to name their babies. Sometimes they were shamelessly overheard takling about whether they were going to get their nipples, vaginas, or their bellybuttons pierced. They laughed about how it hurt to get the area above their pubic hair or above the crack of their backsides tattooed. Girls traded information about their favorite sexual positions, their expertise in oral sex, or how close they were to getting caught screwing on the sofa or smoking dope before their grandmothers came home from work.

Boys discussed sex, too. Which girls perform oral sex on first dates was almost as popular a subject as fighting and dancing at parties. The experimentation with drugs or the drug abuse of their friends and the dangerous behavior exhibited under that influence of alcohol was a common topic.

Students of all races called each other "nigga," "buck-wheat," "Opie," or "Oprah" in affectionate ways, not understanding how dangerous or insulting those names can often be in the real world. Most students could care less about what others thought of them. Their interest in improving their image did not extend into the next minute. Incidents such as these happened so often teachers could not send every student to the office for discipline. Such an incident would have to be extreme before applying discipline. Teachers usually gave students warnings taking the time to explain their constipated juvenile thinking. Students sometimes apologized to teachers, but only to keep them off their backs. A sincere apology was quite rare.

Brent followed Coach Martin around the penalty box watching the paint spit out at the cold turf. He had been teaching all of one day when he knew he would not pursue the profession into a second year. The more Brent experienced as a teacher the less he was impressed. It occurred to Brent he could not save the students from themselves or the ignorance of a generation of parents hopelessly out of touch in an increasingly dangerous world. If the parents did not care, how could the students be expected to? What could teachers, even the highly dedicated and passionate types, do to change a rapidly growing culture immersed in ignorance and lethargy? Brent was continually reminded and his experiences reinforced his opinion that all the standardized testing, school accountability programs, and pressure placed on educators by the federal and state governments did not mean much when an education had been devalued by the inflation of student apathy.

Brent remembered reading a book about one of the nation's leading scientists being asked to speak at the graduation ceremony of his college alma mater. The scientist accepted the invitation, boarded a plane to visit the college town, and was escorted by limousine to the campus by the university's chancellor. En route to the hotel, the chancellor never stopped bragging about the university's prolific sports teams.

As the limousine sped into the city, the chancellor spoke of the university football team's top twenty-five ranking, the bowl victory, and the basketball squad's two parade all-American recruits.

When the chancellor finished bragging about stadium expansions, the scientist asked calmly, "Who is the university's top science and math student?"

The chancellor explained he did not know; that it would take a great deal of paperwork to find out, and why did he want to know?

The scientist replied, "I think sports are great entertainment," he explained, "but I find it difficult to compete in global economics or stop an enemy's nuclear missiles with footballs and basketballs."

Brent had heard the sports media sometimes chide academics because "85,000 people have never showed up to listen to a chemistry lecture." While that is true, it is also certain that winning sports championships has never led to Fortune 500 companies moving to a region and providing high-paying jobs to its college graduates.

Brent liked that story. He also knew a bit of history and believed with all his heart that the American empire would crumble like the Romans before them and for the same reasons. Failure to educate the masses would be part of the failure of that once great civilization. Like the Romans, total devotion and immersion in the entertainment of sport and leisure would, and had, undermined the American lower-class student's reason for being.

Each day, far too many students did not bring pencils or paper to school, even on test days. They would lose fifty-five dollar school textbooks and their parents complained to school administrators asking why they had to pay for the loss. But students, even very poor ones, sported $150 sneakers, owned cell phones most did not need, and utilized iPods and DVD players that were terribly expensive. They spent small fortunes on rap and rock n' roll CDs, and wore the eighty-dollar sports jerseys and caps of their favorite athletes. At the same time, nearly 70 percent of the students at East Side High School stood in free lunch lines and complained about the quality and quantity of the food—an insult Brent thought to the taxpayers whose children had to pay for the same lunch. It was such irony and inconsideration.

Brent believed Leonard's father was contributing to the new Rome and there were many more parents like him, if only indirectly involved. Ed Dawson was gambling with Leonard's future. He was helping his son appreciate a dream that would never be anything more than a dream. In Leonard's life, the strong paternal figure allowed basketball to be victorious over books. Jump shots were more important than vocabulary. Private coaching was more important than tutoring a child failing multiple classes. Parental rudeness, arrogance and indifference replaced responsibility. It was a sick, lazy, ignorant, materialistic world and attitude only Caligula and Nero could appreciate.

> "Sports don't build character. It reveals it."
>
> -unknown

January—The School Orphans

They didn't call soccer the "beautiful game" around the world for nothing. Watching the experienced St. Lucy High School boy's soccer team operate was, indeed, beautiful. They were the sixth-ranked team in the state and East Side High School, very short on quality talent and victories, were forced to play them twice in their competitive district.

East Side High School head soccer coach Joey Martin walked along the soggy sidelines dressed in his royal blue Diadora soccer sweat suit. His arms were folded as he paced along a muddy sideline in his fashionably striped coaching cleats. He was again disgusted at the beating his team was taking. Coach Martin's team's dress code was the only thing his side had to prove they knew anything about the game. His team did not play well, but they looked at least respectable in donated uniforms in the absence of new ones they could not afford due to a budget that mysteriously disappeared. He knew they were out-manned and only offered encouragement to his tired team as the ball moved around the 110-yard "pitch."

He glanced across the field and into the bright Saturday afternoon sunlight now bored with a game that was out of control and counted the number of fans in attendance. It did not take long to do so. Of the forty-three fans showing in the bleachers across the field, forty were supporting St. Lucy. Their fans were well dressed, politely vocal, and knowledgeable of soccer as they chanted and offered advice to their sons and friends fighting for the ball on their side of the field. East Side High School had parents producing children to feed the school sports rosters, but they continually proved not to be fans of most of the sports in which their children performed. To add further insult, the only time the football-mad local news media even mentioned soccer was to poke fun at it and the players toiling in it, whether they were local or professional. Their ignorant comments and neglect of the game hurt young men and women because of their obvious prejudice toward it. Like so many other high school so-called "minor" sports, East Side High School soccer was a school orphan.

"Get the ball to the corner, Nickie!" the St. Lucy head coach yelled with his team comfortably ahead, 4-0, with just nine minutes remaining in the eighty-minute contest. "To the corner!"

The St. Lucy head coach had pulled his varsity players out of the match at halftime with a 3-0 lead and allowed his junior varsity to play against East Side High School's varsity. It was still not much of a contest. St. Lucy's younger players skillfully moved the ball around the pitch. It was a generous move by their head coach to keep the score down, out of respect for East Side High School, but somehow it was also humiliating to Coach Martin. He knew it was not intended that way, but his team could simply not compete and it was embarrassing.

As the St. Lucy halfbacks intercepted the ball at midfield and the clock running under eight minutes, East Side High School senior captain Terrance Wright moved up to "mark" his man. As he did, the halfback simply slapped at the ball with his right foot providing just enough trajectory for the ball to launch over Terrance and into the far right corner of the field near the red corner flag. The East Side High School defense was set and ready for another assault at their goal. But a St. Lucy freshman forward won the race to the silver and blue-colored rolling ball, gained control and lofted a perfect cross pass into the center of the eighteen-yard box. The ball skidded about twelve feet in front of the East Side High School goalie who attacked the pass as instructed. It was a solid defensive tactic in most cases. But the St. Lucy attacking forward stopped the ball at his feet, allowed the goalie to commit full speed, and dribbled around him with two simple steps. With the goalie now on the ground having been faked and his defenders guarding other players nearby with similar talent, it created a can't-miss goal. East Side High School defender Jesus Estevez left his man and ran to help his goalie but the ball was already perfectly struck with a right foot of the player in a different colored jersey. The ball lifted from the ground like a laser about three-feet high with backspin and landed in the middle of the clean white nylon net. It was textbook perfect as the fans cheered and the St. Lucy players celebrated.

The East Side High School players said nothing. To their credit, they knew who they were and where they were in the scheme of things. Their strength was they knew their weaknesses. Six of their eleven starters had never played the game before. They were simply athletes borrowed from other sports learning a demanding game the hard way.

Coach Martin's now sunburned face glanced at the opponent's bench and seven new faces in clean uniforms that had yet to play were now going in. Seven St. Lucy junior varsity players in grass-stained jerseys jogged off the field to the approval of the varsity players now standing and applauding near their bench.

Coach Martin hurt for his players. He knew what they were thinking and he was trying to decide how he was going to explain the beating to his team. Coach Martin was tired of giving rallying speeches, but he was becoming expert at it.

His team was not only losing, 5-0, they were being upstaged by a junior varsity team in the second half. His boys were tired. Their sweaty, defeated faces resembled weather-beaten middle-aged men. They were the East Side High School boy's soccer team. They were all Coach Martin had. They were his team, his fans, and his best friends at a school that hardly recognized their existence.

> "Those that do not set goals are destined to work for those that do."
>
> —Chinese proverb

Early February—"Ever Heard of the First Amendment?"

A red and white Channel 8 news van pulled up along the curb of Iberville Boulevard next to East Side High School in the late afternoon. A long thick red racing stripe from headlight to rear bumper highlighted the gaudy "8" and station call letters stenciled on the outside of the van with the corny slogan, "Your Only Metro News Source" hyped to identify itself as the city's best.

Like many local news stations around the nation, Channel 8's claim was large on verbosity and short on substance. There were other news sources in the city, but it helped to dramatize to the public to make them believe their news station was the only one looking out for the interests of the common audience. In truth, Channel 8 was suffering from an image problem and lousy ratings. Fancy slogans painted on the side of news vans bought from New York City's marketing gurus was not going to save Channel 8 from finishing at the bottom of the ratings game. However, there was always one reporter arrogant enough to believe they could save the station from itself. Around the city, the station was lauded as "flash and trash" news commentary and coverage and its reporter, Dick Preston, was its journalism field marshal, a first-name he ignored due to the obvious jokes aimed in his direction.

When there was not much news to report, Dick would simply embellish what facts were available. It was typical of a reporting style more prone to drama than facts. That lack of style had become his trademark as he tried to put together a tape he could use to sell himself to bigger media markets, his ultimate goal.

Dick was in his mid-thirties and was a pretty-boy to be sure. He was tall, had wavy brown hair with dyed blonde highlights and a phony tan bought in a "cancer coffin" serving double-time as a tanning booth. He had cheek bone surgery to give his chin and jaw line the appearance of authority. He wore blue-tinted contact lenses that gave him Aryan characteristics. He worked out with weights at a local health spa and enjoyed being seen running the busy four-lane streets of the city without a shirt. Although he was married, it was an unhappy arrangement and Dick was as much a flirt with the women as he was a reporter whose reputation for infused drama preceded him. As he stepped from the van and onto the East Side High School campus parking lot, his stiff white button-down preppy shirt and navy-blue pleated trousers with cuffs and tasseled black shoes portrayed him as a professional. He was nothing of the sort. His intention on this day was to make a major story out of something that would hardly be construed as news in any other metro area its size. Dick's current target was the reputation of East Side High School.

Driving the van was reporter Daryl Rheams, a twenty-six-year-old television cameraman for nearly three years. He, too, was looking to make a name for himself in a town where a cheap, insincere station commercial could get one recognized standing in line at Wal-Mart. Daryl thought that was something in a city where a hero was, too often, a nineteen-year-old college football player.

Daryl's idea of being a professional unbiased reporter came from the wrapper of a used box of "Crackerjack" caramel corn. That was one reason he was slowly becoming known around the news station as more of a cameraman, even though he started out as the station's primary reporter. Daryl did not have the instincts for news. The station allowed him to consider himself both a reporter and cameraman, but he had not held the microphone on a news assignment in nine months. Channel 8 liked it that way.

Neither were professional journalists. Meaning, neither of them completed journalism as a major, which should be a requirement to deliver news in a metropolitan area of 700,000. WXBS-TV, Channel 8, made an effort to make the ignorant viewing masses believe its reporters were on the job twenty-four hours per day defending the population from the shady deals that existed in the state capitol, and along the back alleys and boulevards of the sprawling city. Channel 8's problem was it had garnered a reputation among the reputable media and among the more affluent populace as a station on its way to rivaling the yellow journalism at the turn of the twentieth century.

Nonetheless, Dick moved toward the school's main office just before the evening bell rang signaling dismissal. The two men walked onto the campus without permission. School policy held that everyone must report to the office, regardless of time of day, and gain permission to walk the grounds to speak with anyone or to film anything—a school policy ignored by Channel 8 and their so-called journalists.

Principal Adam Berling, a grizzly veteran teacher, administrator and former major in the U.S. Marine Corp, met them at the flagpole near the office before they got too far onto the campus grounds. The school bus fleet was lined up and in place with its doors open awaiting noisy students as the U.S. flag whipped high above them in the cold February wind. Right on cue, the 2:30 bell for dismissal rang and hundreds of students poured from seven campus buildings from numerous directions. The reporters, hoping to be aided by the ensuing chaos, would attempt to ignore Principal Berling. Like troubled teenagers, they believed they could act as ghosts and no one would notice their demonic media presence. Principal Berling, being no one's fool, immediately called out to the television crew in a manner that characterized his reputation as no-nonsense.

"Excuse me, but what is Channel 8 doing on this campus without permission?" asked Principal Berling, already indignant at the reporter's presence and arrogance.

"We don't need your permission to do our job," Dick shot back never making eye contact. "Just stay out of the way and we'll be gone soon."

The news tandem were young puppies in the eyes of Principal Berling. He knew this type. They were, as reporters, bush-league. Principal Berling noted that about six on-duty teachers and office personnel were beginning to gather around him. This situation, he thought, had the potential to be a nasty scene. At the same time, he had never run from a good fight in his life and was not about to allow two young media punks gain a reputation off of him in front of the people he was hired to lead.

"To hell you will," Principal Berling said to the arrogance laid upon him by a news source he thought little of to begin with.

He began to move in their direction with purpose like the Marine he once was, even as the two reporters were moving away from him. He was behaving like an angry dog snipping at the heels of a stranger that entered his yard. Principal Berling was a tall man with hard muscles for sixty-two years old. He was intimidating with his size as much as he was with his intellect and quick-wit. His white hair was close-cropped revealing a military background that had seen action in the early stages of the Vietnam conflict. To him, a skinny news crew was not nearly as tough as North Vietnamese artillery. He had no intention of backing down from the Fourth Estate.

"Let me tell you something," Principal Berling said in a torturous tone. "No one called me and told me you were coming or why. Not you. Not the school system's central office and no one from your station. What is this all about?"

As far as Principal Berling was concerned, the young crew of WXBS-TV was not going to take another step on his campus without his permission or blessing. He was God almighty on this campus and intimidated even the older faculty members. That included the burly basketball coach at the school, a military veteran. If Channel 8 wanted a fight, then by damn, they would get one from a tough ex-leatherneck.

Dick slowed down his pace, spun around, and chose to speak for the station as he slowly made a few steps toward the principal.

"We got a report from a source that a movie was shown on this campus about a week ago that included violence and some sexual innuendo," Dick said with authority. "We are here to interview the teacher who showed that movie."

"And just who might that be?" asked Principal Berling. "Because you are telling me something I don't know."

Dick reached into his right pocket, unfolded a piece of yellow paper, and read the name aloud as if he were the jury in a trial that had already found East Side High School guilty of a cover-up.

"We are looking for a math teacher by the name of Miss Helen Carmeno," Dick answered. "Now, would you kindly tell us where her classroom is located so we can conduct this interview?"

"No!" answered Principal Berling, like he was turning down a request from a NON-COM to go into town for a drinking binge the day before an amphibious assault. "I need to find out what's going on first before anyone can speak to you about it. That may take a few days. In the meantime, I am going to ask you and your cameraman to leave the campus. Now!"

Principal Berling was trying to be nice. It was against his entire genetic code to be nice to the news media. He despised them. He despised their methodology, or lack thereof. He believed it to be true that the news media did not care about the facts, just a story, even an incorrect one. Protocol meant nothing to the news media, but it meant a great deal to the school system. The media thought, because they had a camera and their faces were recognized due to the magic of television, they had a right to go any place they deemed necessary, regardless of the rules and the safety of a high school campus. This news crew wanted to meet with Helen Carmeno. The crew from WXBS-TV believed an old man with a penchant for intimidation was not going to stop them.

Dick then tried to get tough with Principal Berling. No one, he thought, got in the way of the news, especially some high school principal playing the role of Roman emperor.

"Look, we have a right to be here!" Dick explained. "Ever heard of the First Amendment? Just let Miss Carmeno defend herself. We'll give her a chance to explain and we'll leave."

"Son, you don't seem to understand, do you?" answered Principal Berling, with his hands on his hips and slightly leaning over at the waist. "I'm in charge here. I'm responsible here. I just told you when I get the facts, and I don't know what is even going on right now, you would be able to speak with someone regarding the issue, whatever it is."

"So, we might *not* be able to speak with her?"

"You are testing my patience and I don't have a lot of that anyway. Please leave. I have explained myself for the last time. If you don't leave I will have the police called and have you removed!"

With that final word, Principal Berling moved toward the pair like they were cattle at a roundup. He was angry. More so than when students fought on campus, which he abhorred. His outstretched hands created a seven-foot wingspan like that of a basketball player as he gestured they move toward their van parked near the edge of the campus. Dick and

Daryl began to back step slowly not sure what the old man was going to do. Or, what he was capable of doing. At that very moment, Daryl began to roll his video camera and shoot the incident, which they would use in their attempt to discredit Principal Berling when they aired their 6 p.m. news segment in a matter of hours.

"Turn the camera off!" Principal Berling demanded. "There is no news here! You are not acting like professionals! Please leave or I will call the police! You are not invited here! You are breaking school rules!"

The film continued to roll as the crew from WXBS-TV stepped just inches off of the campus and continued to shoot footage of the school, including the large logo along the side of the auditorium so that there would be no doubt to viewers watching which school was in question. It was a cheap and absurd attempt by the news crew to get their way and proclaim news when there was not any. In other words, Channel 8 was on the job.

Principal Berling immediately called Helen Carmeno into his office to get to the bottom of what he feared might become an ugly situation. Helen spent an hour in Principal Berling's office after school explaining that she had her students watch a movie on the so-called Senior Skip Day, a "holiday" students awarded themselves. Quite simply, like many teachers that day, she did not have a quorum to conduct classes. With only eight of thirty students present, she decided to watch a movie one of the students brought to her mathematics class.

To be sure, the movie was not fit for academic consumption. It was a horror film with a bit of mild seedy language and violence. It would have made much better sense to have the kids "study" for an hour rather than to take a chance on a movie that had *not one* instance of redeeming mathematical value.

Unfortunately, one of the students in her class that day, fifteen-year-old sophomore Erin Sanchez, wanted math to be taught despite the low number of students. On top of that, she was offended by the movie's lack of borderline ethics and went home and told her father, Jay, an overzealous Christian, who wanted his child to be in private school to begin with. Jay immediately called Channel 8 and reported the incident hoping to embarrass East Side High School and the public school system. The intent on Jay's part was simply that childish.

Jay would have been better served to contact the school principal first. If he did not get any satisfaction through that vein he could have called the East Baton Rouge Parish public school system. The problem was, Jay did neither. He completely overreacted and caught the school system blindsided by a news crew hell-bent on getting, what they hoped was an exclusive story on a very slow news day.

Helen's problem was she was simply lazy. She was noted for being a strong math teacher, but on this day her poor judgment gave all public school teachers a bad name. She often showed up late for school each morning, and at day's end, had the key in her car's ignition and was seen driving off campus before buses had pulled out with students aboard. She volunteered for nothing, particularly extra-curricular activities, and had now given the scarred public school system another reason to defend itself.

Principal Berling wanted Helen's side of the issue, in brevity, before WXBS-TV took their "story" on the air before 6 p.m. He needed to create a shield of damage control before his school, the place of employment entrusted to him, was dragged through the public mud unceremoniously. The once proud school had suffered enough through the years and this one story, he believed, did not need to be told. He did not believe his effort to be a cover-up on the part of the school. He saw himself protecting the institution from a very poor news source. If the story was told by WXBS-TV and their desperate need for ratings, one could almost guarantee it would portray the school in a very ugly manner.

Hero Status for a Day

At 6 p.m., predictably, WXBS-TV's anchorwoman Dana Shay, with a beaming smile matching the strand of pearl beads around her flawless silky-skinned neckline, led the news teaser with:

> *"Sex, drugs, and violence in the hallways of East Side High School. An exclusive up next at six, only on WXBS."*

Dana followed that up with a smile that gave the aura of professionalism, while the station "promo" played. Immediately after the silly introductory music stopped, Dana began her lead story looking directly into the camera lights and one-fourth of metropolitan area viewers.

> *"Sex, drugs, and violence in the hallways of East Side High School. Good evening, I'm Dana Shay and this is what's happening.*
>
> *"WXBS has learned that an East Side High School math teacher showed an inappropriate movie to students today that included film footage of sex, some violence, and drug abuse. The students involved: twenty-three ninth-graders so upset at the playing of the movie they, and their parents, complained loudly to school officials, who did nothing and attempted to cover up the story.*
>
> *"WXBS news reporter, Preston Swain, and his cameraman attempted to get that story and an explanation from East Side Principal, Adam Berling, but were denied and threatened as they were forced from that campus. Here's more on this shocking story."*

The tape began to roll showing Principal Berling waving his arms at the camera like a madman while Dick narrated the segment. The tape showed the principal moving toward the news crew, as the school office shrunk from the background, onto the grassy area on the edge of the campus near the boulevard in an intimidating manner. Dick's narration reinforced to viewers what Dana Shay had already noted. In short, Dick gained his retribution on Principal Berling in about twenty-five seconds.

Then the segment shifted to the home of the parent who tipped off Channel 8 to the story. There was Dick with his perfect hair, a change of clothing that included a purple shirt and loud yellow tie with his microphone tipped in Jay's direction. The story continued with Dick's narration and questioning:

> *"This parent, Jay Sanchez, was very upset that his daughter, who attends East Side High School, was subjected to what he termed, an unethical movie that possessed no academic value. He said that he did not want to speak with East Side Principal Adam Berling, because the man had a reputation for intimidating those who disagree with the way he conducts school business. When asked, Mr.*

> *Sanchez said he was appalled at the type of education that takes place at the school."*

Jay looked straight into the camera and replied in an indignant manner:

> *"I just cannot believe that this type of movie was shown in a high school classroom. Is this the type of education we are paying for? What was that teacher thinking? And why wasn't she teaching?"*

No sound bites from other school sources were aired. No explanation was allowed in why Principal Berling's behavior was animated. No explanation was granted as to why Jay did not follow the chain of command concerning this issue. From a computer-generated control room and with the push of a few buttons, WXBS-TV made Principal Berling's authority at East Side High School look just like they hoped they could—like a wild man quietly running an outlaw school trying desperately to cover up a story they were trying to deliver to a news-thirsty public.

To their credit, the news crew did go to the school board's central office. Luckily, they caught public school Superintendent Dr. Ralph Maddox as he exited his car. When questioned about the incident, one look told viewers Dr. Maddox knew less than nothing. Dr. Maddox did promise to further investigate. What else could he say? If the principal at East Side High School knew nothing, how could the superintendent be expected to know? If either of them knew anything they most certainly would have communicated their concern to each other. This obvious point never entered Dick's juvenile mind.

Dick's plot was clear on this day. He needed a story. He needed to embarrass someone. Something! He succeeded to the misery of teachers and administrators who toil every day with limited facilities and low pay in their effort to make a difference in the lives of a growing number of apathetic students, most hailing from impoverished backgrounds. At the station, Dick was granted hero status for a day.

The news segment was repeated on Cable Channel 12 seven times prior to the 10 p.m. news and aired again during that more popular time slot.

The strange thing about the entire episode was that the city's only daily newspaper never made an inquiry to East Side High School, Principal Berling, or the public school system. WXBS-TV's rival news station never followed up on their "exclusive" or tried to trump their news story with more details on the alleged incident. Only WXBS-TV ran the so-called story. That led those with credible intelligence to believe, rightfully so, that the high school movie incident was blown completely out of proportion. WXBS-TV never followed up on the story. It simply died as bad stories do. Unfortunately, damage was done to East Side High School's reputation. Principal Berling remained angry. He still planned a personal investigation and had a great deal of explaining to do to his superiors.

"Snakes is more like it"

Principal Berling addressed the school over the intercom the following morning. He knew many of the students saw the news broadcast of the movie incident, as did their parents. He was not interested in giving Channel 8 the information they needed, but the students and faculty, he thought, had the right to know what had transpired and why the school was being held up to ridicule.

When the morning tardy bell rang and the Pledge of Allegiance and voluntary prayer were completed, Principal Berling got straight to the point. He spent about ten minutes telling the students and staff exactly what happened concerning the movie incident and who was responsible. However, the teacher and complaining parent were never mentioned by name. He finished the announcement with:

> "...*Channel 8 is no longer allowed on this campus anywhere at any time. If anyone sees them sneaking around this campus, and that's what they are—a bunch of sneaks, snakes is more like it—then notify me immediately! If you are a student or a teacher and see their news van or anyone affiliated with that news crew on this campus you are asked to stop what you are doing and notify me without delay!*"

Principal Berling then finished the regular morning announcements.

"Are we not invited back to your campus?"

The phone rang in Principal Adam Berling's office at precisely 6:45 a.m. He was not in a good mood. He had arrived at school at 6 a.m., very late by his standards, and found graffiti painted on the side of Building One. Someone in the dark of night misspelled and spray-painted "Fuck the *Huricane*," the school's mascot, near the entrance facing the student parking lot. He had to supervise the school board maintenance crew's removal of someone's despicable, but sexually impossible, call to arms before much of the student body arrived. Principal Berling wanted to deny the artist the pleasure of bragging to his friends or admiring his work as arriving students were alerted to it. If the graffiti artist was not an East Side High School student, he wanted to rob the felon of his intention to embarrass his student body. After all, he knew his students could jump to conclusions as to who did it and which school they attended. That, in turn, could lead to an all-out graffiti war neither side could win or afford to fight.

"It's Channel 8 on line four, Mr. Berling," his secretary, Beth Wray, said to him through the open office doors. "Do you wish to take it? Or, should I tell them to call back at a better time?"

Beth knew Principal Berling well enough that when school property had been defaced, it was not going to be a good day.

"No, I'll take it," he replied. "Hold all other business, Beth."

Hold all business. That was a sign to all in the area code to stand clear of the possible wrath of the principal.

He got situated in his leather chair, picked up the black phone on his desk and placed it to his left ear. He then leaned forward and pressed the button giving him access to Miss Toni Alvarez, program director at WXBS-TV. He had been waiting three days for their return call and wanted to give the brass at Channel 8 a piece of his mind.

"Yes, this is Principal Berling," he said courteously into the phone.

"Mr. Berling, this is Toni Alvarez, the station director from Channel 8 returning your call," she said.

"Yes, thank you for doing so, although it only took three days for you to do so and *we* were the ones that needed to investigate *your* facts," Principal Berling chided her.

There was silence on the other end of the line. It was far too early to get ugly with her, he thought. That inevitable showdown would have to wait just a few more minutes.

"Mr. Berling, what could I help you with?" she said getting right to the point. Toni could smell a fight and no longer cared to attempt niceties with the man.

"Miss Alvarez, I am calling to tell you I thought very little of your report on our school a few days ago," Principal Berling said in a tone only he could use. "Your station did much damage to our school's reputation. I have had to field calls day and night from concerned parents over the last seventy-two hours about your accusations, which I must say are not as close to the truth as you all seemed to report it being.

"I've spoken with the teacher, the complaining student, and parent. I've gotten to speak with about six of the eight students who sat in that class on the day in question, although you reported many more were present. And now I can tell you what I think about this situation from an educated perspective rather than being blindsided by your arrogant news crew, who I must say acted in a very unprofessional manner on my campus—a campus I am charged with protecting and running to the best of my ability. Sending those two journalists, and I use the term loosely, to this school without calling me in advance, I believe, was an injustice. The faculty and I did not appreciate it, but I know that's the way you people over there always do business.

"You see, I spoke with the principal at Pope Pius High, Jean Lafitte High, and FDR High School, and they all tell me they have had trouble with the style of journalism your station practices. In fact, I understand your news teams have been forbidden from visiting those campuses again, and that now goes for East Side. Add us to your list of places from which you have been banished. Now, I'm through. You speak."

Finally, Toni got the opportunity to defend her station's actions. She cited the First Amendment and the public's "right to know." She bored Principal Berling with the "We are the gatekeepers of society" speech that made him chuckle on his end of the line. When she finished her long explanation he was not sold.

"You never did mention anything about your station's need to be accurate," explained Principal Berling. "You told me a great deal about having a right, but you said nothing about your responsibility! You do have a responsibility to be fair and accurate. I think you failed in both instances."

"I don't!" Toni shot back. "We report the news. Did that teacher show that movie in class?"

"Yes, she did, and it was wrong to do so."

"Then what is your problem with our report? We tried to allow you to speak your point of view on the issue, but you threatened my news crew, Mr. Berling."

"I didn't threaten anyone. I told them to leave. That's all. One of those punks told me to stay out of his way and he would leave when he was ready. Now, I have to take a great deal of nonsense from the school system, the state, foolish parents, and outlaw students. I do not have to take it from a group that *pretends* to be a professional news group. I expect more from you than that group, but then again, maybe I can't. As far as my giving a sound bite, I could not do so because I had no knowledge of what entirely transpired until as late as yesterday morning."

"We don't have to alert the world about when we intend to show up to get a 'bite.'"

"That's true, Miss Alvarez, but on a public school campus you must report to the office to gain permission to speak to or film anyone or anything. That's the law. I don't think you are above that, not yet anyway. We don't allow even our parents to roam the campus without permission, an escort, or a badge issued by the office secretary. That's standard operating procedure to protect our faculty and students! You understand that. Even Channel 8 must understand that!"

"I understand it to a point."

"Let's put it this way. Without a doubt, your station will be the first here if a student or faculty member is hurt, or God forbid, killed by a person who strays onto this campus. You people at WXBS would report on how easy it was to walk onto public school campuses. You would also report that administrative policy regarding strangers on campus was lax. You would and you know you would. So when I question your reporters on this campus, I do so following the guidelines set by the public school system and the state of Louisiana."

Toni Alvarez was quiet now. She didn't want Principal Berling to be right, but she knew he was. Saying nothing in rebuttal at this point did not hurt her reputation or that of the news station. Saying anything to this principal might. Principal Berling continued in exasperation.

"We can't win with you people," he said. "Don't you see the trap you've laid? If I protect the campus you make me out to look like a man out of control on your news segment in doing so—a man who was trying to hide something. If I let you do as you please, then I'm not really doing the job I've been entrusted to do."

"But we are the news media!" Toni finally responded with a touch of anger and resentment in her voice.

"On this campus, you are nothing more than an *intruder* until we give you permission to be a visitor," Principal Berling responded with conviction. "You can go to one of the malls, one of the universities, or one of the downtown office buildings and implement your style of ethics if you wish, but not here. The school system will back me up on this 100 percent. So will the Metro Sheriff's Department. I've spoken to them as well."

"Are we not invited back to your campus?" Toni asked.

"I'm not through," Principal Berling shot back quickly. "Where do you get off starting your newscast with 'Sex, drugs, and violence in the hallways of East Side High School?' I've had to address that comment more than anything that has come from your so-called report. You had the public misled into believing our student body was running around our science labs and English departments with needles hanging out of their arms while students pressed their bodies against each other!"

"That was our 'teaser.'"

"You call it a teaser. I call it misleading information."

Both sides began to calm a bit. They needed to. Toni was getting tired of being Principal Berling's punching bag, although she began to realize she deserved it. In turn, he realized he was treating her like he did new arrivals to boot camp back in the early 1960s. He knew there was nothing more to be gained from this unfortunate conversation. He said his piece. She was not anywhere near apologizing. He decided to take a different approach to appeal to her as a parent more than a news director.

"You know, Miss Alvarez, about 50 percent of our seniors went to college last year and earned TOPS, the state's college tuition exemption program for high academic achieving students," Principal Berling explained. "Every year since 1970 this school has raised money to purchase toys for the younger kids that may not be fortunate enough to get a Christmas present. This past year we raised, and our students volunteered to assemble, over 500 of them.

"Prior to each Thanksgiving day, we collect enough food from our faculty and students to feed over one-hundred families in need. We've done this much longer than my being principal here.

"After the September 11 tragedy, our students collected over $2,000 and personally gave the money to a New York City Fire Department official. No other school in this area did that, not even the private schools. And let me tell you something, Miss Alvarez, our students don't come from privileged homes. They really don't have a great deal of expendable income. So now I must ask, where the hell was Channel 8 when we did things like that? Where?"

All the program director at WXBS-TV could spit out was, "We weren't invited?"

Principal Berling became enraged as he screamed into the phone.

"You weren't invited here for the movie scandal, either!" he nearly screamed into the phone. "Since when have you people needed to be invited?"

The conversation ended soon after that. Like the war in Vietnam, the final score ended controversially. Principal Berling admitted his teacher was wrong to show the movie. However, he never got an adequate response from Channel 8 about how they conducted their business, a practice that severely hurt the image of the school and school system.

"Success is like perfume. Its fragrance is to be enjoyed. Not swallowed."

-Unknown

Late February—The Unclear Message

Head coach Debra Annison walked into a smelly locker room and past her belittled basketball team as they sat motionless. She then moved toward the water fountain behind the white-painted cinder block office wall and took a sip of water she really did not need. She was nervous. Drinking water bought her some time and was nothing more than a habit. She stood up over the fountain and wiped the drops from her lips. Out of sight from the team, Coach Annison leaned against the wall and sighed not really knowing what to do next. She had been a coach for twelve years, but had difficulty with moments like these. Nearby Coach Tory Leblanc stood in front of the team and said nothing awaiting Coach Annison's adjustments.

It was halftime and her East Side High School Lady 'Canes basketball team was tired and demoralized. They were losing to a powerful Jean Lafitte High School squad by twenty-nine points, 59-30. Coach Annison walked over to the girls who were sitting on two wooden benches situated in the middle of the room, one in front of the other. The white board behind Coach Annison had a defensive game plan drawn in black and red dry eraser marker. She ignored it. There was no sense now searching for halftime adjustments. The Lady 'Canes were beyond mathematical hope of winning the game. Strategy was no longer a factor. What was left of this game for her team involved the courage and determination to continue to compete.

It was a situation the Lady 'Canes had been in many times and Coach Annison was running out of things to say to her team. Furthermore, her players probably did not want to hear any motivational messages as they soul-searched among themselves. To their credit, they were a quiet team. They were not cursing and blaming each other. Their heads hung low as white towels covered various parts of their sweaty silver and blue uniforms. They drank fluids from plastic water bottles and waited for their middle-aged leader to emerge from behind the wall and say something.

Coach Annison walked slowly toward her thirteen players. She sized them up using their body language as a barometer. The team delivered a poor message to their coach as she spit out the obvious.

"Girls, we've been in this situation many times before and here we are again," Coach Annison said with conviction, but not without compassion. "I'll say it again and again because it's all there is to say. So here it is. You have two choices: you can quit and let Jean Lafitte continue to whip your ass. Or, you can play as hard as you can in the second half and gain a measure of respect. That's it! That's your only choices. I wish I could say something to make the pain go away. I can't. I'm not Jesus. We don't have the talent to play with that team, but they are on the schedule and the game is not over yet."

She paused long for effect and asked the team, "So what's it gonna' be?"

There was silence, except for the gym noise behind the locker room door. Nothing moved. No one stirred. Coach Annison, the school's first and only girl's basketball coach, understood her team was totally outclassed. In the gym, the girls could hear the laughter of about 200 fans, an overwhelming number of which were loyal to Jean Lafitte High School, even though it was a home game for East Side High School.

On paper, East Side High School had a girl's basketball team. That is to say they had uniforms, a gym, a few not-so-talented players, and a modest operating budget. They did not have, in any way, a competitive team or a winning tradition. Their future was as grim as the first half statistics Coach Annison chose to ignore.

The girl's basketball program at East Side High School was in rapid decline. The school had won only thirteen games in the last three years. Two years before they enjoyed their best season, finishing with an overall record of 5-15. Last season they finished 2-18 and lost games by an average of twenty-seven points. East Side High School's girl's basketball squad was merely a collection of physical education students who dared to play in the state's top 5A classification in a metropolitan area noted for fielding arguably the best girls teams in the state.

Opposing coaches shared the unwritten rule when playing East Side High School that the game, by halftime, would no longer be competitive and could be used like a scrimmage, in that a good deal of playing time could be garnered for second-team athletes who rarely got to play. Coach Annison and her girls knew opponents patronized them. They did not like it. They knew opponents considered them to be an easy win, a punching bag on their tough schedule. Only winning could change that image, which was unlikely.

On the other hand, when games invariably got out of hand the Lady 'Canes were glad to have opposing coaches use the opportunity to promote sportsmanship by playing those second-stringers. Understandably, the Lady 'Canes usually enjoyed better success during those second halves against lesser talented athletes. They still lost the games, but they were allowed to attempt and cut the opposition's huge halftime leads. After all, losing any game in the first half was tough enough. The second half was usually the Lady 'Canes only prospect of meeting with athletic salvation.

Jokes attached to their lack of athleticism by their fellow classmates were often brutal. Few fans attended their games, home or away. The Lady 'Canes played, more than anything, for fun and the hope that they could avoid being embarrassed. But the embarrassment was erasing the fun, and everyone connected with the team questioned its season-long participation. All Coach Annison could hope for during games was that opposing coaches extended sympathy when the contest and subsequent beating began.

That being said there was always one head coach who did not get it. Enter the Lady Pirates of Jean Lafitte High School, a public school in Baton Rouge's sprawling suburbs. Their head coach, Philip Wilson, was too young and arrogant to be appointed to the position according to most insiders. Since there was no rush by qualified applicants, Coach Wilson got the job by default. He cared little about that fact. He was proud to be the Lady Pirate's basketball coach often wearing his team's red and white logo on his apparel. At twenty-six years old, he was brash and cocky. His talent exceeded his ability to handle success.

Having played basketball most of his life, including at the college level, Coach Wilson understood what it took to be successful. He would use his knowledge to drive his teenage girls to be as competitive, even combative, on the court. His "take-no-prisoners" philosophy appealed to his young team. Having rarely experienced a winning season in a very tough district, Coach Wilson's first team under his leadership accepted his way of preparation. Even though that preparation was bordering on psychotic to observers, who could argue with his early success? The previous season Jean Lafitte High School finished with its sixth straight losing season. In his first year, Coach Wilson led his team of two seniors and an army of underclassman to a 9-3 overall district mark. They were a lock for the playoffs that began in one week. Their game with East Side High School should have been viewed as a tune-up for the playoffs. Petty vengeance on his part would not allow it to turn out that way.

Like most Baton Rouge suburbs, Jean Lafitte High School had growing pains. Its athletic advantage on the Baton Rouge public schools was significant. "White Flight" had permanently removed a chunk of the Baton Rouge public school system's future. It allowed attendance at Jean Lafitte High School to grow to incredible proportions by the start of the millennium. To remedy overcrowding, the DeGaulle Parish school system built a fifth high school, thus spreading out the student population of four existing schools in two rapidly growing suburbs. Some Baton Rouge public school coaches wanted to believe DeGaulle Parish's athletic programs would be less competitive with a diluted talent base. It did not. Three of their parish schools situated east of the Mississippi River competed well in most sports. They enjoyed financial and parental support, middle schools that continually fed them solid athletes, and a common sense approach to education that was absent in urban parts of the state. In short, DeGaulle Parish public schools were quite healthy in the classroom and on the playing field. The Lady Pirates basketball team was proof of that.

Although her team had improved a bit in the last two games, both road losses, Coach Annison knew her team was no match for the Lady Pirates. On top of that her relationship with Coach Wilson was strained to say the least. The two coaches exchanged words at a preseason meeting over the district tiebreakers system. The first-year coach humiliated Coach Annison in front of the other district coaches asking, "Has your program *ever* had to worry about tiebreakers in the district race?"Coach Annison responded telling Coach Wilson to "kiss my ass!"

Coach Wilson was serving notice to all, at the expense of his reputation, that he meant business. The other district coaches were not impressed with him, but on the court his team was a force to be reckoned with.

Consequently, Coach Annison did not know what to expect of Coach Wilson, except that she painted him as a brat. She did know if he could, Coach Wilson would embarrass her program on their home floor. Now, with such a huge halftime lead, she knew Coach Wilson would continue to play his girls unrestrained—something she chose not to tell her girls in the halftime locker room.

"Any comments?" Coach Annison asked with her hands extended. "Questions? Anything? Anybody? S.O.S.?"

Coach Annison, with palms up said, "Let's cut to the chase, girls."

She then pointed at the wall, "Right now, in that other locker room, they are thinking about the playoffs. They've got this thing won and they know it. Next week they'll be in the playoffs. For us, this is our last game. We've only won three this year. We're probably not going to win tonight. Not unless, Kobe Bryant quietly enrolled this morning and shows up in drag wearing a silver and blue Lady 'Cane jersey."

The girls snickered at that. They partially lifted their heads. There were some smiles. Some shook their heads. Humor can remove unwanted burdens, if only temporarily. Coach Annison even creased a smile and began to perk up. She pressed her personality for additional humor.

"Of course, if Kobe do show up I ain't gonna' be going home to no husband," she said in Ebonics while moving her head from right to left. "Sho' won't! Cuz' dat boy be cute. And he rich, too! Sho' is!"

The girls tried to contain it, but were laughing now.

"Yea, he is, Coach," one girl agreed as she stood to move toward her locker directly behind the benches.

"Coach, you crazy!" another said with calm affection.

The players recognized that their head coach would try anything to take the sting out of their twenty-nine-point deficit. It had worked. Even though they did not say so, they were grateful for the effort.

The team began to talk among themselves. Some discussed plays that were close to working and searched for solutions. Others got up to go to the bathroom. Some changed their undergarments. They were alive. The team did have a pulse. All good coaches know there are times when they should back off their team. Sometimes it is best to leave complex textbook strategy and fancy pep talks for another time. This was one of those times.

Coach Annison walked away leaving them to regroup on their own. She again walked over to the water fountain, giving her team some space. The Lady 'Canes of East Side High School were losing badly and were certainly going to be roughed up even more in the last game of the season. Coach Annison did not know what she was going to say to her players at the end of the game. For now, she had bought time for a team she hoped would not quit playing hard.

Her players gathered in a circle and planted their hands in the center where flesh met. Thirteen sweaty hands melting together into one brief show of verbal force they knew they could not back up on the gym floor. The crowd outside began to get more vocal. The sound system was keeping a rap beat as the Lady 'Canes chanted in unison, "1-2-3-Hurricane!" The team opened the locker room door and jogged to the free throw line on their end of the court as basketballs were tossed and bounced their way by student managers encouraging them to play hard.

Within minutes both teams were out of the locker room. The officials, sensing the route and possible hot tempers, wasted no time and gathered the starting ten players in the middle of the court for the inbound pass.

Standing and slightly bent at the waist, Coach Annison yelled out to her rejuvenated starting five while clapping her hands, "C'mon girls! Play hard! Communicate!"

Coach Wilson followed Coach Annison's call with instructions to his team, "Let's go for the kill!"

As the crowd settled into their seats, Coach Annison looked over at Coach Wilson who looked back at her and smiled. Coach Annison knew he was going to further humiliate her girls at all costs. What Coach Wilson hoped to gain from it, God only knew. But Coach

Wilson had his best players on the court when they took the ball inbounds and raced down the court for an easy lay-up.

The partisan crowd cheered wildly, which made Coach Annison look over her shoulder at the crowd and shake her head in disgust. She briefly questioned why the parents of her girls rarely showed up to support their offspring. It was ridiculous for a home team to consistently attract less crowd support than the visiting team. The Lady 'Canes were sadly used to it. Coach Annison accepted that fact, but could not comprehend it.

Coach Annison shouted and continued to clap her hands together hard, "No big deal, girls! Keep your heads on! Let's go! Set up the offense!"

Sophomore forward Ashley Wiggins tried to get the basketball inbounds for the Lady 'Canes, but the Lady Pirates were "pressing." Coach Annison was livid. Why were the Lady Pirates pressing her offense with a thirty-one-point lead, she thought?

The official held up his hand and blew the whistle, "Five-seconds! White team's ball!"

He then pointed to the wall under the goal signaling to Jean Lafitte High School that it was now their possession.

Ashley bounced the ball to the official who then tossed it to a Lady Pirate. The opposing player held the ball over her head and slapped it as a signal for her teammates to move into position. Someone set a "pick" and got their top scorer, Jeannie Didier, open for a three-point shot. Swish! The ball went through the net without touching the rim. The Lady Pirates were now up by thirty-four points, 64-30.

Ashley tried to get the ball inbounds again. She did not want to again be called for a five-second count. In a panic, she threw the ball into one of her teammates who was not really open to receive it. The pass was intercepted by Lady Pirate guard Tasha Landry at the top of the key. Tasha dribbled to her left and saw Jeannie wide open for a lay-up under the basket with no one guarding her. Tasha looked left and threw a "no look" pass to Jeannie who banked the shot in from about three feet. The Lady Pirates were now ahead, 66-30.

Ashley tried to take the ball in from under the basket for the third time in less than one minute. The Lady 'Canes had not crossed mid-court yet. They could not even take the ball in bounds. In those brief seconds the Lady Pirates had padded their lead scoring seven points.

Ashley finally got the ball to sophomore Jesse Barnhill at the three-point line in front of Coach Annison. Jesse immediately, out of fear more than anything, dribbled as quickly as she could to the mid-court stripe. As Jesse crossed that line, two Lady Pirates, trying to force another turnover, bracketed her. They held their hands up blocking Jesse's vision. Jesse picked up her dribble and looked for someone to pass the ball to. She saw no one. She then threw a two-handed pass over the two defenders and toward her teammates moving toward the Lady Pirate goal. The ball went into the air more like a jump ball opportunity more than a pass to a specific teammate. Several players went up to take possession. Bodies collided. One Lady 'Cane fell to the court. In the scramble Ashley came away with it and moved toward the Lady Pirate defense. Ashley was the team's leading scorer and felt obligated to make something happen. She passed up an opportunity to pass to an open teammate. Instead, she moved into the lane hoping to take a short jump shot. A Lady Pirate defender went to meet that threat and took a "charge" and then collapsed to the hard wood. The whistle blew. The official signaled charge against Jesse.

He then shouted, "White ball!" and pointed toward the Lady Pirate basket.

It was another East High School turnover. Coach Annison was now becoming more concerned about her team's morale than the opponent's score, which mimicked climbing Wall Street stock.

The Lady Pirates took the ball in at half court. The Lady 'Canes were already panting with fatigue. Jeannie took the ball up court toward the East Side High School basket slowly. When she crossed mid-court she began to sprint to the foul line where she pulled up to shoot. Closely guarded by Jessie whose hand was in her face, Jeannie passed the ball around Jessie back to Tasha, who calmly set up to take a shot just inside the three-point line. There was no defense to thwart that effort. Tasha took her time while the tired Lady 'Canes stood and watched in defensive position under the basket. Swoosh! The Lady Pirate lead was now, 68-30.

Lady 'Cane center, Lisa Cappo, then grabbed the basketball as it fell to the floor trying to get the ball inbounds before the Lady Pirate defense could set up. Lisa was taller and could see the floor better. Lisa spotted Ashley near mid-court and threw her a pass like a football quarterback.

"Press! Press! Press! Don't let up! Remember? Take no prisoners!" Coach Wilson yelled with his two hands funneling his mouth as he sat on the bench next to players whose uniforms were not yet sweaty.

It was then that Coach Annison wondered if Coach Wilson was going to play his backups. There were six girls in uniform who had not seen one second of playing time for the Lady Pirates. Was Coach Wilson going to play them at all? What was he up to? Coach Annison could not figure it out. Sure, it was her team's job to stop the opposition. That was true. But any decent coach with even a hint of sportsmanship, regardless of sport, usually played the backup players when so far ahead. Did Coach Wilson not fear injury to his starters in a game that was now hopelessly lopsided in their favor? After all, he had a playoff game in just one week. His strategy made no sense to Coach Annison.

While Coach Annison overanalyzed, Ashley hauled in Lisa's pass and moved down the far sideline. She was closely guarded. Ashley beat her defender to the corner of the court as then moved to attack the basket. The crowd screamed.

The Lady 'Canes on the bench stood yelling, "C'mon, Ashley!"

Coach Annison was on her feet having never sat down. Coach Wilson was now standing and shouting obscenities at his defense for allowing Ashley to get that close to their basket.

"Damn it, stop her! No one gets that close to our freakin' goal!" he shouted.

Ashley then moved off the end line and jump-stopped. Her thin, well-sculpted physique rose off the clean squeaky floor with her shoulders square and took aim at a ten-foot jumper from the side of the basket. The ball sailed through the net cutting the Lady Pirate lead to 68-32.

The whistle then blew stopping play.

The official pointed at a Lady Pirate and shouted, "Foul! Number 23. White team! One shot!"

Ashley pumped her hand in the air returning to the free-throw line for an extra shot. Ashley did not think she was fouled, but she was not going to argue.

As she moved toward the Lady Pirate free throw line, Lisa grabbed her around the waist and asked in a whisper, "Were you fouled?"

Ashley smiled and replied, "No, but we're getting whipped and we need the point."

Lisa chuckled, patted Ashley on the butt, and retreated to play defense with the rest of her worn teammates.

Then the controversy began. It was a controversy that did not need to be given birth. Had a more mature coach been in charge, he would have agreed to disagree with the official's call while realizing his team was going to win the game easily. Instead, Coach Wilson complained to the officials that Ashley was not fouled and should not be awarded a free throw. He was probably correct. Whether the official's call was right or not, no coach in any sport at any level has ever successfully overturned a controversial call with any consistency. In fact, it is very, very rare to force an official to admit a mistake. In this case, Jean Lafitte High School was beating East Side High School by thirty-six points. One would think Coach Wilson would just keep his mouth shut about a meaningless call of no significance in a game that had long lost any drama.

Coach Wilson was now standing and stomping his right foot to the floor for effect screaming, "I can't believe you made that call! That's a ridiculous call! You're an idiot!"

The official calmly handed the basketball to Ashley at the free throw line. The Lady Pirates stood on each side of the free throw lane with their hands extended as every team is coached to do. Ashley steadied herself as the crowd screamed at her to miss the free scoring opportunity. The longer Ashley took to shoot, the louder the gym became. Sportsmanship was absent even among some adults.

"Choke!" an adult in the crowd yelled at Ashley. "You're gonna' choke!"

Some Lady Pirate supporters were yelling in frustration at Coach Wilson, "Sit down, Coach! You're embarrassing us!"

Coach Wilson did not hear the remarks over the noise made by his own supporters.

"You're a sad excuse for an official!" Coach Wilson said as he stomped his foot again. "Damn sad! You'll be hearing from me! Book it!"

One official ran to the Lady Pirate bench urging Coach Wilson to keep calm. Coach Wilson waved him away as a sign of disrespect.

He then paced down the sideline cursing under his breath, "This is bullshit!"

His players and the crowd nearest him heard his every word.

Ashley missed the free throw. The crowd roared its approval.

Tasha grabbed the rebound for the Lady Pirates. She quickly moved up court and made a brilliant pass to guard Dana Hebert in the lane at the other end of the court. Dana turned, took one dribble, and released the shot that found its target. It was too easy. It was now a thirty-eight-point lead for the Lady Pirates and they were again pressing the Lady 'Canes.

Lisa tried to take the ball inbounds and could not find an open player. She then decided to call for a timeout. Lisa placed the ball under her arm and used her two hands to give the sign requesting a timeout. The official's whistle blew. Most of the crowd then stood and roared its approval for Jean Lafitte High School's Lady Pirates.

Coach Annison had now figured it out as her players ran toward the bench. Coach Wilson wanted to break the century mark. That is, he wanted to score one-hundred points on East Side High School and was willing to continue to play his starting five to get there. He was also out to teach Coach Annison a lesson. What Coach Wilson did not understand was that he also was failing to teach his players one. The Lady 'Canes did not deserve the beating inflicted on them by an upstart powerhouse coached by a man with a great deal of growing up to do. But that explained it all, Coach Annison thought. How could Coach Wilson teach his players character and humility when he did not possess those traits himself?

When play resumed following the timeout, Coach Annison watched in horror as her team turned the ball over nine more times in the game's final fourteen minutes. Coach Wilson continued the defensive pressure. He never removed his starters. His substitutes never played a minute's time in a game that begged their introduction. The Lady Pirates outscored the Lady 'Canes, 31-4, the rest of the way and won easily, 101-36.

When the East Side High School team and Coach Annison went to shake hands at the end of the game, the Jean Lafitte High School squad was nowhere to be seen. Coach Wilson immediately shuffled his team to the locker room and even refused to speak with Coach Annison, who had now bypassed angry and was moving into the neighborhood of indignant.

In a perfect world, Coach Annison would love to one day return the favor, but she did not have the athletes. Even if she did have them, she wondered if she was capable of lowering herself to inflict on another team what was inflicted on hers. The simple truth was Coach Annison might never be given the opportunity to confront that chance anyway, especially considering the way the inner city public school system was being bled of students each year. The few athletes who were available to participate in sports were becoming, in increasing numbers, academic casualties.

Time promised that Jean Lafitte High School would get even stronger in the coming years. Time also guaranteed East Side High School would continue to struggle mightily for even a shred of athletic respect; the school's better days having passed on. Instead, all Coach Annison could hope for was that Coach Wilson would eventually grow up to be as successful a person as he was a head basketball coach.

As fans filed out of the brightly lit gym, Coach Annison walked into the locker room glad the season was over. She and her players had done all they could with the talent they had. They had little to show for their effort. It was a humiliating end to another unsuccessful season.

Coach Annison knew that, given the political circumstances in the parish, she was going to be forced to redefine what success was in terms of athletic accomplishments. East Side High School's climate now dictated success as simply year-to-year survival. For Coach Annison it also meant a crash course in improving a halftime rhetoric designed to rally demoralized teenage spirits. She was growing tired of having to perform that task. At the moment, she faced having to make fifteen, sixteen-year-old girls comprehend why an alleged adult like Coach Wilson chose to humiliate them. She had no answers for them. That was an unclear message that left only questions.

It was now 7:35 p.m. Coach Annison's day had begun at 5:30 a.m. After speaking with her players, she would then have to spend the next hour cleaning up the locker room and parts of the gym. There was school in the morning and there could be little evidence of a basketball game played the evening before. When that was done, she then had to load her SUV with six of her players and give them rides home to neighborhoods over five miles away in various parts of the city. Coach Annison had to drop off the girls in dangerous neighborhoods at dark, and on her own time, because parents refused to pick them up. Giving her players rides home each day after practice and to games was her only way to keep the six girls on the team. Otherwise, the players would have to catch the bus home each day at 2:30 p.m. and never make practice. It was a tiresome task, but most inner city coaches in the parish were resigned to doing it for the sake of a healthy roster.

For all her effort and aggravation, Coach Annison received an athletic stipend of an extra thirty dollars per week. Divide that by the time she put into her program from October to early February and she was paid about three dollars per hour. That "payment" was typical for most high school coaches. Coach Annison did not mind it so much when she was single, but she was now a tired middle-aged mother of two. She still had to go home to play mom and wife. She was beginning to question if coaching was any longer worth the sacrifice. After tonight, she had to wonder if it was also worth the personal humiliation and that of her team.

"It's in their nature to choke"

Coach Wilson was angry. With one minute and three seconds remaining in the fourth quarter of his first ever playoff game, his Jean Lafitte High School Lady Pirates were being out-hustled by a veteran St. Mary High School squad. St. Mary out rebounded Jean Lafitte, had better free throw accuracy, and a higher shooting percentage. St. Mary also had a team with eight seniors and four juniors. St. Mary's only deficiency was they could never advance past the first round of the playoffs. Even so, they had been in the playoffs the last four years and knew how to handle upstart teams like Jean Lafitte.

That mattered little to Coach Wilson, who was now showing how much of a punk he really was. The bleachers at St. Mary's gym were still packed. One would think the crucifix situated on the brick wall directly behind Jean Lafitte's bench would limit Coach Wilson's usage of foul language. Not so. His team was losing by sixteen points, 54-38, and St. Mary had their best free throw shooter at the line for two shots.

Coach Wilson, seemingly dressed for *GQ* magazine, sensed his season was coming to an abrupt halt. He had performed miracles with his team completing the season with an overall record of 15-6, 10-2 in district play, and four of his players were picked first or second-team all-District. Two college coaches had visited Jean Lafitte in the last week to make it known they were interested in recruiting two of his players. The news media had taken note of his team's fierce style of play. Coach Wilson should have been proud of his team as the St. Mary player dropped in two free throws extending their lead to 56-38. Instead, he paced in anger, like a man who had been betrayed.

As the clock ticked down to forty-six seconds and a brief timeout, Coach Wilson sent five fresh players into the game who had yet to see action in weeks.

When his starters returned to the bench they were greeted by their coach with, "You make me freakin' sick! I thought you guys were tougher than that!"

His hands were on his hips exposing a silk red tie against a white pressed shirt. His lips were pressed together. He would not even look at his team as they plopped down on the bench in utter exhaustion. Their red uniforms were drenched with perspiration—their bodies exhausted. Their confidence was broken.

On the other side of the court sat a small Jean Lafitte crowd applauding and appreciative of their efforts despite the impending loss. It was always easy for the home crowd to act as good sports when their team was sure of a win, but the fans at St. Mary's had a reputation for always being gracious and proved so again by joining in the applause.

Coach Wilson stood near mid-court shouting instruction to second team players who had immediately turned over the ball, "Foul them! Foul them hard! Leave blood on the floor!"

Coach Wilson then lowered his head as he slowly walked toward his bench. His arms were folded as he muttered, "I'm not Catholic. I don't care about them."

Jean Lafitte's second-string girls were embarrassed for their coach. They could not even make eye contact with the St. Mary's girls as play began. Coach Wilson had prejudiced their public school image. He had justified the negative feelings of private school parents toward kids enrolled in public schools. In fact, he insured those sentiments.

Coach Wilson's players knew St. Mary's was the better squad. His second-string players felt like they should have been in the game five minutes before when the score still reflected a contest they could not win. Despite their coach, they were good girls and decent players. They did not carry out Coach Wilson's instructions to intentionally hurt St. Mary's players when play resumed. Coach Wilson sensed that and became furious. His players had never refused his instructions before, but they suddenly took on a mind of their own. It was overdue.

St. Mary's took the ball inbounds and moved across the mid-court stripe. Jean Lafitte's defense was set up under the basket, but St. Mary's point guard did not intend to penetrate the defense. She simply dribbled the ball alone near mid-court waiting for the clock to run out. The crowd was on its feet counting down the seconds.

"Eighteen. Seventeen. Sixteen. Fifteen…" the crowd chanted as Jean Lafitte's fans filed out of the stands.

Coach Wilson raced to the end line where his defense could hear him and shouted to his players who did not challenge the play, "I said to foul them! Foul them! Damn it! Do as I say!"

The Jean Lafitte players refused his instructions. The players acted like they did not hear their coach over the crowd noise, which made it convenient to passively object.

Coach Wilson was now on the court standing about six feet in front of the sideline.

"Don't act like you can't hear me!" he berated his young players.

"Nine. Eight. Seven. Six…"

Coach Wilson took off his tie and threw it to the floor. His behavior was beyond childish. The official moved toward Coach Wilson and pressed his hand in his chest to move him back to the bench.

"Coach, it's over!" the official reminded him.

"Three. Two…"

"Ref, I want a timeout right now!" Coach Wilson demanded.

"C'mon, you've got to be kidding?" the official asked in disbelief as time expired and the horn sounded to end the game and Jean Lafitte's season.

Players from both sides shook hands at mid-court while Coach Wilson was already moving toward the visiting locker room. He was not a good sport. He was a great coach, but a lousy leader. He knew tactics and strategy, but knew little about maturity. He could motivate his team with a degree of fear, but not with a season's worth of athletic success and comradeship. For every good point he brought to the Lady Pirate program, he brought unwanted baggage. Coach Wilson needed to tell his players to forget about the playoff loss and reflect on their many accomplishments. He could not find it in himself to do that for a bunch of girls who gave more of themselves than they had to give.

As Jean Lafitte's players filed into the locker room, they said nothing. They wanted to chat. They wanted to talk about the game, but they feared Coach Wilson. Success for them came at a very high price. Perhaps the price was ridiculously high considering their ages.

As the girls sat down for what they were sure was a post-game verbal assault by their tyrant of a coach, a voice interrupted the calm as unfamiliar faces entered the cramped locker room.

"Coach, could we see you for a minute?" a young male face asked with his body leaning through a door he was not anxious to enter.

"Who are you?" asked Coach Wilson as he stood in front of his team anxious to address them.

"The Baton Rouge *Daily News*" came the reply. "Coach, I know the timing is bad, but we've got a deadline and I need to get a quote. Is that okay?"

Coach Wilson walked toward the reporter. His ego would never refuse the media's request. As he stepped through the door, two additional reporters greeted him. With his back to the wall reflecting the bright lights from the ceiling, Coach Wilson could see a now empty gymnasium except for custodians cleaning up the floor in the distance.

"Coach, we'll make this quick," another reporter said, hoping the remark would put Coach Wilson more at ease.

"No problem," Coach Wilson said staring at the other end of the court.

Coach Wilson was a tall man and an impeccable dresser. His shirt was still pressed. His tie was still on the gym floor in the distance. His black tasseled shoes were highly buffed. There were creases in his cuffed pants. In his post-game personality there was mildew, scuffs, and wrinkles.

"Coach, if you would, make a remark about the play of your team in tonight's game," a reporter asked.

Coach Wilson stood over the shorter reporters and looked down on their scalps as he thought about what to say. He loved the attention. Addressing the media was one of his favorite things to do. It made him feel overly important and fed an ego that was hopelessly out of control. He cocked his head before speaking the words slowly.

"I thought we played as well as we could tonight," he began as reporters scribbled notes and extended mini-tape recorders up toward his face. He then picked up the verbal pace. "We had a great season and I'm proud of the way the girls handled it all. It was our first trip to the playoffs, but we'll be back. We'll learn from this and get better."

It was common coach-speak, but it was such an easy thing to say to the news media. Why he could not extend that overdue compliment to his tired team was simply unexplainable. Coach Wilson did not understand that people needed to be appreciated. It was human nature to want to be complimented when it was deserved, especially in young people. If a coach could learn to do that it made it easier to scold a team and push them harder when it needed to be done. He had not yet learned that lesson.

Another reporter asked, "What was your impression of St. Mary?"

Coach Wilson smiled, knowing that what he was about to say could be construed as sour grapes, but he was too stupid to care about the consequences of his actions.

"I didn't think too much of them," he said. "I would love to play them tomorrow. Hell, I'd play them right now if you could get them out of the locker room."

The reporters briefly glanced at each other while taking notes. The looks they recorded were ones of shock. Coach Wilson was a great quote, but he was careless. Being interviewed is something in which he did not possess experience and it was showing.

Coach Wilson continued, "I know St. Mary's goes to the playoffs every year, but they also fail to get past the first-round every year, too. They choked last year and they'll choke this year, too. They won't win next week. It's in their nature to choke."

When the brief interview was concluded, Coach Wilson turned and walked back into the locker room. Behind him about one-dozen parents and other supporters gathered to console their children and the team.

"Good job, Coach," one parent said as he patted Coach Wilson on the back.

"Nice season, Coach," another said. "We'll get'em next year."

Other parents politely clapped wanting him to acknowledge them. Coach Wilson did not look at them. He said nothing. He sent another poor message.

Coach Wilson was like some high school coaches who foolishly thought of themselves as being just a few wins away from coaching at the next level. It was especially true of football and basketball coaches who bounced around high school campuses as if the school existed because of their program. Their sense of self was terribly over inflated. They saw themselves as separate from the school, not a part of it. They labeled themselves more important than the librarians or the math and science teachers. They basked in the limelight every Monday morning following victory and reveled in the hallway whispers of teachers warning others to stay away from them following losses. These foolish coaches forgot their constituency was teenagers. They forgot their success was often tied to the commitment of school officials, ordinary teachers, and fundraising arms that made their financial burdens less so.

Coach Wilson's diligent efforts had quickly built the foundation for a strong basketball program. His negative words and actions to his players, however, were creating huge cracks in that slab. The parents standing outside that locker room were miffed. Coach Wilson was proving to be a problem.

"An education isn't how much you have committed to memory, or even how much you know. It's being able to differentiate between what you do know and what you don't."

—French writer, Anatole France

March—"I Finally Figured It Out"

Tory Leblanc sat quietly reading the Tuesday morning newspaper while Brent Masters poured hot black coffee into a small paper cup. The clock on the wall read 9:10 a.m. He was on a thirty-minute break and decided to spend that time in the teacher's lounge trying to wake up before resuming his duties as a test proctor. It was not a normal teaching day. In fact, the week was not to be normal in any sense.

The state of Louisiana designated early March for the mandated Graduate Exit Examination for high school students, a test of state content standards. Students statewide were in classrooms taking tests that, if successfully passed, would allow them to move to the next grade. The effort hoped to continue and monitor not only a student's academic progress, but also that of their respective school and school districts. Students need only score well enough to meet one of four categories: "approaching basic," "basic," "mastery," or "advanced." Only an "unsatisfactory" score would fail a student. Those results would be tabulated and studied, reports and recommendations made, and school districts hailed or criticized publicly.

It was a serious week and a nervous one for many inner city public school teachers like Tory and Brent. It was hardly fair to the teachers, but their reputations would be gauged on how the children they taught performed; a group widely regarded as the most underachieving and laziest in East Side High School history. They had the poor attendance practices and the suspension and failure rates to prove it.

It was the first time Brent had given the test. There was so much painstaking detail involved that it shocked the rookie teacher. Even one error, however accidental, could erase the results for each of the students in which he administered it. Teachers were required to stay after school the previous week for two hours, unpaid, to pour over the intricacies of the test with school guidance counselors. The GEE and documentation of its rules were lengthy and clear, but bordered satanic. Those rules were firm and hoped to ensure that no student gained an unfair advantage due to the ignorance of the teacher.

Brent sipped his coffee and stood over the table near Tory and a folded front page of the newspaper, but chose to read only one small front page headline: "Graduate Exit Examination administered statewide." Brent wanted to make small conversation with the veteran, a person he did not know well. Before he could, Tory took the initiative.

"Well, how is it going in your class this morning, Mr. Masters?" Tory asked the obvious.

"It's hard to tell, Mrs. Leblanc. I just don't know much about this stuff," Brent answered while sipping the steamy cup.

Tory never removed her eyes from the headlines as she folded the newspaper and leaned over an article of interest. She continued the small talk.

"As the years go on you will become nearly an expert at this, trust me," Tory said.

Brent thought about her statement, but knew he would not be teaching the following year, regardless. His first day of teaching was enough to scare him out of the education business and into something else, even if that meant working as a laborer on a construction job. Brent just smiled at Tory's remark, not wanting to tip his hand to that fact.

"Yea, I guess that's true, but I've got some kids who are not taking this seriously at all," Brent said hoping to elicit support and advice.

Tory put the newspaper down on the table and looked up at Brent. She pushed herself out of her chair and moved toward the soda machine situated in the corner of the room. She placed a dollar in the change slot, pushed a button, and the clumsy noise inside distributed to her a cold drink full of caffeine. Tory untwisted the top and began to move toward the table where Brent had now seated himself.

"I know it's early for a Mountain Dew, but you've got your pick-me-up in a hot cup and I've got mine in a cold can," Tory said with a grin as she took a big gulp.

Brent repeated his last statement wanting some sort of validation for the mere fact that some of his students were not spending much time on the individual questions. This, too, he had also witnessed the previous day. He was not experienced in the matters at hand and understood all too well the ramifications of the school's poor performance on the GEE the past three years. East Side High School was rated by the state as a "school in decline." There was pressure on the entire faculty to erase that pitiful performance, but the experienced teachers knew by the attitude and aptitude of the majority of the student body that their efforts were likely, once again, to be routed by apathy.

"I've got three kids who I have to constantly wake up during the early stage of any part of the exam," Brent told Tory in exasperation. "I wake them up and urge them to continue, but they just want to sleep. I've got another kid who, yesterday, took the first ninety-minute test and finished it in five. He simply filled in the bubbles on the answer document with his pencil and went to sleep. That's four kids in one class who are going to help destroy our test scores."

Brent paused, hoping Tory would comment further, but to her this story was a repeat of last year and the year before.

"You know, I spoke with three other teachers yesterday and they told me they are facing the same thing in their classes," Brent added. "Is it always like this?"

"Yep," Tory quickly agreed. "I have two like that myself and there is only so much you can do. I've got three students who are absent today that were here yesterday. I reminded my two sleepers that it's important to do their best and reminded them what is at stake for the school, but they just laughed and laid their heads down. What's important, I guess, is the rest of them are trying, right?"

Now it was Tory wanting reinforcement for the very same thing Brent was hoping to garner. He realized quickly that Tory felt as helpless as he did, but she hid her emotions better. A small group of students in any school refusing to do their best on the GEE could not outperform the hundreds who really tried their best. When two to four students in twenty to twenty-four classes refuse to take the GEE seriously, the school then has a problem of epidemic proportions. That appeared to be the case once again at East Side High School.

"All we can do is teach the ones who want to learn," Tory reassured Brent and herself. "I have to remind myself of the twenty-three in my class who are working as hard as they can to pass this test and move on with their lives. And those twenty-three are really trying. Those are the ones I want to focus on. I cannot save the other two."

With that, Tory once again buried her head in the newspaper. Brent knew her words to be true, but he knew without saying it, as did Tory, that the school would once again be ridiculed for falling test scores. It was hard for educated professionals like teachers to accept, but that lack of character and purpose on the part of many inner city students was a harsh reality.

Tory glanced at her wristwatch realizing she was just moments from returning to her class and another ninety minutes of testing when a medium-sized figure in a clean, crisp, uniform and hat stood in the doorway smiling directly at both of them. The figure removed his hat and tucked it under his right arm, revealing a military "high-low" haircut. His black shoes were shined and reflected the ceiling lights. His green trousers and tan shirt were creased and his tie was perfectly knotted. Tory sat up in her chair. There was something in the face that was familiar. Yes, Tory knew the face, but was not sure. As the young man in the uniform of the United State Marines moved forward, Brent and Tory both stood up. The Marine reached out for a handshake and Brent extended his out of courtesy now realizing Tory was the one being sought.

"You don't remember me, do you?" came the question from the smiling face in uniform looking at Tory for approval.

Brent said nothing. Tory peered deeply into the face of a young Marine belonging on a recruiting poster. His handshake was firm, his jaw was square, and he eventually broke into a light laugh knowing he had his former teacher's attention.

"Okay, I'll give you a break and tell you who I am," the Marine told Tory. "I'm Jason Reese. Now do you remember?"

Tory put her hand over her open mouth before lunging at him. She wrapped her arms around the muscular Marine whose two stripes revealed him to be a corporal in the toughest branch of the armed services. Tory's behavior was surprising because she really cared little for him when he was a student. When Tory released her hug, she backed away to take in the sight of the young man, one she thought she would never want to see again. Tory tried to compose herself. Her eyes were never more awake.

Jason Reese was the class clown from the graduating class of 2003. Tory taught Jason geography twice because he failed so many tests and his attendance fluctuated wildly. Jason was often rude to Tory and many other teachers because he craved the attention. He was thrown off the freshman football team because he missed so many practices. As a sophomore, he was a fixture at the discipline center, a place for habitual offenders of school rules. During his junior year, he dropped out of school—fed up with academic failure and the school's insistence on his compliance with rules. To his credit, he returned the following year. He should have been counted among the class of 2002, but Jason made it through high school, even if it was sliding through. When Marine recruiters made their appearance at East Side High School with weeks remaining in his senior year, Jason knew college offered him no asylum from the mean streets of his neighborhood. His grades were modest, he needed to get away from home and his dead-end friends, and a minimum wage job that was sure to be his in the absence of an education he was too lazy to fight for. In a leap of faith, Jason joined "The few and the proud."

"You look so good," was all Tory could say with her voice rising. "I mean, I am stunned looking at you! And look at you!"

Jason beamed as he told the story about his decision to enlist and how it was the best thing that ever happened to him in a life going nowhere. He had been a Marine for almost one year and was on his way to Iraq sometime during the summer, an infantry job he was trained to do and one he told Tory and Brent he was confident in performing.

"Yea, I mean, I finally figured it out," Jason said. "Those days I was here at East Side I wish I could take back. I mean it. I wasted a lot of time and I was too immature to listen to anybody."

"But the Marines got your attention, huh, Jason?" asked Tory.

"Yes, ma'am, they did. If they didn't I don't know where I would be, maybe in jail. But when I get back from Iraq I want to go to junior college and see if I can't do something positive there."

The two exchanged pleasantries while Brent listened. The conversation was cut short because the two teachers needed to return to their classes. Jason thanked Tory for trying to talk some sense into him, something he said he thought about many times lying in his bunk while in boot camp. For some inner city children, the military is not a last resort. It is the only resort. Jason, an undisciplined child, found a home in the most disciplined military corporation in the world. This student who did not like rules now belonged to a fighting machine whose success depended on recruits who followed every order without question. Jason found his niche, his confidence, and a home. Tory felt validated in a public school where success is measured infrequently. Brent learned that student success is not always defined by walking across a stage with a college diploma. More often life is like Irish author, C. W. Lewis, once defined education: It is "not to cut down jungles, but to irrigate deserts."

> "To take medicine only when one is sick is the same as digging a well only when one is thirsty—by then it is probably too late."
> -Chinese poet, Po Chu-i, 722-846 A.D.

March—Dollar Diplomacy

If the entire episode were not so sick it would be sad, but it was too sad to be sick. Incidents involving drugs and alcohol on high school campuses or while under the banner of "school activities" are not unusual in the nation today. It happens more often than school officials, public or private, want to admit. Teachers rarely know of it and administrators are reluctant to share the news. When occurring in private schools, it is swept neatly away in a place where no one, especially the news media, can learn of it. Therefore, the perception of private schools being "better" than public schools is sold. Most students on both sides, however, know the devil in the details and word can spread quickly.

Marcy Baxter was a wealthy child who wanted for nothing. She possessed a beautiful face accented by rich, dark eyes. Her hair was sandy-brown in color, often wrapped in a ribbon that fell to her firm shoulders. Her tanned body, even at seventeen-years-old, made even adult men stop and take notice. Young men vied for her affection. Even a simple "hello" from Marcy could carry some male students through the day believing a chance for a date existed somewhere in a smile she had become expert at delivering.

Marcy knew of her sexual prowess, too. Even though there was a strict dress code at St. Lucy High School, teachers knew from overheard hallway discussions among students which ones were promiscuous—the way they wore their uniforms was often a tip. Marcy had bought the promiscuous reputation. In fact, she reveled in it. She was one of the many recently leaving the public school system to, according to her parents, rid their daughter of "that element of society that is destroying education." It never occurred to Paul and Mindy Baxter that because their daughter and new friends were hiding behind private school uniforms that they could ever be involved in poor behavior.

On a field trip one cold, blustery early March morning, Marcy got on a school bus with twenty-four other students for a trip to New Orleans' French Quarter for a taste of the city's art and counter-culture. What better place to reflect and discuss lines, patterns, backgrounds, and architecture? New Orleans is dripping with such culture and St. Lucy High School art teacher, Diane Arnault, wanted to turn her students' attention to the world of art in a manner they may have never appreciated.

The school principal, Joseph Allen, approved the trip knowing he could not keep the students sheltered from the real world forever. Not to mention, a trip to the French Quarter on a midweek morning in March was not exactly going to display the weekend seediness for which sections of the Crescent City were infamous. Besides, the trip was not going to be overnight and there were two additional adult chaperones accompanying the group. Buses would depart at 8 a.m. and were to return to the school around 6:30 p.m., traffic permitting.

The only perceived problem with the trip was the return would be in darkness as daylight saving's time was still delivering the Northern Hemisphere sunsets around 5:45 p.m. Marcy knew this when she signed up for a seat next to her new boyfriend, senior David Boyle. The overwhelming number of St. Lucy students could be expected to uphold the reputation of the school and act as adults. Marcy, however, was not sure what she would be able to get away with in terms of unapproved activity, but she was going to keep her options open in an effort to keep her reputation as a "rich bad girl" intact. Life was too easy for Marcy and what excited others bored her. She was always hoping to amuse herself.

The students eventually took in the sights of New Orleans. They walked Royal and Canal streets, Pirate's Alley and Decatur Avenue, while purposely bypassing the immorality of Bourbon Street. They marveled at the people who lived among the city's shadows more than they noticed the French and Spanish architecture. Diane did her best to keep moving while teaching her students and keeping them focused as they stood on the Moon Walk while viewing the Mississippi River Bridge. Huge ships from around the world ducked slowly under her steel beams as they moved upstream to Baton Rouge, Memphis, St. Louis, and points beyond. Ships from the Midwest and Northeast packed with produce and steel made their way downstream to the Caribbean, Central America, or into the Panama Canal for trips to Asian ports.

St. Louis Cathedral was a must stop for the students and many of them, including the few protestants, were in awe of the beauty of such an old church just minutes from their homes that they had never visited. One student admitted aloud her wish to return one Sunday to participate in Mass.

The students walked the above-ground tombs in the aged graveyards, sat in the street cafes, weaved in and out of the ancient oaks lining Carrollton Avenue, visited the city's Catholic university, Loyola, and spoke with the designated locals about the history of the area. Overall, the trip accomplished its mission. Most students initially went to New Orleans as an excuse to miss other classes and get away from the monotony that was high school. But most students actually learned something about the local flavor while enjoying the freedom. Diane had made her point and had done her job.

The return trip was quieter than the morning run. Students were tired, and some slept. By the time the bus made its way out of the rush hour traffic and the bustling city lights past Loyola Avenue and onto the darkened Bonnet Carre Spillway over Lake Pontchartrain, the darkness summoned many more to sleep. Marcy was now ready to make her move.

Marcy and David began to kiss, which was forbidden under school rules. Although there was a school honor code, the church, confession and one's reputation to think about, neither cared little for any of that when Marcy reached into her coat pocket revealing two small bottles of vodka, an alcohol difficult to smell on one's breath. David looked into Marcy's eyes and smiled with approval before unscrewing the top. He looked over the seats in the bus, saw no one looking his way, and drank a large swallow before licking his lips. Marcy kissed him on the neck in the back of the darkening bus, took the small bottle from David's hands and finished the contents of the first bottle in one gulp. She closed her eyes and inhaled slowly wanting the buzz associated with vodka to embrace her.

"Hey, David, you think you could 'light me up' when we get back?" Marcy said in a whisper never opening her eyes.

"What do you mean?" David asked.

Marcy leaned over and laughed as she kissed David's left ear, where he had already placed a diamond-studded earring, against school rules.

David opened the second bottle and drank half before passing the rest to Marcy.

"Look, we'll have to wait until the weekend when my supply gets back," David said.

"Gets back from where?" Marcy asked, mildly interested in the underworld of adolescent narcotics.

"If I tell you, I'll have to kill you," David said before getting serious, suddenly realizing his joke fell flat. "Look, these dudes are mean and I don't want you to know anything you don't have to. All you have to do is smoke it and enjoy it. Okay?"

There was silence as a backdrop to David's reassuring smile. Marcy again glanced at David letting him know she wasn't taking that for an explanation. She was spoiled rotten and was used to getting anything she wanted materially. All she wanted from David was a simple explanation. That was certainly cheaper than anything she would have demanded from her mother shopping the many malls they visited when traveling California over the summer months. David picked up on Marcy's body language and knew he had to reveal more information. She was sitting with her arms crossed and feigning anger toward him.

"Marcy, all I can tell is, well, the guys that sell 'weed' to us are from the public schools and they are a scary bunch, so please let's leave it at that," David said. "I mean, they scare the hell out of me when I give them money. You know what I mean?"

Marcy looked directly into his eyes demanding more information, now more out of needed entertainment than real interest. David hinted a bit more at his source for drugs and the need for secrecy in his next sentence.

"These are thugs, okay? Really tough thugs, do you get it now?" David explained with his hands in exasperation. "I mean, if they get mad at me they will think nothing of taking it out on you. It's best you don't know squat."

Marcy's grin faded. Accepting David's explanation and plea, Marcy then went to sleep on David's shoulder. After two huge gulps of vodka, she was feeling her buzz and getting sleepy.

Within the hour, the bus pulled just minutes late into a dimly lit parking lot at St. Lucy High School that had seen a day's activity without the crew aboard. Diane, tired but pleased at her logistical success, immediately dismissed them. Some parents waited in running cars for their offspring to disembark the bus while other students moved toward their own vehicles sitting in the huge lot full of yellow parallel lines. Within moments, the parking lot was empty except for a few scattered brown leaves dancing in the cold north wind.

"Miss. Johnson, would you please send Marcy to the office at this time," the intercom blared to the fifth-hour geometry class.

"Could I send her down at the end of the hour?" Linda Johnson asked the unseen voice coming over the box situated above the white dry eraser board. "We are taking a chapter test at this time."

"I'm afraid I need to see her right away," the voice beckoned sounding like a terse Principal Joseph Allen.

"I'll send her immediately," came Linda's frustrated reply.

Linda Johnson, a large women in her late forties, was a no-nonsense teacher and did not like the idea that five of her students, grades notwithstanding, had to miss her class for what she considered a frivolous art field trip the day before. Marcy had missed yesterday's lecture that was prominent on today's test. Now, Marcy was leaving in the middle of the exam to attend to matters in the office.

Marcy slowly got up from her desk and moved toward Linda's outstretched hand to get a hall pass for a legal exit from Room 604. Many things raced through Marcy's mind. She had not been in any serious trouble before. She thought about her aging aunt in a Houston hospital suffering with cancer and thought maybe there was word on her health. Maybe, she thought, someone overheard her conversation with David about drugs on the bus yesterday. No, that could not be it, she thought. Everyone, and I mean everyone, was asleep during that time frame. She was sure of it.

Marcy's pace picked up as she thought out reasons why she was being called to the office in the middle of an afternoon test. This was not normal procedure. What could it be? She thought about David and wanted to pass by his nearby class to see if he had been called out, too. But the hall monitor would never let her pass through that part of the campus with the pass she possessed. No, she was permitted to go only to the main office. To make a detour now might get her in trouble. It may even delay her arrival to Principal Allen's office. If the school's hall monitors had to come looking for her she could get into trouble. The administration knew exactly how long it took to move from her class down one short hallway to the office.

When Marcy moved toward the office she could see her mother behind the glass that exposed a desk, filing cabinets, a computer, and two wooden chairs making up the small room. She could see her mother's profile and her look was one of disbelief. She appeared stunned and unmoving in the chair situated in front of Principal Allen's littered desk. Marcy gingerly knocked on the principal's door. Principal Allen waved her inside and motioned Marcy to take the empty chair next to her mother. Marcy carried a frightened look on her face as she sat down. Being spoiled and immature she immediately attempted to wrestle control of the situation.

"What's going on? Why was I called down here? I didn't do anything wrong!" Marcy explained knowing she was about to be charged with something far worse than anything she had ever done before.

"Settle down, young lady!" Principal Allen said in a rather stern voice as his hand was extended toward Marcy in a show of control. "You have quite a bit of explaining to do. We just hope the accusations we are about to discuss with you are false. In the meantime, you must know I have discussed those accusations with your mother and Mrs. Boyle, who just left this office. She was not happy when she left, Marcy, and I think you know why. You should also know your boyfriend, David, has been sent home."

Marcy was stunned. Mrs. Boyle? The drugs? The alcohol? The kissing? Her mind raced. Should she admit her mistake and take the punishment? Or, should she do what most teenagers are born to do when in tough situations—deny everything until the evidence is overwhelming?

"Marcy, at least three students on yesterday's field trip turned you and David Boyle into this office and accused you of drinking alcohol in the back of the bus," Principal Allen explained slowly.

It was true. Several St. Lucy students were quite aware of what Marcy and David did on the return field trip and told their parents of it, who in turn, informed Principal Joseph Allen. St. Lucy's handpicked student body was among the best of the lot. Although the school, like most, had its share of problems, the students at St. Lucy were an inner city public school teacher's dream. The majority of them were polite, religious, and cared a great deal about their future. Even though Marcy was beautiful and intelligent, many students resented her affluent background and the way she flaunted what they only dreamed of having. Privately, they cared little for her. They were not jealous of Marcy. They simply saw her as one giving the school a bad name their good judgments may not be able to erase.

Principal Allen didn't want to trip on his words. This was a serious accusation that would have tremendous ramifications on how the school monitors its student body and how and when field trips would be approved in the future. Principal Allen continued and looked sternly at Marcy.

"Marcy, did you and David Boyle drink alcohol in the back of the bus during a school-sponsored field trip?" he asked while looking directly at Marcy's face for any hint of remorse or guilt.

There was a long silence. Marcy's mother was disturbed awaiting an answer she thought she already knew the answer to. Marcy's brand of silence was used as some sort of defense in the event the adults in charge lost their intelligence in the span of twenty seconds or less. But Marcy knew she was guilty and caught.

She looked directly at Principal Allen and released an embarrassing, "Yes."

Marcy's mother covered her face with both hands. Principal Allen handed her a handkerchief not knowing what to say next. He had been in this situation before as a public school principal in the 1990s. However, alcohol consumption and school participation—whether on campus or off—are strictly prohibited. Period. There was no deviating from that fact. Principal Allen felt sorry for Mrs. Baxter. He knew, like so many parents, that she did not know her daughter's lifestyle to be

231

so reckless or she knew it and ignored the warning signs. Either way, he could only wonder how it must feel watching your child on trial for making a stupid choice. Principal Allen felt very uncomfortable with what he had to do next.

Mrs. Baxter looked up at the principal from her tears of shame and humiliation and asked in as poised a manner as she could muster, "What next? What happens to my daughter now?"

"Mrs. Baxter, with all due respect to you and your family, Marcy is going to have to learn a tough lesson," he explained. "This is not the kind of school where the parents of troubled students sometimes dictate their punishment to a disciplinary council with simple promises that they will learn from their errors. This cannot be ignored. You must know the possibility of termination exists. I'm so sorry."

Mrs. Mindy Baxter lowered her head in shame. She could no longer make eye contact with him or her daughter. Marcy and her mother both nodded they understood the rule. Mrs. Boyle then issued an apology to Principal Allen. He did not respond to the apology. He did not even glance in her direction as he scribbled notes while seated at his desk. A simply apology does not cure the world's ills, he believed. Principal Allen had to give Mrs. Boyle credit for one thing—she did not fight the accusation and make a scene. She simply accepted the fact her daughter made a poor judgment. Still, she pondered whether to call her husband, an attorney and school benefactor.

Marcy was instructed to return to class, a courtesy not extended to David, and await further instructions while Principal Allen agonized over what to do next. Mrs. Baxter had just learned in middle age, perhaps for the first time in her world of swimming pools, fancy vacations, and credit cards, that bad reputations eventually exceed apologies and cheap promises.

Principal Allen was polite to the Baxters, but direct. His words were exact. His words were the law. No lawyer or politically correct cry of denial could rid Marcy of the trust she violated. The school had rules—very old rules—and its standards were not just words as far as he was concerned.

Mrs. Baxter retrieved her arrogance for a moment, sat up in her chair and decided to challenge the school boss. It was a rash move, but it might just work, she thought. She knew how to win her way through life. Marcy learned well from her mother. Behind the pearls and expensive dresses, Mrs. Baxter understood manipulation. She had married well, lived lavishly, and drove a new Lexus that she parked on the family's 3,300 square-foot suburban Highland Hills estate. She now believed, in the company of this $50,000-per-year principal whom she did not really respect, that she was powerless in a world that, until yesterday, she ruled. So she made her move, although a pathetic one.

"For God's sake, Mr. Allen, a little drink is what we're talking about, aren't we?" Mrs. Baxter bluntly asked. "You never did anything like that when you were her age?"

Principal Allen was not comfortable with the question.

"I'm asking a simple question, sir," Mrs. Baxter repeated. "I drank in high school and I turned out fine. Can't we just counsel Marcy and let it go at that? This is so ridiculous!"

He chose not to speak any further. Mrs. Baxter was further complicating things in an undignified manner that made him shift in his leather swivel chair while he decided whether to call Marcy's father, Paul. He wanted the mother to handle the situation, but she was proving to be nothing more than comic relief. Principal Allen was not amused and suddenly understood why Marcy was such a troubled girl.

It was widely known among students and concerned teachers that Mrs. Baxter was throwing drinking parties at her home on weekends for Marcy's friends. The parties started out small with just a few of Marcy's close friends invited. Eventually the parties grew to include boyfriends, their friends, and public school friends, along with anyone remotely socially connected to Marcy. With the hard-working father often away on business, the parties grew so large cars were parked two blocks away from the Baxter home and the neighbors were beginning to get suspicious and complaining. There were beer, wine, and hard liquor served. On occasion, marijuana was provided, courtesy of David. Once, Mrs. Baxter smoked marijuana on a dare to the cheers of the teenage crowds abusing her family's Queen Ann living room furniture and expensive Persian rugs. This mother, acting more like a juvenile reliving her spoiled youth where anything was within reach, retreated to a cheap attempt at being popular with her daughter rather than parenting her. In Mrs. Baxter's view, it was better her daughter and friends drank under her supervision rather than from a bottle in a mall parking lot or in a dark city park where they could get into serious trouble. What Mindy Baxter did not understand was that her living room was no sanctuary from trouble.

Principal Allen did not know whether to believe the rumor, but it was clear to him Marcy had no positive direction except in how to wiggle her way out of embarrassing situations. This time, there was nowhere for Marcy to run. Or, was there? Principal Allen measured Mrs. Baxter's arrogance before deciding to answer her.

"I don't feel that way about that type of delinquency and I assure you David's parents won't feel that way, either," Principal Allen said as he rose from his desk in recognition of the additional paperwork delivered to him by the school secretary for a hearing on Marcy's transgression. "And no, I don't think it's just a little drink we are talking about here. We are talking about and expecting trust at a school that not only teaches it, but expects it of its student body."

"Oh, c'mon, let's stop the nonsense, can we?" Mrs. Baxter chided as she sat on the edge of her chair. "You sent David home and my little girl back to class. Why? Because my husband has bathed this school in money for the last decade. I don't recall you ever turning down a check made out to the school! Standards? What standards? My husband makes one phone call and this whole stupid thing goes away and you know it."

Principal Allen remained standing, hoping his comment would explain his position clearly. Principal Allen did not want to say anything that she or her politically-connected husband could use against the school. The best thing to do was to politely escort Mrs. Baxter off the campus and seek another opinion on his next move.Quite frankly, outside of scheduling a hearing on the field trip matter, he did not know what that might be. He then politely asked her to walk with him outside as an escort off the beautifully maintained campus.

There was nothing further he could suggest to Mrs. Baxter about her daughter's behavior if she was not willing to help him correct her. Marcy had to want to be saved. Drinking alcohol on field trips, drugs, cute boyfriends, and rich parents continued to outpace common sense in Marcy Baxter's world.

Redefining a Code of Conduct

Within two days there had been a not-so thorough investigation into the incident involving Marcy Baxter and her boyfriend, David Boyle. The Discipline Committee at St. Lucy High School, made up of a select group of parents, counselors, and teachers—both on staff and recently retired—decided to expel David Boyle for "conduct unbecoming of a St. Lucy student entrusted to uphold the highest social, moral, and religious standards."

David left St. Lucy quietly and enrolled at nearby East Side High School in mid-March of his senior year. It was easy for the Discipline Committee to expel David. David had been in trouble before at the school. Without ever mentioning it, the Discipline Committee knew that David's expulsion sent a message to the remainder of the student body without harming the integrity of the Baxter family. A below-average student, anyway, David was simply expendable in the eyes of the Discipline Committee. St. Lucy's solution would soon become East Side High School's problem. Private school castaways are common in public schools.

At St. Lucy, it was about the money. Everyone knew it. No one liked to speak about such possibilities publicly, but whispering reference always referred to examination of a family's W-2 form. Students hanging on the fringe of admission usually did or did not gain acceptance unless the financial bottom line had been scrutinized. David Boyle's financial picture was a very small number. His parents could not afford donations.

In reference to the incident, the school had to lay the guilt elsewhere. This episode was too painful for the reputation of St. Lucy and had to be dealt with quickly and harshly, even if that blame was misplaced. The administration found an easy target and Principal Allen's blame always hit the mark of where it was intended, even if it was the wrong target.

Earlier in the school year, ten students broke into one of the school's wings and entered two classrooms by breaking doorknobs. Once inside, they ripped down the posters belonging to teachers, used their considerable expertise to place viruses on thirteen computers, punched holes in the white eraser boards, smashed the glass to an overhead projector, and stole the "key" to several exams. Once the perpetrators were revealed, Principal Allen had to mete out student discipline. After meeting with the parents of the vandals, pressure was applied to ignore the incident for a sum of money to repair the damage. In the end, discipline was applied only to those not able to fix their name to a check made out to the school. Despite the religious theme of the school, the faculty was livid but said nothing.

The school also had a reputation for inflating the grade point average of its students so they could enroll in prestigious colleges and universities nationwide. Never mind that nearly 40 percent of those students flunked out of those colleges within one year; the numbers looked great in slick glossy pamphlets issued to parents considering St. Lucy as a place to enroll their children. Principal Allen played the game of perception well and was in his element when performing it. This was one of those times.

Diane knew all of this and was hardly naïve knowing the way business was conducted at St. Lucy. She could not be certain that those directly responsible would be properly punished or that those indirectly involved, like her, would be vindicated.

Not surprising, Diane was somehow found to be directly, rather than indirectly, responsible for Marcy's behavior, according to the Discipline Committee. True, she was the teacher on duty responsible for the safety and well-being of the students. She was the lone teacher representing the faculty. Diane argued, in vain, that somewhere along the way the teacher has to stop being responsible and the student must exercise some common sense. She pleaded with the Discipline Committee to exact the punishment on those who directly perpetrated the crime and, thus, violated the school code of ethics. In desperation for her credibility as a person and teacher, Diane also argued there should not be an easy way out for the politically and financially connected at a school like St. Lucy, an honest remark but one not taken well by the Discipline Committee. She knew the school went to great lengths selling a naive public on its stringent application of a high standard of ethics. Sitting stone-faced and quiet, the Discipline Committee refused her request or advice. In the end, Diane knew she had been sold out by dollar diplomacy. She could not compete there. Power without conscience always redefines a code of conduct.

No, someone else had to take the fall for the embarrassing field trip. Diane was chosen. She was an easy target. The Discipline Committee's bullet of alleged misconduct on the part of Diane Arnault sailed precise and bore a hole directly through her solid reputation. The only real thing Diane was guilty of was being too sleepy on the return ride from New Orleans to pay attention to the students in the darkness during each and every minute. The Discipline Committee agreed to let her finish teaching the remaining of the year informing her that they would "review your contract and subsequent employment at the appropriate time scheduled in early June." Humiliated, Diane felt utterly betrayed by those she thought would support her as a teacher. As she left the meeting of the Discipline Committee, Diane realized the religion preached daily to the students was from the hollow lips of a paralyzed administration she could no longer respect. But fear it, she would from now on.

Marcy's father, Paul, an attorney, again used his considerable financial influence to the benefit of St. Lucy. He hoped the "donation" would help the administration to rethink admonishing and removing his daughter from the prestigious school. No one knew the exact sum exchanged. In the end, his daughter remained enrolled at St. Lucy's.

Four weeks following the field trip, the school held tryouts for its cheerleader squad and Marcy was included in that number. She was smiling broadly during the color team photo that would be released before football season began the following school year. As a show of appreciation, Marcy's parents threw an impromptu party at the lavish Pelican Country Club in honor of the recently named members of the cheerleader squad. Many parents, members of the administration, and a few from the Discipline Committee were invited and present. The cheerleaders hoisted glasses of punch while the adults enjoyed red California merlot in a toast to St. Lucy. Everyone was emotionally touched when the evening ended with the singing of the school's alma mater.

"No one at St. Lucy is above the rules."

A day later, Marcy heard that her best friend, junior Tonya Krzewski, earned a two-day suspension because she was caught chewing gum and her white, button-down shirt-tail was not tucked into her purple and orange plaid skirt for the second consecutive day. Principal Allen delivered a lecture the next morning to the entire student body following prayer at precisely 8:11 a.m. Principal Allen wanted "to remind all St. Lucy students about their expectations at this fine institution.

"We will not tolerate such slovenly dress or behavior from our students. Dress and act like adults and you will be treated as such. No one at St. Lucy is above the rules."

Marcy thought how hypocritical the entire school apparatus was. She did not know whether to feel lucky that her father was financially gifted in protecting her or to squelch the laugh that was building in her firm, flat belly that held her button ring.

Lately, Marcy thought about David at East Side High School and wondered what he was thinking. Was he safe? Were the gangs beating him up and stealing his money? Marcy's image of the world was shaped by television's embellishment of everything. She knew what she heard about public schools and believed it all to be true.

Marcy's more pressing question was how could she see David again? At the moment she was forbidden to do so. With Marcy, however, there was always a way. For now, she would simply kiss mom and dad's backside for a few months, and eventually, they would get so busy making money, playing golf at the club, and running their business affairs they would again forget to be parents. Marcy was counting on it.

"No nation can survive an ignorant, lazy population. We've been living off the seed corn of earlier generations, but the bin is about empty. The evidence of that is the across-the-board decline in the quality of all of our institutions."
—The American Free Press, January 2006

Early April—Just Plain Vulnerable

Tory Leblanc opened her e-mail and remained perfectly still in her swivel chair. She had taken the first bite of her sandwich during the twenty-five-minute lunch shift when the words nearly assaulted her. As she slowly chewed, she read the brief, but intriguing message:

"Hey, girl, FYI, ESHS student arrested for burglary, resisting arrest, and assault of a police officer. See link below. Big surprise, huh? Margaret Sexy-ton."

Tory's best school friend, Margaret Sexton, sent her a message she was not sure she wanted to open. She clicked on the link provided and waited for her classroom desk computer to download the news. Suddenly, she was staring at the police beat of the Cityscape section of the daily newspaper. What she read was not uncommon for inner-city public school teachers. In fact, some teachers read the police beat as much as they did their lesson plans. Chances were they would know a student, current or former, who was arrested or killed in the hooligan playground in which they happily labored. The report read:

"A Baton Rouge youth was arrested Tuesday night by the Metropolitan Sheriff deputies for possession of a date-rape drug, possession of a firearm, and resisting arrest during a routine traffic stop on Interstate-10. The Sheriff's Department reported John Wilson, 17, was stopped on westbound I-10 near the Acadian

*Thruway exit ramp for speeding in excess of 85 miles per hour.
When stopped and questioned by deputies, Wilson's spare tire was
found to contain several pills of the date rape drug, Ecstasy, and
a loaded revolver. When questioned further by police, Wilson
became aggravated and attempted to wrestle control of one of the
officer's weapons."*

The report continued in two additional paragraphs, but Tory did not
have to read much more to know John Wilson's bad-boy lifestyle had
finally caught up with him. One thing was for certain as far as Tory was
concerned; John's desk would be empty the remainder of the year.

Students like John were scary and they were not in short supply in
the inner city public school system. Students with John's background
were afraid of nothing and no one. The choices between success or
failure and life or death were relative to many students. What scared
Tory more than anything was what John was accused of doing and how
he handled the police during questioning. It proved how potentially
volatile he could have been with her at any time during class. Tory, like
any other teacher, would not have been able to handle him.

Tory never realized how close she was to danger—a danger in *her*
classroom. John had a felony arrest record. Everyone knew that. It
angered her that the school system allowed "students" like John into their
schools and that some feel-good liberal judges allowed such dangerous,
unpredictable students into mainstream classes while awaiting court
dates. What could these judges be thinking? Public schools were not
pseudo prison waiting rooms. One thing was almost certain—those
same judges probably sent their children to private schools.

Inner city public high schools enrolled students accused of rape,
burglary, assault, car jacking, and drug distribution. An increasing
number were in gangs or had affiliations with such. They were in the
hallways and sat in classrooms with teachers unaware. More often than
not, it was the students who usually informed the teachers that felons
existed alongside Shakespeare and the theory of relativity.

Tory was just a thirty-year-old married history teacher. She took the
job as an educator wanting to help students achieve. The students she
now taught, however, were proving each day to be more of a threat to
her safety. Now, she wondered if she should add the word "vulnerable"
to her career resume. It was the way she felt. It was the way it was.

"Pop culture is on steroids now. It's bigger and badder than it's ever been. It's pervasive, inescapable and powerful enough to override good parenting...Any intelligent person who thinks today's pop culture is as harmless as yesterday's hasn't raised a child, or he has a financial stake in the continuation of the cultural genocide."
—Jason Whitlock, Kansas City Star sports columnist

Late April—"Next president, please"

The grass had begun to turn green and the distant humming of a lawnmower was becoming once again the song of spring. The trees and flowers were in bloom. It was not much of a winter for Baton Rouge, even by its own standards. The chirping of the birds outside the windows and the early afternoon sunshine splashing through the panes reminded Joey Martin that school was nearing an end. Although there were four weeks remaining in the school year, the sights and sounds of warm spring afternoons reinvigorated the soul of a teacher. Summer and its ten-week break were nearing.

Most teachers would admit the best part of any school year was the stretch from March until May. Most of the thugs that comprised parts of any student body had been tamed, expelled, transferred, or dropped out. What remained, for the most part, were good kids wanting to be in school, if for no other reason than to hang out with their friends. That did not guarantee teachers would be left with the best students, but the student body of spring had 122 fewer students than when school had begun in early August.

East Side High School began the school year with 1,086 students. By Christmas, thirty-four of those students had been expelled for various violations—most for fighting or possession of weapons or drugs. There was a sizable population of the school entering the month of January, the spring semester, with several suspensions and a sole remaining chance to stay out of trouble or be expelled. The overwhelming majority of those students would eventually get into some sort of trouble and find themselves expelled by the start of Easter break in mid-March.

Joey began the school year teaching 123 students in five social studies classes. By Christmas, his total class enrollment had dropped to ninety-nine students. In all, he had lost thirty-three students, but picked up nine more including transfer students into East Side High School from private schools—students enrolling from out of state, and magnet school dropouts returning to mainstream public schools. Students came and went so often it was hard to keep up with them. The school system was becoming more transient than ever. Instability ruled. It was part of what the school system had become. On one day a teacher could be interrupted in class by a student-worker sent from the office requesting a final grade and the number of absences for any given student that was transferring from the school. The very next day a teacher could be adding a student. The tumult would continue in spring.

Since the first day of the spring semester in early January, Joey's roll consisted of three students who never bothered to show up. One week later, he enrolled one student who had dropped out of the city's lone dedicated magnet school, two others from private schools, and two students transferring from out of state. By the end of January, Joey had to drop three students due to expulsions. Two additional students simply dropped out of school and two more quit to pursue their GED or Graduate Equivalent Diploma. One was arrested for possession of drugs with intent to distribute over the first weekend in February and never returned to school. By Valentine's Day, two students experienced severe family problems which forced one to move to another state and one to run away from home—neither to ever return. Three more moved to other school districts within the city and enrolled at other high schools. One student, only a fourteen-year-old freshman, became pregnant and "temporarily" dropped out of school. As the Mardi Gras season approached, Joey added two students who decided to leave Ascension Parish public schools for Baton Rouge. Two weeks later, they both dropped out of East Side High School to return to their former school. In early March, Joey added one student from another part of the state, but that student missed thirteen of the next fourteen school days before dropping out of school altogether. The very next day, two of his students were expelled for fighting.

The math involving student movement was enough to drive a teacher mad and it was common. To add insult to injury, Joey and his fellow teachers had to prepare this transient crew for the statewide mandatory testing, Graduate Exit Examination-21; a high stakes test in which the East Side High School faculty and administration would be held accountable. It was hardly fair to be responsible for the success or failure of such a motley crew, but little regarding teacher accountability in public education was. In addition, those test results had just been made available to the public and the numbers were disappointing.

To compound problems, now that GEE-21 examinations were completed, students believed they had license to miss as many days of school as they thought they could get away with. Students knew they could miss as many as ten days *per semester* unexcused and still remain eligible to successfully complete the academic semester. They knew exactly how many days they could miss. Many took advantage of the situation, which, in turn, lowered their grade point averages even further. It was not unthinkable for 50 percent of students at any inner city public high school to miss eight to ten unexcused days of school per semester. They walked that numerical borderline considered unthinkable by a generation of teachers who did not miss that many days of high school.

Furthermore, thirteen of Joey's students had missed eighteen days of school in spring or more, but turned in enough "excuses" to the office from home, most legitimate, that kept their unexcused absences under ten days. This semester's group was dangerously close to automatically failing his class because of such. Of those thirteen students, twelve were failing his class anyway, excused or not. Missing school was missing classwork, no matter how many letters momma wrote to the school office in defense of her child. Missing class, regardless of the reason, almost assured failure. There was a correlation.

Joey studied his roll book as the sun and shadows fell on his tired shoulders and found the situation tragic, but there was nothing he could do. Twenty-five students were absent from his classes today alone, which represented 24 percent of all his students. Eleven of those were absent in his sixth-hour class, leaving him just twelve students to teach. Ten of his students were listed as being in the parish discipline center for breaking rules ranging from excessive dress code violations to fighting. Two others were in the school time-out room for excessive tardiness to class. One student was on a school-sponsored field trip.

Earlier in the day, one male student dropped out of school for the second time in two years. He was eighteen-years-old, but still listed as being in the eleventh grade. He had not passed one test the entire year. His highest grade earned on any of the thirty-three, 100-point tests given during the entire school year was 41 percent. After many phone calls to his residence, not one of his seven teachers could get his parents to attend a parent-teacher conference—not once.

One female student was expelled for refusing to go to the office following a simple dress code violation and for not wearing her identification tag—a requirement at East Side High School. When Joey sent her to the office, she chose not to go. Instead, she blended into the late lunch crowd gathered in the grassy school commons area. That way, Joey would not know how the office dealt with her transgression. The office personnel did not know of her school violations and did not know to look for her. It was perfect. She had exercised this plan before and had gotten away with it. Eventually, one of her own friends turned her in and she paid a high price for it. Failing to wear the identification tag did not get her expelled. It was her fourth major "strike" in defiance of the rulebook and the school disciplinarian now had legal grounds to permanently dismiss her.

Another student who transferred from out of state proved to be more trouble than she was worth. Her grades reflected a complete disdain for school. She had grades of 'F' listed in six subjects except physical education, where she posted a grade of 'D.' She had been expelled from school and forced to move from California to Louisiana, where she did not want to be, to live with a father she had not seen in seven years. Her dysfunctional family hoped that the move to Baton Rouge would change her luck. However, students, like adults in the working world, created their own luck and usually caused their own problems. She was rude to Joey upon their introduction, refused to work on any assignment, and laid her head on her desk to sleep each day practically daring him to correct her. Joey had spent seven months training his students on how to think, study, and behave in class to the best of his ability. He was not about to have a late arrival with a chip on her shoulder disrupt it all in the span of just a few days. Eventually tired of her childish antics, Joey dismissed her from class twice in three days. She was suspended for four days, and ordered to enter the parish discipline center which she never attended. Therefore, those four days that were to be spent in the discipline center automatically became unexcused absences and her class work could not be made up. She cared little and then went on to miss seven of the next eight days unexcused. With four weeks left in school, she had earned a grade of 23 percent.

There was a young lady in his first-hour class who had missed eleven days unexcused and had not passed a test in three months. Her overall grade point average was a dismal 1.0. When Joey pressed her as to why she had missed so much school, she confided in him that she did not like to go to school. She simply rolled over in bed when the alarm clock went off at 5:30 a.m. and told her sympathetic mother she did not wish to go to school. Part of the poor test scores posted by many students was directly related to the failure of being able to arise in the morning and attend daily classes. There was no strategy to cure that. Her grade in Joey's geography class was an underachieving 46 percent. What's worse was that she had the potential to become one of Joey's best students, but chose instead to be painfully below average with her mother's blessing.

Joey did have a particular interest in one student, junior Barry Hines. Barry was the kind of kid Joey wanted to help because he thought he could. Every teacher wants to be a knight in shining armor to the students who care to learn and want to improve the quality of their lives. Most teachers want to "save" that type student, not just from a sick society offering too many bad choices, but often, from themselves. Barry had lost his father to prison when he was just nine-years-old for selling drugs. His father was released when Barry was thirteen-years-old, but returned to jail one year later on the same charge, except with the addition of attempted murder. Barry's father was now serving a lengthy prison sentence. Now alone, Barry's mother struggled like most single mothers to take care of her son, but he began to rebel against everything and nothing when he thought he was physically imposing enough to intimidate his mother into complying with his juvenile wishes. The mother became an alcoholic from the pressure. Barry, like an increasing number of high school students in the inner city public school system, had to fend for himself. Barry eventually befriended a suspected drug dealer even though he swore to Joey he had never experimented with hard drugs. His reasoning was the drug dealer in question loaned him the needed money. What scared Joey was what Barry might have to do to pay off that "loan." What's more, Barry was one of Joey's top students. Barry had posted grades of A's and B's throughout the school year. He often told Joey his American history class was the only reason he came to school at all. Barry's biggest problem was his mouth. Barry often verbally abused his teachers. By late April, Barry had cursed his English teacher in class, and had thus committed his fourth major offense—now being recommended for expulsion. Rather than telling his side of the story at a school board hearing and perhaps gaining another chance, he told the East Side High School assistant principal of discipline he was an "asshole." He was assigned to the discipline center until the date of the hearing that would either uphold or strike down the school's request. Barry's disrespect for the English teacher and the assistant principal was the last straw for the school and for Joey. Although Barry's expulsion was still not yet official, word among the students that knew him best was he would not return to school. After thirty-two weeks of solid academic achievement, his failure was now assured.

Joey then glanced at a name that had been scratched out in his roll book many weeks before. Next to his name and a date reading February 20, were the words "dropped out." Joey had never forgotten the story of junior, Rodni Black, who asked to speak with him in private one day following roll call. Rodni was a hard-ass on the street and one of the tougher kids in the school. It was said he never lost a fight. He once started on the school football team as a defensive end and had a reputation for punishing opposing quarterbacks and runners with helmet-ringing tackles. At six-feet, 200 pounds, he was the epitome of what a high school football player should be on the field. He played the game with the same zest manufactured on the wild, late night streets of his high-crime neighborhood. His grades-be-damned, Rodni loved playing football. It was his definition in life and he was good at it until his arrest during the football season for resisting police following a gang fight over drugs at 1 a.m. on a school night. Rodni was eighteen-years-old and classified as an adult. Naturally, his felony exploits made it in the police beat of the city newspaper and the football coaches were forced to drop him from the team in late October. However, to Rodni's credit, he stayed in school but achieved nothing during any given school day except eating lunch. By mid-January, he was nearing his trial date. Naturally, Joey found it strange that Rodni had fear in his eyes, perhaps for the first time in his life, when he approached his desk for advice prior to an American history class. Rodni told Joey of how the police were threatening to throw him in Angola State Prison for resisting arrest, his third felony. Joey eventually learned Rodni played the tough guy image during police questioning by refusing to cooperate until they threatened to do all they could to place him in Angola—a hell-hole even for the most hardened criminal. Rodni did not understand the legalities of the justice system to know that the police could not do such a thing simply because they wanted to. But Rodni listened intently to the probing of an angry city police investigator trying to clean up the streets of his drug-infested precinct under immense public pressure. Rodni had answers for the police they desperately needed and a bargain was offered. The police told Rodni he could return to school and have his latest transgression removed from his record if he turned against his gangster friends. Rodni knew that to cooperate with the police and inform on his drug-dealing friends could get him killed. Rodni was scared and did not know what to do. He turned to his teacher for guidance, but Joey was no attorney and was not his parent or guardian. To turn his back on Rodni, however, would be almost criminal in itself and Joey knew it. He told Rodni, naively, to cooperate with the police. As Joey recalled the sad story, he could see the vision of Rodni's tired face in his green and white-checkered roll book sheets full of names, dates, disconnected phone numbers, and below-average grades. Rodni's was a face of despair. Turning to his social studies teacher was a last resort for Rodni. With no real direction and no easy answers, Rodni chose to disappear the very next day after his gangster friends literally threatened his life after school the very day he spoke with Joey. Terrified at having a pistol placed in his mouth by a gang member and told he would be killed if he talked with police investigators, Rodni disappeared for thirty-eight straight school days. The police did visit the school looking for Rodni, but no one knew where he went or what had become of him. No one offered information to the police, either.

Joey also had five football players, three of whom were starters, in his American history classes. Not one player was passing despite constant pleas to the players by Joey, a coach himself, that their football eligibility was in jeopardy. The players did nothing to enhance their academic performance. With so little time remaining in the school year, it was mathematically impossible for any of them to post the grades needed to pass his class unless they attended and passed summer school. Students were only allowed to take two summer school classes and the five players in question were each failing multiple subjects. Joey could only wonder what their future football fate might be.

When Joey's depressed daydreaming was completed, he immediately went online to view the school and parish test scores. Just like the general public, teachers had to learn how their respected schools fared via the Internet or the newspaper. Word had spread on morning radio shows the GEE-21 scores would be made public knowledge today. Rumor among teachers for weeks was the scores were dismal. Although Joey strongly believed poor scores were not a reflection of his teaching ability or that of his teaching contemporaries, the public would disapprove of their efforts and he knew it.

As he scrolled down the list on the web site he found his school's GEE-21 scores had dropped dramatically after two years of modest improvement. Overall, the school composite score was not as bad as he had heard it might be. The school composite score ranked it sixth among the parishes' twelve public high schools. East Baton Rouge Parish public schools would again be ranked among the lowest in the state. There would be hell to pay for it. Joey knew teachers would be criticized by the public, the media, business journals, the state, the BESE, the school system and parents looking-even needing-to blame someone for the latest decline. Real estate agents could smell additional residential sales to the suburbs. Private schools could expect more interest in enrollment. Someone had to take the fall for the poor performance of a school system in dire need of respect from a population that was abandoning it, from prospective educators that taught in it, and from the media that watched its every move closely. Joey knew teachers would be targeted for professional humiliation—again.

The students, unbelievably, were the only ones seemingly insulated from the poor test results. Teachers would be accused of not doing their jobs and would shoulder the burden for their dismal testing giving parents and students the alibi they needed.

Certainly BESE member Leslie Jacobs of New Orleans would not understand the scores. In past years, she asked publicly why suburban Livingston Parish did so well with test scores, but urban parish school systems like Orleans and East Baton Rouge did not. She never considered that Livingston Parish, with some of the highest test scores in the state, did not have to compete with a private school on every corner and a magnet school sapping traditional campuses of their academic talent. Livingston Parish did well on GEE-21 because they ran an old-fashioned middle-class school system. There was no magnet school or private school leaking the best and brightest from its class rolls. East Baton Rouge and Orleans Parishes, facing extremely stiff competition for students from dozens of private high schools in both cities, were often left with few households of quality. Their students were bused to and from locations all over their respective city. Jacobs was again on record in the newspaper chastising teachers and disqualifying their efforts.

Joey did notice one bright spot in the test scores and wondered if anyone would make note of it. It was a statistic that would vindicate teachers, he thought, but it was unlikely to gain any attention because the media would likely prove too weak to mention it. Political paralysis would not allow it to be mentioned.

GEE-21 scores were categorized by parish, high school, and race. In the race category labeled "non-black" East Baton Rouge Parish test scores were among the highest in the state. Joey was pleased, but perplexed. The cause of the low composite test score in East Baton Rouge Parish came from the dismal showing of its black students. For teachers, this statistic proved their worth. They were working. They did care. They did follow state mandates. Despite all that was said about poor teacher performance in the past, and what was certain to be said in the near future, Joey believed it proved that some students were succeeding because teachers were doing their jobs. How could it be that non-black students comprising Arabs, Orientals, Hispanics, and Caucasians could score dramatically higher sitting in classrooms full of predominately black students? All student races sat in the same classrooms in the same desks with the same books working on the same assignments. They took the same tests and were expected to adhere to the same school and classroom rules. True, some black students would fare well on the standardized test, but why as a *group* did they traditionally score so poorly? It was hard to explain. Joey had a theory, but he did not want to share it aloud even if asked.

Joey knew there would soon be charges by special interest groups that teaching strategies were more suited for other racial groups than African-Americans. There would be more bogus charges that teachers were somehow different toward African-American students. It would be falsehoods, of course, but those special interest groups kept their jobs by selling fear to the masses looking to blame someone for poor student performance.

Even the East Baton Rouge Parish public school superintendent would take sides in the blame game against teachers. Dr. Ralph Maddox was a leader often in agreement with the side going with the wind. He found it politically convenient to sell out his teachers and schools to appease the screaming masses rather than tell the media the truth about lackadaisical student attendance practices and parental performance.

Joey knew for a fact that Southwood Middle School was so dedicated to improving their school performance score on the state's standardized test they assigned each of their forty-seven teachers phone numbers in which to contact the school's 900-plus student body. After school, teachers were instructed to phone parents or guardians and invite them to an after school meeting where they would be informed of the importance of their children passing the test, what failing it might mean, and how to assist their children in preparing for it. Sample test booklets would be passed out and explained to parents in detail. Teachers even baked or bought food out of their own pay to serve to parents during the two-hour presentation. The phone calls to those same parents were followed up with letters paid for out of the school budget. Announcements were made over the intercom in the morning for five straight days prior to the meeting reminding students to tell their parents about such an important function. The teachers and administration were not paid for their effort. They decided as a faculty it needed to be done to better serve their underachieving student body. On the late afternoon of the meeting, parents representing just seventeen students showed up. The teachers and administration of Southwood Middle School were, naturally, disappointed. As expected, Joey took note that their school performance score dipped for the second consecutive year.

East Side High School also made sincere efforts to raise the school performance score. Principal Berling ordered the departments of mathematics, social studies, English, and science to meet after-school three weeks before GEE-21 to formulate a plan to increase their school performance scores. No idea would be subjected to ridicule, they were told. Every idea would be carefully weighted. They believed themselves to be a bright, dedicated faculty, even if they were the only ones that knew it. Surely someone would percolate an idea worthy of a satisfactory academic game plan. The social studies department, which included Joey, decided to offer free tutoring services after school to any of the school's 184 juniors preparing for the high stakes test. The tutoring would take place after school twice a week for two weeks prior to GEE-21 and was to be taught by four of the six social studies teachers. Although only 16 students took advantage of the free service the previous year, the staff still felt it was worth the effort. Only two students showed up for GEE-21 tutoring this year. Of the school's 184 juniors, only two students thought the teacher's efforts to improve the quality of their lives was worth the time. The general public would never learn of that effort by the school faculty. Tutoring normally costs between fifteen to twenty-five dollars per hour, but this service was free. Teachers extended this effort because they wanted to help their students achieve. It would be criminal to label the social studies department at East Side High School deficient in their efforts to prepare their students, but it was certain to be done.

The bell rang breaking the peace. It signaled the beginning of the next class. Joey's slumber was jolted. He still had to teach despite his low morale and the current fever of truancy that had caught fire among the student body. Before he could properly collect his thoughts he stood up, leaned over his computer and logged off the Internet. He stepped into the hallway outside his door for duty, required of all teachers between classes. As the student body walked by the noise level picked up. Vulgarity could be heard, but it was hard to pinpoint who said what in such crowded conditions.

"You's a stupid, nigga'!" one male student yelled to another from down the hallway from where Joey stood.

"Hey, you fuckin' 'ho!" a female screamed.

"I ain't no 'ho!" came the angry response.

"Leave me alone!!!" a female yelled at the top of her lungs.

"Hey, yo, dog! Ain't worried about the 'po po. They can't catch me 'cause I be a gangsta'!" a male voice yelled to another with bravado.

"Po po" was the slang phrase for the police department.

Vulgarity such as "suck," "fuck," "whore," and "faggot" were still the favorites among a student body that also prided itself on slovenly dress. Many young men wore their trousers well below their backsides. They bloused their trousers military style into their untied sneakers. They wore wristbands with NBA and NFL logos on them and some tried, foolishly, to wear earrings they knew were against school rules.

Young ladies wore skirts that were too short. They stretched their tight shirts where they could be barely tucked in, but as soon as they breathed heavily or raised their hands in class, their navels would be revealed.

Two in ten students did not have or discarded the required identification tags. Joey, like many, once believed implementing a dress code would solve many of the school's aesthetic problems making it easier to identify students. It did nothing of the sort. Students circumvented the rules almost daily. It was a rite of passage. If the dress code mandated students could not wear sandals then they would not wear socks with their sneakers. If socks were required the students would not lace their shoes. If lacing shoes were required they would wear different color shoestrings. If they were made to wear the same color shoestrings they would wear different brands of shoes. If they were required to wear the same type and brand of shoe they would tuck their trousers into their shoes. The fight over trousers and shirts was even worse. The dress code was an ongoing battle that teachers and administrators were losing. Many teachers, especially females, simply quit enforcing the dress code, tired of the confrontation that usually followed. Teachers enforcing the dress code were called horrible names by students or chastised for doing their jobs.

A common response from students to teachers about failing to comply with dress codes was, "Miss Jackson saw me last hour and didn't say anything about me not having an I.D!"

Those who chose to be especially ugly would tell teachers as they walked away from them in a show of disrespect, "Get a life!" or "I'm sorry that you're bored, but get off my back."

It was enough for a teacher to want to slap the student. Most students refusing to follow the dress code were repeat offenders. Their punishment was rarely severe enough to drive the point home to them that they needed to follow the school rulebook they were given and signed during the first week of school.

Joey was one of those teachers who reluctantly compromised himself on dress code rules. He decided to enforce the rules in his classroom only. Whatever took place outside of his classroom concerning dress codes was of no interest to him. Tracking down students seen violating a dress code on the other end of the hallway usually involved a student with a bad attitude, sure confrontation, or taking the student to the office while he turned his back on the class he was expected to teach that particular hour. Joey wanted to handle only what he could. Despite his compromise, students called him the "Dress Code Nazi" because of his strict enforcement of the rule. One disgruntled student even wrote on the controversial Internet web site, "Ratemyteachers.com" that Joey was a "Notsi." Joey and his closest faculty friends got a good laugh out of that. Obviously angry with Joey, one student could not even insult him with intelligence, failing to understand the word of choice in that instance was misspelled.

As one young lady entered the classroom, Joey noticed her wearing "jeans," defined as having rivets or sewed-on pockets. Ninety percent of students wore the approved trousers called "chinos." But she was a repeat offender and Joey had to say something or else send out the message to other students he was no longer one of the teachers enforcing the dress code. As she walked past Joey, he could smell her perfume and watched her as she moved toward her desk. Joey then issued his concern.

"Miss Ardoin, what are you wearing?" Joey asked in a tired voice as she moved away from him.

Felecia Ardoin was a slender, beautiful sixteen-year-old who was popular and she knew it. She turned and asked the obvious question as if she didn't know. She looked directly at Joey with bright green eyes and a stunning figure to go with her light complexion. Her look was naturally one of surprise. The look on her flawless face was that of an angel. She could have been a model and certainly drew the attention of the boys. Her plea was one short on acting ability, however. The face of confusion and vulnerability may have worked in the past and probably did work on overly hormonal young men, but not on Joey. He had been teaching long enough to recognize what teenagers were thinking before they even thought of the words to release from their mouths.

"Coach, please don't!" Felicia asked in a begging tone as she placed her books on her twenty-two-year-old warped desk.

Joey pointed his index finger at her when he spoke to her more like a business professional than a sympathetic teacher.

"Miss Ardoin, you knew when you put those jeans on this morning they were illegal, but you did it anyway," Joey said. "You took a gamble when you put those trousers on this morning and you lost. Time to pay up."

"Coach, I'll get in trouble if you send me to the office," Felicia said and now the only student standing as others chatted around her, oblivious to the conversation. "The next time I get sent to the office, I could get expelled. I've been in too much trouble this year!"

"That is not my problem."

"You want me to get expelled?"

"Felecia, if you get expelled it's because of the choices you made—not just today but in the past, too. Not because I sent you to the office today. So, go to the office and see what they do, but you can't stay in here like that."

"But I'll get in trouble!"

"Then you should obey the rules like everyone else in here today. Take off."

Joey's finger was pointed at the door as he viewed her with stern eyes. Felicia picked up her books and suddenly had a change of attitude for the worse. She walked briskly toward the door before bumping Joey with her shoulder as a show of power knowing there wasn't much a teacher could do in response. The class noticed the act of defiance. Joey made a joke of it as the class looked on.

"I'd appreciate if you would not touch me, Felicia," Joey warned. "I'm a married man."

Felicia turned and looked back at Joey as she moved toward the door as if she wanted to kill him. She thought Joey had betrayed her. She was one of numerous females believing she could get away with anything with a pretty smile. The students laughed aloud at Felicia's attempt to intimidate their teacher. Joey's only line of self-defense in the situation was cheap words and the class knew it. Joey decided to make a lesson out of what transpired between Felicia and himself, even though it was very late in the year to remind students of something that has been common knowledge since early August.

"Guys, I don't like sending young people to the office," Joey told them as he sat down at his desk to call roll as the tardy bell rang. "I'm not on a power trip. Despite what you think, I am not here to push you around because I have the power to do so. Just do the right thing. It's so easy to live life that way. It really is. I have a dress code, too, and I must follow it or get fired. That's it."

"Why do they even have a dress code, Coach?" one young man asked. "I mean, it's stupid and has nothing to do with education. When I get in trouble, man, with the dress code, my parents think it's stupid. They don't even be mad at me."

The students grumbled in agreement. Another blurted aloud, "Mine neither!"

"Tell your parents the school appreciates their support," Joey said with sarcasm.

As he adjusted his chair, Joey thought of a better answer.

"Look, wherever you work in your life, and regardless of your profession, they will require a dress code," Joey answered. "I promise you any job worth having has a dress code. Construction workers, plant workers, secretaries, cashiers at grocery stores or fast food restaurants, doctors, attorneys, policemen, firemen, teachers, state workers, military personnel, salesmen, and host of other professions require uniforms. Even workers at Burger King and Taco Bell wear uniforms. School is not just about civics or math. It's about teaching you as much as we can about life, and life has rules. That's a fact! Get used to it. I have a job to do. You do yours, and yours is to be a good student and a better person. Too many of you are failing at that."

Joey paused for effect. He was just as good an actor as he was a teacher and he mixed the two well when need be. This was one of those times.

"Don't like that answer, huh?" he continued as he continued strict eye contact with his students.

Joey then stood up and leaned against the front of his desk.

"Let me tell you something, folks, in the real world if you violate the dress code there is no time out room or discipline center. Nope! They just fire you and replace you. Tell your boss that your work has nothing to do with the dress code and see what he says. You won't like it, and your butt will be looking for a job! And your reputation will follow you!"

With that explanation, the class became quiet. He could only hope at least one student agreed and got the message as he sat down to call roll, which he did quickly. He called out last names only. He never used a student's first name. Even in late April he knew very few of their first names. Students were called "Mister" and "Miss" followed by their last name and he expected and demanded they reply in kind.

Joey rose from his desk and was eager to introduce the day's lessons about John F. Kennedy's term as president and his subsequent assassination. Joey had a clip of the assassination he was prepared to show the class. Most students had heard of JFK and knew he was murdered, but the events surrounding it were not clear or known at all by students. This was a chance to introduce the evidence in the assassination of the president of the United States. Students usually paid attention to the JFK lecture and asked questions about the case in history that may never be fully understood or explained. The assassination itself was controversial, to say the least. Joey would bring out the known facts and let the students comment.

"All right," Joey said as he picked up a dry eraser marker. "Let's get out the notebooks and get started."

"Wait just a minute, Coach," one female said. "I'm not ready."

"I'm not waiting for you to get out your notes," Joey said unsympathetically. "We've been doing this routine since August and you guys still waste too much time. I'm going on."

"No, wait!" another said. "I'm not..."

Joey cut the student off going straight to the white board where he had the day's outline prepared. He reached out his hand to touch the blue eraser mark where the acronym, "JFK" was atop the list. Joey slightly turned, noticing Lartavius Hancock, a very tall student had nothing on his desk and did not appear anxious to do anything. Joey was already aggravated. Now his patience had run out as he addressed the situation.

"Mr. Hancock, please get out your notebook as I asked the class to do several minutes ago," Joey asked in exasperation.

His temper was about to boil and Lartavius either did not see the warning signals or did not care.

"I ain't doin' nothin' today, so get off me," Lartavius said with a calm demeanor that unnerved Joey.

"Mr. Hancock..."

"Mr. Hancock is my daddy, and I told you I ain't workin' today! Do what you gotta' do, but leave me alone, dog."

"All right, you can leave," Joey said motioning toward the door representing the seventh time this year he's had to toss Lartavius from class. "And I'm not a dog. If you're not Mr. Hancock then I'm not a dog."

"Whatever!" Lartavius said as he scrambled rudely from his desk and made his way out. "Do what you want. I don't care."

His ugly comments never stopped flowing.

Joey looked at his wristwatch again and realized this class was fast getting away from him. As Lartavius made his way down the hallway to the office he could still be heard talking to himself. Joey moved quickly back to work as if nothing had happened. It was all he could do. He then continued to make an attempt at teaching.

"His name was John F. Kennedy," Joey said as he turned to face the class. "It was his initials for John Fitzgerald Kennedy and he was the thirty-fifth president of the United States. He ran against Richard Nixon in 1960, whom we will talk a great deal more about later, and won the closest election in the history of the U.S. The election was a very close call for JFK who would go on to be the youngest president to ever serve at forty-three years old.

"JFK had three things going against him and one big thing going for him. Does anyone have any idea what they may be?"

Silence. Joey waited for about fifteen seconds for someone to speak up. Nothing. Joey began to pace the small classroom as he made certain everyone was taking notes, mandatory in his room each day. His teaching style was ancient in the eyes of those experts believing education today should be made entertaining, but Joey decidedly hated that teaching style he considered lazy. He was a teacher in every sense of the word. He knew his material and was preparing students for college or trade school where note taking was imperative.

Joey continued, "Believe it or not, there is prejudice by white people even against other white people in this country. I know we are programmed in society to believe that only Arabs, blacks, gays, and women can be discriminated against, but it's simply not true."

Joey told the class of majority black students about JFK's Irish-American background that did not sit well with many across the nation. He told them of his being the only Roman Catholic that ever held the office in the White House and why many Americans, including protestant Southerners and the Reverend Martin Luther King, did not trust JFK as a potential Catholic president.

Joey spoke of the public's appeal to JFK's youth. He told them of the presidential debate between JFK and Nixon that may have changed the minds of many Americans into voting for JFK and how television helped change American politics forever. He spoke of JFK's handsome features and his appeal to America's youth, a group JFK identified at that time as disconnected from politics.

Most students took the notes and sat eagerly listening to Joey, known around the school as an entertaining speaker. About six students took whatever notes they could, not really wanting to be thorough. They only wanted to take enough notes to keep Joey off their backs. Joey knew it, but could no longer worry about those few students hell-bent on being mediocre. He would not slow the class down for them this late in the school year.

Eventually, Joey got to JFK's trip to Dallas, Texas, on November 22, 1963, the final day of his life. He mentioned the many groups that the young president had angered with his civil rights policies and his being against the U.S. entering the growing conflict in Vietnam. Joey drew on the board the street design JFK's motorcade took that day and where the trees and people were lined up along the curb. He informed them of the location of the book depository and of Lee Harvey Oswald, who worked there. He told them of the errors the Secret Service and the FBI might have made that day making JFK extremely vulnerable. Joey had set the table and most of the students appeared interested. They knew Joey had a knack for grabbing their attention before throwing them a curveball. They never knew what to expect of him. Finally, Joey moved toward the VCR and continued to address the class.

"Watch this film," Joey ordered. "It is the only film known to exist that actually captured the assassination of the president. It was a film taken by a man standing along the curb of the street by the name of Abraham Zupruder. This film is known as the 'Zupruder Film" and is about thirty seconds long. We'll talk more in detail about how it could have happened, who might have been responsible, who was said to be responsible, and what many Americans still believe today. Watch closely."

Joey hit the button beginning the tape, stepped out of the way, moved toward the light switch, flipped the lights off, and moved where he could see and further explain.

On tape the 1960s-era black convertible presidential limousine with small American flags whipped slowly in the breeze. Average American citizens waved and snapped pictures as they called out the president's name. Although the color film was silent, there was much to anticipate. Then suddenly something hit the president in the head forcing him to grab his throat with both hands. The students said nothing. They were too desensitized by hours of violent video games to be moved by JFK's initial reaction to his injury. But when the second bullet hit JFK in the side of the head forcing the president to fall to one side as his wife, Jackie, screamed, the class groaned in unison and disgust, "Ohhhhhhh! Oh, my God!" Their reaction struck Joey. It was obvious they had *never* seen the Zupruder film before. Ever! What had they been doing and watching for sixteen years? This story was over forty-years-old and was obviously new to them. It was a sad commentary on the quality of their life, but Joey was glad to have been the teacher to introduce this lesson in history to them.

The film then showed a third bullet striking JFK in the side of the head. It was the most graphic of the shots aimed at the president. JFK's head blew apart. Again, students groaned. Some sat in horror. It was history that had come alive for those students. Joey was pleased at their reaction and concern. They showed that they did have a conscience and were interested in the subject. Subsequent comments by two students were not what Joey had hoped to hear. He wanted his students to be angry. He wanted them to hurt for the nation, even if it was retroactive.

"Oh, they capped his ass!" Billy Clayton said to another student reaching out for a slap of his right hand as they sat in their desks. The word "ass" was muffled as Billy covered his mouth with his left hand hoping the teacher did not hear it, but he did. Joey was not upset at the student's vulgarity. He was upset at the reaction of these two students over the assassination of an American president, one of the most popular and controversial presidents to ever live. The two boys continued to laugh. The class waited for Joey's reaction they knew would be swift.

"One dead president!" junior Marc Chevalier said aloud stomping his feet like a child in delight. "Next! Next! Next president, please!"

"I wish they do that to George Bush! Bang!" Billy added with glee as he held his right hand like a handgun. He joined Billy in showing his obvious lack of respect for the office of president, the nation, the class, and himself.

Joey rewound the short film and turned it off. He had to address this before moving on. Joey was good at making his point without boring students with tired phrases of, "How dare you! This was the president of the United States who was killed. Where is your patriotism?" Those appeals meant nothing to the majority of students owing their allegiance only to immediate self-gratification, materialism, and insatiable teenage tribal popularity.

Joey did not raise his voice. He was upset and the students knew it. He walked over to Billy, an African-American, and decided to direct his opinions and advice toward him, the instigator. Joey's voice feigned excitement. Joey could get down on their level, a place many teachers chose not to visit. But it could be highly effective if used properly.

"Hey, Billy, guess what?" Joey asked with a quickened pace without waiting for an answer in a dark classroom. "I want to tell you a story about a man that stood for greatness, freedom, and equality when others told him to shut up. Yea, they told him black people were inferior. They threatened his life, but he chose to stand up for his rights. He challenged

America to look at itself and improve while the world watched. His name was Martin Luther King! And you know what happened? They capped him!"

Billy sat quietly with his eyes opened wide not knowing what to expect from his teacher. Joey then busted out in canned laughter. He then walked over to Marc's desk, a white student and Billy's best friend, and pounded it with his right fist. Joey held his sides and howled in mock laughter. Joey was not comfortable feigning insult to the civil rights leader, an icon in the black community held in the highest regard.

"Yea, they shot him in the head!" Joey continued in a loud voice as he looked at Billy before glancing at Marc. He then held his finger like a gun and aimed at Billy before screaming, "Bang! He's dead! Shot him on the balcony in Memphis, Tennessee! Yes they did. Next! Next! Will the next civil rights leader please report to Memphis!"

Joey was roaring alone in mock laughter as students sat quietly wondering what he was up to. They knew there was a point, a punch line, and they waited for it. Then Joey stopped laughing almost immediately. His face changed from one of comedy to seriousness. He stood up straight as he stepped out of character. He then looked around the room at all his students. No one said a word knowing there was a point to his strange behavior.

"What?" Joey asked calmly with his palms held out. "I'm sorry. Did I offend you?"

Joey kept the room silent for effect as all eyes were turned on him.

"Oh, so the assassination, and the death of any man is really not that funny after all, am I right?" he asked the class. "When it was JFK being killed it was funny to you, huh, Billy? In fact, you want the same thing to happen to George Bush, right? When I mention King you got really quiet. Why is that?"

Joey placed his right hand on his hip and acted confused as he scratched his head.

"So, let me get this straight," Joey continued, "when a man gets his brains blown out it's really not that funny, am I right? I mean, this isn't a video game, is it?"

Joey knew by the look on the collective faces of his class, including two underachievers like Billy and Marc that he had made his point, albeit painfully.

"Can we move on now?" Joey asked the two with sarcasm, as if he really wanted their permission.

Joey hated to be disrespectful to the leader of any group or organization in the world. He prided himself in being open-minded and begged his students to look at both sides of any issue. He often reminded them there could be more than two sides to a story and deciding to take part in any issue could be confusing. Joey did not really care about a group's political affiliation, religion, sexual orientation, racial prejudices, or socio-economic background. He strongly believed every group had a story, a reason for being whether one agreed with it or not. When explaining the rise of Adolph Hitler's, Joey explained how Germany suffered more during the Great Depression of the 1930s than any nation and why it embraced the Nazis. He explained why communism was greeted as heroic in some nations and considered tyrannical in others. He explained the pros and cons of trade unions, China's Chairman Mao, and why some believed the United States and terrorist leader Osama bin Laden to be either the world's best hope or greatest evil. He wanted students to open their minds and challenge the status quo with intelligence. It was against everything he stood for to appear disrespectful to Martin Luther King, but it was just as upsetting to him to witness young American students, however cruel and ignorant, to laugh at one of the greatest tragedies in U.S. history.

Before Joey could replay the assassination of JFK and explain it more in detail, the bell rang to end class. Joey was now increasingly frustrated. His momentum had been disrupted. What should have been one of the better lessons of the year was not completed. Students began to file by Joey with their books in hand never saying a word to him. It was too much to expect an apology from Billy or Marc.

As the students moved toward the door, Joey shouted out, "We'll finish this tomorrow!" as if most even cared.

Joey was suddenly left alone in his classroom with twenty-nine displaced desks and paper on the floor left behind by a student population promising to keep Baton Rouge a littered, unkept city for years to come.

As Joey straightened the desks and picked up the papers he found himself exhausted. His teaching day was over at 1:30 p.m. He had taught five classes beginning at 7:05 a.m., had a mere twenty-five minutes to gulp down his lunch, and now was expected to be on duty in the school parking lot in just minutes. In his last hour he had to dismiss two from the class for breaking school rules or being disrespectful. It was the end to a tough, and frustrating teaching day.

As Joey glanced across the room he noticed one of his former students, sophomore Lacee Maxwell, just fifteen-years-old, standing alone at the door as students moved in the hallway behind her. She was obviously despondent by the look on her face and in need of attention. It was an unusual situation and made Joey uncomfortable.

"Lacee?" Joey called out in the form of a question as he picked up class litter. "What's wrong?"

Joey stood up with a fist full of white notebook paper in his hand. He began to crumple it up before asking her again why she appeared so ill at ease. She did not answer, appearing to be near tears. Joey taught Lacee geography the previous year. She was an average student, but never gave him any discipline problems. Most of all Joey liked her because of her sense of humor and the fact that she at least tried to be a decent student. The truth was Lacee was boy-crazy like so many other freshmen females causing her priorities to be unfocused. Joey had not spoken with her much this year and found it strange she was in his room rather than attending her final class of the day.

The tardy bell rang and Lacee was now late for her next class. So was Joey for his duty post. He moved toward Lacee who never made eye contact with her former teacher. Her head was shifted toward the floor never speaking a word. Time was short and Joey had to get to the bottom of whatever was wrong and quickly.

"Lacee, I have to get on duty, so why don't you walk with me to your next class, okay?" Joey said.

Lacee nodded in agreement and they both slowly walked into the hallway. Joey closed the door behind them making certain it was locked. Theft was becoming a huge problem for teachers and students alike. The only defense was to keep a locked classroom at all times. Joey already had an Adidas rain jacket and a radio/CD player stolen during the year already. He was going to do all he could to prevent a third theft of his property from occurring.

He extended his hand and directed Lacee to the double doors at the end of the hallway. He wanted to place his arm around her shoulder as a show of support, but Joey had seen too many teachers on the 6 p.m. television news in orange prison jumpsuits accused of things educators had *allegedly* done. Reputations and careers were ruined sometimes for some of the most innocent acts of kindness. Teachers were always guilty in the public eye until proven innocent.

Joey became a bit impatient. He pressed Lacee asking politely, "C'mon, Lacee, you have to tell me what the problem is. You came to me, remember?"

Lacee broke into a soft sob as she walked.

"It's my mom," Lacee said through the tears that began to roll down her cheeks. "She got arrested last night and…"

"She got arrested?" Joey interrupted before stopping in the middle of the hallway and looking Lacee directly in the face.

Lacee became more upset, "Yes, sir, she got arrested again."

"Again? Lacee, how many times has she been arrested?"

"This is her third time."

"What did she get arrested for?"

"Buying crack."

"Your mother is a crack addict?"

Still making no eye contact with Joey out of sheer embarrassment, Lacee began speaking very slowly, "Coach Martin, my mom's been smoking crack since I was in the seventh grade. Her boyfriend, or whatever he is, gives it to her for sex when she doesn't have enough money. They throw me out of the house when they want to 'do it.' We don't always have enough to eat and sometimes she doesn't pay the bills on time because she buys crack, you know?"

Lacee was over her emotions now. Her voice went more from trembling toward angry. She was speaking to someone she believed to be a friend as well as a teacher. Joey still did not know what she wanted from him, although her problems did suddenly explain a great deal about her average academic performance.

"Lacee, what can I do?" Joey asked Lacee shaking his head in exasperation. "I mean, I don't know how to deal with something like this. I'll do whatever I can, if I can."

"Coach, I'm hungry," Lacee said shyly as she looked over Joey's shoulder at the parking lot. "I didn't eat today and I don't have no food at home. I know the refrigerator is empty. Like, mom's in jail and she ain't gettin' out anytime soon the police told me."

"When did this happen?"

"They busted her last night while I was sleeping. I got woken up about, oh, three o'clock when they knocked on our door and arrested her, you know? I never did go back to sleep. I couldn't eat today because I been so nervous and scared. I don't know what to do when I get home. My grandparents are coming to get me this afternoon. Right now I'm just hungry. I just..."

She stopped speaking as two boys dressed in their baseball uniforms strolled by as they made their way to the rear of the school for the afternoon's home game. Lacee did not want the players to hear her story. She had enough problems and did not need to add social isolation or rejection to her list of problems. When the players passed far enough where they could no longer hear their conversation Lacee continued to speak, but Joey didn't want to hear anymore. He knew what he had to do. He reached into his pocket and gave her a crisp ten-dollar bill. He now realized being late for his duty post was secondary to Lacee's sad situation. He asked her not to tell anyone he had given her the money and urged her to use it to eat supper, not playing around with her friends after school. Considering the seriousness of her tone of voice he knew she would not. Lacee promised to pay Joey the money back, but he told her to forget it. Ten dollars out of his pocket was nothing to him. It was money he would not miss. To Lacee, it would pay for this afternoon's supper.

He decided then to walk her to the guidance office where a counselor could possibly help her in ways he could not. Lacee agreed to speak to a counselor, but both knew there was only so much they could do for her, especially with such late notice in the day. A school could only do so much.

As they reached the small brick building, Joey reached out to grab the doorknob to the glass exterior door of the guidance office and held it open for Lacee. He expected to sit with her as she explained her problem to the counselor that would not be surprised by anything she had to say—having experienced so many terrible stories during her eleven years experience. As both Lacee and Joey walked toward the secretary's desk, Lacee abruptly turned to Joey and asked him to leave.

"Coach, let me talk to her, okay?" she asked as she looked up at Joey's taller frame. "Like, this is going to be hard, you know what I mean?"

"Are you sure?" Joey asked. "I mean, this is pretty disturbing stuff."

"Hey Coach," the secretary said smartly to Joey as she looked at Lacee. "What's up?"

It was as if the secretary was inviting Joey to stay.

Lacee looked at Joey. They both stood still and silent. It was time for Joey to exit at Lacee's request. He patted her on the back and turned to leave. As he pushed open the door, he turned and wished Lacee good luck.

"Thanks, Coach," she said before turning to speak with the secretary.

As the glass door slowly closed, Joey could hear the secretary ask Lacee, "What can I do for you, Lacee?"

Joey knew the answer to that question might not be answered any time soon. From here, it was up to the social experts to help Lacee. Joey was now out of his element and not trained or equipped to deal with such issues, but they were becoming all too common as the years marched on in his career. He also knew he would not ever learn what would become of her calamity because it would very soon be labeled highly confidential. Unless Lacee told Joey of her fate personally, he would never know how it would be resolved.

Despite what politicians and so-called education experts sold to the news media, teachers could not save children such as Lacee. And there were lots of them. Their problems were too big, too complicated, and could only be resolved within their family structure, if they had one. If they did not have family, the problem became that of the state of Louisiana and its taxpayers.

Joey walked briskly to his duty location in the student parking lot about twenty-five minutes late. As he moved in that direction, he remembered a former public school superintendent representing another parish once telling one of the city's magazines that children should be taught with "an interest as if it were your child." The line sounded compassionate and was a great quote, but it was not realistic. What could any teacher really do to help Lacee with her problem? Joey could not take Lacee home and care for her. He did not have the financial resources to help her. He was not her family. Joey believed either the superintendent was a terrific salesman or was truly naïve. Perhaps the guidance office could phone that ex-superintendent and could offer insight and assistance. After all, with the superintendent's six-digit income and a $900 per month car allowance, he was certainly more capable of helping Lacee than Joey could as a $35,000 per year teacher and coach.

Joey was not rich and was not God. Joey would never be mistaken for one of the religious icons in the stained glass at church. He cared a great deal for Lacee and many other students like her. He sympathized with her greatly. It was a damn shame she was born to a mother not able to cope with a substance abuse problem. It was horrible that Lacee could have spent the night alone in a home that may or may not have electricity or food. If the superintendent really meant what he said about teachers treating students as if they were their own there would be better classroom discipline, higher attendance, increased test scores, and fewer dropouts, but only because there would be more discipline in the direct control of the schools and teachers. Joey also knew that possibility could easily be filed away on the public library shelf under "fiction." It would never happen. The superintendent's words were just politically correct salesmanship. Nothing more. Salesmanship and great quotes were not going to solve the problems of a generation of inner city students increasingly disengaged with civilized society. A teacher's job was not only growing more difficult in terms of academics. It was becoming increasingly frustrating to watch an army of high school students lose touch with their hopes and dreams before they reached their senior year. How could Lacey immerse herself in English composition with an empty refrigerator at home or criminals for parents? Teachers and schools are simply not armed to combat problems like that.

Joey opened the wide double door to the main building and entered with only Lacee on his mind. An increasingly common sight quickly jolted him. What once may have been shocking in the early part of his teaching career no longer registered as unusual in Joey's contemporary job description. Two male students were arguing over whom was going to beat up the other and when. As they yelled obscenities and swore, each was escorted by the scruff of the neck by male teachers telling them to keep their mouths shut, as they were disturbing classes in session nearby. One student had a bloody lip and was wiping his mouth with his right palm. While being dragged by lockers he wiped his blood on the hallway wall.

"Stop it, Kendrick!" the teacher warned him as he pulled him more to the middle of the hallway away from the lockers. "I hope they make you clean that up! You disgust me, son!"

"I ain't your fuckin' son, old man!" Kendrick told the teacher with an uneasy calm. "I ain't gotta' do nothin' but be black and die. So get off me! And I'm gonna' get that motha' fucka' who hit me, too. Don't nobody do that to me, 'cause I'm the big dog. I'm the big dog! You hearin' me? You hearin' me, Opie?"

Brett, Kendrick's white counterpart, from about twenty paces behind was being held tightly by another male teacher and responded in a more violent tone.

"Shut up, Buckwheat!" said Brett, as doors opened in the hallway and teachers and students peered out at the noisy display of false bravado.

A show that would almost assuredly get Brett expelled, he was a long-time troublemaker with an extensive record both at school and on the police blotter.

"I ain't scared of you, dog! I ain't scared!"

Brett once hit a police officer during a routine traffic stop for speeding. When suspected of possessing marijuana, he hit the officer in the chin with his fist and ran from the scene. Two days later, he was caught by police near his apartment complex and was sent to Juvenile Detention for a month during the last summer. For Brett, the court's warnings meant nothing to him. He took up residence on society's edge and liked it there. At age eighteen, his parents gave up on him and kicked him out of their house. Living with three other young men in a cramped one-bedroom apartment, Brett was still in the eleventh grade and failing three of seven classes. It was now likely the school would permanently dismiss him with the blessing of the school system. The system was also to blame for Brett's poor behavior. In middle school, he got into a fight with a student and pushed a young female teacher against a locker and to the ground when she tried to intervene. What did Brett get for assaulting a teacher? He was suspended for two days.

In general, Kendrick was no angel. He was a below-average student, but the only trouble he caused at school was having difficulty making it to class on time. He had been sent to the time out room four times already this year for class tardies. So, it was quite a shock to the teachers he was behaving so poorly as he was escorted to the office for fighting.

Joey kept walking. He was not the least bit interested as to why the two fought, although he was told as he scurried toward the parking lot that Kendrick and Brett actually began fighting in the classroom before it spilled into the hallway. The particulars would normally be of some interest to Joey, but on this day his concern was for the teachers nationwide where this type of behavior was becoming all too common. He had once read an article noting that one in four public school teachers could expect to be physically assaulted at least once before retirement. Joey could only wonder when it would be his turn.

As Joey moved outside and along the sidewalk to his duty location, he could hear in the distance the bumping against the ground. More problems. Damn! Would the day's absurd issues ever slow down? Wasn't it enough his last class of the day was a catastrophe? Wasn't it disturbing enough that a former student came to him desperate and as a last resort in a life that was spinning out of control?

The closer Joey got to the parking lot the more he recognized the noise as bass from a speaker. The noise had to be disturbing several classes that were being taught in close proximity. As Joey moved into the parking lot, he stood on the curb with the sun in his eyes overlooking about seventy-five cars. It did not take long to identify the vehicle from which the so-called music came. Joey stepped off the curb and rehearsed what he would tell the occupant he could now see bobbing his braided hair inside. He was a white male with two earrings and a large tattoo on his left bicep seen through the driver's side window. He appeared to be about thirty to forty-years-old. He was either a parent or a guardian waiting to pick up a student. Joey found that disturbing in its own right.

There was no rule against a person of any age waiting to pick up a student at the end of the school day. There was, however, a rule against the occupant of a vehicle on campus playing music so loud it defeated the ability of teachers in classes nearby from performing their duties. Teachers often complained about late afternoon "concerts" from the parking lot, but they were not going to leave their classes to deal with the matter. It was Joey's job at the end of the day to quell this type of disturbance and it was a scary thing to do. Almost always, people agreed to turn the music down when asked. It was shameful they did not possess the common sense to know they might be disturbing the school. Joey thought them deaf, ignorant or just unsympathetic. Joey also never knew if and when a deranged individual might pull a pistol on him, start a fight, or verbally abuse him. So far, he had been lucky. Regardless, it was important to always be polite to people and hope the situation could be resolved peacefully.

As Joey moved closer to the late 1990s black SUV, he could see the occupant make eye contact with him. Joey could now hear the lyrics more clearly and was not surprised by the vulgarity a generation of so-called entertainers and fans called music. The beat was unmistakable as it thudded against the pavement. It was ear piercing and reminded Joey to take his next paycheck and invest it in a corporation manufacturing hearing aids. Along with teaching sign language, Joey was convinced hearing aid products were the business of the future. Based on the lyrics, Joey continued his belief that rap was the enemy of civility.

> *"I'll take you to the candy shop,*
> *I'll let you lick the lollypop,*
> *Give you a taste of what I got,*
> *Keep going 'till you hit the spot,*
> *Whoa!"*

Joey smiled as he motioned to the driver with his hand to roll down his window. The noise continued.

"Hi," Joey said over the excessive decibels.

There was no response. Just a look from the driver as if he were oblivious to the problem he was causing on school grounds.

"Sir, I have to ask you to turn down your music," Joey said as politely as he could muster without showing the fear that churned in his stomach. "It's disturbing several classes and we still have about ten minutes of school remaining. Okay?"

The driver immediately looked away, turned the music down, looked at Joey with disdain and said to him, "Whatever."

He then rolled up his automatic window. No apology. No sign of being from a civilized planet or society; just a "whatever" comment and a disinterested look. Joey could care less about what the man said. He was only glad the music was turned down and he lived to finish the day. Parents sometimes could be as ignorant as their offspring. They could be as rude and uncompromising as any teenager sent to the office for disrupting a class. Too many parents were slightly better in matters concerning self-control than the students. This particular parent was listening to loud, vulgar music in the parking lot of a public high school and cared very little that he had caused a disturbance. That thought meant nothing to him. It would mean even less in the future to the child he was allegedly rearing.

Joey walked back to the curb of the sidewalk slowly. He glanced around looking for suspicious activity and it did not take long to spot it. He sighed as he looked with his peripheral vision at the second floor of a building about one-hundred yards from him. Joey noticed three male students hiding in the stairwell. It would have been impossible to spot them had they not been so noisy. They were not supposed to be there. Every student was expected to be in class. There had to be an explanation, but Joey had to move as quickly as he did cautiously. They could blend into the student body and be lost if the bell rang before he could catch them. Joey could not afford to be seen either, or they would run from him faster than he could blink. It was a game of cat and mouse—a man his age was too old to play, but it had to be played and won. Joey always felt like a child in matters such as these. How many men his age were sitting in offices wearing neckties answering e-mails and taking long distance phone calls for corporations? How many were working with other adults on construction jobs, at chemical plants, or involved in sales and marketing sessions? They were serious people with what many would consider serious jobs. Here Joey was trying to outwit three teenage boys in a school stairwell with only minutes remaining in a tired day. It was part of his job title to play this game he was playing, but there was something degrading and insulting about it, too.

Joey moved toward a different building acting as if he saw nothing. As he made his way under the covered crosswalk, he knew the boys could no longer see him. Joey then quickly made his way to the building where the boys were. They never saw Joey coming. By the time they did they were caught. As Joey approached them they were startled.

"Hey guys!" Joey said in an intimidating voice. "What are you doing here and why are you not in class?"

With that question, one student took off running so quickly he could have made the U.S. Olympic track team. Joey did not give chase in fear of losing the other two. He moved in closer to them and grabbed their identification tags from their necks in case they decided to run away or lie about their names. Joey did not have time to take them to the office with the bell about three minutes from ending the day. He also knew all he needed to do was turn in their names to the assistant principal for discipline and he would investigate why they were skipping class, where they were supposed to be, and who the idiot was that ran from Joey. There was no time for any investigation at this moment and Joey was too tired to pursue the incident any further.

"Seth Johnston and Carver Mandel, huh?" Joey said as he read and took their tags from them without even asking. "Well, you can pick these up in the office tomorrow morning. You've got some explaining to do. You know you can't be out of class until the bell rings. So, why are you not in class?"

They said nothing. They did not even appear the least bit sorry they were caught out of class. Seth, the smaller student, carried a smirk on his face as Joey looked at his wristwatch for the time remaining in the school day. Carver, a husky kid with two gold front teeth, looked only slightly regretful. Joey spoke to Seth who acted as if nothing would really happen to him today, tomorrow, or ever. He was one of a number of students believing themselves to be bullet proof. Seth behaved as if he knew something Joey did not, perhaps hoping he could cause Joey to rethink his performance on duty as a waste of time. Joey hated these kinds of kids. They possessed unearned arrogance. They feared nothing. Joey knew Seth would probably not even attend school tomorrow in an effort to avoid whatever trouble was heading his way. To continue to try and reason with him was a waste of Joey's time. It could only lead to confrontation. It was better to say nothing and let these children believe what they wanted. He had their identification tags and the satisfaction they did not get away with what they had planned.

As Joey turned to walk away and leave the two boys to themselves, Seth could not resist a cheap verbal shot at Joey, a taunt to his authority.

"Ain't nothin' gonna' happen to me, Coach," Seth said with Joey's back to him. "My mom will be up here and you'll be apologizin' to me. I ain't scared of you! You mess with me and see what happens. See what happens, dog!"

Seth then mocked laughter while Carver standing next to him offered no support. Carver stood still listening to his friend wondering just how far he was going push a teacher, a school symbol of authority, a man twenty years his senior. Joey never looked back as he moved down the stairwell on his aching feet back into the parking lot. Seth was still talking trash at Joey, but he no longer tuned in. He wanted to slug the kid right in the mouth, but could not and Seth knew it.

As Joey reached the last stair step delivering him to the ground floor, the final bell rang. Students poured into the parking lot to connect with rides or to drive themselves home or to work. Within seconds, hundreds of students surrounded Joey from all directions. The music forbidden to be heard aloud seconds before suddenly reached decibels of unimaginative levels. The cursing began. Students whipped out cell phones they were not allowed to possess on the school campus. Shirttails came out of trousers or were removed altogether. Shoes came off. Baseball caps went on and colorful bandanas were wrapped on heads in a gangster style. It was an undisciplined sight to witness. It reminded Joey just how out-manned and duped teachers really were.

Just as Joey moved away from the protection of the covered walkway that masked his nabbing of Seth and Carver, a plastic container of bottled water, sold in campus vending machines, went whizzing by his right ear at a high rate of speed. The weighted object narrowly missed Joey's head. The water bottle hit the concrete about fifteen feet in front of Joey and skidded about ten more feet before bouncing away from a curb and rested near a car tire. Joey's immediate reaction was to look at where Seth had been standing, but there were dozens of kids there. There was no way to prove who threw it, even though the logical choice owned one of the identification tags Joey carried in his hand. Joey was extremely angry. Had that bottle hit him in the head he could have been knocked unconscious. Had it hit him in the back it could have injured his vertebrae. Thrown from a second floor location about thirty yards away, whoever threw the bottled water intended to seriously hurt Joey. Of course, he asked a few students he did trust if they saw who threw the bottle at him, but no one admitted to seeing anything.

It had been a hell of an afternoon for Joey. Sadly, this type of day was not all that unusual. There were good days and good kids, to be sure. There were also days like these that made teachers feel vulnerable and weak. It was a feeling teachers did not like. Truth be told, Joey realized teachers really did not have any control. Seth knew it, too, and that thought nauseated Joey.

Joey realized in the last two hours that school test scores had dropped and he feared the imminent political fallout. He sent a female student to the office for violating the dress code and she responded with a shoulder charge. He had his history lesson disrupted by two punk students laughing at the assassination of a president, gave a now orphaned student his last ten dollars following the arrest of her crack-addicted mother, was disrespected by an intimidating man for asking him to turn down his filthy rap music so as not to disturb classes, caught three students skipping class, had one student run away from him, and could have been seriously injured for catching the other two. All this work performed for a lousy $1,000 dollars net salary every two weeks. The summer could not come quickly enough for Joey. He had earned the rest.

And to think, when summer did arrive, Joey would be playfully chastised by his business friends with, "You only work early August through mid-May! I wish I had a job like that! I wish I had two weeks off for Christmas and one week off for Thanksgiving and Easter."

They would laugh at his profession and challenge his abilities. They would joke about public schools, remind him their kids attended private schools, and ridicule him for not pursuing a "serious profession." Joey was fond of telling them he doubted they could survive his job for one week. In turn, they would instinctively argue that they could, that teaching was made out to be harder than it really was. He never knew if they were serious, but it hurt just the same. All Joey could do was laugh at their remarks as if it did not bother him. He wanted to tell them, friends or not, to go to hell.

Hell. It was sometimes Joey's place of employment.

"How have successful schools for low-income, minority students done it? Largely by ignoring education 'experts' and going against theories and practices that reign elsewhere...real teaching rather than 'activities' or 'projects,' phonics rather than 'whole language,' standardized tests rather than mushy evaluations, and in general a back-to-basics approach."

—Syndicated columnist, Thomas Sowell

Early May—"Isn't This Supposed to be Rewarding?"

Gloria Hampton was in a good mood for so late in the day. She had just finished teaching five straight classes and her one-hour daily job on duty patrolling the hallways had been fulfilled. For all practical purposes her day was over at 1:30 p.m. All that remained was her planning period. During that time, Gloria had finished typing a final exam to be given to students in a mere two weeks. She was ahead in her work. Days like these were unusual for most teachers, especially those who sponsored clubs or coached, as was hers sponsoring the Beta Club. That unpaid responsibility was completed and she now had nothing to do but teach the remainder of the year. Those extra five-hour per week club meetings between the beginning of school and early May were, like the subject she taught, history. Even the most enthusiastic teacher found their energy level heavily taxed by this time of year. With just twelve days remaining in the school year, it was a good feeling to be just a teacher.

Gloria felt light on her feet, but her mind was swimming with the idea of retiring. She chose to erase those thoughts for now while feeling as giddy as a schoolgirl. She looked forward to the bell ringing to end the day. She could simply go home without a care in the world or go grocery shopping like a common housewife. She could continue her workout routine she abandoned since school began. In short, she felt professionally liberated. No parents to meet, no club members to discipline, no fundraising to attend to, no assignments to organize for her eighty-eight-member club. For a brief part of the school year Gloria could take care and worry only about Gloria after school.

As she bounced along the aggregate corridor and past the bricked buildings in desperate need of sandblasting, she noticed a student teacher sitting alone in the school's Common's Area. Sitting hunched over a green painted picnic table with her back to Gloria, the young lady was in deep thought; her body language failing to conceal the struggle within her. Normally, Gloria would pay little attention, but as she glanced at her watch she noticed there was still twenty-five minutes left in the day and she had nothing else to do. Gloria took a chance and walked over to her.

As Gloria approached her she realized how beautiful she truly was. She was about twenty-three-years-old and of mixed race. Her complexion was light brown and her hair was long, black and straight. When she turned to meet Gloria's eyes the veteran saw them as brilliant green. She wore a short shirt that seemed all the rage, the kind of garment that when leaning over the table exposed her flat bare midriff. It was hardly professional to wear at work, especially in the company of overly hormonal teenage boys, but she was a vision of loveliness. Gloria looked at her and tried to recall her name, but it was useless. Gloria had seen her before. With the 1950s personality Gloria grew up and felt comfortable with, she called her "Kid" in the Frank Sinatra-style the new millennium would never know.

Before she could wipe the water from her eyes Gloria recognized her as a social studies teacher—Ann Sumrall's student teacher. It was not unusual to never learn the names of the many student teachers East Side High School had during the spring semester. As Gloria began to speak she knew she was taking a chance. She did not know this young lady. She could easily embarrass Gloria by brushing her off, or worse. But it was not in Gloria's nature to ignore people who needed to talk, if in fact, they wanted to. Gloria did not know if she did.

"Hey, Kid," Gloria called out to her as she moved closer. "Are you okay?"

It was the obvious question, but Gloria was never good at small talk. In fact, she hated it because it was so insincere. In her world it was simply better to get to the point concerning everything. It saved time and dealt with issues directly, but it was often misconstrued, in Gloria's case during most of her life, as being unpolished and blunt.

The young lady turned halfway around to look at Gloria while wiping her eyes and replied, "Fine, I'm fine."

She was not fine. She was trying to hide her pain and got caught by a lady more than twice her age. She appeared somewhat embarrassed as she put on a quick smile that accented a gorgeous face. Then she looked directly into Gloria's handsomely wrinkled face and sat up straight. This young lady was going to try and sell Gloria on her poise and cool, but Gloria was too experienced and had lived too much life to buy it.

Gloria paused for a second and remarked coolly, "Yea? Well, when I'm fine I don't have to wipe tears from my eyes."

Gloria realized she was, perhaps, again being too blunt, but she had said exactly what she was thinking and there was no going back now. All she had to do was wait to see how this student teacher would react. To Gloria's luck, she politely snickered.

"I didn't mean to draw any attention when I came out here to think," she said as she sat up straight and looked at herself in Gloria's sunglasses. "I just have a lot on my mind."

"Personal stuff or things you can talk about?" Gloria asked.

"It's..." she started to speak and made it appear she was ready to, but she stopped herself not knowing if she could talk to a stranger.

After all, Gloria *was* a stranger, even if a concerned one. But she continued nonetheless. This student teacher was smart enough to recognize a chance to take advantage of experience, something her college professors did not have in teaching at the high school level.

"I just got a job offer to teach at a high school next year and I don't know if I want to take it," she said softly almost disbelieving her own thoughts. "I applied for the job. Now that I've got it, I don't know if I want it. I'm really confused."

Gloria's analytical mind raced in many directions. The student teacher was not revealing too much about her situation. Was the job out of state? Was it a situation where she was going to have to leave family or a boy friend? With just days remaining before she graduated from college, was life moving too fast for her? Was it all of the above? Gloria needed to pry before he could offer her unsolicited advice. But it would be nice if Gloria could just get as far as learning her name.

"I don't want to appear rude, but I don't know your name," Gloria said while extending her right hand for a shake.

The young lady grinned and then extended five fingers full of gold rings in return and replied, "I'm Jenny. I've seen you around many times, but we never stop to talk. Everyone is too busy, I guess."

"Yea, I've seen you, too," Gloria responded.

Gloria could not help but wonder why she had not visited her class during the semester. Student teachers were required to experience other teachers instructing and interacting with students in classroom settings. It's part of their college requirement before graduation. Gloria had already entertained five student teachers that year, but Jenny was not among them. While Gloria shook her hand Jenny continued speaking about her confusion. All Gloria had to do was listen.

"When I decided to become a teacher I really believed I was going to help kids, you know what I mean?" she said and asked in the same slang-style language used by the new generation. "I wanted to help young people prepare for the world. I wanted to give them hope and, like, be a great teacher that could make a difference, you know?"

Jenny paused to monitor Gloria's face for a reaction, but she gave none as she sat with folded hands on the table's rough, green-painted surface. Jenny then began to get more animated and revealed more of her thoughts.

"Most of these kids don't seem to want to be helped," Jenny continued as her voice began to slightly rise. "I have been here since January and I don't think I've reached more than six or seven kids. I teach three classes and the majority of them don't care if they ever get the information. Ever! I didn't go into this profession to teach two students out of thirty in each class."

Jenny's voice then slowed and she appeared tired in her description of the students. Her facial expressions exposed the rest of her feelings.

"The rest just want to sleep, pass notes, and slide by with the lowest grade possible," she continued. "If they get a D they are glad to get it. They don't do my assigned homework. They don't read. Some can barely read. How did they get to high school with such poor basic skills? No one can answer that for me."

Jenny stopped for a moment and waited for Gloria to answer. Gloria had seen this beast rise from the inner thoughts of more than one aspiring teacher during her thirty-three-year career. These concerns usually occurred to the second or third-year teacher who eventually realized they had been regulated to career baby-sitter who *tried* to teach state-mandated curriculum. But Jenny caught on very early to the traps and trials of considering education as her lifeblood. She had been student teaching a scant sixteen weeks, and only three classes at that, and she had concluded what many seasoned teachers caught on to years before; no matter how hard one taught or prepared, many inner-city public school students did not want to learn. There was nothing anyone could do about it.

The state government could not legislate the importance of getting a good education to the students of today. Oh, they tried with each meaningless legislative session, but those who had never taught a high school class in their lives wrote bills, spoke on them, and passed them believing they had repaired another glitch in education. It would be comical if it were not so tragic. Legislators hired or solicited opinions from state appointed Board of Secondary Education members, many who have never taught or have not done so in a very long time. Gloria used to comment to friends about her frustration with those who called themselves "experts" in her job but were not qualified to do it. Gloria knew they were not experts. What they were expert in was analyzing educational data. Nothing more. Many teachers wondered why the state did not appoint recently retired teachers to those positions. At least they knew what it was like to teach in today's social conditions. It reminded Gloria of her legislator's annual questionnaire to educators asking them to write down views and concerns with teaching. In past years Gloria used to write at least two pages of opinions in response. Disgusted with the legislature's leadership in education, Gloria simply wrote two sentences during the last inquiry:

"There is nothing you can legislate and there is nothing I can do that is not already being done. The state's problems concerning education are cultural."

It was only those cynical views Gloria could offer Jenny as an explanation for her early frustrations. While Gloria believed her view of teaching in today's inner city public high school was jaundiced in opinion and somewhat hopeless in application, it did not make that opinion any less correct. She was going to try to share it with Jenny.

Gloria had been fighting to educate students for years. Like many of her professional contemporaries, she was burning out with each passing day trying to educate legions of students from low socio-economic levels whose parents were also marginally educated. Gloria understood Jenny's situation more than she could possibly know. The funny thing was, both the experienced educator and the student teacher were thinking of leaving the profession for the same reasons. Gloria understood, without saying it, that Jenny was contemplating leaving the profession before it further dulled her.

"I just don't know what to do," Jenny said with her palms extended. "I should be happy that I got the job. The economy is not so great that I could go out and qualify for something else. I wanted to do this. I wanted to be a teacher as long as I could remember. It's what I trained to do. Now I have the chance to do it and I don't know if I want to, you know what I mean?"

Jenny was looking down now. She could sense herself getting emotional and did not want to revisit that side of her. Gloria reached out and patted her on the hand while choosing her words carefully.

"Jenny, did you ever talk to your professors about how you feel?" he asked.

She perked up almost angrily.

"Yea, a lot of good that did!" she said in a mocking tone. "I had one professor tell me I should read more theory to try to understand the psychology of teenagers. I don't need to read psychology to know that many of these kids don't care, you know? They don't care! But the professors don't understand that. Like, they keep telling me to raise the bar and the students will rise to meet the challenge. That's a freakin' joke."

Jenny was becoming salty in her explanation because she thought she might have found an ally in Gloria, who smiled as she listened intently. Jenny picked up Gloria's approving vibes. Gloria had also repeatedly heard the nonsense from the experts about "raising the bar" and students would meet the challenge. The problem was the students were not meeting the old bar of expectations. The test scores were proof of that. The idea that raising a new bar would excite, frighten, or challenge students to do more, always more, was sheer folly. In fact, it was outright ignorance. The idea appeared sound and she thought the effort should be made, but Gloria had seen many students look at the proverbial bar and refuse to attempt the jump or choose to go around searching for an easier way. Gloria agreed with Jenny's every word and attempted to appease her.

"Jenny, who ever said this job was going to be easy?" Gloria explained. "No one."

Jenny interrupted with her finger raised, "I never said that! I never thought for one minute this was going to be easy. No job is. But isn't this supposed to be rewarding? Aren't we supposed to be in the business of guiding students in the direction of success? That's what I signed on to do, you know?"

Gloria shot back calmly without taking a breath, "And you realize now that teaching high school is not like it's shown in the movies where the job starts out overwhelming and ends up a terrific feel-good story where the teacher makes a point and the students all respect them for sticking with them through thick, thin and thinner, is that right? This is not the movies."

Gloria was on a roll. Jenny's eyes were wide now.

"I am not going to sit here and tell you about all the wonderful success stories sold at school board meetings for television cameras," Gloria said. "You're right, Jenny. Many of these kids don't give a damn. Neither do their parents, sad to say. And now you are bummed out that you are not Academic Jesus. You cannot save them, even though it is in your nature to try.

"Some of your college professors gave you very lame advice on a job they themselves have not done or cannot do. They study education fads, graphs, charts, and liberal testimony about how tough it is to survive academically, especially for the minority students. But what they don't tell you is that 50 percent of your success depends on how badly the student wants to succeed."

Gloria waited for a response from Jenny who stared blankly back at her. The look on her face told Gloria she was on the right track and had

Jenny's complete attention. A few months ago Jenny would not have believed Gloria's testimony, but she knew it to be true because she had experienced it firsthand. Gloria's words were gospel and Jenny was the congregation.

"Back in January, if I would have told you what I just did what would you have thought?" Gloria asked.

"I would have listened to you and thought you were a burned-out old fart," Jenny said with a shy laugh. "I would have thought to myself, 'God, I hope I don't become her.'"

"Yes, and I know you would've, too," Gloria returned with a laugh.

In fact, they both laughed at the absurdity.

"I wanted to make a difference, plain and simple," Jenny said returning to the subject. "I want kids to care about what I have to offer them in the classroom every day."

"You still can make a difference, Jenny, but you may have to amend that blueprint," Gloria advised. "Look at what the public school system *is* and not what you want it to be, or, what it once was. Because what it was will never be again. That's the harsh reality of it all. You can either accept it or reject it. Don't believe that "No Child Left Behind" fantasyland the bureaucrats advertise. Some kids are behind and plan on staying there because they are comfortable and the government is caring for them anyway. You, however, are still young enough to make changes."

Gloria stood up making it known she had to attend to other items before the bell rang to end the day.

"Jenny, I can't tell you what to do," she said now standing over her. "I'm not your mom or dad. We don't even know each other. But I can tell you a few hard facts and there is no straying from their reality. You want to hear them?"

Gloria asked because she was no longer certain Jenny wanted to hear additional cynicism.

"Yes, go ahead," Jenny answered, now looking up at Gloria. "I'm sure I need to hear this."

"Okay, here it goes," Gloria said. "Number one is that the public school system is in decline. White families are bailing out and taking their money, power, influence and kids with them. Whether the NAACP or the other parties that have sued the school system want to believe it or not, they ruined the public schools in their attempt to save them. Test scores will continue to decline. Budget cuts will be the norm. Louisiana teacher pay will remain behind others states. Despite all, if you can improve the life of just a few kids per year you would have well earned your keep. Quit trying to save the world because the world does not notice a teacher's efforts, only our failures.

"Number two is do this job because you love it. Don't do it for any other reason. If you do it for another reason, you will destroy the very being of your existence. Don't deny your talents. If you think you can contribute to the profession then do it. But you need to be realistic about what has become of young people in society today. And you are not always going to get the support from parents to stem that tide.

"Thirdly, you cannot save the world. When bad education news strikes, whether it appears in the newspaper or on TV, try to put it in perspective. You will learn many people will blame teachers for almost every ill in the school system today. If their kids fail it's because you didn't teach them well. If teams lose it's because you didn't coach very well. If they drop out of school it's because the teacher did not take the time to reach them. People will tell you how overpaid you are because you get three months a year off. Even though you don't get paid for that time off they will throw it in your face every time there is blame to claim. There is almost no respect from society for what you do.

"Lastly, everyone has got the answers to what makes an effective school, but they will never ask your opinion. You are expected to perform as teacher, coach, baby-sitter, parole officer, psychologist, sociologist, police officer, narcotics officer, bouncer, fund-raiser, counselor, mother, father, and advisor. Did I leave anything out?"

Gloria paused. Jenny laughed.

"If you perform well at your job, as most teachers do, rarely will you be thanked," Gloria continued. "If you choose to join our ranks you will be one of the best-educated people in this nation, but don't expect to be rewarded for it. Understand the only reward you get is that which you bestow on yourself at the end of a tiring day. Then if, by some chance, one of your students makes it through college and has the education to build a rocket that will go to Jupiter, they *might* remember you as the one inspiring them."

Gloria was now out of breath explaining thirty-three years of experience in a short outburst of advice. Jenny sat motionless. Both sides quietly weighed each other. Gloria was not sure if she was able to reach Jenny any better than she did her students. Jenny did not want to believe Gloria's prognosis, but she was afraid it was correct. After all, Gloria possessed the experience and the despair. They bid each other a good day, shook hands, and promised to talk later. Both knew they never would.

As Gloria strolled the hallways back to her classroom she thought about her own words. She was not only defining the job to Jenny, she was reminding herself about the hoops of fire through which she jumped each day. She began to think of her current students for the justification of her recently spoken words to Jenny.

She thought of senior Norah Wadel, a skinny girl with an incredible singing voice whose very existence at school was about singing in the school choir. Norah loved to solo at church, school plays and functions, and competitive festivals. She was an incredible talent. But it was not unusual for her to miss one or two days of class per week. In fact, not only was Norah failing Gloria's class for the second time, she had already missed eighteen days during spring semester unexcused. She had also checked out of school eleven times after choir class was completed at 11 a.m. missing all of her afternoon classes. With days remaining in the school year, she was now in jeopardy of failing all classes and not graduating due to lack of attendance. Teachers contacted Norah's mother, Ann, as early as February to help get Norah on the right track. For a few weeks, it worked, but by March, Norah's grade was worse. Ann then contacted Gloria begging for her daughter to receive extra-credit, which Gloria would not extend. Gloria would not allow Norah to get what other students were denied. Not seeing the logic in that argument, Ann called the principal complaining, but the administration supported their teachers to the fullest. Changing strategy now, Ann sent a note to Gloria the following day asking for her child "to be excused from the final exam so Norah could study a few extra days and take it the day after students were dismissed for the year." Gloria had no authority to do such a thing and refused the request per the school rules. Students were expected to take exams the day they were slated. Ann wanted to circumvent those rules for her underachieving daughter.

There was sophomore Casey Evers, a physically large girl with long brown hair who spent more time trying to be cool than trying to get educated. Every class has one of these personality types who thinks they know more than the teacher, which only proved they didn't. But the joke was on Casey and she did not get it. Casey was in her second year trying to pass history. Going into the final exam, her grade was a solid 54 percent. She would have to pass the final exam with an 'A' to pass the class with a 'D.' Given her track record it was unlikely she would do so. Many times Gloria tried to contact Casey's parents and did so only once with success. The mother promised Gloria her daughter would improve by threatening not to buy Casey a new SUV if she failed to raise her grade. Casey made a 'C' on her fifth six-week progress report and mommy came through with a new Nissan X-Terra. After gaining possession of the SUV, Casey predictably spiraled downward academically. Gloria considered how ineffective Casey's parents were. How could a 'C' impress parents enough to spend $22,000 on their daughter? Why couldn't they wait until final grades were submitted before buying the vehicle? It was inconceivable. How could any teacher reach Casey by impressing upon her the value of education with a parental reward system such as that?

There was freshman Shonika Williams, who turned in test papers with nothing more than her name on them. She wrote her name on the last seven tests and turned them in blank. She earned, predictably, seven straight grades of zero. Gloria tried desperately to contact her parents. When someone did answer Gloria's phone calls, the young voice on the other end of the line had an excuse as to why the mother could not be reached. In eleven phone calls to her work and home, Gloria never got in touch with Shonika's mother.

Beverly Hall was a slim, beautiful girl with an incredible figure for just sixteen-years-old. The boys loved her, but her eyes were on college-aged young men. Academically, Beverly had straight A's but she was morally bankrupt. Behind her "Yes, sirs" and "Good morning, Mrs. Hampton" was a sexually active girl playing dangerous games. While lecturing in class the previous week, Gloria intercepted a letter Beverly was writing and read it after class. The letter was as graphic as anything she had ever read. Apparently Beverly was having sex with two college-aged boys at the same time and neither knew about the other. According to the letter, one of the boys became suspicious while in the act of sex with Beverly and questioned her loyalty. Beverly's letter was to her best friend soliciting advice on what she should do. Gloria threw the letter away knowing the parents would never believe their daughter would engage in such action even if evidence were available. With so few days remaining in the school year, Gloria did not wish to get involved. Many teachers, particularly males, knew dealing with sexual issues was asking for more trouble than it was worth.

Gloria recalled being cursed by a parent for not seeing the warning signs of their drug-addicted son. Never mind that the parents missed those warning signs. They expected Gloria, who only saw the addict one hour per day, to notice something erratic in junior William Donovan's personality. What was Gloria supposed to notice? William had a strong 'B' average in the class and seemed interested in learning. But when he disappeared for six straight school days just three weeks before the end of the fall semester, the family called the police. William had bought a bus ticket and left the state, his destination unknown. He missed one chapter test and the mid-term exam, which dropped his grade to a low 'D.' Gloria thought it was remarkable William could pass at all having missed so much schoolwork. When William returned home his parents looked to dole blame. They called Gloria at home four days before Christmas wanting answers she could not provide.

William's mother, Jan, asked in a demanding tone, "I want to know why you didn't call us when William had a drug problem? How can you enjoy the Christmas holidays knowing you failed our son? You did, you know! Teachers are supposed to be trained to know the warning signs of drug addiction in teens and you missed them!"

Gloria said little as Jan promised to contact everyone from the school system to the pope. Gloria did not feel responsible for William's problem any more than Jan would feel responsible for some of the problems she had in the classroom. Jan acted in a ridiculous, and irrational manner. Gloria was never given a chance to explain and eventually hung the phone up on Jan when she became threatening. Jan never took responsibility for her failure as a parent. Such was the nature of teaching.

As Gloria moved closer to her classroom, her thought process was interrupted as she heard a student outburst aimed at a teacher from one of the many rooms she passed.

"I ain't did nothin'! You don't know me to be talkin' at me like that!"

"Please sit down now!" came the reply from a teacher's voice Gloria could only identify as being female.

Only God knew from where it came or who was guilty.

"Nobody talk to me like dat!" the troubled student continued. "You ain't my momma! Don't you ever be talkin' to me like dat! Keep talkin' to me like dat and see if I don't get you!"

Gloria considered the threat she heard from a student to the teacher and sighed. It was all reruns in the inner city. She returned to her thoughts.

Gloria remembered first-year teacher Brent Masters, who on his first day of teaching found a note on his laptop computer from a female student wanting to have sex with him. Feeling highly defenseless, Brent did nothing out of fear of having any investigation turned against him as an alleged pervert. He was considering quitting the profession at year's end. What she did not know was Brent had already laid the groundwork for an exit.

What advice would a college professor give a student teacher in dealing with the matters in which Jenny was faced? What theory could Brent explore to remedy his problem? What book is available for such advice? Their respected teaching certifications did not help them here. Their education degrees were now proving to be hollow shells.

Gloria thought of junior Ken Simon who had earned himself an arrest and a parole officer for gang fighting in early summer, but stayed out of trouble until two weeks before school began for fighting at a shopping mall after breaking the back window of a car for no other reason than he felt like it. The owner of the car was walking out of the mall as Ken crashed a baseball bat through his back windshield. The pair began to argue. Ken, at eighteen-years-old and a former football player, was one of the toughest students in the school. He attacked the owner for daring to challenge him. The two began to scuffle and Ken beat the thirty-seven-year-old badly while his two high school friends cheered and watched. Ken was arrested, posted bond, and began the school year while awaiting his court date. At his October trial, the judge sentenced Ken to five years in a correctional institute. Gloria, who taught Ken until his court trial, did not know until after the sentencing what was in Ken's background.

There was junior Adam Clavelle, a wiry kid with hardened muscles and curly black hair that had been tossed out of a private school in early February. No longer able or willing to tolerate his unpredictable nature, the private school solved its problem by making it East Side High School's problem. He was assigned to Gloria's class. Adam tried to sleep every day and every day Gloria woke him up trying to make him pay attention. It did little, however, to improve his grades. During those precious minutes he was awake, Adam constantly bragged to anyone who would listen about how tough he was. He outlined every detail of every fight he was involved in over a given weekend. He stayed out late on school nights, smoked, and drank a great deal of alcohol. Rumors were he was dealing drugs and running with a very rough group. Gloria never had any major confrontation with Adam in class, but many other teachers did. Adam once left campus during the school day after an argument with his second-hour mathematics teacher over his refusal to conform to the school dress code.

When the teacher pressed him to remove his baseball hat one morning he told her, "No fucking way."

The teacher told him to go to the office. Adam did more than that. He left school. He then went to visit his girlfriend at a private high school before officials there had him arrested for trespassing. He eventually returned to East Side High School one week later woefully behind in his schoolwork. Later, he got into a fight during physical education class and broke another student's nose. Adam was then expelled.

Adam's expulsion counted against East Side's "School Report Card" monitored by the State Department of Education. In reference to the national "No Child Left Behind Act" that pressured schools to extend the academic life of its most-at-risk students, what advice did President George W. Bush have for Adam's teachers in dealing with him?

There were sadder stories.

Gloria remembered junior Wesley Wren, a kid whose parents divorced during fall. His mother left his father because she fell in love with a man on the Internet from Thailand, traveled to meet him, and promised to marry him after she moved to Bangkok. She made good on her promises. Not able to accept his wife leaving, Wesley's father quit his job and began to drink heavily. He then squandered the family saving's account and Wesley and his nine-year-old brother were having trouble eating. In effect, the kids were abandoned. Wesley quit playing sports at school and took two part-time jobs, one of which ended at 2 a.m., to insure his survival and that of his brother. With only four hours of sleep each night, Wesley's grades dropped dramatically. Too tired to keep up the pace of being both a student and breadwinner, Wesley quit school. Eventually his uncle in Georgia learned of Wesley's fate and approached the state court about gaining legal custody, which he was able to do. The last Gloria heard of Wesley was he and his brother were enrolled in a rural Georgia high school living as normal a life as one could under that bizarre circumstance.

No teacher is equipped to deal with such situations.

Gloria could only laugh when remembering freshman Kyle Moore, a tall, gangly kid with a smile of Hollywood flavor. He was handsome and he knew it. He thought a quick smile and small dose of manners could get him anything in life. During the month of March, Gloria gave a chapter test in which students were given three days notice to study.

As students filed into class on test day, Kyle quietly told Gloria, "I'm not really ready to take this test so I'm going to take it tomorrow, okay?"

Students like Kyle were growing in number. They were con artists who over-estimated themselves while attempting to master the art of negotiation. Students thought everything was under negotiation, including grades. It was becoming a real problem. Students like Kyle never understood that tests were given on specified days to *all* students, not just a selected few. Gloria, of course, objected to Kyle's plan so he refused to take the test, instead, opting to sleep while other students labored. At day's end, Kyle went home and told his abrasive mother, his personal pit bull, he was not *allowed* to take the test. The mother phoned Principal Berling and blamed Gloria for everything explained to her by a spoiled rotten son. Gloria was obligated to explain everything to the principal who then relayed his findings to the mother, who refused to believe Gloria's side of the story.

Gloria could not forget junior Lyle Conner, who had more problems than a team of psychiatrists could handle. His mother, a prostitute, was murdered when he was seven-years-old. The father's contribution to their relationship before she was killed involved being nothing more than a sperm donor. Lyle was raised by his aged grandparents who were so out of tune with the reality of raising kids today they were often fooled by Lyle's sweet talk of innocence. Bless their hearts, the grandparents tried to raise Lyle properly, but the street called Lyle's name each night to the filthy strip clubs, and late-night bars in which even the police would not dare routinely venture. Pimps, gamblers, hustlers, and gangsters reared Lyle. They wore outrageous clothes and always had money to spend, dope to smoke, and gorgeous woman to sleep with. No teacher's sales pitch on the importance of an education was going to compete with Lyle's lifestyle. So it was no surprise that he was eventually expelled from school for drugs, arrested, and got out of jail on a plea bargain. Now loose on the street, laughing at the judicial system's handling of his case, Lyle decided to prove himself to his street tough buddies. Within one week, he had broken into the home of a forty-one-year-old mother of two, robbed her, tied her up, and raped her repeatedly. Lyle was eventually arrested again and faced a lengthy prison sentence. The court sentenced Lyle to juvenile life followed by twenty-five years in prison beginning at age eighteen. At the time of the rape, Lyle was only sixteen-years-old.

Gloria wondered how the Board of Elementary and Secondary Education expected her to handle and motivate Lyle.

Gloria remembered watching East Side High School's first baseball match of the season versus St. Lucy High School back in late February. Gloria loved baseball and promised the six players she taught that she would attend. Gloria knew as a teacher and fan that when playing private schools that society believed they were the social elite. The baseball coach often cautioned his players during pre-game that others "expected public school kids to act like savages. Don't let them be right." Rarely did the players say or do anything to embarrass the school, but no one told the mother of Brad Hoffman, East Side High School's starting catcher.

Just ten minutes and one inning into the new season, St. Lucy's best hitter smashed a home run over the right field fence. Some St. Lucy's players began to taunt East Side High School's pitcher, who chose to act like a man and not respond. Except for Brad, who shoved one of the celebrating St. Lucy players to the ground and told him to "fuck off" loud enough to be heard all around the field. With the umpires watching, Brad took a swing at another St. Lucy player who ran to his teammate's aid. The entire situation threatened to get out of control when both head coaches began yelling at each other. In the end, the umpires ejected Brad and both coaches from the game. St. Lucy went on to pound East Side High School into submission, 13-2, in a game called off after five innings. At the end of the shortened game, East Side High School's team morale was low.

As if things were not bad enough, Brad's mother stormed across the infield in plain view of all in attendance shouting at the assistant coaches, "You don't know how to coach a team or handle my son!" she screamed at the top of her lungs.

A confrontation ensued with coaches telling her, "Get off the field!" as St. Lucy parents and players looked on.

It embarrassed the school as all watched in horror at a psycho parent attempting to undermine authority.

Maybe, Gloria thought, an educational theory could have remedied the situation, but it was doubtful.

Gloria remembered in January how freshman Buster Johnson, with four gold front teeth, called her an "old bitch" in front of the class before throwing his heavy book sack against a cinder block wall. That behavior was prompted because Gloria told Buster to leave class after repeatedly telling him to sit down during instruction. Sent to the office, Buster was assigned to the time out room by the school administration for a day's worth of punish work. When Buster's mother found out what her son had done, she phoned Gloria wanting to know what she did to make her darling behave that way. Gloria was outraged. The parent did not call to apologize for her child's behavior. She called to criticize the school's disciplinary tactics. On top of it all, she told school officials her son was not going to the time out room. The school would not relent. But every time Buster was scheduled for his time out visit the parent refused to send Buster to school. He missed eight straight full days of school over the incident, and never served one hour of detention for his horrible behavior. His grades did suffer, however. With no viable excuse to fall back on, Buster was scheduled to fail all classes due to twenty-two unexcused spring semester absences.

Maybe Gloria should have called the NAACP on how to deal with such matters concerning the young minority population they purport to serve.

Gloria recalled a fight between two girls in late January that resulted in bloody uniforms. The fight was over a male student both claimed as their boyfriend. It took two male teachers and a student to break up the fight. Until it was interrupted, about thirty students stood around and cheered watching them beat each other senseless. Both teachers took several powerful hits to the chest and back. No student or parent apologized or issued regret.

Maybe the legislature has a solution on how $35,000 per year teachers should deal with this type of all too common violence.

There was the fight in late February, too, between a girl and one of the school's top basketball players, Jerrell Cardiff, a six-foot-two, 200-pound hulk of a young man. Jerell lost his temper one morning when his girlfriend, Latisha, told him he could not have sex with her "until you straighten your shit out!" Unfortunately, it was a conversation displayed loud enough for the entire Central Time Zone to hear. Jerrell took a swing at Latisha's face with an open hand and knocked her to the ground. It took three physical education teachers to hold back Jerrell.

While three grown men held Jerrell down on the ground trying to calm him, Latisha stood over the four and taunted her boyfriend with, "You ain't so motha' fuckin' tough now, is you bitch? Yea, say somethin' now!"

While she was taunting Jerrell the coaches were fighting for their lives to keep him from beating them all to death.

No Child Left Behind?

There was junior Neal Clark who had a 'B' in Gloria's class and appeared to be most interested in writing—a rarity among students. When the Mardi Gras holiday began in earnest, Neal went to New Orleans to party and never returned. Students joked aloud in class about how Neal said he would not return to school until the two-week carnival season ended. There were reports of his drunkenness and rowdy street behavior in the Crescent City. The students told Gloria that Neal would not be coming back until Fat Tuesday, the final day of the Mardi Gras celebration. When Neal did return, his grade point average had been decimated. He spent one day at school calculating what it was going to take to remedy his academic situation. He chose, instead, to drop out of school.

Where were Neal's parents? Why did he choose to engage in criminal mischief and permanently damage his grades? Were Gloria, Neal's six other teachers, and the school really expected to be held accountable for him? Raise the bar of expectations? Neal probably threw up on that so-called bar somewhere in the French Quarter. No pun intended.

Gloria shook her head when remembering seventeen-year-old Orleans Parish transfer Farley Vaughn, a six-foot-two, 270-pound mammoth of a young man the East Side High School football coaches believed was born to play offensive line. Farley, however, never showed even a little interest in playing the sport.

Each autumn day he would be asked to try out for the team and Farley always gave a rude reply to the coaches like, "Why don't you get a clue! I don't wanna' play, get it?"

Eventually, Farley's freshman English teacher figured out he could not read. When called on to participate in class, Farley refused to read aloud even one sentence of any literature book. Only then was it more clearly understood why Farley did not want to play. The fact was he could not play football because he was failing all seven of his classes, including physical education, and would never be eligible to play any sport at East Side High School. It was further learned he never played football in Orleans Parish for the same reason. The coaches at his former school simply could not get Farley eligible and gave up trying. What's worse, he never tried to improve his academic performance. All he wanted to do was eat lunch and shoot basketballs at an iron hoop behind the gym that did not have a net. Violent by nature, Farley was in his own world and the East Side High School teachers were content to let him stay there.

How could teachers be expected to integrate a seventeen-year-old violent, illiterate into their classroom discussions without slowing down a legitimate class to a crawl?

There were continuing discussions by the laughable experts to consider linking teacher pay increases to student performance. To give the state an idea of how she felt about that idea, Gloria always joked to teachers that legislator's pay should be tied to how many professional workers, students, and businesses leave the state of Louisiana. Based on that deal, she guessed legislators would soon be paying the state out of their personal bank accounts.

That's the way the educational game was set up, and it was a game.

An example of a game would be the way six of Gloria's twenty-five students took the standardized test, GEE-21, in March. They took a three-hour test in about fifteen minutes. They simply penciled in answers in the multiple-choice section quickly, ignored the essay questions, and went to sleep. When it came to the writing part of the test these students wrote about three poorly structured sentences and quit. Their test scores were figured into the school performance score. How could teachers impress upon such lazy students how important it was to the school for them to do well on the test? How could anyone reach these types of students and make them understand the stakes?

Despite the sorry state of the majority of the student body, East Side High School's performance scores did go up in *some* categories. Despite the limited success, no one from the school board or the news media took note of the effort or improvement, except Principal Berling. Superintendent Dr. Maddox said nothing, perhaps because he was interviewing in another state for the same post.

Gloria spared Jenny these stories as she put the key into the heavy wooden door of her room and walked toward her desk. Strange, she thought. This entire year she had not seen the top of her desk calendar, but she was, indeed, caught up on her work.

She began to think about Jenny and wondered if she would follow the multitudes of young, disgruntled teachers who planned to leave the school system. She knew of several younger veterans wishing they had left the state to teach when they had the chance. Gloria, however, began teaching when the public school system was outstanding. When her career began, she had no idea society would create and feed such dysfunctional inner city public schools. All she could hope was that Jenny was smart enough to solicit other opinions and take some time away from school when summer began to rethink her situation.

Out of the quiet solitude came a blaring call over the room's intercom situated above Gloria's desk.

"Mrs. Hampton?" came the crackly sound.

"Yes?" came the obligatory reply.

"Would you come down to the office? There are some former students of yours who wish to see you before the bell rings."

"I'm on my way."

Gloria picked up her satchel, locked her room door, and moved quickly down the hallway before the bell rang and hundreds of students poured into the corridors. Almost immediately she noticed a slightly built male with the face of a baby. He was loitering near the double doors to one of the main buildings. Gloria glanced at her wristwatch. There were five minutes remaining in the day and she knew this young man had no business outside of a classroom. Students were either supposed to be in class or off the campus. There was no other choice for them. Gloria was in a hurry, but she had to inquire why this student, who was not making eye contact with her, was trying to make himself invisible.

"Young man, what are doing outside?" Gloria asked in a firm tone.

"I'm waiting for the bell," he said without making eye contact.

"But the bell doesn't ring for a few more minutes. You shouldn't be out here. Why aren't you in class?"

No answer. That was a sure sign of trouble and this student was not quick enough for a comeback comment to sway Gloria's investigation.

"Who is your teacher this hour?" Gloria asked.

"Mr. Rabalais," the young man replied.

"What's your name?"

"Calvin."

"Should we go and ask Mr. Rabalais why you are out here loitering instead of in his French class?"

"What's that?"

"What's what?"

"That word. 'Loitering?'"

"It means you are hanging out where you aren't supposed to be."

"Oh."

Suddenly the student gave up some information.

"Mr. Rabalais threw me out," Calvin offered.

"Why?" Gloria probed.

All the young man did was shrug his shoulders while still refusing to make eye contact as his lone social defense.

"Let me guess," Gloria continued and would orally deduce for Calvin. "You were bad in class. Mr. Rabalais threw you out and sent you to the office. But with just a few minutes to go before the bell rings you hoped to jump on the school bus instead and lose yourself in the after-school crowd. That way, Mr. Rabalais *thinks* he sent you to the office. You don't have to get in any trouble today and the office knows nothing of your behavior problem in seventh-hour French class, so they don't know to look for you. Does that about sum it up?"

Calvin was impressed. He smiled broadly and finally made eye contact with her.

"Yea, how'd you know?" Calvin asked.

"I've been doing this a long time, son, and we teachers are not as dumb as students want to believe," Gloria said as she motioned for Calvin to move his body toward the office.

But the final bell suddenly rang. Calvin looked up at Gloria and smiled.

"I guess it worked, huh?" Calvin laughed as he back-peddled toward the safety of the buses. "Safe for another day! Too bad."

"I'll get you tomorrow, Calvin," Gloria promised as she extended her index finger toward Calvin with a grin. "You can book it!"

With that, Calvin turned his back on Gloria and began sprinting toward the long line of buses waiting for teenage passengers to ride home.

Indeed, Gloria would inform Mr. Rabalais and the school disciplinarian of the situation. But whatever happened to Calvin was none of her concern. She would let the law of the school extend whatever punishment it deemed necessary.

Calvin's entire makeup revealed how a growing number of young people think today in society. Calvin was not sorry for his actions. He offered no worthy response or explanation. Calvin did not promise to never break school rules again. Calvin played and beat the system, at least for the day. Calvin actually laughed as he walked away caring little that his actions might get him in further trouble in twenty-four hours. Students like Calvin lived in a dangerous world extending no further than the end of their fingers. If they could not eat it, touch it, smell it, wear it, or control it, then it meant nothing to them. They lived in a world of immediate self-gratification. It was the law of the street. It was Calvin's form of twisted survival in a cruel world that he would have to deal with sooner or later. He would not be prepared for it. Gloria knew Calvin's problem was not about grades. It was not about Shakespeare, the Bill of Rights, integers, or the mass of an object.

It was about character and Calvin displayed less than zero. There was no class to teach that could explain to Calvin what he did wrong. Teaching that class, if it existed, would be a waste of time. Decency, character, morality, humility, perseverance, dedication, and other words to describe what an adult should be, and what teenagers should strive to reach, seemed a mental defect to many inner school teenagers teachers encountered during a day's work. It was sad that it was no longer taught at home. But given the many parents Gloria met in her years of teaching it came as no shock the parents often displayed the same poor character traits.

How did society degenerate to this? Gloria and her high school friends would have never behaved in such a way. Why did the class of 1968 keep their pants pulled up and their shirts tucked in? Why did they do as their teachers told them, even if they disagreed? What had happened to society in the last twenty-five years? Gloria could sum it all up in a radio commercial she recently heard advertising a digital scanner to beat police radar. The commercial stated:

> *"Tired of driving the speed limit? Got too much to do in the day to stay stuck in traffic? Then you need the Digital Scanner that's guaranteed to beat police radar detectors!...We're so sure you'll be pleased with this product! And if you are not satisfied with this product we'll pay for your speeding ticket! You can't beat that offer! Besides, how else are you going to keep from getting speeding tickets?"*

How else are you going to keep from getting speeding tickets? It was simple. Don't speed down the highways! But to the students Gloria encountered, the world was about doing what one wanted and what one could get away with. That was the mark of a champion—more importantly, to brag about it if one got away with it.

Most students proved they could beat the system each day during lunch shift. Nearly 80 percent of the students at East Side High School were on free or reduced lunch programs subsidized by the government. Students complained about the length of the line and the quality of the food while wearing gaudy $150 basketball shoes. They owned cell phones and "blackberries." They were beating the system. These students learned young. Some had money, but it was not to be spent on necessities. They did not live a world of "business before pleasure" or the "Protestant Work Ethic" or the American ideal of "Rugged Individualism" of which the nation was built. No, it was a new day for young Americans. Pleasure and leisure were the name of the game. The Romans called this phenomenon "Bread and Circus." A little over 1,600 years later it was still alive in the growing failure of the young American character. Just like Rome's government, the U.S. government subsidized, even promoted, a great deal of that living standard that was a drain on society.

Teachers could not possibly expect to make a student like Calvin understand what he did wrong when most aspects of the society that relates to him sent him horrible messages of greed, immorality, and excessive materialism. That message was on TV, radio, newspapers, the Internet, billboard advertisements, magazines, and on the street in which he lived. Calvin was surrounded by it. It was all he knew. He was not likely to change as he moved into adulthood. Unfortunately, students like Calvin brought that simple-mindedness to school and his behavior and grades reflected it. Students like Calvin did not care even a little.

Gloria eventually made her way to the office and opened the glass door as she gazed upon a heavy-set woman. She was middle-aged, stood about five-foot-nine and must have weighed over 250 pounds. Her fingernails were about four inches long and painted bright red. She was wearing sandals and a dress too short for a woman of her age, revealing legs as large as seventy-five-year-old oak trees. She was talking loudly and angrily on her cell phone to someone about how she felt her child had been mistreated by the school administration.

Gloria walked over to Dr. Marie Pellington, the school band instructor, and asked in a very quiet voice in the back of the room, "What the hell is going on?"

Marie was shuffling papers she had just pulled out of her teacher's mailbox. She was pretending not to notice the scene beginning to take place in a crowded office as hundreds of students milled around just beyond the large plate glass windows separating them. Marie was looking down, but her peripheral vision was allowing her to watch the terrible show just beginning to take place.

"I don't know, but this woman is about to lose her mind and doesn't mind us knowing she is angry about something," Marie said never looking up.

"Believe me, they gonna' fix it the way I's want it fixed or they gonna' be havin' to see me talk to the news about this shit!" the woman and parent complained to the person on the other end of the phone and to the entire civilized world. "They obviously can't control their damn classroom and they want me to believe that my child, my baby, is the reason the other kids can't learn. I ain't listenin' to that. I ain't believing it. I know my child. She don't be actin' like that at home and I know'd she not be doin' that crap here! Do these fools think I'm a fool like them?"

Whoever was on the other end of that phone line could not get a word in. This parent was wound up like a top spinning out of control. She could not be calmed. No teacher was going to make the attempt to calm her, even as some students filed into the office to make phone calls home for car rides.

The woman continued to pace back and forth with the small black phone still attached to her right ear near a dangling silver earring large enough to shoot a basketball through. Out of the corner of her eye, Gloria noticed the students she was there to see. It was two girls she had taught nine years before, now in their late twenties. She smiled at them as she put her finger over her lips instructing them to keep quiet while the angry parent rambled on. They smiled back at Gloria agreeing it was the right thing to do.

"Girl, I will either go to the news or to the newspaper, but I'll be damned if they gonna' lay this on me!" the woman continued. "I'll tell you what…"

Gloria and the many teachers that had slowly filed in at the end of the day to check their mailboxes quit listening. They had become uncomfortable. They had seen this type behavior from parents before. It was little wonder the students acted the way they did given this was one child's idea of a mother and a role model. The assistant principal tried to stem the embarrassment.

"Miss Baker, would you like to come into my office and discuss this further?" the assistant principal said to her from a distance in an effort to diffuse the situation.

"No, I would not like to talk to you again!" Miss Baker replied shaking her neck from side to side with the phone never leaving her ear.

"Miss Baker?" Gloria asked Marie for clarification as she still shuffled papers.

"That's Lanisha Simpson's mom," Marie realized and explained to Gloria. "Do you know her? She's a sophomore."

Did she know her? Every teacher knew Lanisha whether they taught her or not and not for the right reasons. Lanisha was a lot like her mother. She was obese, rude, loud, and craved attention. Lanisha was also a horrible student having earned four F's and three D's at midterm. Her grades had changed little as the end of the spring semester drew near. Lanisha had already spent as many as nine days in the time out room for various offenses ranging from dress code violations to cursing a teacher who dared to ask her to wake from her sleep during a class review of a math homework assignment she did not do. Lanisha had already been suspended three times, once for leaving campus without permission, once for excessive tardies to class, and once for fighting. Even though the school system once sold the public the idea of "Zero Tolerance" and an automatic expulsion for fighting, teachers understood the school system committee reviewing such infractions did not always enforce it. Nevertheless, Lanisha was being suspended a fourth time, which now granted her an automatic expulsion. Lanisha's mother was at school for the first time all year, raising hell about her child's fate and protesting her innocence to a school administration sadly well-acquainted with this type of parental behavior.

"The apple does not fall far from the tree, does it, Marie?" Gloria asked quietly.

"Nope! Catch you later," Marie replied before walking off bored with the entire episode.

Gloria motioned for her two former students to go outside where they could talk. The two girls retreated outside to the thinning crowd as school buses roared away. Gloria had to walk past Miss Baker to get to the door and it was all she could do to keep from shaking her head in utter disgust at the barbaric woman posing as a concerned parent.

The day slowly unfolded as it sometimes did in the hot afternoon sunlight.

"Creative genius dwindled…the pen, the graving tool and the pencil produced highly spiced work, able to attract and amuse the mind but incapable of elevating and inspiring it."

-From Mikhail Rostovtzeff's book, Rome

Early May—"I Need to Pass"

The bell rang at 12:30 p.m. sharp to end fifth-hour class when a student moved quickly toward mathematics teacher Coach Ed Stallworth, who was standing next to his open door awaiting the arrival of students. Sophomore Brandon Wilson had just finished his lunch shift and sprinted down the shining-waxed hallway to speak with his math teacher before the crowd grew too large to converse with him. It was a conversation he wanted in private.

Brandon was an aimless sophomore who, lately, had been assigned to the time out room due to numerous in-class infractions. He was one of those kids who could never keep his mouth shut and had the natural habit of only speaking in insults. Rarely did he have anything nice to say to anyone. He always played off his ugly manner explaining "it was a joke." But humor has a pointed edge and usually hints more at a nasty truth. Brandon's truth was often cruel, especially to his teachers, which made him unpopular among the decent students. His real friends could be counted on one hand, even though he believed he was the life of any party.

Coach Stallworth was a highly polished ex-football coach in retirement. Although Coach Stallworth had not coached any game in any sport in over four years, the students and faculty still called him "Coach." He wore thick brown glasses that were no longer stylish and looked he like he played linebacker in today's version of the game. A bit over weight and now a grandfather, it was hard for some to believe, based on his physique.

Coach Stallworth was once a hard-nosed high school defensive lineman. He earned first-team all-state honors in 1967 and 1968. He was second-team all-district in basketball helping his school win their only district title. He was on the honor roll in both high school and college and completed his master's degree in 1973. He was, by all accounts, a successful man with a streak of morality that was the envy of his peers. His students knew none of that background. If they had they might have respected him more. But Coach Stallworth was not one to tell them of his exploits.

He was also among the rank and file recruited by the state out of retirement to teach in "critical need" areas, like mathematics, his specialty. He was a very likeable fellow who, quite frankly, did not need to teach any longer. He simply liked teaching mathematics and wanted to stay in touch with the sights and sounds of public high school academia until he reached a point where he could not take it any longer. Besides, the idea of collecting a salary and retirement simultaneously was a great lure. The events of this day, however, were the kind that could send any well-intentioned teacher over the edge.

Coach Joey Martin, from across the hall, stepped outside of his room to either offer quiet support with his presence—a common move among teachers—or, to watch the show as students moved around them on their way to sixth-hour.

Brandon was a tall, well-built kid who owned a look of sincerity. He was pleading with Coach Stallworth for help. During their noisy conversation it was obvious from Coach Stallworth's tone he had no intention of helping this kid with just five days of school remaining.

"Coach, I need to talk to ya', man," Brandon said in a near begging tone. "I be in real trouble."

"First of all, I'm not your 'man!'" Stallworth noted calmly to Brandon as he waved his fifty-eight-year-old finger in front of the young man's nose. "I'm Mister or Coach Stallworth. Second of all, you not 'be in trouble.' You think you may have trouble. Use the English language, Brandon. It's really a beautiful thing. Now what do you want?"

Brandon, age seventeen, who filled out a size twelve basketball shoe in his six-foot-three frame and a good five inches taller than his teacher, either ignored the request from Coach Stallworth or was too ill-mannered to understand he was being asked to reconsider his use of words when addressing an adult.

In any instance, the pair had never really gotten along well at all. The only thing Brandon took seriously was sports, particularly basketball. There was really no other motivating factor for Brandon to get up in the morning and Coach Stallworth knew it. Brandon had never exerted anything beyond answering "here" when his name was called during roll. He never did any homework, never participated in class, and thought the idea of being a good student was reserved for the "dumb white boys who can't play 'The Game.'" Brandon thought he had life all figured out, which only proved he had nothing figured out. He was one of millions of foolish young men who believed they were special enough to make it to the NBA and live a high profile life.

On this warm May afternoon Brandon found himself near desperation. He had never shown this side of his personality to anyone. Brandon was the class-clown and pseudo street-tough, when he wasn't sleeping. He had begun to realize with just five days remaining in the school year that he was going to fail mathematics.

Why moments like these came over students during the most obvious times is beyond even the most experienced teachers. Brandon had received five progress report cards in Coach Stallworth's freshmen class since school began on August 11, and had earned five F's for his work. Furthermore, he never took part in the extra credit provided for those students needing a bit of extra help.

Perhaps Brandon finally figured it was going to be next to impossible for him to participate in sports next year unless he attended summer school. Brandon never went to summer school because it got in the way of AAU summer camp for prep basketball stars on the rise. Most every notable college coach from the Gulf and East coasts would be there or would send their assistants to watch and chat with these athletes in efforts to interest them in attending their school in the years to come. Brandon was one of those players. He could jump, run, move laterally as well as anyone and had a great presence inside the lane. During basketball season he averaged thirteen points and six rebounds per game for a losing East Side High School team that finished 12-16 overall. Brandon, a second-team all-district selection, knew he could not miss AAU camp. He had too much to lose bypassing AAU camp to focus on catching up academically. But he had only just begun to worry about that prospect. Coach Stallworth saw Brandon's request coming.

Brandon's luck was fast running out on him. He was not going to be able to stay in school very long as a "promising" sophomore. He should have been counted among the junior class, but had failed too many courses to earn that distinction. Brandon *had* to produce academically this year. He had not.

Coach Stallworth was tired of the silence between the two. He had a class to ready for final exams and was growing irritable spending time on a kid whose ignorance and apathy knew no bounds.

"Get to the point, Brandon," Coach Stallworth asked in a polite, but an almost sarcastic tone.

"Coach, I gotta' pass your class," Brandon pleaded with his hands extended toward his knees. "I need to pass this class. Ya' see, I gotta get outta' this class with at least a 'D.' I can't fail another class. Can it be done?"

Coach Stallworth retorted rather quickly at his pupil. He was agitated with the kid's nerve. His request was all too predictable.

"Brandon, why are you wasting my time with this?" he asked. "Your grade in my class is the lowest among the 101 students I teach in any given day. Your grade is not just an 'F.' It's a very bad 'F.' It's not even competitive. The last time I looked you were at around 43-44 percent overall. What do you want from me?"

Brandon's face registered defeat. He even turned his head away from Coach Stallworth and did not offer a word. Brandon was not stupid. He knew the conversation would come to this. He just knew it. There would be no pity from Coach Stallworth who had sent too many real student-athletes into the college ranks and, from there, a number made it to the professional ranks in two sports. Coach Stallworth saw Brandon as an athlete that did not understand his primary job at school was to be a student. Coach Stallworth moved to get around Brandon so as to see his face more closely.

"And you know what bothers me the most, Brandon?" Coach Stallworth asked looking directly in Brandon's eyes. "You didn't tell me that you wanted to *learn*. You told me you needed to *pass*. There's a big difference in the two. You don't want to *learn*. You want to *pass*."

Coach Stallworth had Brandon's attention for perhaps the first time all year. Too bad it was under these circumstances. Brandon was asking Coach Stallworth to do what some teachers in his past had done. That was to look the other way and pass Brandon under the pretense he was a basketball star in the making. That type of thinking is precisely what got Brandon in his current academic quagmire.

"Brandon, you should have worried about your grade in February," Coach Stallworth continued as his voice began to rise in protest at Brandon's indirect request for academic asylum. "Why didn't you worry about your grade after you got the first 'F?' No, not you! You were too busy sleeping in my class or mocking me or going to the office happily when I sent you out of class for refusing to do your assigned work. Now you want to pass my class. Now you worry, but it's too late.

"When Coach Jarreau asks the basketball team to run extra laps, you do it. When you are asked to work out every day in the weight room, without fail, you do that, too. With no qualms!"

Brandon looked up from staring at the floor and registered a strange look.

"What's a qualm?" asked Brandon.

"Are you serious or messing with me again, Brandon?" asked Coach Stallworth.

"No, coach, I don't know what that is. I figure if you gonna' chew me out I might as well know what you be calling me."

"I'm not calling you anything, Brandon. I'm simply stating how you will lift weights after school, run laps, and take extra shooting practice in the gym if you need to improve your game. You'll perform that function all night, on weekends, and holidays. Am I right?"

Brandon shook his head that it was true.

"I hear your mom spent a hell of a lot of money so you could get a private basketball coach to help you improve your defense," Coach Stallworth continued. "Is that right?"

"Yea, and it worked, too," Brandon replied.

"So, why did she not get you a tutor to help you with your grades? Why not summer school?"

There was another long pause between the two as they stared into each other's eyes. Coach Stallworth was not backing down and could only guess Brandon was making his rounds with his other teachers

307

about getting some unearned assistance. Coach Stallworth continued his stern lecture.

"Nothing would embarrass you more than to be seen on the basketball court being outdone by a member of the opposition," Coach Stallworth stressed to Brandon. "But the idea of going through life not knowing how to add, subtract, multiply, or divide fractions is not of any interest to you at all. I don't understand that about kids like you.

"Sorry, Brandon. I won't help you. Get inside the classroom and take what life dishes out."

With that final word, Coach Stallworth opened the heavy wooden door to his room and escorted Brandon inside. Brandon felt beaten on this day by his math teacher.

Coach Stallworth had seen too many times in his past as a successful coach at Huey Long Lab School that an athlete could excel outside of the lines if he wanted to. In sixteen years as head coach in both football and basketball, Coach Stallworth had sent many student-athletes to college. His teams not only won state and district titles in the Louisiana's 2A classification, he knew for a fact those students also earned degrees from some of the nation's finest institutions while participating in sports. Many of these former student-athletes didn't come from backgrounds as good as Brandon's. Brandon was just lazy when it came to schoolwork. Coach Stallworth proved to be a full-court press after Brandon "picked up" his dribble. Brandon was trapped and now had to live with that choice. Today was Brandon's payday.

Brandon, with his baggy trousers falling about halfway down the crack of his backside in the so-called popular style of the day, lazily walked to his desk to the jeers of some of the students that heard the hallway discussion that Brandon hoped would not last long enough for anyone to hear.

"Haaa, hotshot!" laughed one black kid whose grades were only slightly better than Brandon's. "Look like you and me be goin' to summa' school!"

Brandon threw himself in the faded twenty-year-old plastic desk and put his head down in disgust. He then, predictably, went to sleep as he had much of the year. Coach Stallworth ignored him.

"All right, class, let's continue preparing for the final exam," Coach Stallworth said to the class of twenty-two underachievers. "Turn to page 121 in Chapter 19."

With his head down as he flipped through the large textbook, Coach Stallworth wondered if he had done the right thing in dealing with Brandon. Yes, he knew he had. Was forcing Brandon to retreat back to the tenth grade really the right thing to do? After all, sports was really all Brandon had going for him. Basketball, perhaps, really was Brandon's ticket to success. However, Coach Stallworth could not use that as justification to socially promote him.

God gave fifteen-year-old Jesse Hester the gift of consistency. Jesse did not know his multiplication tables when he entered Coach Stallworth's room in August. Sitting in the front row and with the great effort of an after-school tutor, Jesse managed to overcome that deficiency. It helped Jesse in every facet of mathematics this year and he passed with a 'C.' Coach Stallworth was as pleased with Jesse earning that "C" as he was an honor student accepting the school's top mathematical award. Sometimes it's not the grade one earns; it's the effort one puts forth.

Brandon only chose to understand effort when it came to basketball. Coach Stallworth tried in vain to force Brandon to understand there was more to life than basketball. Too many kids did not make a living playing basketball. They put all of their eggs in one basket, so to speak. These so-called high school "phenoms" were offered terrible advice from non-faculty coaches interested only in using a prep star's talents to further their own aims. In short, Brandon swallowed every nice compliment made to him by a strange coach or scout about his talent. Brandon never considered the remote idea he might not make that certain team that would either kill or continue his athletic career. He never considered that there were others pursuing the same dream that may be better adept at the playing the game at the next level. He never considered his competition on the basketball court might also have the grades to attract a scholarship that would certainly be denied him. Brandon, like many inexperienced gullible athletes, believed everything said about him, except that he was not worth being promoted to the eleventh grade.

Coach Stallworth paused and grinned remembering who he was and what he was hired to do. Brandon knew the stakes when he entered

Coach Stallworth's room nine months before. Brandon chose failure. He would get the grade he earned.

While Coach Stallworth scribbled math problems on a thin plastic sheet to be seen by students on the overhead projector, sophomore Chas Albright began to give Coach Stallworth his predictable trouble. Chas was like a daily menstrual cycle. His teachers could count on his pains almost each and every day without fail. And there was no pill for, or break from, his misery. Brandon's disruptive appeal in the hallway almost insured Coach Stallworth's mood to be shaky. Chas did not pick up on that possibility, nor did he care.

Chas was of average height and build with shaggy blonde hair and piercing green eyes. The girls considered him cute and he dated females from both races. He craved attention and would do anything to get it, including faking an injury on the football field in which he practiced four months per year. He was also unpredictable. One minute he was a bit of an introvert with a passion for school, mostly out of the same need to succeed as Brandon. The next minute Chas could prove distressing. Any guidance officer could tell this was one of the many signs of drug abuse, but no one had proof that Chas was experimenting with illegal narcotics. On this day, Chas chose to be difficult and his timing could not have been worse.

"Chas, please sit down, son, and turn to the page I requested," Coach Stallworth asked firmly while looking right at him as he stood near the rear of the class.

"Hey, I'm not going to work today. Okay?" Chas laughed, which of course gathered steam and allowed others to join in the mocking of Coach Stallworth.

"Yea, we not gonna' do the work today," a Hispanic female student repeated with a laugh.

Coach Stallworth never acknowledged her ridiculous declaration.

"Chas, I'm not in the mood for any of this today," explained Coach Stallworth, who was standing near Brandon's sleeping corpse. "We've already wasted about ten minutes of time already. So why don't you just step into the hallway and we'll send you to the office with a referral."

"Good. I don't want to fucking be here anyway," Chas dared to explain.

"What did you say?" Coach Stallworth asked shocked by the audacity.

"You heard what I said. I know you can't see too well, old man, but I didn't know you couldn't hear either."

More class laughter.

"Step into the hallway while I fill out your referral slip," Coach Stallworth asked.

With that, Coach Stallworth motioned Chas to the door.

Chas slowly walked to the door leading into the hallway and lazily gazed at Coach Stallworth's writing out the referral to get an idea what he would have to defend once he made it to the office. But Coach Stallworth saw Chas attempting to look at the referral and quickly snapped it up from the desk.

"Get into the hallway and I'll take you down to the office personally," Coach Stallworth said as he pointed to the door.

"Yea, well, will you hurry it up, Coach? I've got things to do and places to go," Brandon added, as if he weren't in enough trouble already.

Coach Stallworth discontinued his effort to fill out the referral. He would simply ask Coach Martin to watch his class while he took Chas to the assistant principal of discipline to explain the situation personally.

As Coach Stallworth and Chas walked down the hallway to the office, Chas had one last word for his math teacher as they moved away from the classroom.

"I was hoping you would touch me in some way so I could kick your bi-focal ass before I left," Chas admitted with sincerity.

Coach Stallworth said no more to Chas and refused to even look at him. Chas had been in trouble before and probably always would be. Coach Stallworth's only private question was why Chas waited so long to get thrown out of school? He knew his behavior today almost ensured his dismissal from school. It was obvious that was exactly what he wanted to do. Why wait until there were five days of school remaining?

Maybe it was because Chas, a reserve halfback on the soccer team, was on Coach Martin's black list and was no longer allowed to play because of his unpredictability. Coach Gatewood of the football squad desperately wanted Chas on his team as a cornerback, but warned him that next season his grades would have to improve drastically to be eligible to play. Coach Gatewood made Chas a deal after the season finale that if he kept up his grades and was eligible for the beginning of next season, he would make him junior varsity captain. Chas, with his eyes wide open with surprise and excitement, promised to live up to his end of the deal.

Within three weeks following the season finale, Chas was up to his old tricks. He routinely disrespected his geography, math, and physical education teachers.

He got into at least one fight in the hallway, finishing the confrontation, telling his adversary in a crowded hallway between afternoon classes, "I will find where you live and kick your ass!"

These incidents bought him time in the discipline center totaling eleven days—time he missed being in actual school keeping up with his assigned work. When Coach Gatewood learned Chas was failing to live up to his end of the deal, and was again failing in all seven of his classes three weeks prior to the end of school, he quit speaking to him as if they never had a deal. He simply gave up on Chas. Not really having anything more to look forward to, Chas looked, found, and pursued an exit from school.

"Man, I don't know you!"

Three days later, the daily school attendance report was issued to teachers in their mailboxes. Chas' name was listed under the title "Expelled." School rules stipulated that any student expelled during the final ten days of school must see that expulsion through to the next year as well. It was a mechanism used to keep students from thinking they could act as they pleased in the school year's final days. Without such a rule the truly bad students would make an attempt at intimidating the entire student body and administration without any fear of repercussion. Therefore, Chas was dismissed from East Side High School for what was left of the year *and* the following year. Coach Gatewood would simply have to find another cornerback. Chas would have to find another whipping boy for his failures and begin work on Plan B, if he had one.

When Chas' father, Ben, went to pick him up from school within an hour following the incident with Coach Stallworth, Ben was dumbfounded that his son had been recommended for expulsion. In fact, he told Principal Berling in their subsequent meeting he didn't know Chas was a problem in any class or to anyone. It shocked no one to learn Ben had not seen his son's progress report since the first one was issued back in mid-September. It proved how little he knew or really cared about Chas. It was always amazing how school administrators and teachers never meet the parents of their problematic or underachieving children until it was far too late to administer any punitive action. Chas was a school menace and the only person who seemingly did not know it was his father.

While Chas waited in the office for the meeting between his father and the principal to end, he talked to himself in an effort to be as disruptive as he could in his final minutes as an East Side High School student. When the school secretary asked him to stop making a fool of himself and allow them to work in peace, he ignored her. Chas then began to sing as he tapped his fists on either side of his thighs as he sat in a cushioned chair near the office's glass door.

The fact was Chas was the eighty-first student expelled from East Side High School since August. The overall number of expulsions for the calendar year had not beaten the record number asked to leave the school in past school sessions, but it was close.

Suddenly, Chas' father opened the door to the principal's office. The meeting had not lasted long. Ben was angry in a quiet sort of way. Whatever Principal Berling told Ben made him extremely upset. Whether he was mad at Chas for being so foolish as to get thrown out of school or at the school as an excuse for his failure to properly parent his out-of-control son was hard to know. When he saw Chas singing in the office, he stopped and glared at his son, who had the nerve to smile.

"I'm hungry, dad, let's go get something to eat," Chas said to his father with a toothy grin from a half-cocked face.

It was obvious Chas was still pushing the proverbial envelope. He had no excuse for his behavior and, like so many others at East Side High School that had been expelled before Chas, he had no remorse for his actions. For the moment, Ben really seemed to care about being a good parent to Chas, who lived with a mother that obviously had lost control of him. That presented Ben with the additional problem of having to fight with his ex-wife over Chas' future or lack thereof. There were so many things running through his mind he did not know how to react to his arrogant son that was a stranger to social mores. Ben was fuming, but to his credit he did not curse the principal or the school, make a scene or promise to sue. He simply looked on angrily at the spectacle of his son and asked the obvious question.

"How could you get thrown out of school, Chas?" Ben asked with a terse ring in his voice. "I never got thrown out of school. Never!"

"Oh, shut up!" was the only explanation Chas could offer in a nonchalant manner.

Principal Berling stood directly behind Ben, but knew it was wise to say nothing even if Chas was rude to him. Chas was no longer a student and Principal Berling was professionally regretful, but personally ecstatic. Chas' family could no longer use East Side High School as their baby-sitting service.

"Don't talk to me like that, Chas," Ben demanded with his index finger pointed at his ungrateful son. "Not after all I've done for you."

"What the hell you done for me? I don't have a car! I don't have new clothes. Who are you to act like my dad? Man, I don't know you!"

Chas waved his father away, stood, and turned to open the door and make his way outside in full view of many teachers and administration members watching nearby. Before Chas could take more than a few steps toward the door, Ben grabbed his son by the left arm and spun him around in an effort to get his attention. It was a bold move by a father with much to lose in a situation that threatened to spin out of control. Chas did not like it.

"Look, son, don't walk away from me when I'm talking to you," Ben said sternly.

"If you grab me like that again, old dude, I'll kick your ass in front of the whole school, you getting' this?" Chas warned as he violently pulled his arm from his father's grip.

Chas then walked out of the door as the final bell rang to end the day. He moved toward the parking lot where many students were soon to wait for rides while talking loudly among themselves.

Ben stayed motionless in the office and then exited watching his son walk away from him. He was further stunned to the lengths Chas had gone to ensure his tough guy reputation. It was now clear to him that everything said about his son was true. He didn't want to believe it, but Chas was providing the evidence with his terrible behavior at his father's expense. Ben was afraid his next move would result in a heated argument that could not be won. The school administration was watching carefully from inside the paned glass nearby. It was certain to be one hell of a show; one they did not want to see unfold.

"Chas?" Ben retorted weakly hoping to gain his son's sanity as he walked briskly behind. "Chas! I'm talkin' to ya, son!"

When Ben caught up with his son the two exchanged words no one in the office could hear. But the physical actions of the pair told all watching it was not a pleasant conversation. As the two argued, Chas looked over his father's shoulder noticing some of his friends were watching and decided to regain control of the situation. After all, he had a reputation to protect. Without warning, Chas grabbed his father by the shoulder blades and pushed him against a parked car which sent him backwards onto the hood in a spread eagle position. Again, Ben was still as he was further shocked at his son. Ben regained his footing and composure immediately and attempted to wrestle control of the situation. He was humiliated and stunned, but regained his poise. He moved toward his son and grabbed him again by the arm. Before he could say a word to his son, who he had underestimated in terms of strength, Chas hit him in the jaw with his right hand. Chas followed that with a punch to his father's chest with the left hand as Ben was forced back up one step. The damage was more psychological to Ben than it was physical, but it left him standing alone looking very foolish as his son walked away cursing.

Chas' mouth became even more vulgar. He verbally abused everyone within earshot. He would not listen to reason. Chas continued his walk off the campus leaving his father and whatever adolescent dreams he never had permanently behind. Chas then began the long march home down the tree-lined street.

The school year was nearing its end. It was time.

"It is the mark of a higher culture to value the little unpretentious truths."

—Fredrick Nietzsche

Early May—The "Survivors"

Tory LeBlanc chatted quietly with her dear friend, Margaret Sexton. It was casual conversation about nothing. They sat cross-legged as formal ladies will. They were wearing new dresses and high heeled pumps with empty metal folding chairs all around them. They awaited other educators in Section IV of the River Center, a space reserved for the East Side High School faculty and staff. In the arena above them parents and friends of the 204 seniors of the Class of 2004 were filling dirty multi-colored cushioned seats and talking a bit too loud for such a special event. Naturally, the level of noise appeared to be worse than it was in such a cavernous place. The bright lights in the high ceiling seemed to be miles above the shiny, smooth, dull concrete floor. The scoreboards sat blank on either end of the arena. The large colored advertisements at each end appeared out of place for a high school graduation ceremony.

The River Center is located in downtown Baton Rouge adjacent to the civic building offices that is part of the government complex serving the city. The River Center is not an attractive building. From a distance it looks as if it is still under construction. The granite making up the exterior always looks dirty and the structure, from the bottom floor up, does not flow well. For those who favor the city's increasing love affair with its traditional art deco style, the River Center is a reminder that the architects designing it disregarded simplicity and taste. The entire structure is a contemporary nightmare revealing its age far sooner than it should. The arena itself is poorly kept, but is the only place some local high schools can use for graduation exercises in lieu of on-campus facilities that do not have air conditioning or enough seating. It is hardly an ideal place for graduation exercises.

Tory and Margaret talked as they watched the crowd slowly flow out of the cramped portals above and then stop before taking in the arena view as to where they would choose to sit. There were already about 1,000 in attendance and the parking garage outside had a line of vehicles to enter about two blocks long as rush hour traffic filed out of the downtown area. It was just fifteen minutes until graduation began and several teachers were late arriving to the faculty area. Greetings were exchanged, but not overdone as teachers had seen each other just hours before. Some male teachers wore neckties and suits. Others chose to wear short-sleeved sports shirts to combat the 6 p.m. heat that was manufacturing temperatures of ninety degrees in the bright sunshine. The females dressed professionally, but comfortably.

Few teachers really enjoyed graduation these days. There was a time when graduating high school was an impressive milestone in one's life. The academic challenges were rigorous and most students aspired to do something with their lives. Their dreams were grandiose to be sure, but in past years students wanted to make life after high school special. They wanted to stand out academically and took defeat in the classroom and in life personally. Today, too many inner city students consider academic failure an option—a way of life offering second chances that don't always exist in the real world.

Conversely, today's inner city public high school diploma is hardly worth the paper in which it is written. Most students aim only to get by. So very few actually take school seriously enough to be truly prepared for life outside of high school. But the lack of student preparation was not all the fault of the students. It was a system failure giving students an easy way out of true preparation. The system allowed students the choice of not wanting to be challenged. While federal and state pressure mounted on teachers and administrators to raise test scores, the system itself failed to support the very teachers entrusted to repair the academic problem.

To graduate, students need only take three math classes or "units," four English classes, three science classes, and three years of social studies. In all, students need to pass twenty-three units to graduate high school. Being that most inner city public school students took seven classes per year during their first three years of high school, they could complete the majority of those requirements in three years. Their senior year involved taking nothing more than two or three classes. In fact, roughly 90 percent of East Side High School seniors finished their day by 11 a.m. That was a sad, but a perfectly legal fact. Considering about one-half planned to attend college within the year it was nothing short of absurd to spend one's senior year *not* adequately preparing for college-level work. The private, parochial, and magnet schools did not allow their seniors to leave school early following completion of their units to graduate. They believed, rightly so, the more education a senior student attained the better prepared they would be for life after high school. Mainstream public school seniors did not always have that extra preparation, choosing instead to vacate their school campuses in the morning hours for part-time jobs or sleep. Graduation exercises were becoming hollow springtime rituals.

In the rear of the arena, students began to group in their silver gowns and blue caps with silver tassels near one floor level portal. Among the seniors was David Boyle, formerly of St. Lucy High School. David graduated with a 1.9 grade point average, continued proof that private school transfers to public schools were not universally better. His girlfriend, St. Lucy's Marcy Baxter was in attendance, despite not being allowed to see David again.

Tanner Liwinski and Terrance Wright stood near David as others chatted nearby. Tanner's football future was uncertain. When the college football signing period elapsed in early February, not one college or university offered a scholarship to the hulking senior offensive lineman. Days later, Tanner reluctantly agreed to "walk on" to a small in-state school and try and reinvent his high school gridiron successes. Terrance, captain of the soccer team, decided to leave Louisiana for Texas, where he would move in with his uncle and enter a community college.

Tailback Lester Hayes, a poor student, was not among the senior class on this night. Hayes dropped out of school in mid-January and was never heard from again.

About six teachers were frantic, trying to organize students to line up alphabetically for their entrance onto the arena floor.

The noise level began to climb as the crowd grew in size. It was an unimpressive crowd. The atmosphere was not cozy. It appeared the crowd was better suited for a summertime minor league baseball game. Cell phones were ringing and the subsequent conversations were annoying. Children ran around the concourses without the supervision of their parents. It was not unusual to hear screaming in the distance as two parties attempted to communicate.

"Come sit over here, girl!" one female yelled as she pointed with her finger across the arena at another. "We gonna' sit down here!"

"Okay, but I gotta' go to the bathroom first!" the other responded.

It was hardly classy and it made Tory and Margaret chuckle.

"Now everyone knows she has to go to the bathroom," Tory said matter-of-fact to Margaret who was holding her face in both palms embarrassed for the girl, the school, and what promised to come for all concerned. "I'm just glad she wasn't on her 'period.' God knows what she might have said."

The attire of the crowd looked like a freak show. Many middle-aged parents and friends wore clothes that were better suited for a night of dancing. Some dressed appropriately, for sure, but too many adult females wore blouses revealing belly buttons the size of donut holes in a midriff full of flab. The color combinations of clothing and gaudy jewelry adorning them were atrocious. Some wore hats nothing short of obnoxious or sequenced gowns better suited for a five-star New Orleans hotel on New Year's Eve. The younger girls dressed like common whores as if competing for the attention of soldiers and sailors on leave from Baghdad.

Many of the younger boys almost made no effort to look nice. They wore bandanas in every conceivable way. They wore them on their necks, tied them around the heads with the knot in the front or the back. They covered their heads with them and they talked loudly on their cell phones. They wore baseball caps sideways and backwards to highlight their freakish haircuts. They wore un-tucked football and basketball jerseys too long for their frames. They wore sandals or pricey sneakers crisscrossed in colors complimenting capped gold teeth.

Somewhere along the way, most making up the River Center crowd forgot the night was not about them. Graduation was not a fashion show, a place to see or be seen. This night was for the students. Instead, it unfortunately appeared the night was a chance for too many patrons to show off whatever they were tired of showing off at the local mall.

For both sexes there were simply too much jewelry, hats, earrings, cell phones, cameras, and video equipment. They were, to be sure, an overly aggressive group with little concept of what this night was supposed to be about. The idea was not lost on Margaret.

"You know, I have never seen this many people at any event we've had at school this year, not one!" she said to Tory who was nodding in agreement. "Not even at one of our football games have I seen this many people. There must be nearly 2,000 people here, and they're still walking in! We only have 204 seniors. Where do these people come from?"

Tory shook her head in amazement adding, "We can't get these folks to attend parent-teacher night, a sporting event, a concert, a play, and we can't get them to help us help their kids fundraise. But, oh, on graduation night they come out of the woodwork! Where have most of these people been for four years?"

"I don't know, but you can look at the way they act and dress and understand why they are like they are,'" Margaret said. "Let's just get this over with before something terrible happens."

Something terrible had already occurred at too many high school graduations around the state and it was becoming epidemic nationwide. In Baton Rouge the previous year, a graduation ceremony had to be evacuated because of a bomb scare. In 2003, there was a gang fight in the parking lot forcing the cancellation of a New Orleans graduation. In Baton Rouge just a few nights before, one school opted to have their graduation exercises on campus, but concerned students told their principal they heard rumors of a possible shooting that was to take place during commencement. Nothing happened, thankfully, but it may have had something to do with additional East Baton Rouge Parish sheriff's deputies on campus. East Side High School never had to worry about violence at its graduation. The only violence at the River Center on this afternoon was the current suicide of the school's culture and tradition.

With that, Tory and Margaret turned and faced the stage arranged with chairs, a large table, and a podium set up for the ceremony. Most of the faculty was now present and talking among themselves when the lights began to dim to 50 percent candlepower. The twenty-three-member band was now properly composed sitting upright as the school band director, Dr. Marie Pellington, waved her plastic white baton and led them in the traditional song, "Pomp and Circumstance." From the rear of the arena graduates began moving toward the faculty and the stage in one long line. Unfortunately, the noise from the much larger crowd now grew even more obnoxious—so much so, they drowned out the band music.

"Shateshia! Shateshia!" called out one mother as she waved madly in recognition of her daughter. "Go girl, go!"

"There goes my baby! There goes my baby!" another mother called out as she stood jumping and waving and making a scene.

"Martin! Martin! Martin!" three boys chanted in unison while stomping feet as their friend stepped onto the arena floor.

Martin waved and smiled before the student behind corrected him with a gentle shove.

"Dante! I'm over here!" yelled another as a camera bulb went off in the distance.

The chants and impromptu greetings from the crowd to the students ranged from childish to sublime. Camera bulbs blanketed the floor. Either way, it made East Side High School's graduation ceremony closely resemble pre-game tailgating on a college campus on a drunken football Saturday night. But this was not Saturday night. It was not a sporting event. This was not entertainment. It was a graduation exercise that should have been dignified, solemn, and respectable. It was starting out to be nothing of the sort.

After the students made their grand entrance and stood in front of the dull metal chairs, they were asked to remain standing for the playing of the National Anthem followed by prayer. During the playing of the "Star Spangled Banner," many in the crowd continued to talk. Some of the younger individuals did not even bother to stand, remove their hats, or cease speaking on their cell phones. The poor strains of the school band were difficult to hear. Only when there was prayer did the arena finally become as quiet as it should have been throughout the entire ceremony.

Tory leaned over and whispered to Margaret, "The band is terrible, bless their hearts."

Margaret nodded her head in agreement and then placed her finger over her full lips reminding Tory to be quiet for a minute longer.

There was a time when the school band numbered nearly one-hundred strong. For the public school system in the here and now, that was nearly ten years and 14,000 students ago. So many students had left the public school system in East Baton Rouge Parish it was next to impossible for most school bands to comfortably exhibit the parts played by all instruments in the brass or woodwind sections. Still having nearly the same number of high schools as twenty years before, the number of students available to participate in extra-curricular activities was stretched to the absolute limit. It was one reason Dr. Pellington chose to not only lead the band in playing, but to play one of many instruments herself in an effort to make up for any part left not played. On this night she was seen playing a baritone, a part normally played by a graduating senior now sitting with his peers.

The future of music in the public school system was not promising. The school system no longer granted band directors even the small, insulting, annual $1,000 operating stipend they once assumed to keep their feeble band departments going. Consequently, the instruments fell into disrepair, uniforms fell to pieces, and band parts for instruments were scarce. The East Side High School band did what it could to live up to the expectations, but they fell woefully short. It was left to overworked band directors to fundraise on weekends to keep the department going.

As the band played on following the prayer, head girl's basketball coach Debra Annison strolled in late after the graduates were seated. She sat beside Margaret and Tory. At first Debra kept to herself feeling somewhat guilty for her tardiness, but soon realized she was in good company as other teachers did the same. It was not lost on Debra as she stared around the arena for the first time and noticed that there were incredible numbers of people standing along the railings, a crowd now numbering nearly 3,000. Debra could only dream what it must be like to play her basketball games in front of such crowds. Her feelings were stated aloud to gain the attention of Margaret and Tory.

"If we could get this many people to the girl's basketball games during one season, I could pay the bills for our team for the next two seasons," Debra said staring straight ahead and in a whisper to both teachers. "Where do all of these people come from?"

Margaret did not know Debra well, never having attended a girl's basketball game, but she was not uncomfortable with her and did not wish to appear as being snotty.

"Coach, we were just saying the same thing," Margaret said.

"I mean, do the math here," Debra continued as she pointed at the seated graduates in front of her. "If there are about, oh, say, 3,000 people here and just over 200 graduates, it means there are fifteen people here for every student. Now you know there is no way these kids have that kind of support at home! It just isn't realistic!"

Margaret and Tory knew she was right, but didn't think to put the situation in mathematical terms. Since Debra did, it made the scene all the more shocking to witness. It left a lot of questions unanswered concerning student discipline, the lack of which would show as East Side High School Principal Berling then stood and walked toward the podium to deliver his speech that promised to be to the point. He was dressed conservatively in white shirt and black suit and tie. In his hands he held the written version of his speech. As he adjusted the microphone to speak to a crowd that had grown unhealthy in size and restraint, applause mixed with ugly comments greeted him.

"Boooooooo!" came the greeting from a handful of former students seated high above the arena now exacting revenge on their former principal.

"Sit down, old man!" another shouted loud enough to be heard by all.

"Hey 'Burr-head,' you suck!" came the voice of a recently expelled student as the crowd's applause slowly appreciated in decibels and began to drown out the ugly comments that continued to flow.

Principal Berling simply ignored the verbal abuse. He gave the ugly retorts no weight.

Not known as a good speaker, much less captivating, Principal Berling was great at getting to the point at graduation and faculty meetings. He prided himself on serving graduation like cafeteria food; he was quick at the expense of being great. But the faculty loved his brevity and appreciated the demands this night had on his teacher's personal time. On this night, however, he would surprise his faculty with his best speech ever.

"Good evening all, and welcome to the 2004 East Side High School graduation," he began uncomfortably.

"You suck!" came a call from the stands behind him.

There was some laughter.

"Tonight, we say goodbye to 204 seniors, a group I like to call 'survivors' because they endured four years of high school education," he continued having never acknowledged the interruptions. "They endured. I like to use that word, 'endure,' because that is what they really have done. To emphasize how much I admire their persistence, I want to remind them that the freshmen class to which they belonged just four short years ago had 325 students. What happened to the other 121 students? For many reasons, and there are a lot of them—some legitimate and many not—this group sitting before me is the reason I get up every morning and go to school. They are the reason for our being."

"Shut up, dude! You makin' me sick!" came the call from the right of the stage where most of the crowd were sitting.

There was no police officer on duty to stop the insults and the faculty had no power off the campus to put an end to the display of disrespect and ignorance.

Principal Berling continued without a stutter, "Our institution is about their success, their leadership, and their dreams. If we, as a faculty, even played a very small part in their future success, then our job as educators is worth the myriad of problems we face each day in educating the masses. And make no mistake, we educate masses, not individuals. Our faculty educates groups, not individuals. Most public high schools do. So it is all the more impressive when a student performs above and beyond the call in preparing for life after high school."

"Who cares what you think, dude!" came a cat call from the same group of thugs seated high above the arena floor.

The crowd near them noticed the group and was becoming irritated with them. Some began to tell them to keep their mouths closed as they were irritating many, but the thugs just laughed louder.

Principal Berling continued to speak and ignored the eight poorly dressed white-trash troublemakers. He wished a River Center security guard would escort them out, but they did not. The lack of security in the arena gave these punks license to abuse a man who had served in the military and was in possession of twenty-four years of educational experience. They had gained most everyone's attention. Many of the East Side High School coaches were angered by the rude behavior, but they were not on school property and were rather helpless in dealing with it. All one could hope was they would refrain from their juvenile remarks of their boss after they had sufficiently amused themselves. But Principal Berling was no pushover, either. He was very much used to unruly students and uncompromising parents. He had broken up enough fights on campus in his time to qualify for a bartender's job in a blue-collar bar. His next sentence was a subtle verbal jab at the noisy eight students now chastising his every word.

"In fact, it is all the more impressive when we can call our students 'graduates' rather than the punks too many want to be because society tells them it's cool to be that way," Principal Berling said leaning slightly toward the crude behavior of one group behind him.

The crowd laughed politely.

"The students sitting before me are not all scholars," he continued, "and that's okay. It really is.

"Some of the young people sitting here tonight in cap and gown are just graduates. They did not excel in school. For them, however, just being here took overcoming incredible odds. No, not all of our seniors' test scores were exemplary. They will not be attending college. But they overcame incredible odds just to get to school and participate in the educational process to graduate. That alone is a success that will not make the newspapers or qualify as a success story. If you knew how hard it was for about forty of these young people just to finish high school, you would give them the same standing ovation you are going to give our very brightest students. I can't delve into their hardships. That would not be appropriate. But the faculty is aware of those hardships and we are just as proud of those students as we are the 32 percent of the senior class that qualified for the state academic scholarship, TOPS."

There was more polite applause. Principal Berling looked up and smiled at the crowd.

What Principal Berling said was painfully true. Success is often defined as rising test scores, college scholarship and academic awards accrued, which university one attends, and grade point averages. This is vital for success in a competitive world, if not mandatory. However, there are often unforeseen circumstances that inhibit students from performing even below grade level. Increasingly, too many students find it a struggle just to go to school given the problems with which they are forced to deal each day. It's a struggle they should not be forced to reckon with at fourteen to nineteen years of age, if at all.

Of the 204 seniors, nine were already mothers and seven were fathers. Sixteen had already served juvenile time for various felony charges. Another eight students were on probation—their probation officers seated in the arena verifying their graduation. Ten had recently shaken off alcohol or drug abuse and three were taken from their biological parents who were physically or sexually abusing them. Seventy percent of the senior class qualified for free or reduced lunch and about one-third of them had to work full-time jobs to financially assist their struggling families. Seven seniors had been expelled at one point in their high school careers, but returned to school the following year with a renewed enthusiasm and a better sense of what was right and wrong. Twelve of the graduates were age nineteen. Over half came from single-parent households, and about half of those students were reared by aging grandparents. Eleven had recently signed on the dotted line to join one of the five branches of the U.S. military, mostly because they had nowhere else to go. These painful statistics were not tabulated and were not unusual in public schools. These stories would not be counted as successes by the pencil pushers at BESE who failed to understand just how difficult it was for teachers to do a job in which they really had no control—a job that was sometimes rewarded by a struggling student's simple commitment to finish high school with a mediocre passing mark.

Principal Berling continued, "We did, of course, have stellar students who will move on to college. Despite what many choose to believe these days, students can get a great education in a public school. You see, ladies and gentlemen, public school is the real world. It's a world that is often so ugly we don't want to hear about it. We don't always want to hear the truth about our society because it is so painful. We feel helpless and vulnerable in dealing with those problems and no one likes that feeling. So instead of admitting the society we have created is quite often the major problem with educating our young people today, we simply blame the teachers, the administrators, and even the school itself. Those schools are labeled 'failing schools.'

"What is a failing school, by the way? I never did understand what a failing school is. Is it bricks, windows and doors that are not working?

In fact, they don't open and close on demand, so it stops our students from learning. Maybe it means when the water fountains don't shoot cold water into waiting mouths on a warm day it's made it tougher for our students to pay attention in geometry class."

There was mild laughter from the audience. Principal Berling now had the crowd's attention. He began to relax in front of the largest crowd he had ever spoken to in his career. The thugs, thankfully, had finally relaxed having grown tired of amusing themselves.

"Some of the people I answer to are always telling principals to raise our 'school performance scores' or risk being labeled a 'failing school,'" he continued. "I chuckle at that. Schools perform or fail because of the students in it. Public schools do not get to pick their students. We teach whatever students get off the bus in a particular year. We do the best we can and maybe I'm a fool, but I still think we do a great job.

"Just like anything else in life, you get out of something what you put into it. Graduates, don't ever forget that simple fact. You are here today because you chose to educate your mind. You chose to improve the quality of your life. Your teachers have always been there for you. It took a commitment from you to make good on that partnership between a student and a teacher. No matter what people will tell you, the education you received at East Side High School is not inferior.

"Sure, no, we don't have perfect lawns and flowers flowing out of terracotta pots costing more than what some of your parents make in a week of work. No, we don't have a state of the art sports complex or alumni that raise tens of thousands of dollars for us each year. I wish we did, but we don't. Very soon, you will be sitting next to students just a few months from now who attended some of the most expensive high schools in the state, and maybe the entire country. Do not be intimidated by that! Just because a student comes from a more impressive school or their parents make more money than yours does not make them better than you. But you still must prove it, just as they will. You must prove you are as good as they are. There is no better feeling in the world than to accomplish something you dream of and doing it when some people believe you cannot. Some will tell you your public education will not serve you well. Don't you believe it!

"The last thing I want to tell you is, life is not fair. We tell young people when they are in kindergarten they can be anything they want to be. That is still true. What we don't tell you in kindergarten and what we wait to tell you until your high school graduation is this: What are you willing to give up to reach your goals? Oh yes, there is a heavy price to pay for achieving your dreams. That is why some people still call it 'dreams.' All some people do is dream. You are not going to be able to accomplish your mission in life by doing things the same way you have always done them. What are you going to give up to get what you want? Some students study so much they sleep less. Others go out less frequently with their friends because they are totally committed to their studies. Some live at home a bit longer than they want to. What price are you going to pay to be successful after tonight? If you want to succeed in life, trust me, you will have to pay for it. Nothing is free. Whoever told you that some things in life are free probably lied. Even if something is free to you, somebody somewhere that you don't know is paying for it. You college-bound graduates, please pay that price! When you are my age you will be so glad you did. You must trust me on that one. And remember, your future is not a place you are going. It is something you create.

"For those of you not going to college, get licensed or certified to do something. Don't spend your time waiting to get your big break in life. No one is going to invite you into a world of success. You are going to have to crash that party by being so good at what you do they can't help but notice you.

"There is no crime in hard physical work. We need blue-collar workers as much as we need college graduates in society. There is a role for you to play and there is money for you to make. Go and earn it by being great at whatever it is you choose to do. Be a bricklayer, an electrician, plumber, welder, carpenter, or hairdresser. Dedicate your life to it. Marry it. Excel in it.

"Lastly, I invite all graduates to come back to dear old East Side and visit me, or your now ex-teachers in ten years and tell us what became of you. Brag to us of your successes. Tell us of the places you have traveled. Tell us about how much money you are making. Tell us that you are making more money than us. We'll be both thrilled for you and jealous. We want to hear of your successes. We need to hear of them."

There was more laughter and applause. Some of the graduates slapped the palms of those sitting next to them as a show of support for Principal Berling's challenge.

He continued as he picked up the pace of his rhetoric.

"Come back and tell us about the hospital you work in, the office you run, the business you began, the invention you are working on, the book you are writing, the master's degree you just completed, the military rank you attained, the building you helped build and design, and the exotic places you have seen. Brag to us! Because when you brag to us you are really telling the East Side High School faculty the job they did was good enough because you were good enough. Even if the general public does not know it, the Class of 2004 is as good a group of young people I have ever been around. I mean that when I say it. Those of you who stuck it out were a treat to be around. You are the survivors. You will be missed. I will miss you."

Principal Berling began to draw tears from some in the crowd. The crowd was nearly at a hush for the first time all night. He was brilliant in his speech. The crowd applauded again, but with more enthusiasm. Whether Principal Berling wrote the words himself or even believed them mattered little. His words were the highlight of the evening, words the faculty wanted to believe. He paused for a second before continuing.

"Now, I turn the mic' over to our valedictorian, Seth Andrews. Seth finished with a 4.2 grade point average. He will be attending the University of Mississippi in Oxford, or 'Ole Miss' as some of you know it, and will major in pre-medicine. Ladies and gentlemen, I give you, Seth Andrews."

The applause was approving at both Principal Berling's speech and Seth's worthy accomplishments and introduction—proof the night was moving toward a swift conclusion. As the applause continued, Debra, Margaret, and Tory stared at each other in silence.

"I can't believe what I just heard," Debra said in utter amazement.

"Did anyone write that down?" asked Tory. "That's the best graduation speech I think I ever heard."

"I didn't know the old man had it in him," Margaret added.

The three teachers, like the students near them, were in shock that Principal Berling could muster enough words to produce such a strong speech. He was entertaining, blunt, factual, and brutally honest. They were all very proud of his effort. Whether the students were mature enough to take heed of his well-crafted words or even remember them after a night of beer busts and champagne to follow was another matter.

As Seth spoke his own words, the noise level in the arena reached such a level almost no one could pay attention if they wanted to. What the noisy crowd did not know was Seth did not enroll in East Side High School until the middle of his junior year. He was the success story the federal government bureaucrats wanted more of.

Seth attended a high school labeled a "failing school." Under President George Bush's "No Child Left Behind" Act, students from such failing schools were free to transfer to other schools to facilitate a better education for themselves. Over 400 students were invited to leave that so-called failing institution and enroll in one of four other high schools, including East Side High School. Sadly and shockingly, only eighty-five students parish-wide chose to leave their failing school and transfer, a statistic that said a great deal. The media did not pick up on that revealing story.

Of the twenty-seven high school students who took the president's plan to heart in December 2002, and enrolled in East Side High School, twenty-five returned to their original school before the grass began to turn green in early March. Most of them attended East Side High School as failing students falsely believing their fate was tied to poor teacher performance. That is what the students and their parents were told to believe and they took the bait because it provided another excuse for their poor academic performance. What those struggling students learned at East Side High School was more about *why* they were failing, not *who* was failing them. In short, they simply did not want to learn. While it was true East Side High School challenged the students more, they were forced to admit to themselves the problem lie with them. It was not the school failing the student. Just like before their transfer, it was the student failing in the school. Outrageously, teachers were, again, the obvious targets of a dictatorial government's educational policy responsible for most of the public school system's failures nationwide.

Ironically, one student mentioned to Tory in February she wanted to return to her "old school" because she could pass her classes with

B's and not really work that hard. Therefore, her chance at a TOPS award was virtually assured. At East Side High School, she was failing every class except physical education and art. Seth was one of only two students transferring to East Side High School from that "failing school" that actually graduated from it. Whatever happened to those students leaving East Side High School returning to their original institutions no one knew. The guess was most graduated with inflated grade point averages, earned TOPS, and were preparing to enter college woefully unprepared at the expense of the Louisiana taxpayer.

Seth was now wrapping up his speech, and the crescendo gained the attention of a crowd growing tired.

"Remember, class of 2004, the words of former British Prime Minister Winston Churchill. His words applied to his nation's fighting Germany during World War II, but can be applied to us as we leave the security of high school life. Churchill said, 'This is not the end. It is not even the beginning of the end. But it is, perhaps, the end of the beginning.' We should remember that high school is not the end of the journey. It's just one small step into what we all hope is a life we can be proud of."

There was only polite applause for Seth's obligatory speech. Churchill's quote was the climax of an otherwise dull dialogue, but it had its moments.

"I'll miss kids like that," Tory said to Margaret and Debra as she clapped her hands. "There aren't many of them. Not like Seth."

Tory then paused and sighed.

"Well, I guess this is as good a time as any," Tory said to Margaret as she looked at the floor and adjusted herself in her chair.

Tory had bad news to deliver and was not sure of Margaret's reaction or her own emotional manner as she spit the words out.

"Margaret, I'm moving to Texas at the end of the school year," Tory explained.

There was silence between them with a noisy arena serving as the background to the new drama. Margaret said nothing. Her stomach suddenly grew tense and she felt as if she was running a fever. She waited for her friend to tell her it was all a joke. The look on Tory's face said something else.

"I was going to tell you, but I was waiting for the right time," Tory said to Margaret as if she was speaking to an emotionally torn teenager upset over losing a lover. "My husband applied for a job transfer to any city in Texas just before Christmas. He wanted to further his career. We were willing to move to San Antonio, Dallas-Fort Worth, Austin, Houston, and even as far as El Paso. He was just waiting for a call and he got one. It just happened all so quick."

Margaret was stunned. Tory registered her pain and sighed, trying to make light of it all.

"Come on, Margaret, Baton Rouge is nowhere if you are looking for white-collar work," she said touching Tory's shoulder. "A career person can only go so far here. If you really want to make it in the big time, if you're serious about your career, you have to leave this place. Even the college students know that. They're leaving by the thousands. There's a reason. There just isn't much here to offer professional people."

Margaret looked right at Tory finally feeling strong enough to remark.

"When did you plan on telling me?" Margaret asked Tory, still reeling a bit from the sudden news. "I mean, did you tell Mr. Berling? Do you have a job to go to? Have you been house shopping?"

Tory cocked her head from one side to the other to respond to the last question. She smiled and gave away the answer without saying a word. Margaret picked out the answer to her question easily.

"You've been using your sick days to go to Texas and take care of your business, haven't you?" Margaret asked with a smile.

"Hey, I can't take the sick days with me to Texas," Tory said with a laugh. "I've got forty-three sick days accrued and I'm not going to get paid for them. I used some of them. I earned them."

The two girls moved closer together to talk as the noise and applause level grew from honor students giving speeches.

"We found out about the transfer during spring break," Tory continued. "We got a call from the home office in Dallas and they offered Bob a transfer over the phone. We hopped a plane the next day, Bob signed the transfer papers, and we went house shopping. The company is going to buy our Baton Rouge home from us and we signed the mortgage on another home last week. It was really too easy."

"It sounds it," Margaret replied staring at the floor to keep from becoming emotional. "Things have been moving fast, haven't they?"

"Yea, they have, but what choice do we have? Bob has gone as far as he can go in Baton Rouge. Dallas has so much to offer! I mean, Margaret, you should see the place. It's clean. They keep the grass mowed. The roads are nice. There's hardly any litter. The schools are unbelievable. The city moves and there are jobs everywhere. There's plenty to do. It's a place people are moving to, not from. Bob got a nice raise. Hell, he's been working there two weeks a month since Halloween already. We were just waiting for the end of the school year so I could join him. I told Mr. Berling about a month ago that I was leaving and told him not to say anything until I did."

"Are you still going to teach?" Margaret asked.

"Oh, yea, but I haven't really been looking too hard," Tory said as she waved her hand in front of her face. "I did fill out an application at the school system office there and I'm waiting to hear from them. They assured me I would have a job. I just don't know when. And let me tell you, honey, their pay scale will make you ill. I'll make about $11,000 per year more than here for my experience level. The schools are state of the art. We work in a dump compared to what they have to offer. Margaret, it's a move we have to make."

Both girls finally began to focus their attention on the stage of graduates. Margaret had her information. She knew Tory was right, but it hurt to hear that another teacher was leaving Louisiana. Many have done so over the years and she thought nothing of it, but this time it was a close friend. Margaret knew no one would care. Tory would be replaced and that would be that. Tory was truly outstanding at what she did in the classroom. Teachers are not interchangeable cogs in the education machine. Like all professions, there were good ones and bad ones. She was beyond good. Tory was great. Her leaving would be Louisiana's loss and once again, a gain for Texas, a state racing into the twenty-first century while the self-proclaimed "Sportsman's Paradise" slept on its bed of corruption and apathy.

The graduates were then given the word to now slowly move from their seated rows toward the stage, and up steps decorated with ribbons and flowers to collect their diplomas. Although the students sat patiently, the crowd did not. Many continued to yell out the names of graduates they knew at the top of their lungs. The milling about of spectators in the arena now resembled that of a basketball game. Decorum was absent. Good taste had deceased. The teachers were now resigned to what the graduation had become, more like a spectator sport, instead of what they had hoped would be a return to common courtesy.

Tory, Margaret, and Debra did not speak during these final moments. They refused to be part of the mob. They each possessed enough respect for their soon former pupils to not further disgrace the ceremony with additional unnecessary verbiage. Instead, each of them watched graduates collect their diplomas, reach out to shake the hands of the school administrators, temporarily pose for the camera that would forever catch the moment in time, and depart the stage. With each passing face they recorded in their minds both the good and bad times they had experienced with them. They remembered awkward freshman faces with gangly bodies, the discipline problems, the lost games, the failed tests, the feeling of academic accomplishment, the warm smiles, the victories, late night bus rides from field trips and ball games, the fund raisers, the tears, the confrontations, the unsolicited advice, the fights, the absurdity that marked their unremarkable home life, broken hearts, and successful completion of standardized testing. Teachers would remember their voices and match it with faces that would constantly change as they grew older, but would be forever frozen in black and white yearbook photos. Mental photos of their "children" that would serve as ghosts in a classroom now filled with mere memories of them and fresh faces needing to be led.

Not all students from the class of 2004 would return to visit East Side High School in the future. For many, they would never return owing allegiance to nothing being grateful to no one. They would disappear in the crowded class struggle that defined American life and culture. Some would survive it. Others would blame it. Too many would struggle to stay afloat in it. There were a few in the group who would go on to great things, despite their backgrounds. They may or may not know that the proverbial "deck" was stacked against them. Either through hard work, street bluff or a forcing of a reshuffling of the cards, some would learn enough to draw a lucky hand that would allow them to compete.

Even though most graduates did not know it, they were the ones that made a teacher's job satisfying. They made it through public high school. To date, they defied the pull from the materialistic culture's credo that happiness could be bought with government assistance, a drug, a song, a dance, and a cheap version of *laisse-faire*. They refused to be part of the state's horrendous high school dropout rate. They followed the instructions of their teachers, and some parents, and persisted when too many among them chastised the effort. They were the survivors.

"We have more educated people than at any time in history; we have more people with college degrees, yet our humanity is a diseased humanity...It isn't knowledge we need; knowledge we have. Humanity is in need of something spiritual."
-Morehouse College President Dr. Benjamin Mays, 1964

Late May—A Playground of Mediocrity

The faculty was on edge. Students had completed final exams and left school in a hurry on this final half-day. Teachers wanted to administer those exams, grade them as quickly as reasonably possible, tally the overall grades, and submit other paperwork to the office before the end of the working day.

Unfortunately, some teachers also had another problem to deal with. The school system had announced at the end of April that the budget, once again, was not adequate to sustain the school system for the next year. For the fourth consecutive year, the budget ax was to fall on the backs of the teachers. Meaning, the school system decided to save the needed operating monies in question by firing nearly 200 teachers at the end of the school year. Few in the community took notice, especially the news media, that in the last three years the school system had relieved nearly 500 teachers of their jobs. Classroom sizes had gotten larger. Faculty workloads had grown. Raises were not forthcoming and the cry from the state's so-called experts would lament of a fictitious inner city teaching shortage.

Retiring teachers would absorb the majority of those job losses. Some positions left vacant would remain so. However, there was still no getting around the fact that many teachers would be going home unemployed. For teachers, dodging the unemployment bullet became an unfortunate year-end ritual. The hardest hit would always be the newly hired teachers. They were the future of the school system, had the most energy and enthusiasm, and still believed they could make a difference in the lives of young people. When selections were made, usually by principals, as to which teachers got cut from the faculty and shoved into the unemployment line, those teachers classified as minority, or those possessing seniority, were usually left poised to return. It was the rest of the teachers who needed to worry.

Such was the case for seven non-black teachers lined up against the wall of East Side High School Principal Berling's office. He called a selected group into his office via the intercom as soon as the last students had exited the campus for the summer. Every teacher in the school could only guess why those teachers were called as they slowly made their way down the staircases and into his office and uncertainty. When they arrived, they stood like soldiers lined against the wood-paneled wall. It was to be a career firing squad.

Lined up and awaiting the verdict was Greg Tally, a twenty-four-year-old unmarried science teacher only in his second year. Fully certified in his subject matter, he was the most popular with the students. His charm and good looks did not hurt his credibility, either. The fact was he could hypnotize students when teaching. That was all the more impressive when considering he was placed in the school's worst science lab with the fewest amenities. He never complained knowing one day he would rise to the top of the science faculty and inherit the better classroom. That was his long-term hope. In the meantime, and out of his own pocket, Greg bought some newer equipment and got local companies to donate money to purchase other needed items. Greg bought and erected his own white board for better visual instruction and got his former college science professor to help him prepare for a sequence of lectures. Greg made it work.

Next along the wall was Dr. Jay Anders, a middle-aged biology teacher in his first year. Jay was not certified, but he did carry a doctorate in his subject area. That was good enough reason to hire him the first week into the school year when there were *no* science teachers to be found. Dr. Anders was right out of college and needed a job. For the school and for Dr. Anders the situation worked out more than fine. When he started teaching he had every intention to look for other types of employment. Teaching was simply something to do until he landed a research position somewhere on the West Coast nearer his San Diego roots. Like a native Californian, he loved to surf and scuba dive. Strangely, he found teaching more fun than he cared to admit. Educating students was a new love in his life and he wished to continue doing so. San Diego would simply have to wait.

There was Terry Achison, a thirty-three-year-old history teacher who got his job after another instructor was fired in the middle of the school year. Terry, who was substitute teaching at the school the day of the firing, learned of the job opening from a group of students who loved his teaching style. Terry did not simply pass out assigned work when substituting, he actually taught the subject matter when he could. He got involved with their lives and soon became known as "that cool substitute." The students urged Terry to apply for the job. He did apply. The next day, believing he had no chance at all at the position, Terry was asked to return the following morning for an interview. Within twenty-four hours he was hired to teach three preps for the remainder of the year. For his hard work, he was awarded with two additional years of employment. Twice he had organized trips to Europe chaperoning thirty-five students to eight nations from the U.K. to Greece. He helped officiate and coach intramural football and basketball games after school. Terry fell in love with teaching and the students in his life. He hoped to make it a career. He had two college degrees, one of which was in the subject he was teaching, and was to be certified by summer's end. Unmarried, he considered the hallways of East Side High School his second home. He had taken multiple college courses the last eight college semesters, including past summers, to earn that certification and hopefully entrench himself in the teaching corps.

Twenty-nine year-old Mike Hammonds was one of only three East Side High School alums. He was uncertified and had degrees in journalism and English. Since most high schools did not have journalism or mass media classes, he was resigned to teaching English. However, he integrated some journalism into his course matter. The students loved learning about the mass media more than they enjoyed writing poetry and reading literature. Mike, a newlywed, had spent the last six summers writing and editing numerous articles for various football magazines. Many local area fans began taking a serious interest in football during those certain hot summer months ahead and Mike made extra money helping feed that fan interest while keeping his writing skills sharp. Any teacher who could get students interested in writing had more than earned his keep at any high school. Mike pulled off that magnificent feat. His reward from the school system was anonymity. No one at the school board office knew of his keen gift to students. The school system did know that he occupied a position and they knew it must be taken from him for reasons beyond his control.

Mary Ann Samson graduated college with her heart set on teaching mathematics. She graduated college with honors and was proud of her ability to teach when most of her friends and family working in the public sector scoffed at her talent. Her parents begged her not to enter teaching because they perceived it as a thankless profession administered by unknowing, so-called professionals with hidden agendas. Mary Ann's father told her tales of family and friends that found themselves fighting with corrupt school officials over trivial items, only to be forced to quit the profession or take transfers against their will to undesirable schools. Mary Ann's father even told his daughter he would not pay for her college tuition as long as she majored in secondary education. Mary Ann and her father had a wonderful relationship, but this was the first time the pair had such strong feelings on an issue. Undaunted, Mary Ann applied for and was awarded some financial aid. Along the way she earned a partial academic scholarship. When she graduated it was her father that cried tears of joy. He still did not approve of his daughter entering the teaching profession, but he was amazed and impressed with her tenacity to enter it anyway. At the time, she was living at home to help pay off some of her college debts. Now after one year of teaching, she found herself lined up against Principal Berling's office wall like a criminal awaiting a verdict.

Claire Metz was a recently divorced forty-four-year-old mother of two. After nineteen years of marriage her husband walked out on her after his business failed. She could not sue him successfully because all he had was debt, which legally, was the only thing he left her with along with two school-aged children. Claire had taught mathematics in the mid 1980s, but quit to help her husband with the business. She never regretted the move. Her husband's computer business did well and she sensed the public school system was faltering. She did not like or approve of private schools because they paid teachers poorly and seemingly felt preordained to interfere into one's personal life. During her separation from her husband and with nowhere left to turn, Claire decided to support her family on a teaching salary. Not having taught in over three years, state law automatically stripped Claire of her certification. She had just begun taking night classes to regain it. Like the others in the room she nervously awaited her fate.

Doug Waters, a thirty-six-year-old uncertified physical education coach, had plans to be married and certified in the coming fall. Doug coached the boy's and girl's swim team as well as girl's softball, and like Terry Atchison—without pay—stayed after school to help with intramurals. He was one of the more popular teachers. He knew how to talk the language of the students. He never gave in to their silly dramatics, and yet, had a calming influence on them—so much so, many students admitted they wanted to be more like him. In a student's eyes he had a strange mix of being authoritarian and cool.

The only noise heard in the office was the squeaking of Principal Berling's chair. There was the hum of the window air-conditioning unit. A polished man only when convenience allowed, he was not known as a fair man. He played favorites. A rule enforced on one teacher may be ignored when dealing with another. Hallway rumor was he was somewhat sexist and did not have the guts to confront coaches in dealing with controversial incidents. It was a hard thing to prove, but that was the talk among teachers. No one wanted to believe it. However, there was evidence if one believed the stories told within the walls of the faculty washroom.

Principal Berling was polite, but firm, in dealing with his faculty. He did not embarrass his teachers publicly. He spoke well, dressed even better, and had a reputation of fighting for his teacher's rights, if liked, in the face of school system that treated its teachers as social security numbers. But not even he could fight the Consent Decree that mandated the race of a faculty ratio to be as near to 50 percent black and 50 percent non-black as reasonably possible. It was the school system's version of Affirmative Action.

Few schools were exactly 50-50 in percentage of racial makeup, but they had to be very close. Consequently, many white teachers did not get hired until the first day of school as every consideration was given to hiring minority teachers first and foremost. White or non-black teachers understood the unspoken rule when learning of a job opening. It was demoralizing for qualified and certified teachers to wait until the first day of school to learn if they were to be employed. Many just quit applying. That was a major factor in the so-called teaching shortage.

Principal Berling took too long to give the bad news to his teachers. He tried to be professional, but the teachers knew he was the bearer of bad news before the first words left his lips. He slipped his glasses down his nose and read from a document faxed to him from the school system office.

"I called you seven in here today because I received a letter from the school system yesterday afternoon concerning the employment and racial makeup of our current faculty," Principal Berling said slowly and deliberately. "Unfortunately, due to the Consent Decree laid down by the courts, the faculty at East Side High School is deemed as having too many non-black teachers. In fact, only one other high school under the jurisdiction of the city's public school system has more white teachers than do we. And now the system insists, without further delay, that we remedy this problem."

The teachers knew their fate had been sealed. They never saw their employment or teaching career as a problem, but it was to someone with too much power. Within another long spoken paragraph or two from their boss they would be the newest teaching refugees driven from the public school system.

"It is my unfortunate duty to inform you all that there is no longer a position available for you to continue teaching at East Side High School," he continued. "I am to begin looking for your replacements immediately and, yes, before you ask, I must replace you with minorities. This is completely out of my control. Please understand, I must answer to others. However, I want to tell each of you how much I have enjoyed being associated with you. You have performed admirably and should be proud of your achievements here."

Principal Berling's final salute to them fell on stunned faces. It meant little. It was something he wanted to say and might have felt compelled to say. Either way, they were out of work for no other reason than they were guilty of the crime of being part of a generation born in the segregated South. Now, because of the sins of others, they were paying the price with their young careers.

Claire Metz walked out of the room in tears. She had a family to care for and more problems than any solitary person should have to deal with at one time. Now she had unemployment to add to her list of problems. When she left the office and entered the hallway, tears had rolled down Claire's face and onto her white blouse. Teachers were milling about in the hallway when Claire briskly walked past three female teachers as she moved toward the double doors leading to the back parking lot.

They called out to her, "Claire! Claire! Wait!"

The trio knew by her reaction she was relieved of her duties. Claire never stopped walking. In fact, she picked up her pace as they called her name. She fumbled with her purse in an effort to remove her car keys. Once under control she slowly pulled out of the parking lot. The three teachers watched helplessly as she drove away. One teacher, who hardly knew Claire, decided to verbally attack the root of the problem.

"I hate this damned school system sometimes!" she said angrily before catching herself and calming. "Soon or later it's going to catch up with all of us. Today, it's Claire and God knows who else got fired today. Next year it could be any of us. This is just not right. The school system does not give a hoot about any of us!"

"Nope, they don't," said Dale Addison, one of the school's guidance counselors who had just walked in on the group of females. "Did you hear?"

"Hear what?" the female teachers asked in unison.

"Old man Berling had to cut six others," Dale said before beginning the roll call. "He cut Doug Waters, Mary Ann Samson, Dr. Anders, Terry Atchison, Greg Tally, and Mike Hammonds."

With each name called out by Dale, the female teachers sighed in dramatic disbelief. In other professions employees get laid off when a business closes, falters, or an employee fails to live up to expectations. In the inner-city public school system version of the teaching profession, one could gain or lose employment based on nothing more than skin pigmentation. Credentials and experience sometimes meant nothing.

Greg Tally walked out of the principal's office without saying a word. He was a self-assured man. He had a lot to offer and had no one to answer to in his life. As he paced outside by Dale and the other teachers that had gathered at the edge of the shaded parking lot, Greg walked out with his brief case and a smile. He gave the group of teachers the thumbs up sign and never lost his stride.

"Hey, Greg, I'm sorry about your job," Dale said in a sincere, apologetic tone.

He had hoped Greg would stop and speak with him, but did not.

"Don't be," Greg said as he continued walking toward his car. "I have friends in Texas and I'll be working there next year for more money and less bullshit."

Back in Principal Berling's office, Dr. Anders moved closer to Principal Berling's heavy wooden desk that, at the moment, served more as protection to him than as office furniture.

"Is there any chance I might get to come back next year, sir?" Jay asked candidly.

"Jay, I know you've got a doctorate, but you are not certified," Principal Berling said. "Unless you get certified over the summer there is doubt about whether I can hire you back."

"Mr. Berling, it would take me an additional twenty-four hours of college class work to complete a silly certification process when I have the highest level of education on my resume. It's absurd to spend that kind of money to get certified. I can teach at a major university, but not here at the high school level. This is all *so* stupid!"

"At best, I may be able to hire you back because you, like Mary Ann Samson, teach science and math respectively. Those courses are labeled 'critical need' areas. But because you are both Caucasian I won't know if I can hire you back until the first week of school. Every effort must be made to hire minorities first. If I were you I would not turn down any offers from other schools."

Jay and Mary Ann walked out of the office together after shaking Principal Berling's hand. The principal was handcuffed in making decisions for his school. There was no need to question him any further. This decision-making process was not about education. It was about race politics. And they were the wrong color in the wrong school system in the wrong city.

Now moving in position to stand in front of the principal's desk was Mike Hammonds. Principal Berling answered his question before Mike even asked it.

"Mike, I would love to keep you around here, but you heard what I told the rest," he said. "It's a bit worse for you, I'm afraid. Math and science teachers are in big demand. I *may* be able to hire some of these people back. Social studies and English teachers are a nickel a dozen. I hate to tell you this, but your chances of being employed here next year are not good. I'm sorry."

Without saying a word or making eye contact Mike extended his hand for a shake and walked out. He didn't know whether to be angry, insulted, rejected, or discriminated against. Mike told his now ex-boss he was not even going to bother to apply for another position.

Terry Atchison was hurt and angry. He always believed the school system's methods was unprofessional, even sneaky. He had no love or respect for them. He was the most outspoken of the seven fired in his outright hatred of the public school system.

"Mr. Berling, I found this job on my own and excelled at it," Terry said in a demonic tone as he stuck his finger into the desk hoping it would go right through like a knife. "And now they fire seven of us and don't even give us enough notice to find another job! Most available jobs were filled last month!"

It was true. Most hiring of teachers takes place in March through early May. Any prospective teacher looking for employment after that time is usually selecting from the bottom of the barrel with few exceptions.

"Hell, they did not even have the courtesy to offer us employment elsewhere," Terry continued. "The school system is always bitching that there is a teacher shortage! Hell, they created it! They are chasing half of us out of this profession!"

Terry's voice was rising as Doug Waters stood behind him with his arms folded and nodding in agreement. Terry continued.

"We invest in this school system, but they refuse to invest in us. It's not right and one day they are going to have hell to pay. They cannot continue to function treating us like this! They cannot do it!"

Terry calmed himself, pointed his finger at the door and finished with, "I know I am not going to be back here, Mr. Berling. The school system doesn't like 'us.' And that's my only crime here. I was born white. Not one of those school system clowns knows what we do or how well we do it. All the NAACP cares about is re-winning a Civil War the

South lost in 1865! This is about revenge as far as I can see! It's not about school, or kids, or improving test scores!"

"Terry, I know I'll be able to hire another teacher to take your place, but I'm equally sure I'll never be able to hire another teacher as good as you," Principal Berling assured him. "Teachers with your passion are few and far between. I mean that deeply."

Terry did not shake his hand, but he did thank him for three good years. Terry was passionate about his job. He wore his heart on his sleeve. He was either your friend or your enemy. There was no between with him. The public school system had made an enemy and Terry was not likely to forget what they did to him on this day. Principal Berling was right about Terry's ability. Every school *needed* a teacher like Terry.

All that was left in the office was Doug Waters. Doug pulled his roll book out of his leather satchel and tossed it on the principal's desk. He then slowly stood up and let his six-foot-three frame do the rest of his speaking.

"Tell those clueless idiots down at the school board office I won't be coming back tomorrow," Doug said quietly but deadly.

"Doug, you know tomorrow is the last official day of school for employees," Principal Berling said. "All school system employees…"

Doug interrupted him.

"Yea, well, tell them tomorrow at this time I'll be looking for another job," Doug added with a touch of sarcasm.

"I understand," Principal Berling said in a respectful manner. "I don't like doing what I was forced to do here today. This is the toughest part of my job and it never gets any easier."

The two shook hands. Doug was going to the school board office and his mood was not a good one.

Being middle-aged with little experience he did not think it proper to say anything more. He was angry about leaving. Deep down he was not sure teaching was something he would stay in long-term. But he wanted to continue teaching at least one additional year before making a final decision. If he did *not* want to continue he wanted to resign rather than be fired. Either way, the school system did him a favor. Any thoughts he had about staying in the teaching profession were washed away by a fax and a lesson on the Consent Decree. He saw the impact it had on a group of professionals he knew during the year as his teaching comrades. He saw in them what, perhaps, could have been him in future years. Doug was smart enough to know what he just witnessed was something not seen or noted by the public. He hurt for the teachers that just cleared Principal Berling's office. He did not want their present to be his future.

Principal Berling looked at Doug's face and did not know what to say. Sounding defeated in a tired tone, he looked at his shoes with his swivel chair pushed far away from the desk. He chose no further eye contact with Doug, a man he feared would produce an immaturity he could not handle, but would soon prove unfounded.

"I guess you want a piece of me, too, eh, Doug?" asked Principal Berling staring down at the floor with his hands clasped.

"No, Mr. Berling, I may be the only one here today who was not sure he wanted to stay in the profession," Doug answered calmly with perfect diction. "I wanted to stay at least one more year, but the school system forced a decision on me. I had no idea this was going to happen. It all caught me off guard."

"It's the second or third year they have done this to teachers, Doug, and it makes me sick," Principal Berling said. "It makes it really hard to recruit teachers because of the reputation of the school system. You see those teachers walking out of here?"

Doug nodded that he did.

"Trust me, they are either going to leave the profession, leave the state or parish to teach, and they will almost certainly tell the world of how poorly they were treated," Principal Berling said with a sigh of pain and a tint of disgust in his voice. "Just as bad, Doug, is that somewhere there are black teachers being fired because the faculty at their school has too many African-Americans. Who cares about such things? I just don't know."

"I do have a question, Mr. Berling," Doug asked.

"Shoot," Principal Berling asked, glad there would be no confrontation.

"Are these teachers being replaced due to race considerations or because of budget cuts? I hear both. Which is it?"

"Does it matter?"

"I would like to know before I leave the school. I mean, I'm not coming back into this profession. So, I'd kind of like to know what makes the school system tick."

"What makes the school system tick, huh? I don't have an answer for you because the answer to the question is complicated, but I'll give you the abridged version. Those teachers released today are being replaced because race is a factor. In some schools, teachers of all races are being removed for budgetary concerns. It simply depends on the whims of the school system and the order of the Consent Decree and it all stinks to high heaven. It really does."

Principal Berling was looking directly into Doug's eyes now. Doug said nothing more because the stupidity of it all was overwhelming. There was nothing more to say or ask. In more than one way, Doug was thankfully through with it all. What he saw in one teaching year made him realize the problems within the system itself were almost too much for anyone or any school to handle. His future lay elsewhere and he was eager to begin it, whatever it was and wherever it may be.

"Thanks for working with us, Doug," Principal Berling said as he stood for a handshake. "I knew keeping you over the long-term was a long shot, but I would have liked the surprise. On the other hand, I do feel as if I betrayed you. I hired you and you came through for us when we needed you. And your reward for that effort..."

Principal Berling's voice trailed off. He did not want to tax his already strained emotions. Doug took his rising from the chair as a signal to leave.

"Thanks again, sir," Doug said.

The two shook hands again and Doug left the office.

When the room had cleared, Principal Berling leaned forward in his chair, pulled off his glasses, and rubbed his hand through his graying hair. He hated what he was asked to do. He knew all seven teachers were outstanding in their fields. Their rapport with the students was excellent. A school could build itself around their talents alone. He simply could not understand why some of the teachers took out their frustrations on him. Perhaps it was because he was available. Like it or not, he was asked to exercise the orders given to him by the school system and he carried out those orders.

What he didn't know was if those teachers knew of at least two uncertified teachers who were not called into the office to be relieved of their duty. When they received word to meet in the principal's office they fully expected to see geography teacher Margaret Chase and physical education teacher Charles Starkey. They were not there and both got to keep their jobs. Neither taught in a critical need area. Margaret was white and uncertified, but she coached the girl's soccer team. Charles was black, uncertified and had only one year's teaching experience. Principal Berling never knew that the exiting teachers understood he was protecting the two coaches for his absurd, misplaced respect of sport.

No one liked being fired for reasons beyond their control. The least the school system could have done in doing so was to be fair and consistent in their reasons for relieving teachers. Politics. The school system reeked of it. It was the playground of mediocrity. The public school system was overwhelmed by it. Now Principal Berling had the additional headache of spending his summer replacing teachers he had just relieved.

Pawns on the Chess Board

"**May** I help you, sir?" asked the lady with a smile as she stood behind the counter at the school board office.

"Yes, I am here to resign," Doug said firmly.

"Sir?" she asked again.

"I said I am here to resign and I want to fill out whatever paperwork I need to do so," Doug repeated.

There was not a hint of remorse in his voice. Doug wanted to make a scene. He wanted retribution. He had lost his job and did not wish to surrender it in the manner in which he had experienced. Besides, he had nothing to lose. He was angry and he wanted everyone to know it, including those prospective teachers sitting at nearby tables filling out teaching applications.

"I just lost my job at East Side High School. No, I just had my job *taken* away from me," Doug insisted in a nasty tone. "Just give me the papers, I'll sign them, and get the hell outta' here!"

"Sir, if you don't calm down..."

Doug interrupted.

"Lady, don't get me any more angry than I already am," he continued. "You have a job! Don't pretend to be one of those people here at the school board office who thinks they are better than me! I can do your job, but you can't do mine!"

"Your name?" she asked hurriedly realizing she was getting nowhere.

"Doug Waters."

"And you say you are employed at East Side High School?"

"*Was* employed, lady! Was employed!"

She returned to the back of the office and typed a few items into the computer within full view of Doug. She watched the monitor, gathered her information, and returned with Mincy Adams, the assistant director of school system personnel.

Mincy had the reputation for being callous. There was no other way to describe her, except that she was a short woman in her forties, still quite attractive, who wore expensive suits, and had too much power according to many teachers who had crossed her path. With the stroke of a pen, she could make or break your career. She loved the power entrusted to her, and now she saw an angry Doug Waters as verbal competition—a sparring partner to be tamed in the company of dozens of onlookers. She was about to be outgunned by Doug's temper and she was too arrogant to know it.

"Sir, I am Mincy Adams, assistant director of personnel," Mincy explained in that sassy tone that was an attempt to reduce the opposition to civility. "I understand you lost your job today. Is that correct?"

Doug said nothing. He simply eyed her the way a hungry gorilla eyes a rabbit. He wanted to strangle her. He knew she cared less about what had happened across the parish on this day. To her, the removal of teachers was a mere statistic that would feed the financial engine of the public school system. Doug knew her type. She underestimated his anger and nothing she could say, not anything she had learned in college, could stymie it.

She went on speaking without a hint of cooperation from Doug.

"Mr. Waters, many teachers lost their jobs today," she said.

"Yea, then tell me why these teachers are filling out applications around me?" Doug said as he looked around the crowded room.

In the corner sitting at a metal table was St. Lucy High School art teacher, Diane Arnault, filling out an application for a job in the public school system. Diane's meeting with her school's Discipline Committee was in one week. Her plan was to secure a public school job, the $12,000 per year raise that came with it, and resign from St. Lucy before the school could fire her.

Doug stared at Mincy and continued his tirade.

"Tell me why you will cry like a ninny baby to the gullible news media about the perceived teacher shortage this summer? You can't answer that and I really don't want to hear your silly explanation. Tell me, Miss Adams, have you ever taught? Ever? Anywhere?"

Mincy shot back in a bit of a tough tone, "Sir, if you must speak to me do so in a professional manner!"

"Lady, I didn't ask you to come to this counter!" Doug said angrily with both hands on the counter. "I asked the other lady to simply give me the paperwork I needed to exit this school system. Then she went and got you. I don't know why you people can't follow simple instructions. You would fail my class. Give me the papers to sign and I'll leave!"

The conversation between the two quickly resembled two drunk college students fighting over a woman in a cheap campus bar. Mincy tried to be the professional Doug was refusing to be.

"Sir, we may be able to hire you back in about seven weeks," Mincy explained in a nicer tone. "We have not gotten all the paperwork back from those who plan to retire. We may be able to give you one of those slots."

"Yea, and in the meantime I can't sleep or eat while I wonder how I am going to pay the bills when the paychecks stop coming to my address in late August," Doug said. "I'm too old for this, lady. I'm college educated and qualified to do other things. I resent the dictatorial-hold you people have on the lives of teachers! We teachers are in the profession to help young people. We are not pawns on the checkerboard you call a school system!"

"Sir, we need male teachers in the system," Mincy continued as she glanced at his file. "Please understand that we are under a Consent Decree and are simply following the instructions presented to us by the U.S. Justice Department."

Mincy stopped speaking for a second to collect her thoughts, and plan her next move. She looked at Doug hoping she had finally calmed him.

"It says here in your file you also coach," Mincy continued. "Your qualifications suggest to me that you may well be employed by us sometime in late August."

"Justice Department?" he asked. "That's a contradiction in terms."

"You are angry, I understand," she finally said in a tone of surrender. "I'll get you that paperwork, but I hope you'll reconsider."

Mincy turned and made a simple gesture to a subordinate. Within one minute she placed a legal-size sheet of paper in front of him and urged him to read it. Doug refused. All he saw on the resignation paper was the spot that indicated where he was to sign. He put down a most hurried signature and dropped the pen on top of the document.

"Miss Adams, this school system is racist!" he said with a now calm conviction while slightly leaning forward toward the counter separating the two. "Don't call me if you have a job. I am through. And I will never teach in this school system again."

Doug spun around and walked out. He left Mincy feeling criminal. He created questions for the teachers filling out applications. Everyone in the office stood in uncomfortable silence. One secretary had her hand on a phone attempting to dial the police. There was not a word said by anyone. Doug was quick in his resignation and thorough in his definition to Mincy about his feelings. He meant every word of it. He did not want to go through the official ceremony of resigning on the school system's terms. As he walked out of the school system building, he wished he had not shown up at all, but paperwork and money hung in the balance and closure could not take place without his signing an official resignation document.

The legal points in a Consent Decree had stolen from Doug what he had chosen as his livelihood. Federal judges and nameless attorneys raped him of his profession while hiding behind the law they hashed out behind closed doors. It is a law that takes from one man and gives to another with no explanation other than what is outlined on a document in a briefcase unleashed by a $500 per hour attorney who had his kids in private school.

Within two weeks, Claire Metz would leave the state with her two children and move in with her parents residing in Texas. Claire did not want to leave Louisiana, but she knew if she could be cut from her job due to race considerations once, it could easily happen again. She had enough of her own problems. She could not solve the school system's problems, too. Claire walked out of East Side High School feeling emotionally devastated.

Greg Talley eventually landed a science position at an upscale high school in Austin, Texas, for nearly $6,000 per year more than he was making in Baton Rouge. He never regretted leaving and planned to never return.

Dr. Jay Anders waited all summer for a phone call to return to teaching biology at any school. He never got that call. With so many teachers out of work, Jay would eventually find all avenues to employment exhausted. He returned to suburban San Diego and landed a research job in marine biology. He never returned to Baton Rouge or to teaching.

Mary Ann Samson returned home to a forgiving father. He never told his daughter "I told you so," but in the end she knew he was right. From then on, Mary Ann promised to listen to any advice he had. Mary Ann threw caution to the wind and went to school to learn to teach, her first love. She now felt divorced from that love. Like a marriage that had gone badly, she did not know if she wanted to trust the teaching profession again. Her father advised against it. In the end, she knew she did not want to leave Baton Rouge or her parents. Not surprisingly she, too, never taught again.

Mike Hammonds decided to never step foot inside of another classroom again. All anyone knew was that he moved to Houston. Mike and his multiple talents, like a ghost, had vanished.

In the end, Terry Achison was the only teacher fired on this day who remained in the teaching profession. His fight, however, against small-town public school politics in other parish school systems and school nepotism would haunt him throughout his career. He would be fired once more in his career for being the last teacher hired when another school system announced budget cuts. He would struggle for years to gain tenure.

Doug Waters never did teach again. He eventually took a state job making nearly the same amount of money. He soon married and told those close to him he never regretted his exit from the school system or the manner in which he did it. However, regret it, he did. He missed teaching terribly, especially his interaction with the students. He missed the smell of dry eraser colored markers he used on his white boards. He missed practices and washing team uniforms. He missed the view from his room and the smell of freshly applied wax in the second-floor hallway that shone so brightly in the early morning light. For the next two years, the school system's central office would leave messages on Doug's answering machine offering him a teaching and coaching position. The voice sounded like that of Mincy Adams. Doug always erased the message and went on with his life.

"We started them to school. They learned to read. They learned to work simple arithmetic problems. Now some of our plantation owners can't figure the poor devils out of everything at the close of the year."

Louisiana Sen. Huey Long, 1934

Late May—The Last Day of School—The "Key" to Retirement

Gloria Hampton was pushing sixty–years-old, and was growing very tired of trying to keep up with seventeen-year-old world history students. It was one thing about teaching that never changed. High school teachers grew one year older each year, but the students they taught were forever fourteen to eighteen-years-old. Sooner or later even the best teachers would find themselves out of touch with the student population and be forced to consider retirement. Keeping up with students required an enormous amount of energy. Every teacher reaches a point in their career when they question if they can mentally and physically stay in that race. For the first time, Gloria felt as if she were reaching that career plateau.

It was the final day of school for teachers and Gloria had just completed her twenty-first year at East Side High School and only recently she began to routinely question her ability to do the job. In all, she had been calling roll in public high schools for thirty-three years.

The school campus was Gloria's home away from home. Room 228 had carried her name above the door since the Gerald Ford presidency. She knew every inch of it. Every tile squared above her head and every pane in the window knew her lectures on Caius Julius Caesar, the Crusades, Napoleon Bonaparte, President Woodrow Wilson, Gandhi, Franklin Roosevelt, Huey Long, Vladimir Lenin and Chairman Mao, President Harry S. Truman, JFK and the Cold War as well as she did.

Sitting at her desk and glancing to her right she could see a tree in the distance towering over the large sidewalk as it approached the main entrance to the school. It was a postcard view of shade covering a large enough area to keep an entire class comfortable when teachers chose to hold class outside on those splendid days of fall and spring. She remembered when the school Beta Club planted the tree. It was a small token of appreciation to the teachers of the school from the Class of 1983. Underneath its trunk an inscription read:

> *"To Thine Own Self Be True,*
> *And It Must Follow as The Night, The Day,*
> *Thou Cans't Not Then Be False To Any Man*
> *From William Shakespeare's, Hamlet*

> *Dedicated to the pleasant memories of its visitors, especially the young.*
> *Dedicated to the faculty of East Side High School from the Class of 1983"*

Lately, Gloria had been spending more time under the shade of the tree alone. She remembered the students of days gone by and was thinking of them more often.

She remembered Bobby Dantin, a gangly kid with a face full of acne who entered her class in the fall of 1985. He was tall and thin and shy and the girls did not notice him. He tried out for the basketball team and was cut his freshmen and sophomore years. He was so awkward the other students nicknamed him "Superstar," in reference to his lack of athletic prowess. In his junior year he finally made the basketball team as a backup forward, but playing rarely. By his senior year he was the team's captain, although he never started a game. He simply never quit trying. Bobby was made of substance. He had character and a will to succeed, even if he was rarely mentioned in the sports section's box score following a game.

Bobby worked even harder in class and earned enough academic honors to attract attention from the best colleges in the South. By the time he left East Side High School he was a tall, blue-eyed, senior that won "Most Handsome" and "Most Likely to Succeed." He finished with a 3.9 grade point average having taken a curriculum that was most challenging. Bobby could have left school and gone to work at 11a.m. each morning his senior year, but he wanted to take physics, journalism, and honor's chemistry. He was terrified that his success in public school would not translate into success in college. So, he overcompensated and diligently prepared for his own academic agenda.

Gloria remembered his last day of high school. When the final bell rang on the last day of school for seniors, it was her he sought out. He hugged her and acted as if he did not want to let her go. Bobby *was* what East Side High School once stood for. He embodied everything that a high school student was supposed to be or was supposed to *try* to be.

At graduation exercises, Bobby was one of two students who gave farewell speeches to the 347 exiting seniors. At the end of his speech he thanked his parents, a small group of friends, and Gloria "for her sticking by me when it was not cool to do so during that emotional time in a teenager's life-storm when success and its brethren, 'motivation and desire' can only be inspired with a smile and a nod only a dedicated teacher can deliver."

There have been so few like him since. What's more, society's standards have dipped to new lows through Gloria's old-school eyes. Many students today would actually poke fun at those like Bobby whose character would not allow them to be merely mediocre. If anything, those succeeding today are rarely popular in public school. Today's vernacular terms those who embody diligence and organization as "anal," a millennium explanation for what was termed in the 1970s as hard working and dedicated. Calling one "anal" is intended to be as much an explanation as a social defect. It was a sad definition *from* society and *of* society.

Five years later, Gloria received a graduation invitation from Vanderbilt University in Nashville, Tennessee, from Bobby. He graduated with a master's degree in business administration. Gloria could not make that trip, but five days later he had delivered to her a bouquet of roses with Vanderbilt's logo "V" and his simple signature. Today, he lives and works in Atlanta and visits East Side High School when visiting Baton Rouge.

How could she forget Joseph Daily?

Joseph attended East Side High School with more problems than any teenager should be allowed to have. He was a New Orleans native having been born and reared in the Paris Housing Projects near the bend in the Mississippi River in the city's Warehouse District. It was a dangerous place to visit even in daylight. Violent crime was as common as humidity. By the time Joseph was six-years-old, he had witnessed four men shot to death in separate incidents. One involved his older brother, Jacob, then a fifteen-year-old high school dropout who had gotten into an argument with a member of his own gang.

His mother was a "crack head" who routinely and illegally spent the family's welfare money on drugs and alcohol. Joseph remembered the refrigerator often being empty and going to bed hungry, but the pungent smell of marijuana coming from the living room of their one-bedroom high-rise flat was always there as he tried to sleep, which he learned to do to the sound of police sirens and gunshots in the night sky.

By age ten, Joseph had still never gone to visit Santa Claus during the holiday season. But he had been to the downtown city police lockup after his father had been arrested for assaulting him too many times to count. Joseph was such a regular at the police station some of New Orleans' finest eventually would know him well enough that they raised a few dollars each year to buy him a Christmas gift.

Eventually the father left the family and the mother's drug addiction got so bad she turned to prostitution to pay for her daily drug "fix." Joseph's Baton Rouge grandparents grew so worried about him they sought, and were granted, legal custody of him.

He was immediately enrolled in Lewis and Clark Middle School, but was expelled. He returned to the school the following year and failed every class by the time midterm grades arrived. Joseph's grandparents were confused as to what to do. They were the only thing between Joseph and his being another angry, lost, young, black child with no education on mean streets with a hapless future. The grandparents turned to a higher power. Joseph was enrolled in Sunday school where his introduction to Jesus Christ opened his eyes and turned his life around. All at once he quit sleeping in class. He paid attention in school and delivered respect to his teachers. He went from being a troubled kid with a parole officer for a baby sitter to an honor student.

He eventually attended East Side High School continuing his academic success. However, Joseph would suffer a devastating setback. During his junior year his grandmother died suddenly. With no female figure in his life, Joseph volunteered Gloria as his surrogate mother. The two had nothing in common, but Joseph went to see her regularly during the school day until she offered him, and his grandfather, an invitation to dinner at her home. Over time, Joseph became so close to Gloria and her husband he would often drop by uninvited and stay for hours watching sports or movies with them. Gloria did not mind being Joseph's adopted mother. In fact, she began to worry when he did not visit. Joseph eventually graduated high school and accepted an academic scholarship to his hometown, Tulane University. Gloria was as proud of Joseph as she was of her own son, now married with children and living in the "North Shore" New Orleans suburbs. East Side High School and Gloria helped Joseph return to New Orleans as a victor, not a victim.

Gloria remembered Beth Townley, now in medical school at the University of Texas. There was Robert McKimson, who recently graduated from the University of Louisiana at Lafayette in English with plans to begin his teaching career in Atlanta. Gloria stared blankly at the manicured school lawn thinking of Capt. Kilwana Anderson, a 1996 graduate now serving as an officer in the U.S. Army. William Smothers, a 1999 graduate, was now a member of the Memphis Police Department while working on his bachelor's degree in communications. She remembered her entire first-hour class from the 1992-93 school year and how wonderful they were as students and young adults. Like many teachers of quality long on years of experience, Gloria had touched many lives. How she missed them all.

There were so many students of quality, Gloria thought. She began to wonder what happened to that species of student. Were they now extinct? Sure, there were still good students in the inner city public school system, but they were beginning to be heavily outnumbered by those seemingly forever mired in ignorance and apathy. Gloria looked out at the oak tree as the late afternoon sunshine fought to peek through its heavy branches and a clouding sky. It was corny she thought, but she always saw trees and teaching as being similar. Teachers plant a seed, nurture it, and hope to see it grow to a healthy maturity. She looked out of the windowpane at the oak's now heavy limbs that, like the students marching under the nameplate above her door, matured during the educational process.

Gloria had always felt richer for having been a part of their achievements. Now, she did not know if the time had finally come for her to walk away from a profession she so loved.

A knock on Gloria's door broke her off from her thoughts and ended the cold silence in the darkened room.

"Hello, Gloria, did I catch you at a bad time?" asked Nancy Whitmore, the French teacher from directly across the hall. "I wanted to borrow your pencil sharpener so I could finish up my bubble-sheets and turn in my final grades."

Nancy, in only her second year of teaching, was everything Gloria once was. She was beautiful, bouncy, energetic, and very much in tune with the students she taught. She even listened to some of the same music as the students and dressed like they did when they were off school grounds and out of uniform. Nancy still had her trim figure to go with her long, dark brown hair and an inviting smile. Gloria and Nancy had become good friends over the last four semesters and talked openly about many things, despite the obvious generation gap between them.

"Are you okay, Gloria?" asked Nancy, still standing in the doorway. "You look hurt."

Silence.

"Is something wrong?" Nancy asked.

Nancy went to turn the lights on and Gloria stopped her before her tiny hand touched the switch.

"Leave them off, Nancy," Gloria asked reaching for a tissue to wipe her eyes.

Nancy moved closer to Gloria stopping halfway not wanting to intrude on Gloria's space. Only Nancy's footsteps could be heard on the old tile floor.

"You might as well be the first to know, Nancy," Gloria said softly not wanting to mean it. "I'm through."

Nancy's perfect face changed expressions while staring at Gloria, obviously upset at having made a painful decision.

"Gloria, what do you mean you're through?" Nancy asked.

"I mean, in the last few minutes I have been over-analyzing my career," Gloria said slowly. "I have concluded that I have had enough of teaching. Thirty-three years. I wish it didn't feel like this, I really do, but I think it's time I pass the torch onto someone else."

"That's silly," Nancy said as she sat down in one of the student's desks knowing this conversation was witness to the end of an era at the school.

"No, it's reality," Gloria said still staring through the windowpanes. "I'm not looking for sympathy when I tell you this, Nancy, but I don't feel like I'm getting through to the students anymore."

"Gloria, it's not you, really it's not!" Nancy said in perfect English. "It's the kids today. It's not you. You are still doing a fine job here. Some of the kids still think of you as one of the best teachers in the school."

Gloria scoffed at the idea she was popular and waved her away with one hand at the mere suggestion. That's one thing Gloria liked about Nancy. She was so polished and polite for a twenty-five-year-old. But now, Gloria was interested in harsh realities, not an obligatory verbal pat on the back for her long service record to the educational establishment.

"Nancy, I…" Gloria started to explain further before being interrupted.

"Gloria," Nancy continued. "Maybe you just need a break. Maybe the summer off will help you get some needed rest and rethink this. You know, by July you may change your mind. Why don't you give it some time before you decide? You have the entire summer to think things through."

For the first time Gloria looked directly in Nancy's eyes revealing her pain. She rose and moved slowly toward the window with her back now to Nancy.

"Because if I make the decision now, then Trent Baer will get to keep his job by replacing me," Gloria said in recognition of that teacher's removal due to budget cuts. "He is a great teacher with a lot to offer. I can save his career by terminating mine."

"Is that the reason you are doing this?" Nancy asked.

"No. I have seen many teachers terminated by this system in the last five years. I like Trent a great deal, but this is not about Trent. This is about a teacher who does not like what she sees in the educational system any longer. I was foolish enough, even at my age, to believe I could overcome any obstacle. Maybe it was arrogance on my part, I don't know. I do know one thing, Nancy. I did not begin this year even thinking about this being my last year of teaching."

"What made you change your mind?"

Gloria turned and looked at Nancy but still kept her distance staying by the windowsill. She still used a tissue to wipe tears she wished were not there.

"Oh, it was a couple of things that happened in the last two months," Gloria explained. "Things that should have no place in education and are becoming all too common. I'd rather remember the good times. There were lots of those. If I stay in the profession any longer I'm afraid I'll be condemned to remember only the bad. There's been a lot of that lately. I don't want that. I've loved this career. It's been good to me."

"Can I ask what made all of this come about so sudden-like?" Nancy prodded.

Gloria was hesitant to speak about it, but figured she had nothing to lose at this point. She retraced her steps and sat down in her heavy wooden desk leaning back in her swivel chair staring at Nancy, who was not yet born when she entered the teaching profession. Gloria sighed not knowing where to begin.

Gloria thought of Julie Lambert, a sassy, undisciplined, seventeen-year-old with dyed blonde hair. Julie got caught cheating on the last regular chapter test before final exams and was forced to take a zero. With her overall grade already in serious danger, her grade point average dipped to where she would need a 'B' to pass Gloria's class with a low 'D.' Having not made a 'B' on a test all year, it was highly unlikely Julie could make it on a cumulative final exam that included seventy-five multiple choice questions and five short essay questions. Gloria explained all the details to Nancy.

"When I picked up Julie's paper and her cheat sheet, I said nothing to her," Gloria explained. "I just turned around and she said to me in front of the entire class, 'So, when's the last time you got laid, bitch?'"

"What?" Nancy exclaimed in shock.

"I didn't know what to say," Gloria continued. "Everyone in the school knows my husband died last year of a heart attack. She thought that remark was cute or, a way of getting back at me. Well, you know what, Nancy? It did get back at me. I hurt so bad I went home. Everyone thought I was sick. I wasn't. All Julie got was a warning from Principal

Berling. She also promised the disciplinarian she would apologize to me, but that was Julie's way of squeezing out of the problem. Of course, she never apologized. Like it would have meant anything to me anyway.

"That night I called Julie's parents and set up a parent-teacher conference for the next day. I wanted to explain the academic side of the trouble Julie had gotten into so her parents would know the score. When it was over her mother called me a 'fat, old, bitch' and told me her daughter was right to defend herself.'"

Gloria extended both of her hands asking Nancy and herself the same question.

"Defend herself from what?" Gloria begged. "This kid cheated on a test, insulted me in front of the class, and took a shot at the biggest emotional loss in my life!"

Nancy was beyond shock. She sat motionless in the desk not knowing what Gloria had been going through. Gloria, now sitting up straight, registered the shock on Nancy's young face and continued.

"When I got out into the parking lot after school that day, my new car had been scraped with a key," Gloria explained partly with a smile and pain. "There was a scratch line from bumper to bumper. The body shop totaled the damage at around $3,500. The car was only three months old. I needed a car and bought it with some of the insurance money my husband left me. I considered that car the last gift my husband gave me."

Nancy shook her head in disgust before asking, "I assume Julie did not pass your class?"

"Of course not," Gloria said. "She failed the final and failed the class. No surprise there. On top of that, at least twice this year the head football coach has attempted to intimidate me into changing the grades of two players in my fifth-hour class."

"Intimidate?" questioned Nancy.

"He has his subtle ways," Gloria said. "And I won't do it. I won't! That's not what I signed on to do, Nancy. One of his players failed my class this spring and is ineligible to play in fall unless he goes to summer school."

"Yea, but that's no problem for him because he gets to go to summer school and become eligible for fall," said Nancy. "Maybe he learned a lesson from this."

"True," Gloria agreed, now in better mental form than minutes before. She then pointed directly at Nancy. "But now this football hotshot can't go to summer football camp at some Mississippi university. No, he's got to pass the classes he failed instead. You would think that would be a lesson for him, but, no! His parents called me at home asking me to 'revisit his grade.'"

"You mean change it."

"Exactly."

Nancy then suggested Gloria take the matter to the principal. Gloria then let go of a light-hearted laugh for the first time on this painful day.

"Dear Nancy, welcome to the real world of education," Gloria said in a cocky tone with her hands outstretched. "The principal wants me to consider the player's attendance as a factor in his overall grade. His overall grade in my class was 63 percent. A bogus 'A' for attendance would pass him. Coach Gatewood and Adam Berling know he's missed only one day this semester. Hell, Nancy, he slept most of the time in class. The only reason he missed one day was because he played basketball and baseball, too. Those two sports take up the entire spring semester and athletes can't play or practice if they miss a school day, you know that. That's the only reason he came to school. That was his only motivation."

Nancy, like most teachers, knew it to be true about many athletes at the school. There seemed to be an unwritten rule about athletes being able to get away with things other students could not. It led to major friction on campus between the athletes and the non-playing students. If regular students were sent to the office because of trouble they were quick to point out incidents where athletes got off easily. The teachers and regular students strongly resented the school's administration for its double standard. Some teachers, like Gloria, refused to accommodate that standard. The bigger problem for Gloria lay in the ethics of the problem. If she granted one student an opportunity to factor in attendance into his overall grade she would have to do so for all.

The most notable of these incidents took place in early November involving junior quarterback Ricardo Holmes, who was caught having sex in the physical education shower with a senior cheerleader one evening after practice. Apparently, Ricardo did this on a fairly regular basis, according to players who offered the information to the school administration only it were off the record. When this information was made available to the school's administration, they didn't even investigate the incident until the football season was over two weeks later. They claimed they "needed all the facts" before getting involved. The truth was obvious to everyone else with an IQ above second-grade level. The timing was too precarious and Ricardo too valuable of a football commodity to risk losing to expulsion or suspension at the time.

Nancy felt outraged at an incident that occurred six months before. Her hands had fallen by her side while she sat. She knew about the unhealthy attitude toward football pervading throughout the institution. However, there was still so much she did not know. She felt stupid for not knowing. She felt powerless in that she could do nothing about it. What's more, Nancy learned something about the administration she worked with and looked up to. An administration she always believed would stand behind her in tough times such as the one Gloria was suffering through. Now, she wasn't so sure.

"So, what are you going to do?" asked Nancy.

"I'm not going to extend Ricardo the courtesy of including attendance in his overall grade and pass him," Gloria said calmly and firmly reassuring her judgment. "I cannot, in good conscience, give him what is too late to extend to the other students. Some coaches around here may use a double standard, but I will not. No, Nancy, I am going to uphold Ricardo's grade and retire before Julie burns down my house and Ricardo becomes ineligible to play next season."

Gloria then reached into her desk drawer and pulled out a folded piece of paper. She extended it to Nancy, who got up from the desk to retrieve it. Nancy's heeled shoes clumped across the floor before she took the paper from Gloria's shaking hand. Nancy was now sitting closer to Gloria as thunder began to rumble outside the window. The note read:

"Mrs. Hampton,
Thank you for teaching me so much this year. I think the key to being a good student is unlocking your fears and going for it. I think I succeeded in that. Don't you? Have a nice summer. Julie."

Nancy looked up at Gloria with even more shock on her face than before. She didn't know what to say or think. Nancy wondered how teachers could defend themselves against this type of terror. Julie was cruel, weak of character, a cheat, and spoiled. Her parents proved no help at all. The system had nothing in place to help. Gloria was alone and Nancy never understood just how vulnerable teachers were until now. She had never experienced anything like this before.

"Nice little bitch, huh?" Gloria offered, more as conclusion than a question.

Nancy could only shake her head as she folded the paper and returned it to Gloria. The sky began to crackle with more thunder. It was growing dark outside. It was a typical Louisiana rainstorm that kidnapped an otherwise beautiful day and attempted to turn it into an afternoon quagmire.

"More rain," Nancy said to Gloria as if she didn't notice.

"It's like clockwork," Gloria said quietly looking at the large raindrops beginning to hit the panes.

She was now more relaxed appearing at ease with her impending decision. Gloria walked to the window. One by one the drops formed against the glass until the weight of one raindrop slowly slid down until reaching the bottom of the pane. The window was getting more difficult to see out of as the rain began to fall with more intensity. The wind began to blow in unison with the crackle of thunder. It was an otherwise beautiful view considering the mood in the room. And somehow, the view of the now wet East Side High School campus was the mood. At least it was in Room 228.

"So what will you do now, Gloria?" asked Nancy as she moved closer to where Gloria stood, but not enough to crowd her. "Are you going to tell Mr. Berling this afternoon. Or, just think a bit more about your prospects?"

"Adam Berling?" Gloria repeated with a chuckle. "If I told our esteemed principal I was leaving for good he would be on the phone trying to recruit a football coach that just happened to teach social studies. He's all about football, Nancy. Don't ever forget that. He talks a good talk in faculty meetings about the need to push our kids to be more stable academically. But it's lip service. Nothing more."

It was true what Gloria revealed to Nancy. Principal Adam Berling had been in charge of East Side High School for fifteen years, having once been the football coach and physical education instructor. Principal Berling could have retired at any moment he so chose, but would not have known what to do with himself in retirement. So, he stuck around the school system, pulled a few political strings, and landed an assistant principal's job, which he kept for only two years. When the principal's position became available there were twelve deserving applicants, many of whom were true academicians from more prominent institutions. But, true to political form, Adam Berling was deemed "the best qualified applicant," according to one powerful member of the school system's human resource office. Translation: Adam Berling was expected to be a catalyst in helping resurrect the school's failing sports reputation.

When hired to run the school, Principal Berling removed many good teachers against their will. His pal at the school system office helped facilitate his controversial moves by making room for the displaced teachers at other schools. As expected, each of the newly created positions at East Side High School went to seven assistant football coaches, two of which were non-certified, who chose to leave five other metropolitan area schools. Principal Berling, along with head football coach, Ray Gatewood, created a list of coaches they intended to hire and then removed the true teachers holding those positions in their need to create space. In regards to sports programs at the high school level, it was not an uncommon practice. The teachers have always hated the systematic purges that hurt teachers in order to help a sports program, but it was a fact of life in some high schools, including public, private, and parochial.

"So you mean, even if you retire it's not guaranteed Trent Baer would get your job in the social studies department, is that right?" Nancy asked.

"That's what I'm inferring, yes," Gloria said, still watching the rain descend from a black and gray sky. "I guess what I'm saying is, I'd like to *not* tell him of my plans until I absolutely have to. Otherwise, God knows what he would do with the open position after the party."

"What party?" Nancy asked as she cocked her head slightly revealing curiosity.

"The party Adam Berling and some of the football coaches are going to have when they learn of my impending retirement," Gloria said in a smug way. "So the less they all know right now the better, okay Nancy? Keep this between us for now."

Gloria turned and looked at Nancy for approval before Nancy nodded her understanding. All that was left in the day for both of them was the final faculty meeting of the year, just moments away. That meeting always spelled the official end of the school year and the beginning of the long, hot, boring, wonderful, monotonous summer. They both walked out of the room and made their way down the staircase to the library where the faculty meeting was to be held.

Often ignored or easily forgotten

The faculty was spread about the library waiting for Principal Berling to arrive, speak, and dismiss them for summer vacation. All fifty-three teachers representing five major subjects and a host of other electives chattered away with their book bags, purses, and leather briefcases at their feet. In their own wonderful way they were a group of overachievers whose names the public would never know unless there was a controversial incident to be aired by the media.

Despite their list of personal and professional accomplishments they understood all too well what the public thought of the job they were performing. The short sound bites and fast pace of any newscast made concerning education kept the television masses truly ignorant of how hard their jobs were and how little they had to work with in order to achieve what was expected of them. Individually and collectively, these teachers—like many across the state—had been cursed, booed, ridiculed, disrupted, challenged, intimidated, and some even physically assaulted by disrespectful teenagers in ways corporate office professionals could not fathom.

Many teachers, especially those in charge of sports teams or academic clubs, had routinely averaged workweeks in excess of sixty to seventy hours for much of the year. Several were "robbed," for lack of a better term, of their weekends and holidays as they graded papers, coached teams, or fundraised for needed items their students and players simply could not afford to supply. Much of that extra effort was not financially rewarded.

They rarely complained about their fate or their place in the grand scheme of it all. They toiled in a state where public school education was considered among the worst nationwide, in a parish where its future was, at best, dismal, and in a school system that was nothing more than a empty shell of its past. They were underpaid, poorly staffed, and poorly led. They were legally handcuffed by a system that was soft on discipline and financially strapped. In overcrowded classrooms, they were forced to teach students from low socio-economic backgrounds whose parents cared little for their educational proficiency.

These teachers got up every morning and met the challenge with the best they had to offer. They were not always at their best. They were not always right. They made mistakes. There were things they wish they could have done differently. Despite the looming budget cuts for the fifth-straight year, many teachers were upbeat even though their contemporaries in suburban parishes were making roughly $4,000 to $7,000 per year more to do the same job in better situations.

Public school teachers were the best of the lot. On average they were responsible for teaching roughly 100-150 teenagers per day. They taught a student body that included some who thought nothing of missing as many as ten to twenty days per semester and then questioned why they were failing a subject. More students than they cared to know had parole officers or felony arrest records. Some belonged to violent gangs. Some were mothers and fathers before age sixteen. An increasing number of students were diagnosed and labeled with Attention Deficit Disorder (ADD), by doctors for parents looking for an option to not having to parent and an excuse for their child's failure to perform simple academic functions. Most students were contemptuous of authority or discipline, having never experienced it.

For these teachers, their victories were often ignored or easily forgotten. Their defeats were blown hopelessly out of proportion.

It's like a former college head coach once remarked when he took over a hapless sports program, "The good news is nobody cares. The bad news is nobody cares."

In his trademark starched white shirt and gaudy tie, Principal Berling finally entered the library and stood over the many wooden tables that seated his employees. He held his right hand in the air to get their attention and a hush fell over the anxious group.

"Thank you," he started. "I'll be as quick as I can with this so we can all go home and enjoy the summer. I know that's paramount on your minds.

"First, I want to thank you for your hard work this year. I know working in public schools has its challenges, most of which you cannot control. But I thought we handled our problems and challenges well this school year, considering.

"Secondly, I want to give kudos to our sports teams for the hard work, especially football, and uh, what else? Oh, yes, cross country, for their winning season. That was a highlight in our school year to be sure."

There was obligatory applause. Gloria looked over at Nancy sitting across the room and rolled her eyes.

Head football coach Ray Gatewood smiled at one of his assistant coaches who, in turn, nodded in tacit approval. Principal Berling's almost forgetting the boy's and girl's cross country team's district title proved how proud he really was, or cared, which he did not. Funny, though, East Side High School's boy's tennis team made it to the second-round of the state playoffs and he failed to mention that to his faculty. In the back of the room, tennis coach Mike Donnelly was steaming about his team being, again, overlooked. When the tennis squad put together a couple of wins in the state playoffs during spring, Principal Berling did not even mention their accomplishments to the student body during morning announcements, as he did other sports. Mike brought up that oversight to his boss later that day, but the principal's explanation appeared hollow calling tennis a "minor sport."

To which Mike replied, "There is no such thing as a minor sport, Adam—only sports not supported by the school's principal."

The two men rarely spoke after that exchange. Perhaps Principal Berling's omission now was an attempt at getting even with Mike in a petty way.

Principal Berling continued, "Thirdly, our ROTC and choir did well again, as usual," he said, lumping those two entities together to save time.

Never mind that the performances by the choir placed them among the state's elite, although he was oblivious to the fact. He could not sing and never played a musical instrument. Therefore, his admiration for any performances of the arts was only compulsory.

"We graduated 204 seniors," he continued. "According to our guidance department almost half of our seniors were qualified for the state-sponsored scholarship, TOPS. We struggled with our GEE-21 scores. However, I am certain we will remedy that next year. So we should all be proud of our accomplishments."

It was not lost on the faculty that Principal Berling mentioned sports before academic accomplishments. His agenda was different than the faculty, even though he was expert at acting out the part to prove his academic concerns. He did not know he insulted the people upon whose shoulders rest the backbone of the school. They were accustomed to it and now only wanted to leave. The final day of school should have been a proud moment for the teachers, but the principal blew it. The teachers grew increasingly restless.

Geography teacher Matt Zeno began to quietly reflect on the tumultuous year. There was no better way to define it. He thought about his students and their 180 days together and questioned whether the year had really been a personal success.

Matt began the fall semester teaching three "preps" or subjects in five classes boasting 153 students. By Christmas, six students had been expelled and four students never showed up for class even one day and were dropped from the roll. One student had been arrested for drug possession and placed in Juvenile Detention. He started the spring semester with 142 students, but four dropped out of school for reasons unknown and three transferred to private schools. He added five new students that were dismissed from private and other public schools around the parish, and two additional students that moved in from out of state. That pushed the number of students he taught beginning January 4, back to 142.

By early April's spring break, another six students had dropped out of school for various reasons. Two quit going to school due to pregnancy, two more were arrested, one decided to get home-schooled, and three left the state. Seven others were failing due to lack of attendance having missed more than twelve unexcused days of school during the semester and quit school. By mid-April he was down to 121 students. Of that group, 37 percent failed his class; three of those forty-five failing students did so for the second time.

Another 22 percent earned a 'D,' which Matt thought was nothing more than glorifying failure. He always thought the letter grade 'D' should be stricken from the grading scale. He believed strongly if a student could not be at least average in Louisiana public schools, then that students failure should be recognized in need of special attention he could not provide. Some students needed to be taught individually in order to save them academically.

Of the 41 percent making reasonable efforts earning them grades of 'A,' 'B,' or 'C,' only fifteen students earned the top grade. A whopping 59 percent were labeled below average.

Matt remembered in September how one student, Derrick Austin, and his mother, Donna, chastised all seven of her son's teachers because they were "ill-prepared or trained to deal with my son's problems!" Her son's only problem, as Matt and the other teachers agreed, was he was seventeen-years-old and in the ninth grade. Every time Derrick faced a common problem, Donna ran to her son's defense like a sidewalk pit bull. Rather than forcing her son to grow up and deal with simple matters, Derrick learned to play the system as well as he did his mother's emotions. The only thing Derrick learned this school year was that Matt was not the pushover his mother was. Derrick was treated fairly, but he was not extended any courtesy that was not granted to other students. He failed four classes, including Matt's.

Matt thought of Altaisha Allen, a transfer student from Riverside High School who attended East Side High School against her wishes. Altaisha's mother no longer wanted her daughter attending Riverside High School because of the classroom element. Naturally, Altaisha hated the change. Therefore, Altaisha's mission the entire year was to be thrown out of school in lieu of not being able to change her mother's mind. Altaisha wanted to hang out with her Riverside High School friends and was going to any lengths to make that wish come true. In the end she was expelled for cursing three of her seven teachers during the school year. Matt was one of them. While on lunch duty during February, Altaisha was caught breaking in line. It appeared she did so *wanting* to be caught. When Matt asked her to return to the rear of the line he patted her on the back as a gesture of good will.

She used the opportunity to get attention spinning around and yelling at Matt, "Get your motha' fuckin' hands off me!"

She was expelled from East Side High School with seven "F's." Whatever became of her no one knew.

Matt remembered Mohammad Barca, an Arab who called him a "silly bastard" during class for no good reason. Matt did nothing to instigate being called such a thing in front of his students, but this was also a kid who laughed out loud in class when discussing the September 11, 2001, tragedy when terrorists blew up New York City's World Trade Center and the Pentagon in Washington D.C. Matt nearly begged his students not to take action against Mohammad because, "not all Arabs are terrorists," he told them, "just like not all white people are members of the Ku Klux Klan." Apparently, Mohammad forgot that nice gesture on Matt's part. Mohammad was sent to the office six times during the year and assigned to the parish discipline center for a total of thirty-four days, to which he never reported. Not able to make up work, he began failing classes, and thus became a classroom disruption.

He remembered one student who did pass some subjects, but under suspect circumstances, although perfectly legal ones. Joshua Morgan was a "504" student, a label placed on students having difficulty learning and requiring learning modifications, some of which bordered on absurdity. Students under this banner were given extra time on tests, allowed preferential seating in class, were given repeated instructions, and given extended time to turn in homework assignments. Too often, all it took for a student to be labeled such was an emotional parent and a physician too afraid to inform the parent their child really just needed discipline. Matt was not heartless. He knew some students really needed the extra help. Joshua was not one of them. Twice in March, Matt gave a U.S. map test Joshua failed because he could not spell states like "Texas," "Florida," "Utah," "Iowa," and, sadly, even "Louisiana." He spelled it, "Louziana." He even incorrectly spelled the state of "Virginia," which happened to be his mother's name. Virginia, the mother, wanted enough credit for Joshua's "effort" that he would be able to pass the class and avoid summer school. Matt refused on the grounds that he had given the same test five times during January and February. At the end of one day in March, Joshua took matters into his own hands.

He went home and immediately phoned the assistant principal screaming into the phone, "Mr. Zeno is an asshole! He is not fair!"

When the assistant principal investigated the matter noting Joshua's "504 Modification" required he be *allowed* to misspell as many as 60 percent of any words required on a test, he asked Matt to give Joshua another chance. Matt reluctantly did so, but Joshua failed the map test a sixth time. Joshua then quit coming to school, but not before Virginia threatened to turn Matt and the East Side High School guidance department into the State Department of Education for failing to accommodate her son. Joshua failed four of his seven classes, including Matt's geography class.

Matt laughed to himself when he thought of Edgar Robertson who retorted to his English teacher following classroom instructions one morning in early March, "That's b.s." The teacher automatically sent him to the office. When Edgar arrived at the office the assistant principal naturally requested he explain his vulgar verbal actions. "I didn't say 'bullshit' aloud," Edgar explained calmly. "I only said the *syllables*, 'b.s.'"

Edgar failed three of his classes.

Then there was Misty Yarborough, a sassy sophomore who missed thirty-six days of school during spring semester due to unexcused absences. On average, she reported to classes about twice per week. She finished Matt's class with a grade of 32 percent. Matt could never figure out why she attended at all if that was the only effort she could provide. Matt tried to speak to her about the problem, but she proved to be a con artist telling him, "I'm going to straighten out my life. I know I need to do that. I can't keep missing school like this."

Misty knew the right words to say, but would never attempt to back them up. Eventually, she dropped out of school in late April. Rumor among students was she got pregnant. Others said she was arrested for selling drugs. The truth was she had a one-year-old daughter at home. The baby was *not* the reason she failed to attend school. The welfare check the government awarded her was supposed to remedy any babysitting problems. All Misty had to do was prove to the judge she was in high school to continue getting the stipend. Misty attended the minimum days allowed per the court agreement and split the money with her father, who cared little for Misty's education or his grandson. It would not be farfetched to suggest many students statewide consistently abused this alleged system of alleged financial support.

How could Matt forget "Asshole" Douglas. *That was her name.* Matt initially thought it was an error on the roll when he received it in early August, but no, it was the name of a living, breathing individual. The name was pronounced "Ash-oh-la" and was as sad a commentary on the parent that named the child as it was on the society that accepted it. Matt would not. He insisted on calling her "Miss. Douglas." The guidance department alerted Matt one afternoon in April she was transferring to a school in Arizona where her aunt resided. Apparently, Asshole's mother was a drug addict who forced her fifteen-year-old daughter into prostitution to support her addiction. Because of her mother's substance abuse, it was later revealed the young girl lost her virginity at age twelve. When her aunt learned of the problem after the mother was arrested for the fourth time on possession of narcotics, a judge agreed to remove the girl from her mother's custody. In Arizona, her first name was legally changed and the young woman thankfully began a new life.

Matt taught Carolyn Arceneaux, only fourteen-years-old when she snuck out of her bedroom window to attend a party which her mother forbid her to attend. Carolyn had excellent grades, but was not innocent by any stretch of the imagination. Carolyn got drunk at the party, was sexually assaulted by seven boys under age seventeen in a van parked on the curb of the street, and ended up pregnant. The boys laughed and videotaped the act of intercourse, and placed it on the Internet. Humiliated and extremely angry, the mother withdrew Carolyn from East Side High School and placed her in a boarding school in Massachusetts against the child's will. Matt never learned what happened to Carolyn, except that she ran away from the Massachusetts school at least once. The episode did not end there. The police called two East Side High School boys into the office two days after the incident to inspect their cars for criminal activity in the case. They were found to be in possession of pornography, consistent with the night in question, and were arrested. The pair in police custody began to inform on their peers and other arrests were made at other schools, including one eighteen-year-old at St. Lucy High School charged with contributing to the delinquency of a minor.

Matt also taught freshman Wayne Winston who was so computer literate he became expert at changing grades on his report card from 'C's and 'D's to higher marks. It took his parents and teachers until February's fourth six-week progress report to get wise to what he was doing.

When Principal Berling was through speaking about the year's successes and next year's mission, Matt Zeno politely applauded with the rest of the faculty before glancing at his wristwatch. It was 11:12 a.m. and many wanted to beat the Friday lunch crowd to the bars and taverns in which they had planned to meet. Principal Berling had been speaking, but Matt had tuned him out snickering to himself at the absurdity of the students he taught during the year.

"Finally, I want to announce that two teachers will not be with us next year," Principal Berling said as the faculty sat up in their uncomfortable chairs better suited for teenaged students. "First, I want to call up Matt Zeno, who has accepted a position teaching math at the prestigious St. Andrews Prep School in Rhode Island."

Matt walked up to the front of the faculty while teachers applauded. Principal Berling extended him a handshake and the plastic wrapped gift of a heavy, long-sleeved black school sweater with the school's silver and blue logo on the front, the same gift given to every teacher leaving or retiring. Matt took the sweater and held it up next to his torso. The garment was too large. Everyone in the library laughed. Somehow the heavy crew neck sweater explained the principal—the gift was out of season and Principal Berling's interest in the proper sizing was immaterial. His lack of attention to detail in such matters was notorious.

The fact was, Matt, only completing his third year of teaching, was sick of the inner city public school system's version of education. Sometime during late fall he began to realize no matter how hard he worked, the majority of students he taught could give a damn. He got tired of trying to motivate what could not be motivated. He grew weary of phoning parents he could not reach or parents seemingly helpless to discipline the offspring they created. Matt was one of those special people who tutored students after school for free, even though services for such a practice were expensive. Matt performed them free to any student who wanted to improve. Sadly and revealing, Matt never had more than two students in his class on any given afternoon. In fact, it was common four afternoons per week for not one student to show up at all. At thirty-years-old, Matt could restart his career elsewhere and still retire at fifty-five.

Matt was as motivated as he was frustrated and everyone around him knew it. However, it was clear to him that his best efforts as an inner city teacher were never going to be good enough. Maybe the truth was the students Matt taught were not good enough for him. So when a position making an additional $8,000 per year, teaching four classes with no more than fifteen students per class became available to him, he could not accept the job fast enough. His exit was a huge loss for the state, the school, and the school system.

"I also want to extend my gratitude to math teacher, Trevor Roth, who just completed his master's degree and will now begin teaching at the Governor Claiborne Magnet School," Principal Berling continued. "Trevor has been with us at East Side for fifteen years. That's a long time. He's been teaching twenty-three years in all and has decided to move on. We will miss him terribly."

The faculty again applauded. Trevor was a man who once coached almost every sport known to the school system. He was always a great deal of fun, heavily involved in school activities, avoided social cliques like the plague, and had been a very popular teacher over the last two decades.

Trevor liked to recall when East Side High School was of the neighborhood variety and his job was considerably easier and more rewarding. Over the last fifteen years, he noticed a trend that could no longer be ignored. He saw the interest among students wanting to self-improve disintegrate. He loathed this generation of students viewing education as an impediment to their good times. Trevor did not want to admit it for a long time, but he acknowledged that an overwhelming number of students only cared about immediate self-gratification. Having taught mostly seniors, Trevor witnessed each graduating class prove more ignorant than the last, despite higher or lower test scores.

Trevor did not want to teach rocket scientists. He did not have to teach Ivy League-bound students to give him some self-worth about his occupation. No, Trevor wanted to teach students who made the *attempt* to improve. If all a student could make was a 'C' in a course that was fine with Trevor if they had really given their best effort. Now education "experts" were getting more involved, not in just what was being taught, but in how it was being taught. That was too much of a restriction for a professional like Trevor. He looked for a way out of the inner city public school system he liked to call "a sinking ship even the rats are abandoning." He found it.

Trevor was also growing up, even as late as forty-nine-years-old. Locker room humor was no longer in vogue. Coaching winning football, basketball, and baseball teams was no longer satisfying. He needed more substance in his life and found it traveling the world during each of the last nine consecutive summers. Trevor had visited Italy the most, having landed on those ancient shores six times. He had also been on trains and buses crossing eleven European nations. He had gone to England just once and was planning to visit again next week with a brief stay in Ireland. Travel moved him deeply. He would never admit it to his coaching contemporaries, but base hits, match-up zones, and draw-plays did not stack up to Greek and Roman ruins, Irish Sea cliffs, the Eiffel Tower, or the museums of Vienna. He had matured at middle age and liked the change. He began to coach less while taking night school classes to complete his master's degree. Now it was time to change where he practiced his profession.

Trevor collected his sweater from Principal Berling and although some of his close friends on the faculty shouted, "Speech! Speech!" he refused them and sat down quickly before he got emotional. He knew they wanted to only embarrass him for their amusement, but it was harmless fun.

Principal Berling did not mention Tory Leblanc's impending move to Texas at her request, but Tory's friend, Margaret, sat stone-faced during the meeting still not able to cope with the idea of not having Tory around for the next school year.

"On to more distressing news," Principal Berling said almost in disbelief as the room went from loud to incredibly quiet in seconds. "Now, you all know the school system has got to cut seven million dollars from the operating budget. I don't know where it's going to come from. I expect class sizes to once again grow slightly larger because we've been asked—principals have been asked—to cut two members from each faculty. We won't have to do that because we have two who are retiring. Unfortunately, I don't expect this trend to discontinue. It's almost a summer ritual for teachers to expect budget cuts, larger class sizes, and job uncertainty for the less experienced on any faculty.

"Some of you also know that we have been forced to drop some teachers due to race considerations. Many of those teachers are not present today after having turned in their grades. They are looking for other jobs, effective immediately. I do regret having lost them. You must know it was not my choice to remove them. Those teachers include Greg Talley, Dr. Anders, Terry Achison, Mike Hammonds, Mary Ann Samson, Doug Waters, and others. That's where we are as a school system."

Principal Berling could not remember the names of all those removed from their posts against their will. He also sensed naming the teachers further undermined morale. He ended the roll call abruptly. There was silence. Everyone was uncomfortable. Rumors had swirled in newspapers and in the faculty lounge about these very issues. Their principal had just confirmed those rumors. Privately, they understood next year could be the year they were mentioned at the final faculty meeting as being ousted or transferred.

"One other thing, we are looking for someone to step up and assume the head coaching job for our soccer team," he added.

In the corner of the room, head soccer coach Joey Martin was looking forward next year to being called "Mister" and dropping the affectionate title of "Coach." The soccer program would be looking for its fourth head coach in as many years. Then again, he knew Coach Gatewood would pressure his henpecked boss to simply drop the soccer program, "that Third World Sport," as it was called in the athletic department.

"Our girl's basketball coach is retiring from coaching, but we look forward to adding Coach Philip Wilson from Jean Lafitte High School to our faculty next year where he will assume Coach Debra Annison's former post," Principal Berling continued. "He is an outstanding person and we think he will bring instant credibility to our girl's basketball team."

Debra Annison sat in silent shock at the announcement. Her lip quivered in anger that the girl's basketball program had been handed to an athletic outlaw. Principal Berling continued.

"Lastly, I think I should let you know that beginning in August the school system will no longer allow any school to use our own funds to buy coffee for your consumption in the teacher's lounge."

There were many groans from the caffeine addicted masses.

"It seems the school system can spend tens of thousands of dollars on out-of-state experts to tell us our student population is apathetic and our buildings are crumbling, but we can no longer furnish you with coffee. If you know of a sponsor that would be willing to help us with this problem next year, please contact me.

"Any other business?" Principal Berling asked before pausing. He glanced around the room. "No? Your schedule for next year will be e-mailed to you over the summer. Have a great summer. I'll be here Monday through Thursday through the summer if you need to talk or have suggestions. Be careful. Bye-bye!"

With that, there was a scramble by some to leave as quickly as possible. Other teachers hugged and shook hands. The conversations grew louder in the library. The bright sunlight began to sneak though window blinds in the back of the room as a promise from late spring that summer was to be uncompromising with its heat index. It was time for a much needed recovery period for the teachers and they welcomed it.

Some teachers, however, would teach summer school, conduct coaching clinics, or take jobs performing tasks that would temporarily take them from the classroom. They sold insurance or real estate, painted homes, landscaped yards, interior decorated homes and offices, worked on construction jobs, or simply loaned themselves out to part-time work through hiring agencies. Teachers called the sudden professional change a chance to live a double life. Most teachers simply needed the money, despite the notion they were paid during summer months. They were not, of course. Some teachers collected summer paychecks through their choice of deferred payment. In effect, the money mailed to those teachers in June and July was already earned. But many, by choice, chose larger paychecks during the year. Subsequently, during summer they had to either stretch their budgets or get a second job.

However, the public loved to remind them they had the entire summer off. That's what Matt heard on a popular radio talk show en route to his home just minutes after the faculty meeting. As he pulled out of the parking lot, the radio topic was teacher pay raises up for vote in the Louisiana legislature. In the last few weeks there was debate in the state capitol about whether teachers deserved pay increases in lieu of poor test scores and if the state had the money to grant that fiscal wish. Phone callers to one Baton Rouge radio station displayed both sympathy and ignorance toward teachers.

"Hell, I don't know why we should pay teachers more money," one caller explained. "They get the whole summer off with pay! I wish I could do that at my job!"

Or, "Teachers knew what they were getting into when they signed on for the job," another caller said. "Now, they want pay raises? Poor pay is something they are used to living with and the state can't afford to change it."

Or, "When more students graduate, then give teachers more money."

Another explained to the radio audience, "When the school system stops busing students around town then they'll have the money to pay teachers. There's money to pay teachers. It's being used in the wrong way."

Another reminded listeners that the fact they could read, write, and debate even this topic is proof that teachers were doing their jobs. The caller went on to say, "We can criticize teachers all we want, but very few of us could do their jobs, or would want to. Very, very few people in this state are qualified to do what they do and they still make more money than teachers."

Then came the strangest call of the afternoon.

"Let's go to line four, where I understand school board member Nathan Weems is waiting to give us his opinion on the subject," the radio host said. "Let's not waste any time. Mr. Weems, thanks for calling the show."

"Thank you for letting me set the record straight," Nathan said.

Nathan's voice sounded consumed with concern. Matt knew as he stopped at a traffic signal Nathan either got word from a friend who monitored the show that he needed to call. Or, Nathan was listening and could not allow callers to bash the school system he represented.

"All I want to say is there is no busing going on in East Baton Rouge Parish," Nathan said adamantly. "There has not been busing in this system in years. One of your callers said if we stopped busing then the system could produce the money to pay teachers a competitive wage comparable to what their counterparts are making in the suburban parishes. We don't have the money to pay our teachers what they deserve, that's true, but it's not because we are busing students."

Nathan was interrupted.

"So there is no busing going on in the East Baton Rouge Parish public school system, is that right, Mr. Weems?" the host asked in clarification.

"That is correct and that was the only point I wanted to clear up," Nathan said sounding relieved that he did.

"So, what do you call sending kids to schools five miles from their homes? I mean, some of these kids are at bus stops at 5 a.m. to catch buses!"

"We have community-based schools, not mandatory court-ordered busing."

"It sounds like nothing more than clever semantics to me, Mr. Weems."

"I'll tell you what, call me at the school board office and I'll explain it in further detail, but we are not busing students any longer."

Nathan and the host continued to discuss the teacher pay issue, but Matt tuned out now shaking his head in disgust as he turned his wheel onto a busy boulevard. Nathan Weems was exercising propaganda. Matt was immediately reminded of his dear friends, Bart and Cathy Distefano, whose two daughters were in the public school system. They lived on the eastern side of the city. The two girls lived closer to Woodlawn High School, but were not allowed to attend there because they did not live in the zone drawn up per the court-ordered Consent Decree. They, instead, attended Tara High School about seven miles away. On the way to Tara High School each morning they passed right in front of Broadmoor High School, which was about one and one-half miles closer to their home. Technically and politically, the Distefano girls were *not* being bused. Their east side neighborhood was shaded on the city map legally delivering them to Tara High School each morning at 6:45 a.m. However, the girls lived closer to Woodlawn High School and Broadmoor High School, but were not allowed to go there. Geographically, the girls were being bused. The lines dictating school attendance zones were drawn radically horizontal across the city. Some of those lines stretched as much as six miles across the city map.

Yes, Matt thought sarcastically, don't dare tell the whole truth to the population. That truth was, a host of attorneys with their kids in private and magnet schools simply redefined what busing was. To the ordinary citizen whose children waited each morning at 5 a.m. to catch a bus to school, the public school system was still busing.

Nathan put out the school system party line. The radio host agreed, for the moment, to swallow it. Matt turned off his radio and promised to forget about it all for ten summer weeks.

"For the good of the football team"

Trent Baer was nervous as he stood in front of Principal Berling's secretary, Denise Bridgewater. The school office was empty during summer months. In fact, it was so eerily quiet Denise put the radio on to chase away an office calm she was not used to. Trent fidgeted as he waited for his 11 a.m. appointment to speak with Principal Berling. Although he had been teaching at the school for just one year, Trent desperately wanted to believe his presence and loyalty would be enough to keep his job. Yet, somehow, he felt like he was going to have to impress the principal of his abilities all over again. It was a weird feeling. It was as if Trent had never taught at the school. Denise did not make the event any easier treating him much like a stranger instead of one of the school's instructors. It was an omen.

Gloria Hampton had turned in her resignation to Principal Berling two weeks after school ended. She wanted to believe a cooling off period would be beneficial to her mindset. She had hoped her teaching friend, Nancy, would be right; some time away from the students and the rat race of teaching high school may allow her to clear her head and make a better decision concerning her future. But when Gloria heard the television news confirming pay raises were not forthcoming, she knew it was time to retire.

She surprised Principal Berling with the news of her retiring. Gloria actually informed the school system of her intentions just minutes before she told Principal Berling in person. She planned it that way in case he surprised her by talking her into teaching an additional year. Gloria was not shocked when, instead, he extended a simple handshake thanking her for her long service. Gloria was no one's fool and Principal Berling always underestimated his teaching corps. She knew exactly what he was thinking when she left his office, collected her things, and walked out of her classroom for the final time, a truly difficult and final assignment for retiring educators. Principal Berling didn't even help Gloria down the stairs with the twelve heavy boxes full of teaching tools and memorabilia that she kept in her room.

Before leaving school, Gloria did put in a good word for Trent Baer. She knew he was the future of the school and had his heart in the job for the right reasons. Principal Berling assured Gloria it was his intention to phone Trent as soon as possible, but he lied to her. He was not above it.

Gloria wanted Trent in her old job. He was young, energetic, handsome and athletic. Gloria even went as far as to call Trent to inform him of her decision so he could visit the school and put some pressure on the principal to hire him permanently. Now Trent waited to meet with Principal Berling while the air-conditioning system hummed overhead and the radio softly played a well-worn "Beach Boys" tune:

"...Don't worry, baby. Everything will work out all right. Don't worry, baby..."

The rhythm reminded Trent of the difference between the summer-life he wanted to live as a teacher opposed to the life of uncertainty he currently faced. Like every teacher, Trent wanted job security so he could enjoy his summer and rest his concerns.

Trent hummed to the aged music.

He hoped the lyrics were a good sign, but Denise interrupted him with, "Mr. Berling will see you now."

Denise's voice was too business-like. She made brief eye contact with Trent as she extended her hand toward the principal's office door, as if he did not know where it was. Something about her behavior toward him was wrong. Trent got bad vibes. Just a few weeks before, Denise was like a friend to him. They were educational allies. They traded jokes and were on a first-name basis. Now, Trent was treated as if he was one in a dozen candidates for a job he held just a few weeks prior.

As Trent walked through the narrow corridor leading to Principal Berling's office, he heard the familiar voice of Spanish teacher, Brent Masters, thanking the school for the opportunity to teach at the school.

"Brent, you did us a favor when we needed a teacher and you did a fine job," Principal Berling told Brent. "The best of luck to you."

Trent waited outside the office door for the two men to release their handshake. Brent turned away from his former boss, immediately caught Trent's eye, and extended his hand. Trent was somewhat surprised as he gripped Brent's hand while accepting his brief explanation for it.

"I'll be seeing you, Trent," Brent said. "Best of everything."

"You're leaving?" asked Trent.

"Yea, this is not for me, you know, the teaching thing. I thought I might like this, but it's much harder than people think. I don't mean to sound spoiled, but this is a rough gig."

"What are you going to do now?"

"I've just accepted a job working for an investment firm in Houston. The money is just too much to pass up. I have friends there. It's a bigger city, too. There's a lot more to do, and more opportunity. This just isn't for me."

There was irony in the chance meeting. Trent wanted desperately to keep his job and did not know if he was going to be able to keep it. Brent was not in the rumor mill as one leaving the school and he wanted out. As Brent walked out of the office, he heard Principal Berling call his name like a hunter stalking a turkey.

"Trent? Come on in!" Principal Berling said with a mix of laughter and approval.

When Trent walked through the door, Principal Berling continued smiling, stooped over from behind his desk, and shook hands with the man about half his age. After the two explained pleasantries it was time to get to business. Trent could not wait another minute knowing if he was to be employed the following school year. There was a teaching position available. Trent once occupied it. He wanted to reclaim it. Trent cut to the chase.

"Mr. Berling, will I be able to return to teach here next year?" he asked with more respect than was really deserved to extend. "I've been waiting to hear of Mrs. Gloria's possible retirement or for any change that may allow me to return. What have you decided?"

Principal Berling sighed, sat, and leaned back in his leather chair. Somehow he appeared at ease with the situation. He was too at ease. It was almost as if he had made such a decision weeks ago and had learned to justify it. Trent, on the other hand, stood in front of the principal's desk with his nervous hands and arms folded. There was so much at stake for him and he had been kept in the dark long enough.

"You know, last year we did not do well on the football field," Principal Berling began in explanation as he wiped lint from a shirt that did not expose any. It was obvious he was now very nervous. It made Trent even more so.

Football was not the subject of interest to Trent, but it may have held his fate. Trent knew at that instant he was a dead man as he watched the principal explain what other teachers told him he might do. Being young and naïve, Trent did not want to believe such things as sports were really that strongly considered in teaching hiring practices, especially in light of the school district's poor academic showing. He felt like a fool watching this ex-football coach attempt to justify what Trent had so feared. Trent heard so few of his words. His mind raced. He simply stared at the principal's lips while thinking what a son-of-a-bitch he really was.

To further illustrate Trent's anger, Principal Berling considered himself a religious man, a born-again Christian who never cursed. He liked to tell everyone so. His actions over the years, however, proved otherwise. Trent may have never heard Principal Berling curse, but that did not make him a good man. Principal Berling would rather hide behind the crucifix and play political favorites and destroy careers, of which he was infamous. Trent was now accruing firsthand experience of the principal's lack of judgment, which was the talk among more veteran teachers.

"Trent, you've done a heck of a job for us, no doubt," he said. "I've heard nothing but good things about your teaching style and knowledge. I don't think you'll have trouble finding another job, I really don't."

Typical. Principal Berling did not directly inform Trent he was not returning to East Side High School. He simply made an end-run around that painful fact. In any event, Trent got the message. He had only one question and dared to ask it.

"So, are you not filling the position?" Trent asked knowing he did not really have a right to do so.

"Well, we hired an offensive line coach from the College of Louisiana and we picked up a defensive back coach from a private school just last week," Principal Berling stated flatly and with a hint of a chuckle as if he were lucky for such a find. "Trent, they teach social studies and coach. You only teach. I need someone who can do both. It's really that simple."

Trent was confused. The new coaches had already been hired? Where was Principal Berling going to place the coaches in the event Gloria had not retired? Trent could only guess not only would he be removed from the faculty, but another teacher comfortably at home for the summer foolishly believing they were safe in their position would have been fired at a later date. The entire episode was tragic.

The bigger story involved Trent realizing he was never really considered for the job. Why didn't Principal Berling tell him about this weeks ago when he could have been exploring other job opportunities? Did Principal Berling ever plan on telling him he was not in the running for the social studies position vacated by Gloria?

Questions! Trent had a ton of them. Before he could ask even one more question, Principal Berling uttered the most absurd thing he ever heard, or would ever hear, come from the mouth of an alleged educator.

"Trent, sometimes academics and good teachers have to suffer for the good of the football team," he stated with conviction as he leaned slightly forward over a desk full of papers. "That's a hard fact. I don't like it, but as an old football coach myself, I understand the need for a balance between football and education. If I were you, I'd start thinking about coaching."

Trent wanted to leap across the desk and hit him in the mouth. The advice was as bad as it was unsolicited. Trent loved football. He knew a great deal more about the game than most men. He was a student of gridiron history, tactics, and strategy. But he did not join the teaching corps to be a coach. He wanted to teach and it was being denied him because he chose to immerse himself into the complexities of the U.S.

Constitution and the fall of communism rather than the intricacies of the triple option.

Trent knew football coaches were needed as much as any other discipline. There was nothing wrong with coaching as far as Trent was concerned. His problem was that sports took precedence over academics. In his case, a football coach took priority over academics. Trent also knew too many coaches, especially of the football species, actually spent class time watching game films and drawing X's and O's on the chalkboard rather than teaching subject matter. Some students loved having football coaches for teachers because it sometimes meant teaching would be forsaken, especially on autumn Friday game days.

Trent's mind became a blur. He had almost hoped he was incapable of doing the job. At least that way he could understand why he was not rehired. Hiring a fired college football coach in a shameless effort to revitalize a poor football program should be the lowest priority for any principal.

"When they get certified we hope they'll be as good a teacher as you, Trent," said Principal Berling, now offering further insight into his latest decision. "I mean that. You are as good as they come. Best of luck to you."

As the final insulting words left his lips, he stuck out his right hand for a handshake. Trent was more bewildered than ever. The pair he just hired to take his job were not even certified! How could this hire be justified? It would be, of course.

The hiring of a former college football coach would be so prestigious for Principal Berling. He could brag about it to the other parish principals when they routinely met for breakfast or for meetings at the central office. Oh, how Principal Berling would be the envy of the other school principals, even if it didn't help the football program. As for teachers like Trent, Principal Berling really believed they were expendable and easily attainable. As far as he was concerned, there would be more Trent Baer's who would come along and deliver the educational material. But a guy who could teach cross-blocking and better pass protection in Coach Gatewood's new "Run-and-Shoot" offense was just too good to ignore.

As Trent walked out of the office, Denise did not speak with him. She never lifted her cute little head to say goodbye. Trent was a ghost. She knew the score of this game long before it began, no pun intended.

As Trent walked down the silent hallways and through the school's massive double doors for the last time, it was not lost on him that Louisiana turns out more college and professional football players than most states. In fact, Louisiana, with a small population of just 4.5 million, turned out almost as many stars as state football factories like California, Florida, Pennsylvania, Texas, and Ohio. It was also not lost on Trent that Louisiana was among the nation's worst in high school graduation rates, teen pregnancy, teacher retention and pay, and its ability to halt a "brain drain" of fleeing educated residents that was destroying the state's tax base. Trent wondered if Principal Berling knew of those painful facts. If he did, he probably did not care. A principal's Breakfast Club-ego and reputation among his contemporaries was at stake and he had to make a coaching hire he believed was going to make a difference. Trent was the sacrifice.

A sad excuse for religion

Trent Baer did learn in ensuing days about a job opening at St. Lucy. It did not involve coaching and for that he was relieved. If Trent were lucky enough to get the job he would have to take a $5,000 per year pay cut. Despite their wealth, the Catholic Diocese did not have a reputation for compensating teachers well. But Trent needed a job and a change of luck. He was Catholic, belonged to the parish church, and knew many of the members on a first-name basis. However, Trent doubted his familiarity with St. Lucy's Parish would be enough to give him the edge he needed. Politics were politics. Many Catholic schools were drowning in it.

Trent knew his job at East Side High School was in jeopardy before school ended. Two weeks before in a phone call to St. Lucy Principal Joseph Allen, Trent was informed there was no job opening. In the last two days, however, Trent learned a social studies teacher had quit the profession and gone into private business. St. Lucy did not want to advertise the position and create a flood of inquiries. Instead, they chose to move quietly and slowly concerning filling the position. Principal Allen did not know Trent was going to visit his school armed with such information.

When Trent arrived at 1 p.m. the school secretary, who acted more like a guard dog, told him in a terse tone that he needed to make an appointment. When Trent told the secretary he was there to apply for the social studies job, she quickly excused herself and returned with the message that, "The principal will see you as quickly as he can."

Trent waited anxiously to see Principal Allen. By 2:10 p.m. he began to wonder if they simply wanted him to become frustrated and leave. By 3:05 p.m. he was sure of it. The office was empty. No one was waiting ahead of Trent. He was simply left waiting for no other reason than those in power made him wait. So much for Christianity and love thy neighbor, Trent thought to himself.

Trent was at his wit's end. He needed to work. Time was running short. School was going to begin for teachers August 4. Very few teaching positions were available in any public, private, or parochial school at such a late date. Trent was becoming desperate. Even though he learned some social studies positions were available in East Baton Rouge Parish public schools, three principals informed Trent he could not be considered for hiring until all minority applicants had been given first preference. In short, Trent could not be considered for a position in a public school until after the first week of classes. Trent was now learning to be less of a liberal fool. Learning now that racism went both ways, Trent decided to try the private schools.

Principal Allen finally emerged from a narrow hallway from the back offices. He did not appear to be in a friendly mood. A short balding man, he was also painfully blunt because he had the power to get away with it. His lack of style did not endear him to his associates or his faculty, who thought him to be rude when he could have been a friend. He often chose to be a snob when he could have made a loyal boss. Principal Allen also held grudges and was a sad example for his religion.

Trent thought Principal Allen might have been angry that he did not leave in frustration while promising to make an appointment at a later date. Trent was very nervous knowing the private school decorum and expectations were quite different from the public school system. Trent did not consider himself inferior to any private school teacher. But there was no denying he was intimidated with the idea of teaching in a Catholic school. That's exactly the emotion in which Principal Allen wanted to bathe Trent.

"I'm Joseph Allen," came the unfriendly voice as he moved toward Trent with no promise of a handshake, "What can I do for you?"

"Mr. Allen, I'm sorry I didn't make an appointment but…"

"This is quite unusual, I must say," Principal Allen said unsympathetically while looking directly into Trent's eyes for a trace of inferiority. "We advertise for job openings here through the diocese. You need to fill out an application with them and they will put you in touch with us. That's the process."

Trent wanted to shake the man's hand. That Principal Allen did not attempt to do so made Trent even more nervous. He was already sorry he came.

"Sir, I understand that, but I wanted to meet with you in person before you filled the position," said Trent, not wanting to appear nervous but knowing his effort to do so was in vain. "I hear there is a social studies position available and I want to apply for it. If I need to go to the diocese to fill out the paperwork then that's what I'll do. But I wanted to meet you face to face. You can understand that."

Principal Allen was intrigued. He had no plan to encourage Trent. He only wanted to be rid of him so he could hire whom he wanted. Principal Allen was upset that his prized low-paying job made news in such as a way as to attract a young man like Trent.

"Have you ever taught before?" Principal Allen asked.

"Yes, sir, I just finished one year at East Side High School," Trent explained as he fumbled for his resume stuck inside a large yellow manila folder.

Trent placed his one-page resume on the counter and spun it around so Principal Allen could study it immediately. The principal never picked it up and glanced at it only once. A piece of paper summing up Trent's entire life's work lay on the pristine countertop like a dead animal on a rural stretch of highway. Trent wanted to run out of the office where a picture of Pope John Paul II hung on the wall near them. It was ironic. Trent thought if this was what Catholic education was all about he was ready to study Judaism or become a Muslim. Principal Allen was not a leader. He was a tyrant. It was little wonder fourteen of his teachers quit at the end of the school year. It was leadership like his that made the teaching experience tougher than it had to be. Principal Allen should have learned a lesson from the army of teachers that abandoned St. Lucy under his tutelage. One would think he would get the message that "unhappy people vote with their feet" and change his leadership habits.

He did not. Principal Allen was cut from the same cloth as East Side High School Principal Adam Berling. That was no compliment.

Trent's fear was becoming uncomfortable even for him. He had been through a lot in the last few weeks and began to resent the way he was being treated by everyone. Unfortunately, Trent could not afford to fight back. It made him feel weak. He had no control of his life and he was becoming angry.

"We try to hire individuals closely tied to the diocese," Principal Allen explained. "Did you attend Catholic school?"

"No, sir, but I am Catholic and I go to Mass at St. Lucy," Trent replied.

"Sorry, we only hire those who have a Catholic school background. We also want to hire those with more experience than you offer. I'll keep your resume on file for six months and if I have a position for you, we'll be in touch."

Trent knew his resume would be in the garbage can before he made his way into the parking lot. He thanked Principal Allen for his time and again apologized for not having made an appointment.

As he left the building, Trent could not help but notice how much real-world public schools were unlike St. Lucy. The hallways shone with fresh wax reflecting senior class photos that hung along the interior corridors. The lockers had no graffiti on them boasting the consistency of being painted one color. There were colorfully planted flowers, white crepe myrtles, and statues of various saints fixed in perfect symmetry in the courtyard framed by the glass door at the end of a short hallway. Everything in the trophy case shined with not a hint of dust. The exterior grounds were as perfect as the first tee on the golf course at the City Country Club. There were no trash or potholes in the parking lot. In the distance, he heard the sounds of basketballs hitting a wooden floor in a gymnasium he could only imagine as immaculate.

As Trent drove his car from the parking lot he realized there was no sense wondering "what if" because he was not sure if he wanted to work for power-mad individuals like Principal Allen, no matter how badly he needed a job. Of course, he always thought he could be one of the most educated employees at Wal-Mart if all else collapsed around him. He practiced the greeting as he put on his sunshades in an attempt to mock himself, "Welcome to Wal-Mart! May I help you?" How silly he would look in a blue vest with a big yellow "Smiley Face" on the back.

He was now going to make the ten-minute trek to Louisiana University's Department of Education to speak with his friend, Dr. Fabian Ross. Perhaps he could give him some leads on a job or at least keep him in mind just in case a principal phoned looking for a good teacher. No, Trent thought, he was a great teacher trying to swim in an ocean of mediocre leadership. It was also two good hours of his precious day shot to hell. It was not the hell the Catholics preached in their gospel, but the potential was there.

Barbie Dolls and the "urban challenge"

Sure enough, Channel 8 and its so-called "Education Team" were reporting on the state teaching shortage and how it may affect the public school children in the coming school year. Education Team. It was a moniker given to news reporters to make them look and feel more authoritarian to the common viewer. When the weather was severe the same group of news reporters suddenly became the "Storm Team." If the legislature was in session they were the "Political Team." Only an idiot would believe the same group of $25,000 per year news reporters in their mid to late-twenties could be experts in education, medicine, food, weather-related items, crime, politics, sports, and God knows what else.

As usual, Channel 8 had not done its homework. On the air was public school Superintendent Dr. Ralph Maddox answering questions and worrying parents about his concern on whether he would have enough qualified teachers to begin the new year, just eight weeks away. The Channel 8 reporter on the story, Callie Bowman, looked more like a Barbie doll than a qualified television reporter. She was over-dressed in the latest off-the-rack fashions worn by every high school and college-age student wanting to look like a Las Vegas hooker. Callie interviewed the superintendent as she nodded her head in agreement for the camera as each word flowed. Dr. Maddox brought up the issue of poor teacher pay in comparison to that of suburban school districts. When asked what his strategy was for attracting teachers, Dr. Maddox gave a line that would become a teacher's lounge joke for many months to come.

"We hope to attract qualified teachers by issuing them the urban school challenge," Dr. Maddox said plainly and seriously to Callie, still nodding her head in agreement as her large hoop earrings danced around a head full of hairspray and makeup.

A now unemployed Terry Atchison was at home watching the 6 p.m. news when Callie's report was aired. He could not believe the nerve of the superintendent. He could believe how naïve Channel 8 could be, who never once interviewed a principal or sought out a teacher at any public school in the parish. If they had dared they might have had a real story; a human-interest "piece" that low-lighted and destroyed the careers of many fine teachers in the last few weeks. No, Callie wasn't equipped to delve beneath the surface of the obvious and ask anymore of the superintendent on such a serious issue. She thanked Dr. Maddox on the air for his time before issuing herself a verbal pat on the back by saying to the anchorman at the news desk:

"This is Callie Bowman reporting this live exclusive. Back to you at the studio."

With that, Callie had done her job, she thought. She was so proud of her efforts and her bleached white smile proved it. What she did not know was that her report did a disservice to the many teachers out of work whose stories were never told. Callie unknowingly proved to be nothing more than a parrot.

The following day Terry phoned Callie about the story and gave her his side of what really was happening parish-wide to many unfortunate teachers. He told her of the teachers at East Side High School, one with a doctorate, relieved of their duties over race issues. He outlined the politics surrounding the entire situation. Terry gave her more news on the issue in ten minutes than she could accrue in a week. When he finished giving her the truth, hoping she might follow up on it and begin asking those in charge the tough questions, Callie told him flippantly, "Well, that story is now old news, but I appreciate your calling and filling me in on it."

Which is to say "Barbie" was not interested or appreciative at all. In fact, Callie did not want to do her job thoroughly. She wanted to file a story and move on, no matter how weak or shallow her reporting proved to be.

There is a huge difference between reporting and promoting. Callie did not report on the alleged teaching shortage. She simply promoted what the superintendent would insinuate. The superintendent was not a bad man, but he was not telling the entire truth either.

Callie, not a qualified journalist to begin with, did almost nothing to press the issue for those fired teachers like Claire Metz, Greg Talley, Mike Hammonds, Dr. Jay Anders, Mary Ann Samson, Doug Waters, and Trent Baer who didn't have a voice. No, Callie was not hired by Channel 8 to carry the banner for those unfortunate educators. She was, however, hired to find human-interest stories that recognized abuse in a struggling public entity like the school system. Callie failed horribly.

"I don't have to worry like you do, I coach football"

Trent sat in the waiting room of Louisiana University's Education Building hoping to speak with his dear friend and former professor, Dr. Fabian Ross. They had not spoken for exactly one year. It was Dr. Ross who helped Trent secure a position teaching social studies at East Side High School. Trent hoped to be able to catch that same magic in a bottle while he began to entertain, for the first time, thoughts of leaving the state in an effort to stay in the teaching profession. Many teachers were abandoning the state every year and Trent knew some of them. Perhaps it was time for him to shed the chains of Louisiana's version of public education and finally get on the winning team, even if it meant changing license plates on the back of his car.

The waiting room was full of young students. Most of them were teachers or aspiring to be. Most were reading or studying as they sat so painfully close to each other in cramped quarters. It was all they could do to keep from kissing. Trent became concerned at how long it might take to see Dr. Ross. He had no appointment and there were so many people ahead of him. Nevertheless, Trent had no intention of leaving. Gaining some insight and maybe a lead on a teaching job was more important to Trent at this moment than anything in the world. In fact, seeing Dr. Ross was Trent's last shot at staying in Louisiana and teaching before picking up the phone and calling ex-college classmates about advice on how to apply in Texas public schools. Trent was willing to wait as long as necessary.

Trent picked up a magazine on the glass table in front of him where the toe of everyone's shoes rubbed. There were so few magazines to chose from and most were aimed at a female audience. Trent was not picky about what to read. He just needed to kill some time while assuming a long wait was imminent. Under the mound of colorful slick glossy magazines was the tabloid "Baton Rouge Business Report's *Real Estate Report 2004*" issue. Trent knew so little about business and its inner workings, but this looked more like a magazine the upscale, better-educated classes would read. Skimming through its pages might offer him an education into a world he admitted he should know more about.

Trent turned the pages as fast as he could searching for any article that might entertain him and pass the time. There were no good-looking color photographs of gorgeous women in this black and white tabloid and something needed to catch his eye. But on page nine, Trent began to read about how Baton Rouge residential regional sales were growing. The number of building permits and the value of construction were up. Trent nodded his head in approval to himself, even though he did not fully understand what it meant. But what Trent read next about home sales gutted him because he was directly involved:

> "*...two factors make East Baton Rouge different from outlying parishes...One, the parish is running out of open land...Two, private schools add $5,000 per year per child to the cost of living...*"

Trent now sat up straight in his chair with his eyes fully focused. Both hands clutched the magazine. This article had his attention. He was somewhat saddened to read the declarative statement. It was a statement of fact. Trent reluctantly admitted to himself it was the truth. This type of magazine, Trent knew, was one that garnered respect throughout the metropolitan area. It was a magazine read by businessmen and women, powerful attorneys, construction contractors, the chemical and oil industry representatives, real estate developers, and physicians. It was found on the coffee tables of most city, state, and regional politicians and corporations throughout several parishes and many states. It was a magazine most connected with the metropolitan area business community could not afford to be without.

So, when it was implied that moving to East Baton Rouge Parish meant public school was not a viable option, it hurt Trent deeply. The paragraph did not disguise the understanding among those associated with Baton Rouge business that public education was one of the city's weaknesses. Simply put, public education was a problem a family would be forced to reckon with when relocating to the Capitol City. The article explained that when building a home in East Baton Rouge Parish a family had better anticipate finding entrance to a private school to be just as important as interest rates, financing, blueprints, and the color of wallpaper installed in the master bath.

Those two sentences on page nine were tough to read. It appeared that all Trent had worked for and hoped to be as an educator was considered by the business class to be nothing more than a system in thorough disrepair. His effort in raising school test scores meant so little to some. Those two sentences explained a great deal to a young teacher like Trent trying to establish himself in a career for a hapless public school system that was embarrassingly acknowledged as a deficiency to quality living. Trent read no more. He now had something more to think about.

Trent began to feel sorry for himself. He knew that feeling was counterproductive and, in the end, no one really cared. What bothered him so much was that he did care. He knew of countless individuals that cared about the perception of public schools as much as Dr. Maddox. Trent was so proud of his modest accomplishments during the past year. He was proud to be a teacher and swelled with pride when telling others of his chosen profession. Now he found himself unemployed in a public school system a local print reporter identified as something to be bypassed when shopping for a home. If St. Lucy Principal Allen failed to make him feel inferior, the paragraph on page nine finished the job.

Trent watched three individuals get up to leave the office tired of their wait. Four others were called to the back offices to meet with other professors. Suddenly, Trent was alone with one other person and he wanted to speak with that person to keep from going mad. He also wanted to see if the middle-aged face with whom he was about to speak was ahead of him in line to meet with Dr. Ross. Trent took a chance on being polite to a stranger. It had been a horrible day and he needed to speak with a friend, even a new one he did not know.

"Are you here to see Dr. Ross?" Trent asked shyly.

The man looked up from his magazine and studied Trent. He looked around the room recognizing now they were the only two remaining in what was once a crowded room. Both men realized it was more comfortable to speak aloud. Trent noticed the stranger was wearing a green and light blue coaching shirt with no identifiable logo on it. He was slightly balding, well tanned, and appeared physically fit for his age. He placed the magazine on the table apparently as bored with reading as Trent was in need of positive reinforcement.

"Yea, I'm here to ask him about finishing up school," he offered without being asked. "You?"

"I'm next, if he'll see me," Trent replied.

"Why wouldn't he see you?"

"I don't have an appointment. That seems to be a problem today."

Trent leaned over and extended a handshake, "I'm Trent."

"I'm Daniel," he said. "Daniel Ellis. Are you a teacher?"

"I guess you could say that," Trent said without a trace of enthusiasm.

Daniel cocked his head to the right and looked strangely at Trent as if to suggest he explain more. Trent obliged him needing to talk with someone in a therapeutic way.

"I was a teacher for one year and lost my job to a football coach," Trent said flippantly hoping Daniel would empathize. "I had the job and I thought I was going to retain it, but my principal—and I use that term loosely—gave it to another person. I am not a happy camper today. I'm officially unemployed. Certified. Experienced. And unemployed."

Trent thought he might have sounded pathetic. Perhaps he had offered too much information to this stranger. And at the same time he cared little if he did. It had been that bad of a day for Trent. He was no longer interested in being politically correct.

"Not to make light of your situation, but I got a job today because I did coach," Daniel said leaning over and scanning the table for something to read.

"What do you coach?" Trent asked.

"Football."

"Where did you land a job?"

"I just got hired at St. Lucy's. I'm going to be their secondary coach. That's on the defensive side of the ball, you know?"

Trent was blown away. He was insulted. Shocked. Stunned. Saddened. Despondent. Through all the emotions, Trent noted that Daniel never did mention what he would be *teaching*. Daniel mentioned only that he was coaching the defensive secondary. Trent prodded. He had to. The fact that Daniel mentioned St. Lucy made him inquire further. Trent was not really interested in Daniel's resume. Trent was investigating St. Lucy's hiring practices.

"Ah, they told me I'd be teaching social studies and maybe some P.E.," Daniel said in answering Trent's question. "I'm not real sure. It doesn't matter. I don't care. I know some of the coaches over there and they hooked me up with the job interview. They interviewed me and I got a call this morning that they wanted to hire me. It was too easy."

Daniel then released a chuckle only he could appreciate. It was not intended to be rude, but Trent noticed most people adopted the habit of faking amusement with themselves when they finished speaking to strangers.

"Who hired you?" Trent asked as if a bomb were about to explode.

"The principal," responded Daniel. "Nice guy. What his name?"

Trent obliged him, "Joseph Allen."

"Yea, that's it. You know him?"

"Yea, better than he thinks."

Daniel perked up not understanding Trent's cheap shot at St. Lucy's leadership. He began talking more comfortably with Trent. He felt like a celebrity. Daniel was foolish enough to think his new job title as assistant high school football coach was truly interesting to Trent. As Daniel spoke he never understood he was killing what little enthusiasm remained in Trent's now beaten psyche.

"Yea, I told Mr. Allen, is that his name?" Daniel asked already forgetting who his new boss was to be. "I told him…"

Trent was no longer listening. He lowered his head, stared at the floor, and nodded his head for Daniel. He wanted to scream and cry. He could not decide which.

Daniel continued speaking rapidly in excitement, "I told Mr. Allen I had never taught before and that I'm just starting the certification process. That's why I'm here to see Dr. Ross. I want to know exactly what I have to take to finish this up. I want to do it fast. Football is going to take a lot of my time, you know?"

Football was also taking up a lot of Trent's time. All Trent could remember was Principal Joseph Allen rudely telling him he did not have enough experience for the job and he needed to fill out an application through the Catholic Diocese. He was also humiliated into waiting two hours for a job that did not exist only then to be told he needed to make an appointment. Daniel, on the other hand, had no experience and no certification, but was hired on the spot. Daniel was so unaware of the information he provided Trent, who now felt as low as at any time in his young life.

Daniel continued speaking about football and the district race his coaching buddies had told him would be competitive. With each word spoken Daniel was pushing Trent one mile closer to the Texas border.

"Yea, I guess I don't have to worry like you do," Daniel said as if he had an edge in the educational job market. "I coach football. As long as I do that I know I'll always have a job. That's what I'm told anyway. It makes sense, too. Especially if we win some football games."

With that Daniel let out a laugh. Again, he had humored himself because he knew that statement to be painfully true.

Trent then knew that both East Side High School and St. Lucy sold their souls to win football games. Although it would probably cost some unknowing students a solid social studies education, the parents who paid the $4,500 per year tuition at St. Lucy would convince themselves they were getting their money's worth. Perception was reality. And no one sold it better than St. Lucy in their glossy pamphlets and summer tours of their sterile school.

Trent had heard it all. He got up, shook Daniel's hand, and wished him luck. Daniel was dumbfounded Trent was not staying around to see Dr. Ross.

"I'm not going to be that long in there," Daniel assured Trent as he moved toward the door. "I'll be out of his office in about ten minutes and he's all yours."

"It's not that," Trent said to Daniel. "I need to go. By the way, good luck. I know you'll be successful."

Trent's words to Daniel were hollow and rang from the mouth of a young man who was temporarily beaten.

For Trent, the day's events were the end of a line he no longer wished to straddle. His "need to go" meant leaving the state of Louisiana. There was no denying it now. Trent had to go. In this one day he learned more about how corrupt the hiring in the educational system was than he cared to experience in two lifetimes.

Trent also learned some painful truths. He was not the right color to work in some public schools. He was not politically connected enough to gain an edge in certain jobs. His not being a football coach was crippling his career and his desire to be a teacher. In short, the system currently deemed him unworthy of a job or the respect he hoped would attach itself to the profession. Trent felt like a fool. There was so much he did not know this morning. He was wiser now.

What he did know was he had bills to pay and a career to launch. He knew somewhere a principal would be eager to hire him because of what he knew and experienced as an educator. There was a teaching position out there in the world and he was going to locate it.

When Trent got to his car he promised himself he would use his cell phone to call friends in Texas about teaching posts. He was serious about it now. No looking back. Trent had been pushed around by an unimpressive group of men and it was time to fight back in the only way he knew how. It was time for a change of luck, a change of scenery, and a change of residence. He would not waste another minute searching for a teaching post in Louisiana.

The state was on the verge of losing another brilliant young mind. Those allegedly in charge of educating young people guaranteed his departure. The final score for Trent's Louisiana teaching career read: Football 7, Serious Education 0.

MFP's and Legislative shotguns

The Louisiana legislature had just adjourned after twelve grueling weeks. It was not a productive legislative session as most go. It was not an election year and *most* of the good-ole-boys that purport to run the state conducted business as usual, which means Louisiana's image as a business backwater, politically corrupt, refugee-fleeing state that could not keep the grass cut along the interstate highways, was not in jeopardy of changing.

The session also did little to help public school teachers in most districts. One would think the state's doling out any additional money for teacher pay raises would be a fitting gift to all educators. When money for such raises was found and approved, the problem was not every teacher in the state was guaranteed even a small pay increase.

According to a very complex formula known by the State Department of Education as the "Minimum Foundation Program," or MFP, teachers in certain parishes would be awarded raises based on the number of students taught and how affluent a parish was. For teachers in East Baton Rouge Parish and elsewhere, they would get no additional pay increase this year. None. According to last year's MFP, each teacher in East Baton Rouge Parish was awarded a mere thirty-two dollar *per year* raise. The MFP, and teachers believed the acronym to stand for other things, reasoned East Baton Rouge Parish was considered affluent with its strong chemical industry and availability of white-collar jobs. Never mind the overwhelming number of public school students were at or near the poverty line, the MFP considered the parish prosperous. Therefore, the MFP reasoned its school system could afford to pay their teachers more, budget cuts or not.

On the other side of the Amite River separating East Baton Rouge from Livingston and Ascension parishes, respectively, those suburban teachers—already $3,000 to 7,000 ahead of East Baton Rouge Parish public school teachers on the pay scale—once again got additional money. The MFP awarded Livingston Parish teachers an additional $1,400 pay increase for the second consecutive year. Never mind that over 80 percent of the Livingston Parish residents work and collect paychecks in East Baton Rouge Parish. The MFP graded that parish less affluent. If the MFP were a person, it needed to be murdered.

It was an unfair system to be sure. Some legislators sought to even the pay scale and change the MFP formula by taking other items into consideration, but legislators representing those less affluent districts vetoed it.

When the session was completed some legislators felt so good about their overall efforts they chipped in and bought one of their outgoing contemporaries a double-barreled shotgun and presented it to him in the state capitol on the floor of the House of Representatives. The *Baton Rouge Daily News* took a photograph of the "ceremony" and carried it in the following day's edition. Greg Tally could not believe that a photograph of such an event was in the newspaper for all to see. He was not angry with the *Daily News* for running the photo. It was their job to follow and report the news. Maybe the news photographers took such a photo for the same reason Greg was upset. Perhaps the photo was meant to get readers upset, although many of the state's legions of undereducated may never have caught on. Greg was angry that legislators thought such a publicly extended gift was appropriate. He also hoped most readers would find it as inappropriate as did he.

Greg hated Louisiana's image. He had to defend it and himself almost everywhere he traveled. He was growing tired of doing so. The more he traveled Greg slowly came to realize that maybe all the jokes about the image of the state were closer to being true than he cared to admit.

Greg believed seeing a photograph of a legislator admiring a shotgun inside the state capitol premises sent a very poor message to the young people he had been teaching. With violence on the rise statewide, a serial killer recently captured, and another recently arrested Washington D.C. sniper murdering for sport, the timing of that "gift" could not have been worse. Greg hoped the Associated Press wire did not send that picture out. Oh, how the people in Los Angeles, New York, Miami, Chicago, or Boston would get a laugh out of it. It would confirm their stereotype of a state mired in an image its politicians could not, and seemingly refused, to dispel.

For Greg, there was more to that unfortunate photograph than most could know. In the previous day's newspaper Greg read about a student he taught during the past school year that had been murdered five days before outside of a Baton Rouge bar at 1:30 a.m. on a Sunday.

Eugene Merchant, eighteen, was standing outside of a bar in the northern part of the city when an unknown assailant weaved his way through a crowd numbering about 150, according to witnesses, and placed a .38 revolver at the base of his skull when he was not looking. The fired weapon nearly blew Eugene's head off. The assassin fled. Eugene's final moment of life was spent in a pool of his own blood in a dirty parking lot on a seedy side of town surrounded by strangers who refused to cooperate with police investigators.

Eugene was not a good kid. He was a failing student that missed many days of school. He was a thug. No amount of grieving or reminiscing about his death could change that fact. Eugene was very bad news to everyone around him, including teachers he regularly disrespected. He had been expelled from school his sophomore year for physically assaulting and breaking the nose of a fifty-four-old male special education teacher twice his size when the teacher attempted to break up a fight.

After Eugene's sucker-punch sent the teacher to the floor of the hallway, he leaned over and taunted, "How did you like my punk-ass elbow landing in the back of your head, college-boy?"

Eugene returned his junior year and was expelled again for threatening to kill another student over an incident involving a female who did not attend East Side High School. After that he drifted back into the neighborhood cesspool from which he came. He sold drugs, participated in gang activity, and carried a pistol for either status or protection. In the end, it was not enough protection for Eugene.

Strangely, Eugene did have a small amount of respect for Greg. It was not very much by any teacher's standards, but Eugene was a very real threat to his immediate environment. He could go off at any moment and the explosion could be as dangerous as it was unpredictable. However, he never uttered a word in Greg's science class. The two simply had an unspoken truce. Greg helped Eugene *if* he wanted it. If Eugene didn't want that help, and he never asked for any, he would do nothing to upset the flow of Greg's class. Everyone who taught and knew Eugene believed his gangster lifestyle would eventually defeat him, but his murder did not make Greg hurt any less.

Watching some of the state leaders unveil a high-powered weapon to an exiting Legislative pal as a gift indirectly condoned the violence that paralyzes teachers and students with fear, in some school districts on a regular basis. Greg knew legislators could conveniently hide behind the weapon as being one of a hunting variety. They would spew their right to wave the weapon on the House floor under the protection granted under the Second Amendment. Greg simply saw the ceremony as continued legislative moral flatulence. It was constipated thinking.

Either way, bullets from a rifle kill deer, rabbits, and young teenage boys with the same prejudice.

Greg also considered how the legislature had delivered in one brief so-called lighthearted moment a horrible message to the nation as well as to the youth of a state desperately struggling for a change of image. A moral compass that, in Louisiana, too often pointed toward the pole of unenlightened rural mannerism.

June-"That's your problem, not mine!"

Bob Woods was punishing himself pushing his lawn mower across his well-kept lawn near the noon hour on a brutally muggy June afternoon. With the entire summer off at his disposal to do as he pleased, Bob paced himself as best he could pushing his mower in row after row of tall St. Augustine grass. When he finished the front lawn, he cut off his mower at the foot of his sidewalk that cut through his Napoleon Estates middle-class neighborhood. He pulled off his wide-brimmed tanned straw hat protecting his balding head and wiped the perspiration as it streamed down a face creased with worry lines. Next door he noticed his neighbor of three years, Lyle Vickers, hammering a "For Sale" sign into his front yard under the only large shade tree left standing after last season's Category-1 hurricane. Bob hoped it was not what he feared. Needing a break from the monotony of yard work, he ambled over to visit his neighbor to gain answers to the reason he was putting his lovely home up for sale. Bob did not want to lose Lyle as a neighbor, but it appeared inevitable.

"Lyle!" Bob called out as he moved in his direction.

Bob picked up his pace as he got Lyle's attention. Lyle stood erect with the hammer in his hand a bit embarrassed to have been caught putting his home up for sale and having to explain why. But good neighbors always wanted to know why they would lose a good neighbor and to what.

As soon as the two shook hands and exchanged greetings, a green Mazda SUV placed itself on the curb of the street. On the door panels for the world to see was a magnet advertising "Guilbeau and Associates Real Estate, since 1966." The two men laid eyes on the beautiful brunette lady in her early thirties emerging from the vehicle. She wore a long skirt that had to be too warm for the time of year, but it was professional as it was intended to be.

"It's my real estate agent, Justine," offered Lyle before Bob could even ask the obvious question.

She exited the SUV and ambled up to the sign placed in the ground the day before and attached another that proclaimed her company's logo. She then turned and approached the two men who never took their eyes off her gorgeous figure. She then moved toward the men before extending a handshake to Bob, who was clearly shocked she spoke to him first rather than the head of a family she hoped to do business with. Maybe, Bob thought, she wanted to use the moment to promote the possibility of selling him on purchasing another home. Real estate personnel are aggressive, especially in a region exploding in growth with interest rates plummeting. Justine was a tiger in real estate and her body mechanics proved she was afraid of nothing but failure.

"Hello, I'm Justine Anderson of Guilbeau and Associates," she said. "Pleased to meet you. Are you interested in the house by any chance?"

Bob was a bit embarrassed at the question as he shook her small hand because he looked like white trash looking for a handout. He was wearing a sleeveless shirt and dirty shorts covered with fluids recently leaked from his worn body while toiling in the 105-degree heat factor over the last ninety minutes. He was definitely not interested in the house, but she was making small talk with him and trying to be nice.

"I'm sorry about the sweaty palm," Bob said apologetic. "I live next door and I just came over to see why Lyle was selling his home."

Bob looked at Lyle for an answer as Justine tossed her head up and then down slightly to show her understanding of Bob's somewhat awkward presence. She then smiled and nearly melted both men with her presence.

"Hey, Lyle," she said, "believe it or not I may have two couples interested in looking at your home this weekend."

Lyle smiled at the immediate interest shown to his home. For him, it was justification in hiring Justine and her agency. He was lucky to have Justine on his side and he knew it. She then turned to Bob, now more self-conscious than ever to be in the conversation. She was so incredibly beautiful and he looked at his absolute worse.

"Oh, well it was nice to meet you and if you know anyone that's interested in the home please call and let me know," Justine said as if in a television commercial.

She then pulled her card out of her brief case and excused herself as she turned and greeted Lyle's wife making her way outside. The men continued to watch Justine as the two women shook hands and moved their way toward the front door and an air-conditioned living room to conduct real estate business. Bob then turned to Lyle with concern.

"Man, I hate to see you go!" Bob said in earnest. "I mean, we don't know each other that well, but everyone knows what a great neighbor you are."

Bob meant it, too. Lyle kept his home in immaculate condition. He and his wife, Becky, had recently spent nearly $14,000 updating the home in the last two years. The small French-style home had recently been painted and had new shutters installed. The yard belonged on the cover of *Southern Living* magazine. The grass looked like carpet rather than freshly cut turf. The home boasted new hardwood floors, paint, wallpaper, and one bathroom had a newly installed old-fashioned bathtub sitting on a new reddish-colored stone floor. The patio had been bricked and a fountain installed with French Quarter-style lampposts. The couple had gone out of their way to steer their suburban cookie cutter home toward something different, even if it was simply a traditional south Louisiana style.

Lyle and Becky were quiet and proved to be the kind of people who would watch one's house when away on vacation, whether one asked them or not. They were good people and Bob knew it was most unlikely that whomever bought the house could ever live up to their standards. That bothered him more than anything.

"Yea, we hate to leave the neighborhood, Bob, but Becky wants a baby and we need to start planning for that," Lyle said.

"I don't understand," Bob asked with his palms extended for effect. "You can't plan for a baby in this house? You've got over 1,700 square feet and three bedrooms to work with. And you've invested so much in the home."

"True, but five to six years from now our child is going to be going to school," Lyle said, "and there's no way I am going to place him or her in the public school system. Neither Becky nor I make enough money to consider private school. Becky is going to have to quit working when she gets to be about seven months pregnant and we'll be living on one income until the child gets to about two-years-old. So, you know, we are moving to one of the suburban parishes while interest rates are still low."

Lyle continued with a shrug of his shoulders, "Who knows if interest rates will be as low as they are now by the time the baby is ready to go to school. So, we're going to make our move now."

Lyle registered the look on Bob's face and remembered he was a public school teacher living in the district where his offspring would attend high school if they stayed in their present home.

"Bob, no offense intended, I assure you," Lyle said respectfully hoping he had not hurt Bob feelings.

"None taken, man," Bob said waving his hand in front of his face suggesting it was no big deal, but it was.

Bob worked hard teaching English and coaching track at East Side High School. He wore his school T-shirts while working in the yard as a display of pride lost on East Baton Rouge Parish residents. Bob was no fool. He fully understood that Lyle's opinion and the reason for his move were quite common. He had read too many stories in the newspaper over the nineteen years he was an educator about what Lyle was doing now. Lyle and Becky's imminent move to one of the suburban school districts continued to brand him with the reminder of his school's hardscrabble reputation.

East Side High School did not have the highest test scores in the metropolitan area, but they did not have the worst. What's more, people like Lyle—and there were regiments of them—were indirectly telling teachers like Bob that regardless of their efforts they did not believe their children could get a good enough education to sustain themselves in college or in working class life. It hurt Bob deeply, but he never indicated to those type of well-intentioned individuals, many of them his dearest friends and family, how much that message cut him.

"Everyone is moving to the suburbs, man," Lyle said shaking his head cooperating with himself. "It's no secret that you can get a good public school education out there and not have to pay a dime for it. Look, I don't have to worry every time the news comes on if the NAACP is going to continue to play their 'successful victim' routine and muddle things up to a point where I have no say in what goes on. I want some stability for my kids and I don't want to have to worry about them in school."

"Lyle, you can get a good education in this school system," Bob said in defense of public schools. "It's not *that* bad. We send lots of kids to college. Our kids do not fight every day. The gangs do not control our hallways. We do a very good job with what we've got to work with..."

"I know," Lyle retorted with both palms up and nodding in agreement before Bob got on a roll. "And I wouldn't want to do your job. I couldn't do your job. I know you are forced to teach what the school system delivers to you. I know your facilities are poor. I know you are underpaid. But Bob, God love you, that's going to be your problem and that of any parent who puts up with that. I don't have to."

Lyle was beginning to raise his tone, not so much at Bob, but at his frustration with the school system over the years. He also began to realize he might have overstepped his bounds by indirectly insulting his neighbor. Bob stared blankly at Lyle. He remembered how angry Lyle was back in January when they talked about the public school system in the very spot they were now standing.

Bob flashed back to two years before when the NAACP agreed to meet many concerned parents for a locally televised debate about the state of the public school system. Lyle was engaged to Becky at the time, but the two knew they would soon marry. Both attended that function hoping to understand the roots of the system's problem and look into the eyes of those who had decided the fates of a generation of parents, teachers, and students covering over two decades of court-ordered forced busing. After listening to the televised arguments on both sides for over one hour, Lyle and Becky got up to leave before being caught in the overflow crowd making an exit.

When they finally entered the darkened parking lot they spotted Theodore Johnson, head of the Baton Rouge Chapter of the NAACP, a party in the nearly fifty-year-old lawsuit against East Baton Rouge Parish public schools. As they passed near the first row of parked cars nearest the building, Lyle overheard a private conversation between school board representative Lori Chambers and Theodore about the long-running case. What Lyle overheard disgusted him. It also explained to him why the school system was faltering and why he decided on that evening that it would never again prosper.

"Theodore, how can you tell these people tonight that this case will continue until the school system is fully desegregated?" Lori asked with a touch of shock in her voice. "How can we desegregate a school system that is 70 percent black?"

Theodore looked directly at Lori and said callously, "That's your problem, not mine!"

He then walked away leaving Lori alone in the dark as cars pulled out of their parking spots all around her. Lori was dumbfounded. Just having overheard the remark, Lyle felt betrayed. He heard what Theodore told the television cameras and the interested parties what they wanted to hear that evening, but in the parking lot it was obvious to Lyle and his fiancé the NAACP had quite a different agenda. What it was Lyle did not know, but it was nothing like what he told the interested people at the televised debate.

Some three weeks later at a televised school board meeting, Lori would tell that story publicly without mentioning Theodore's name. The shock in her voice from that conversation still registered as she explained her thoughts and feelings about that remark. Despite her best efforts and that of the school board, Lori felt politically betrayed and she made those feelings known. The news media conveniently ignored Lori's story. Lyle never forgot them.

Lyle continued, "Bob, I don't mean to hurt your feelings. I know if you taught my kids you would do one hell of a job. But I don't trust the public school system. They have broken too many promises. I'll never forget that meeting I went to two years ago."

Lyle pointed at his chest and explained how he took time out of his busy afternoon to at least consider sending the children he was planning to eventually conceive to public schools. Lyle recalled the story about his visit to the televised meeting to Bob as if he had forgotten. Bob listened politely, but didn't hear a word. He was not upset at Lyle. He was becoming increasingly aware that his efforts, like those of Lori Chambers, still meant very little to the parents of the students they hoped would repopulate a school system in obvious decline.

Suddenly the front door of Bob's home opened disrupting their conversation. Becky leaned under the shaded green doorframe with Justine standing just over her shoulder.

"Honey," Becky called to her husband. "Justine has another appointment in one hour and needs to speak with us about the house."

Becky then instinctively waved at Bob to be polite.

On instinct, Bob walked Lyle slowly toward the two ladies still standing near the open door. Bob shook Lyle's hand and both promised they would stay in touch long after he was gone. Of course, they agreed to meet for dinner before he left the neighborhood for good, but both knew they never would.

"Becky, I'm going to miss you guys," Bob said as he mocked a half-hearted wave. "Hate to see you go."

"Do you and your wife have any children, Bob?" interjected Justine.

"No. Why?"

"Well, there are some really fine houses in the suburbs for families in a similar price range of what you are living in now, but the lots are bigger. There are more shade trees and less traffic."

"No, Justine, thank you, I'm quite happy here in East Baton Rouge Parish."

No one responded, but broke out in smiles nonetheless.

Lyle told Justine that Bob was a public school teacher.

Justine was curious in as nice of a way as one could be.

"Oh, Bob, are you a teacher?" asking the obvious.

"Yes, I am," he replied.

"Bless your heart. I know that's a tough job."

"It is, but I still love it despite its shortcomings."

Lyle joined the last of the conversation as Becky disappeared into the living room.

"I was explaining to Bob that it's those unfortunate shortcomings that are forcing us to leave the neighborhood and Baton Rouge," Lyle said to Justine letting her in on their conversation.

"Bob, I admire your loyalty, I really do," Justine said. "But about 45 percent of all my business is moving Baton Rouge parents into Livingston, Ascension, and even West Feliciana parishes. The increasingly common complaint from people is their dissatisfaction with the public school system. I don't mean to sound cruel, but as long as the school system stays in chaos the real estate business in the metro area is going to boom, regardless of the economy."

Justine stopped speaking hoping she did not anger Bob as she registered the look on his sweaty face. He stared back into her eyes with no malice. There was no emotion in his eyes. Bob felt like the student for a change. Justine was his teacher and her lesson was of a reality that squashed his hope for a rebound in the direction of the public school system. Justine had also just delivered a verdict on his future. It was an ugly pronouncement from Justine's beautiful face, but Bob realized it was an honest one. It pained him to hear it from a real estate agent making part of her income from Baton Rouge refugees running from the public school system in which he worked.

Justine quickly changed gears quite suddenly.

"In any event, if I can help you in any way, or, if you know someone who may be interested in Lyle's home, please call me," she reminded him.

With that everyone said goodbye. Lyle followed the two ladies inside as the door closed leaving Bob alone with perspiration running down his face and onto his soaked shirt.

As Bob made his way back to his own lawn he thought about the fact he had never taught any of the children of his family or friends. Many of those offspring were of high school age and not one of the seventeen he could count attended a public school. Not one.

Bob's brother-in-law and younger sister both lived in the city. Between them, they had five teenagers. They all attended private schools. They were all in honors courses and were heavy participants in extracurricular activities.

His neighbor across the street had a sign fixed in their front yard flower garden proudly exclaiming allegiance to a private school. The sign read, "A John Hancock High School Eagle lives here!" Bob never really gave it much thought until now. Down the street there were similar signs proclaiming allegiance to several private schools. Someone was always proud to be a Raider, Warrior, Eagle, Bear, Kitten, Red Sticker, Knight, Cub, or Wolf. He suddenly remembered leaving for school in the early morning hours and seeing many students on street corners serving as bus stops in private school uniforms more so than those of public schools. The evidence was irrefutable. It was also disheartening.

His older brother, now living in suburban St. Louis, refused a job promotion and a chance to return to Baton Rouge because he did not want his two boys in the city's public schools. Not wanting to spend money on private schools and doubtful he could gain admission for his honor roll sons, he opted to stay in Missouri.

His fishing buddy living on the street behind his home reluctantly sent his fifteen-year-old daughter to live with his ex-wife in Livingston Parish because he wanted to avoid placing her in Baton Rouge public schools. His best friends recently sold their home in the River Oaks section of Baton Rouge and bought a home in Livingston Parish, like most, to avoid the inner-city public school system.

There were numerous stories. For every story Bob knew about the Capitol City's academic refuges there were probably one-hundred he did not know about. Sad stories. Expensive stories. Inconvenient stories delivered to the doorsteps of an urban population in spite of their disdain of it all. Many Baton Rouge parents did what they felt they had to do. They simply left the urban parish for the suburban variety. They were leaving by the hundreds each year at the expense of the city. Justine was one of many real estate agents taking advantage of that still fledgling market.

The toughest part of it all was Bob listened to their disparaging words about his choice of employment knowing they were right. It made him realize just how disconnected the public school system was from the middle-class population. Despite public proclamations to the news media, new school construction, and the best efforts of the East Baton Rouge Parish public school system, Bob realized there was no hope in its salvation. The exodus of families with school-aged children from Baton Rouge was more pronounced than he knew. The out-migration of students went from a trickle to a flood in the last twenty years and its waters spread out over many parishes. While Livingston and Ascension parishes complained of too many students enrolling in their fast-growing school systems, East Baton Rouge Parish was closing schools, planning to close more in the near future, and trying to explain to an increasingly disinterested public of their latest plans to improve it all.

"Don't get too attached…"

As if on cue and one week later to the day, Bob returned home from running errands on the hot streets of the city and saw the word, "Sold" posted in bright red on the sign in Lyle's front yard. Bob could see the word from nearly one block away as he turned the corner onto Louvre Street where they lived. One week later, Lyle and Becky Vickers pulled their moving van out of Napoleon Estates having bought a home in the suburb of Prairieville, about two miles to the south of the East Baton Rouge Parish line.

When Bob's new neighbors moved into Lyle's vacated home two weeks later he and his wife, Amanda, made it a point to make an introduction. The husband, a chemical engineer, and his wife, a legal secretary, were young and obviously affluent. As Bob and Amanda spoke to the newest arrivals to their street, they could not help but notice the couple had a four-year-old son. When introductions were complete, Bob and Amanda excused themselves, but agreed to meet later in the week for a barbeque hoping to get better acquainted. As Bob strolled home with his wife of seventeen years he felt as if he once again lucked out in gaining neighbors of quality.

"They seemed like really nice people," Amanda said to Bob as they made the short walk home. "We even know some of the same people. Small world, huh?"

The irony, Bob thought.

"Don't get too attached," Bob warned his wife while staring straight ahead. "They'll be short-timers to the neighborhood, too. Did you notice the age of their little boy?"

"It will be private school for him with the kind of money they probably make," Amanda said in agreement.

"Either that or they'll leave for the sanctuary of the suburban school system. One thing for sure, sweetheart, I'll never have the privilege of teaching him."

"No dear, you won't."

"Don't let (a child) whine and pester you for treats; give rewards only for good deeds or for promised good behavior. When he is thrust into competition with children of his own age, don't let him sulk or become angry...Never let the child become accustomed to the soft and easy life...For the child who has been denied nothing, whose tears an anxious mother always dried...This child will be unable to cope with the harsh realities of life."
-First Century Roman philosopher, Lucius Seneca (the Younger)

Late June—"You've Got to be Kidding?"

He simply could not believe it. Coach Joey Martin and his wife, Carolyn, were on their way to a late Saturday afternoon movie to kill the monotonous summer boredom, and he was still attending to school matters. When a cell phone message was left from a concerned parent about her child's grade in one of his classes, Coach Martin suddenly had more questions than answers.

The caller identification flashed the number and the name, "Rebecca Seals." Coach Martin did not know the name. That mattered little because so many children of the millennium were raised by stepparents, grandparents, and legal guardians that it was impossible to know which child belonged to which adult based on a last name. Seals? The name did not register in Coach Martin's brain.

To compound the confusion, he no longer had possession of his roll book. That was turned in on the last day of school for teachers. Those attendance sheets and grades were filed away at the school or school board office. There was no way Coach Martin would be able to hold a factual conversation with any parent about a child's grades at such a late date.

Why would any parent want to speak with a teacher about their child's grades now? School had been out for over five weeks! Report cards had been issued. Any challenges to grades at this point should be taken to the school principal. In his entire teaching career this was the first time Coach Martin would call a parent about a child during the middle of summer. Coach Martin knew he would not get into any trouble if he did not make the call. At this point he was under no obligation to do so, but he was too inquisitive not to call. So he picked up his cell phone and punched the number in as he drove along in traffic. The phone rang three times before a woman in a gravely voice finally answered.

"Hello?" the lady answered.

"Yes, I'm looking for Miss Seals," Coach Martin said while his left hand handled the steering wheel. "This is Coach Martin from East Side."

"This is she," she responded as if she did not remember why she initiated the inquiry, but her mind picked up the slack. "Oh, yea, thanks for calling, Coach! I know calling a teacher is unusual at this time, but I wanted to know what Malika's grade was in your class."

"You've got to be kidding?"

"No, I'm afraid I'm not kidding," she said with a touch of laughter. "You see, Malika was a senior this past year and she failed your class and one other. She told me she thought she passed your class this year, but the report card came to me a few weeks back and proved she failed. What was the percentage?"

Malika Spears. A senior. Coach Martin knew he had told this student before seniors retired from high school in early May that she was in serious danger of failing his class. He had warned her as far back as February that her refusal to turn in assignments was going to destroy any hope she had of graduating. Malika always verbally shot a nasty response to Coach Martin designed to draw attention to her case and make the class laugh at the teacher's expense. Malika's remarks were rarely so harmful they warranted writing a referral and sending her to the office for disciplinary action. Instead, her witticism drew just enough blood to wound Coach Martin, never to fully humiliate him. Students were expert in that game, especially females.

Malika often laughed at her predicament. She lost academic ground faster than he could compute it in his roll book. She did not take three tests during spring due to lack of attendance and did not produce an excuse to retake them. She never turned in homework assignments and did not show up on days when extra credit was assigned. When Coach Martin attempted to reach the mother for a conference he was always informed she was not available and no one knew when she would return. Often, teachers did not have the time to endure it. Coach Martin never did reach the mother and began to believe she was pure fiction. He was reduced to repeatedly reminding Malika she would not find the situation funny if she did not graduate from high school. He even had three of Malika's progress reports coded with the chilling reference, "Parent-teacher conference requested." Coach Martin was never contacted.

In the end, Malika failed just as Coach Martin predicted. That much he knew about Malika's case. What this parent wanted now was details and he had not any to offer. Parents, however, tend to think their children are the only important student a teacher instructs during the entire day. They speak to teachers as if they are surrogate parents understanding each nuance in their child's character. Truth be told, when a public school teacher is responsible for over one-hundred students per semester their characteristics are not so distinguishable. It takes three months just to learn their names. Now, he finally had the truant mother's attention on the phone.

"Miss Seals, I don't know how to tell you this, but I don't have any idea," Coach Martin said honestly. "I turned in the roll book at the end of the year. I don't know what Malika scored on the final exam, how many days she may have missed, or the exact academic situation she was in prior to the final exam. My memory is not that good. It would not be wise for me to even guess at this time what percentage she earned."

Earned. That is the key word veteran teacher's used when speaking to parents. Earned. It let parents know that the conversation about their child's grade is about how they performed in class. Earned. It's not about what the teacher "gave" a student. What a student earned and what a student was given as a grade by a teacher needed to be clarified immediately.

Every parent with a problem concerning their children believes their situation is unique. Any problem a parent has with their child is not unique to the teacher. An experienced teacher has visited the same problems dozens of times over. It was like being a police officer stopping a vehicle for speeding on the expressway. When a driver is questioned about why they were speeding, the driver may think they are offering the police officer an unusual story that may explain their way out of the traffic ticket. The fact is, the police officer—like the teacher—has heard every conceivable excuse imaginable. Rebecca Seals fell right into that category. She believed with all her heart Malika's not being able to graduate was so unusual it demanded immediate attention. To Coach Martin it was all reruns.

As she continued to talk to Coach Martin at a rapid pace about Malika's situation, several items ran through his head while driving the sunny streets. Malika's being a senior means she would have left school three weeks earlier than the underclassmen. Why did this parent not contact Coach Martin when this news was fresh back in May? She could have met with him at school during that time and he could have explained to her in painstaking detail why her child failed his class. No, she did not take that kind of time.

Malika also did not "walk" with the other seniors at graduation exercises. It was proof she failed. So why was this parent phoning now? If there was a legitimate explanation for Malika's grade, why did the parent wait seven weeks after seniors received reports cards to notice a problem? Nothing added up to Coach Martin. Apparently the rank of "senior" may have been applied too liberally to an obviously immature student like Malika. Her high school business was not completed and her mother had to finish it for her. Coach Martin thought it all to be a bad joke.

"...So, Malika said she passed the class," Rebecca continued rambling, "but I don't understand the 'F' she got. I know she's not the best student, but I know she did enough to graduate. Malika told me she did. Can you explain to me..."

The rambling continued and meant nothing to Coach Martin. He was already sorry he phoned as she told the same story over and over and over. He did what he had to do. He interrupted her in what had become an exercise in futility, an argument he feared he could not win because he could not explain it to such a ridiculous parent.

"Ma'am, I do remember Malika missing several days over the legal limit," Coach Martin said. "In fact, I could swear she missed something like, oh, seventeen to twenty days, if my memory serves me correctly. Any student receiving a number of unexcused absences over eleven or maybe twelve gets an automatic 'F.' The teacher has no say in that. That is the school's rule."

"We got those unexcused absences taken care of."

"So I was right in that there was a problem with her attendance?"

"Yes, but we went down to the school board office a few weeks ago and appealed those when school was out for seniors."

Coach Martin was onto something now.

"Well, ma'am, if your child failed due to the number of unexcused absences there is no way I could know that after school let out," Coach Martin said.

"That's why I'm calling you now," Rebecca said. "I need to know if appealing those absences will give her a passing grade. Or, should I put her in summer school for the July session? I want her to graduate and go to college in the fall. She can't do that unless she finishes high school. Malika swears to me she passed with a 'C.' We need that 'C!' We must have it!"

Not only was this parent being lied to by her daughter, she was late in attending to business nearly two months old. She also failed to get such business attended to in time for summer school's June session. Now she was being demanding with only the July summer school session remaining before college classes began.

Coach Martin pulled into the crowded movie theatre parking lot. He needed to end this conversation. He simply did not have the answers for her.

"Ma'am, Malika is not telling you the truth, I hate to tell you that," Coach Martin said to her rather uncomfortably. "No student can miss as many days as she did, excused or unexcused, and pass my class. There's no way. I also told Malika many times during the school year she was in danger of failing and she just laughed. I really think she expected her teachers to socially promote her because she was a senior. She just didn't think we were going to uphold our word. Malika did not do the work! She earned a grade of 'F.' I don't know the percentage, but I know she failed. That's the harsh truth. I hate to be the one to tell you so."

"That's not what I'm being told!" Rebecca said, getting more upset, her voice rising. "My daughter would not let me go to bat for her unless she knew she was right!"

"Miss Seals, did you ever get Malika's progress reports?" asked Coach Martin not waiting for an answer. "I placed remarks on each of her last two or three progress reports suggesting we meet for a parent-teacher conference. I never heard from anyone."

"Why didn't you call me?"

"I did phone you and I was told you were never home."

"Did you call me back? Who told you I was not home?"

"I called many times. Many, many times."

"Who did you speak with?"

"I have no idea. That was long ago."

"Seems to me you should remember something important like that."

Rebecca was beginning to get pushy. Her tone had changed from docile to rude. Coach Martin knew where this was headed and he had to terminate the conversation fast. All he wanted to do was take his wife to a late movie in the middle of his summer vacation. The school year was over. Instead, he was arguing with a tardy parent of a lying child about a predictable situation that slowly unfolded to their dissatisfaction from February to late June. Coach Martin had grown tired of the entire episode.

"Ma'am, this is what you can do," Coach Martin instructed as if he were handing out homework assignments. "Go to the school Monday morning and tell our principal, Mr. Berling, your story. If everything is excused as you say, then they will call me. At that time I will be required to go to school and double check that grade."

"Okay, that's good," Rebecca said satisfactorily and now backing off her stance. "I'll call the school Monday. So, expect to hear from them and me soon. My child passed your class. I know she did!"

"Very good. Goodbye."

Coach Martin hung up the phone quickly. He knew he would never hear from East Side High School or the parent again for the remainder of the summer. This parent did not understand it mattered little if her daughter turned in excused absences or not. Malika had failed too many tests. It was mathematically impossible for her to pass his class. That much he knew for certain. But this parent needed to find that out on her own. In the end, Coach Martin did witness the incredulous behavior of a parent hoping to browbeat a teacher into verbally committing to change her child's grade out of desperation. The idea of Malika being successful with a college level workload with her terrible study habits was almost pure comedy. More and more, Coach Martin felt less like a teacher and more like a child at home playing school. Coach Martin turned to his wife sitting next to him as they prepared to exit the vehicle.

"It's true what they say, you know," he said as he unbuckled his seat belt and cut off the ignition. "Insanity is hereditary. Students get it from their parents."

His wife did not respond to the humor. Their minds quickly turned to the movie they were to see, one Carolyn had selected. As Coach Martin exited his vehicle, he closed the door and set the alarm with the push of a button from his key chain.

He placed his arm around his wife's neck with the fading orange afternoon sunlight as a backdrop before asking, "What are we going to see?"

"It's called, *An American Haunting*," Carolyn replied knowing her tired husband did not appreciate being phoned about school business during summer.

"Hey, it might remind me of school," Coach Martin said amusing himself as they walked toward the movie theatre's entrance.

"No, this is a movie about scary people and things."

"Same thing."

"Honey, this fear is based on a true story."

"So far, we're talking about the same thing."

"No, sweetie, in this movie the people are very afraid, especially for their future."

"Funny. So am I."

421

Printed in the United States
131011LV00013B/82-96/P

9 781434 366528